JERSEY DEVIL

MATTHEW EARNEST

SEVEREDPRESS

JERSEY DEVIL

Copyright © 2024 by Matthew Earnest

WWW.SEVEREDPRESS.COM

ISBN: 978-1-923165-18-2

Devil devil in the woods,
See Him, run away you should.
Trust your instincts, trust your fear,
Or it's you who'll disappear.

PROLOGUE

Small droplets of cold rain fell onto the paper cheeks of children who were stapled upon overcrowded telephone poles. Their static tears were all overseen by the same text: MISSING. It had been some time since the evenings were filled with the playful laughter of kids and the arguments they would have with their parents to stay out for just a smidge longer. Not many people were out after dark. Troubled parents bought cameras for their houses. The state itself had a curfew put in place. Of course, there were those who didn't take it seriously–said it was all a myth. They wouldn't be too far off. Everyone had their secret theories on what exactly had been terrorizing the towns in and around the pine barrens. Truth is, the terror didn't care about curfews, cameras, or night patrols. The pressure of national attention wasn't enough either–the tragedies continued and showed no signs of slowing down. Grief became epidemic; it was thick in the air. Many assumed the worst–serial kidnappings, human trafficking, etc. Why must it keep happening? What were the authorities even doing? What could possibly make it all stop? Many were desperate for answers, and even if they knew they might never get any, they still clung on to whatever hope they had left. The yearning for justice was almost tangible throughout the state.

Some things, some "myths," lie within the truths and untruths of tales and legends of old; they have serpentined their way throughout history, inconspicuous and tactful. And one such legend is said to exist deep within the pines of the Garden State. A legend waiting to unravel into further blood and chaos.

CHAPTER 1

It wandered about the woods, carrying a heavy emptiness, trampling upon a carpet of pine cones, leaves, and nettles. Roaming about, it bathed in the moonlight with a dark serenity, steam coming out of its nose from the low temperature. The cold never bothered it. Prideful eyes peered over its expansive territory–a monumental space filled with trees, wildlife, and history. But there was one nasty, barbed thorn that embedded itself so deep into its mind, it felt impossible to get out. That thorn existed as a space within the pine barrens that made it feel like *it* did not belong–a clearing with a colossal white oak tree in the middle. It approached with apprehension–a rare feeling to be felt for such a domineering creature. Nearing the tree, whispers danced inside its head. It approached closer and closer and the whispers became clear chatter. Even closer now, enough to touch the tree, and disembodied yelling rang in its head. It came in fragments, some explicit, some confusing. All it could make out was: ...CHILD? ON THE TREE...SOON. Among the splintered, screaming voices in its head were screams of a baby, children, men, and the distinct yell of a woman. She was not afraid but filled with rage. It made no sense to the creature, but it kept attempting to calm down the voices and unwelcome aura surrounding the oak tree. Every attempt had been a failure thus far. How was *it* the interloper? What audacious presence made it feel such an awful way? Whatever it was, it would not stand. It held something limp in a frustrated, yet determined hand and smashed it into the tree with a wet crack. Another one added to the pile. It waited for the voices to subside, but they didn't. It headed out yet again on its mission with no clear direction, prepared to haunt and beset anything in its way, using any means necessary.

CHAPTER 2

Albert Lawless' alarm clock let out jarring beeps. He gave it a few inaccurate slams before it shut up. Albert woke up angry for a split second, but the feeling vanished after he remembered it was a perfect Saturday morning in historical Hamberton Township, New Jersey. His wife, Lily, also woke up feeling angry. Conversely, that feeling persisted after she remembered it was a *Saturday morning*. She had been putting up with this for longer than any sane woman should. *Who the hell sets an alarm for 5am on the weekend!?* she'd think. The sentiment came out as an upset groan, however, but at that point Albert couldn't hear it; he was already in the bathroom spraying doe urine on his hunting clothes.

There he goes with the deer piss again, Lily thought as she rolled her closed eyes so hard she thought she was staring straight at her brain. On the rare occasions he did hear her groaning or complaining, he thought it was equal parts annoying and funny. Lily always told Albert she hated the smell of the deer urine he put on for hunting. He'd retort by telling her she sure would love it if she were a deer. When asked if she looked like a deer, Albert held back from taking the banter any further. He knew better. He still attempted to squeak out of bed as gently as he could, disregarding the loud beeping that happened seconds earlier. He couldn't help it; his mind had already drifted off elsewhere–his next big kill. Albert loved hunting, loved fresh protein, and *loved* trophies–the big, furry, taxidermied ones.

Heavy steps banged on the wooden floors after their bedroom door erupted. Albert was especially excited today, as he heard rumors of the presence of some serious game from his friend who owned the property he hunted on–game with at least eight-pointed antlers. His son, Hunter, shared his mother's grumpiness, as his father's heavy footsteps startled him awake. His daughter, Hannah, on the other hand, slept right through it. Hunter stretched, rustled his sheets back over him, and tried to get back to sleep. With a faster beating heart and some adrenaline in his system, however, it would be a challenge. He could sympathize with his mother's tired, groggy irritability on most mornings.

Albert began his morning hunting ritual. The aromas of coffee and a toasted bagel danced throughout the house. With an abrupt crinkling, he pulled some potato chips out of the pantry and began munching on them. After all, Albert would say, you just gotta start your mornin' off with a good, greasy crunch. He ate them straight from the bag to his mouth so he didn't get any grease or crumbs on his fingers. He would never compromise the pristine beauty of his weapons or equipment by getting stains on them. *Pop!* The toaster scared him as it let him know his bagel was ready. Albert had been training for years not to be caught off-guard by the toaster, but it seemed like that toaster always knew when to go off and spook him. Even when he dedicated a month of mornings staring directly at it, anticipating it to pop out whatever golden-brown goodness was inside, it would still make him jump. He pointed at it with a snarl and squinted eyes. *This ain't over, you son of a bitch*, he thought. This battle of man versus machine had been decided, but the war had yet to be won. Obstinate Albert wouldn't have that.

Strawberry jam. Strictly for muzzleloader season, of course. Albert's go-to bagel spread depended solely on which hunting season he was in. This was sacred. A sacrosanct ritual. He always made sure there was enough jam of each flavor stocked up for his hunts. Apricot was for bow season and blueberry was for shotgun season. Even though seasons involving firearms were shorter, his favorite jam was strawberry. It was an extra treat for him. The superstition started after a particular morning where he got not only the first big kill of his life, but won five hundred dollars off of a scratch ticket at the convenience store beforehand. He'd been a firm believer ever since. He'd do anything to keep lady luck on his side.

Albert sat up faster than he should've as he felt his consciousness start to slip away before the blood equaled back out in his head. After a surprised sigh, he wiped off the bits of breakfast that were left on his mustache and started packing up his equipment to put in his truck. He slowly started to realize as he got out of his morning daze that there was a constant noise coming from outside. A cacophony of caws and chirps. He could hear them from his kitchen. A winged, twitching mass was on his lawn. Black drops upon a green canvas, close enough together that they took on the form of one great inky splotch on the grass. A collective.

"Lot more of ya than usual, that's for sure. My yard got that many bugs or whatever you eat in it? If you're havin' such a banquet, I'ma start chargin'!" Albert said with a chuckle. He couldn't hold in the temptation to run at all of the blackbirds and scare them away, dispersing them into a black, squawking cloud in the distance. For a brief moment he feared what could be revealed on the ground after they flew away. The morbid side of his brain went to thinking about there being a whole bunch of carrion or decaying fingers in the place of dirt and grass. He dismissed the thought, and with a smile went charging at them.

"I'm the most handsome scarecrow you'll ever see! Wha-whoa!" The blackbirds surprised Albert. None of them flew away. They stayed right there and he ended up stepping on one and hearing a crunch. He threw himself off-balance trying to come to an abrupt stop and fell face down into them. He felt the unfortunate ones who hadn't been granted an instant death still squirming underneath him. Their beaks like blunt spikes against his clothing. He turned his head over to the side and a bird stood there. It gave him a piercing look like it was ready to peck out his eye. He sprung up and was bombarded with frantic chirping. He saw the ones who hadn't died by the 215 lb mass dropped onto them still writhing in pain. Then he looked down at himself and saw some blood and feathers on him. Unlucky.

"What the hell? You shoulda moved, damn it! What's wrong with you guys, huh?" A sadness took over him for a brief moment. Albert had no problem killing animals, but he always did it in a way that would honor and respect them. This killing didn't feel right. His sadness turned into an uneasiness. He stepped forward and the birds made way for him. It was the darndest thing to Albert. He was the opposite of a scarecrow. He got towards the center of the mass and they closed the path on him. Stranded on his own little island in the middle of a bunch of blackbirds. Their sounds were making him sick. They echoed in his head and he couldn't think. Albert panicked, but didn't want to step on any more birds. The ground was so concentrated that it was impossible not to step on some if he wanted to get out. Albert kept looking around, pacing back and forth. The blood was drying on his shirt.

"Y'all got a death wish or somethin'? Get outta my way! Gahhh...I can't waste this day trapped on bird-fuckin' island! I got deer to hunt, and you sure as hell aren't ruining that." He could barely hear himself shout. Albert pointed out a straight line on the ground to his truck. "This is where I'm gonna step and run to get outta here. I'm tellin' all of you this now so you can't say I didn't warn you when you're a mess of blood n' feathers on the bottom of my boots! You hear that?" Albert got only more chirping in response. He looked down at himself and wiped off some of the remains. He took the first step running and all of the birds immediately took off flying. The black torrent fluttered up with such a viciousness, you'd think they were trying to force Albert into the ground with the sheer force of the wind made by their wings. They perched up on some nearby trees and left Albert on his ass so frightened and embarrassed that he looked around hoping nobody was watching. Of course nobody was watching, there were mostly just woods and fields around him. His neighbors' houses that were in visible range were all facing Albert from their sides with no windows, so no witnesses there either.

With a hard blink and shake of the head, he got up and walked his way back to his truck and hopped in the driver's seat. He looked in the rearview mirror and noticed feathers and some corpses of the birds he fell on gently rustling in the wind as a black, feathery splatter on the ground. He looked at it for a while. The longer he looked at it the less it was a splatter. It became an imprint of a headless body on the ground made out of dead blackbirds.

"Christ…that's not a pretty scene," he said as he drove out of the driveway. He wasn't about to waste any more time on those damn birds. *Maybe they won't be there by the time I'm back. Wind'll blow it all over or something*, he thought. He drove off, looking to kill something a little bigger than a bird or two.

CHAPTER 3

He pulled up to his usual spot back off the side of the road and hopped out of his truck. He opened up the large utility box at the front of his truck's bed and took out his gear. His hunting stand in the woods was a thirteen-minute walk. Albert thought of that stand as a holy place. A place of escape. Of concentration. There was no one else in the world in that spot besides him. Removed from humanity. Just him, the lesser fauna down about twenty feet below, and the bugs creeping and buzzing about. He took the break action muzzleloader out from its case and put in a primer and fired it. He got his field rod and bullet starter out, but couldn't seem to find the gunpowder to pour down the muzzle. He checked his backpack. Nothing. He looked all around his truck. Nothing.

"Damn it, I really left my gunpowder back at home, didn't I?"

After a bit more aimless rummaging he was convinced. He thought about it. He didn't want to return home right now, not after what happened earlier. Those birds were the reason he up and left in a hurry in the first place.

"They really made me forget my powder." He didn't blame himself. It was far from a typical morning, after all. He pulled out the shotgun he also had in a case in his utility box. "Not in season..." He sighed. He knew it wasn't a good look for a hunter like himself who prided himself in holding a clean reputation.

"...but I guess I'm gonna have to use you today. No one'll know. No ears out here besides mine. Whatever I shoot today I'll skin n' gut nice and clean." The muzzleloader went back into its case and that was that. Shotgun season for a day. Double-aught buckshot.

Albert made the trek to his hunting stand. It remained a perfect November morning. It had rained the day before, and the petrichor smell was calming. The clouds did not threaten nasty weather today, though. The air he breathed energized and refreshed him. From the pines to his lungs. Fragrant, plain beauty was all around him. Copies among copies of pitch pines as far as his keen eyes could see, each looking the same en masse, yet so different individually. Each paramount in the making of the barrens, which were not barrens at all, but a sea of greens, grays, and browns, all wading and warping in the wind as he weaved and wandered through them. Black, scarlet, and southern oaks were abundant among the pines as well. Their branches twisted and turned in sinister ways away from their thick trunks. The walk to and fro was just as delightful as the patient waiting game of the hunt to him. He had already almost completely forgotten about the awful and strange event that happened earlier this morning. He traversed his way to his stand. It was a sight seeing such a large man climb up that tree. Like a drunk, determined, out of shape bear. He bent one of his screw-in steps on his way up. They had seen wear and tear in their years of service, driven into trees and bearing his weight every climb.

He left everything behind once he entered those woods. He was The Hunter. A predator. An apex towering above in the trees, almost perfectly camouflaged save for the high visibility orange of his hat. He didn't see the orange as out of place, however. Not a flaw at all, but instead a primitive, Darwinistic device. After all, many dangerous animals have something that stands out. Some of the most deadly snakes and frogs possess the brightest, unnatural colors. An anglerfish beckons its prey with its alien, bioluminescent lure. Many birds have dashes of reds, blues, and yellows about their feathers. And Albert Lawless had his cap of bright orange, a deadly drop of paint on the forest canvas.

His human issues disappeared in the pines. He saw himself as more of an animal at that point. His gun might as well be a fatal stinger of some sort. A single sharp tooth, precise enough to do the job. A razor sharp claw ready to slice the jugular. His worries of the future, his children, what was for dinner, and this weekend's big game on TV–all vanished. It was a complete escape into a realm that never dealt with such trivial things. The pine barrens were the pine barrens and that is all they would ever be. Albert respected that. Embraced it. The chirping of the birds and rustling of the trees brought him further peace. The cold breeze kissed his face. He did not allow his mind to wander. This state of mind aided him when it was time to take the shot. He almost never missed.

An hour passed. A doe trotted by. He watched it with an appreciation, knowing that she may be the mother of a beautiful buck one day–like the ones he heard were rumored to be around already. The ones he *really* wanted. It would be another successful hunt under his belt, as well as a bragging point to bring up to his rival hunting buddy, Clint Morris. Ever since that elk hunting trip he and Clint went on in Montana, Albert had something to prove. Albert had been tracking an absolute titan of an elk for a few days. It was pure white. He thought it must've been some kind of rare albino variant. Clint mentioned to Albert how it was so ethereal and enchanting that it could have been revered as some sort of forest deity to the natives. Its antlers must've easily been over 3-feet long. Albert was all about having the head of a god stuffed and on display in his living room, though. Clint, an avid hunter himself, was disturbed at the thought of an eventuality where Albert killed this elk. He wasn't sure if he wanted it for himself or was just hypnotized by its divine aura, but whatever it was, it possessed him to slip 10mg of melatonin powder into Albert's drink the evening before he was getting ready to kill it. Albert overslept so long that, by the time he woke up, Clint had gone out, took a shot at the prize elk himself, missed, hit its antlers by accident, and wasn't too far from the bullet ricocheting back at him. Its antlers didn't even look damaged. They almost seemed to glow for a moment. He couldn't believe it. It didn't run, either. It stared straight at him for a while, exhaled a good amount of steam from its nose, and skipped off. As bad as Clint wanted to tell anyone that story, he had kept it to himself to this very day. Albert, waking up late and clearly pissed off, had his suspicions of Clint, but never said anything either. It was still a fun trip overall. A nice, relaxing time between old friends, away from the wives and kids.

Two more hours passed. Not much. Albert was struggling to stay in his focused, comfortable hunter state. He couldn't shake the thoughts and images popping up in his head from this morning. The barrens reflected this mental state, feeling more unwelcome and unfamiliar to him than ever before by the minute. Blackbirds circled above. Or was he just imagining them? The creeping, dark shroud of night would approach before he realized. More and more time passed. He was getting hungry. No big kill was on the horizon today so he decided to throw in the towel. He climbed his way down the tree and was getting along just fine until his foot slipped on the bent screw-in step about five feet from the ground. His balance was thrown off and he fell the rest of the way down. His head made contact with a broken stump on the ground and he was out cold.

He woke up even hungrier. The sounds of night filled his ears. It felt like just a second ago it was around dinnertime.

"Ugh, shit." Albert managed to sit up and rubbed the back of his head. "God damn step." He stood up with a grunt and went through his bag for his flashlight. He picked up his gun from the ground and started making his way back to his truck. He staggered a bit, still dazed from the fall. He stopped and stretched out his palms against a tree. He took deep breaths to regain his composure and then continued on. It was only a few minutes later that he noticed something strange. The racket of the night came to a halt. The crickets stopped chirping. The birds of the night stop cooing. The rodents stopped squeaking. Even the breeze rustling through the trees seemed to vanish. The sounds that gave him peace were now lost in a mysterious void. Albert only heard noise coming from himself– his breathing and footsteps–and it bothered him, as he thought it was not natural at all. He tried cupping his hands over his ears and tapping them to see if a little percussive maintenance would do the trick. It didn't help. A heightened anxiety caused him to begin walking faster. Never in his life had he heard such an abrupt stop to the sounds of nature. It was as if everything left–raptured into eternity, leaving him behind. Or did everything stop and keep quiet? What would they keep quiet from, though? Something they feared. Or revered? Albert thought the only thing in the woods they needed to respect was him. The hunter and apex predator. The badass outlaw pushing open the batwing doors with authority that had the whole saloon looking at him quietly. But no, something was wrong. He started walking even faster and that's when he noticed a different noise. It was hard to notice because every time he took a step, something else also took a step. Every time he breathed, something else breathed too. The subtle difference was that the steps being taken not by himself were hitting the ground harder with less surface area than his own foot. The breathing was deeper and had an ominous energy behind it.

Or was it all just his imagination getting the best of him? *What could possibly be following me and mimicking me near-perfectly?* he thought. *You're losin' it, Albert. Just get home and get something to eat. Lily will check out this bloody bump on your head and it'll be okay. I ain't with Schwarzenegger in the goddamn jungle right now being stalked by Predator.* He laughed it off and continued on, only another ten minutes before he reached his truck. He still couldn't figure out why it was so silent. Most of the time the barrens were *more* alive at night. It didn't sit right with him. Desperate to come up with a logical explanation, he thought about something he saw years ago that could be a terrifying answer as to what the mimicking movements were. It was a few years ago around summertime and he was sitting in a deer stand in a further northern part of the barrens. Around 7 PM. The wildlife was active that evening. So much that Albert saw an odd and unlikely thing happen. A black bear, which had mostly been hunted out of the barrens, had made its way far off to the right of his vision. Albert, knowing how adept bears are at climbing trees, kept completely still and readied his gun just in case. There was something strange about the bear, however. Its movements were abnormal. It came closer and he realized it was walking on two feet rather than galumphing around on all fours. It surprised Albert just how well the bear could walk on two legs, too. It got about thirty yards from him and, relieved, Albert lowered his weapon, now knowing he was not in any immediate danger. The bear was laboring one of its menacing paws. There wouldn't be any tree climbing for this big bruin anytime in the near future. He couldn't shake off the strangeness of seeing such a large, hulking beast go all bipedal on him. It felt so unnatural.

He stopped again and shined his flashlight around. He wished he hadn't. The seed of fear had been planted in his mind and disoriented him. Its roots were growing deep, fast. A light in the darkness can be something necessary and something hopeful, but Albert had wished he remained in the nescient abyss of night. As he pointed his light around, familiar shapes and shadows danced around, twisting into something new, unfamiliar, and frightening. Fear can fill in the blanks of what is seen and what is not with horrors sudden and dreadful. A cat opening a door late at night, for a split second, becomes a stretched out wraith barging in, ready to reap your soul. The wind animates a twig into a creeping claw, about to scurry up a tree or rip out your throat. Shadows from a flashlight turn mean and reach out, grabbing at you with a corporeal grip. Albert's own horrors manifested inside his head and made him question his surroundings. The vulnerability he felt was foreign and terrifying. There was no angle in which he did not feel exposed. Everything had eyes–the trees, the fauna, the brush. There was no hiding any action or thought. Every imagined eye stared with a gaze that shot into the depths of his being. Soul scrutiny. The trees closed in on him. He shone around his flashlight, looking for a way out, but the pines gave him no opening. The light picked up two glistening orbs in the darkness. They glowed a dead, opaline, hollowed-out light. He held the light there and readied his gun in his other hand. Roots spread fast along the ground and entangled him. His eyes darted around. The menacing eyeshine disappeared. Where did it go? What was it? Whatever was happening, it wasn't just a trick of the mind. The footsteps were approaching closer and closer. Their heaviness grew. He struggled, but it was no use, the roots around his limbs were unmoving and cold. He held on tight to his gun, but was in no position to aim and fire it. He could barely move his flashlight around, as his wrist was tangled. A lone, diagonal beam of light shot up towards the sky. A prey's beacon.

Albert knew roots didn't move like that. He thought he must still be unconscious, it must be some sort of nightmare. How could this be reality? He'd heard of the legends before, but that's all they were–legends. Just fun stories to tell around the fire to creep your drunk friends out while you make another s'mores. He closed his eyes and waited to wake up. His head was flooded with the sounds of screeching birds. He shook his head and took deep breaths, still denying he was awake. Whatever was walking towards him was now right in front of him. Albert's brittle denial was shattered by the steaming breath hitting his face that came from something staring closely at him. He opened his eyes and beheld a legend.

CHAPTER 4

Hot. Its breath was moist and unpleasant. Rancid. As if the fumes of hell itself were pouring out, wrapping around his face. Even on a cold, crisp November night, the warmness was unwelcome on his skin. He moved his head down and to the side to stop from breathing in as much of it as he could. It felt toxic, and the very thought of it entering into his lungs disgusted him. Albert was a big man–6'2 and with a good amount of muscle. Not too fat but still had a belly. He wasn't used to being looked down upon. It was a shameful, demeaning feeling, yet a feeling of bravado rushed over him, a defense mechanism as a result of the sheer and utter terror that came with the realization that he was not, in fact, dreaming. He opened his eyes and looked up.

"I got some Tic Tacs in my truck. Just let me go and I'll go get some for you. Trust me, you need some, you fuckin' freak of nature," he said. The cheeky smile he wore only lasted for a second. His line did not come out nearly as badass as he thought it would, for when he saw what was in front of him, he was horrified. "W-What the hell even are you?"

He was hoping his levity wasn't going to get him in trouble, as it did so many times in the past. He got a real good look at it. It was indifferent to his comment, still standing there breathing on him. It stared at him with awful, yellow-brown irises laid on top of striking white eyes. Tiny red veins divided the whiteness into pale rivers. Horizontal, beady goat pupils were transfixed onto Albert. The large, spaced-out eyes matched the head of a giant black goat, with inward-curved horns. A sinister, perverse horn curved more than the other and poked into the side of its head. Its protruding lower jaw revealed thick, menacing teeth.

"Listen, I know I got a charming face, but what are you try-"

"THIS IS MY DOMAIN."

Albert, still tangled up, had a confused look on his face. The sounds that came out of its mouth were deep, twisted, and contorted. They were not sounds of any animal or human he had ever heard in his life. He could only equate it to a strange language conveyed by some unnerving blares of creatures he had experienced throughout his hunting tenure along with his upbringing on the farm. The screaming of a goat mixed with the chilling yowl of a mountain lion, perhaps? No, add in a dash of dying elk with its intestines all scattered and tied up in the branches and maybe then you had a combination of what it sounded like. The most jarring thing for him, though, was what entered into his mind–language he could understand. It was verbal and telepathic at the same time. From those noises, he understood its message. Its warning. Its proclamation. Albert was scared and cold sweat dripped down his neck and back. He struggled in the tangled mess of living limbs. He let go of the flashlight and managed to squeeze the trigger of the shotgun with his other hand. The sound stunned the creature for a second and it put roots up around its body as a defense mechanism. Albert broke free. He grabbed the flashlight and took off in a sprint. He tried to dash and serpentine in various directions so as to confuse the creature and not get tangled in any roots, but everywhere he turned, it was there. By either the gleam of its wild eyes to the sheer presence he felt, he knew he wasn't making any distance. Leaves swished and crunched underneath his desperate feet. There was no outrunning this thing. He was getting winded and decided to cut off its angle of attack by having his back to a tree. He aimed the gun in front of him, trying to point the flashlight to wherever its eyes were. Backing up against the tree was a mistake. Roots crept up from behind the tree and tangled around his body, strapping him to it. More branches padded him in, stifling his sight and movement even more. Then two long, black, nightmarish limbs wrapped around the tree. It grabbed the shotgun and bent the metal barrel upwards. He was trapped again and this time without a functioning weapon.

"I'll leave-" Albert was still catching his breath. "I'll leave and never come back! Just let me go!" he said. He dropped the gun hoping to gain a semblance of trust or at the very least show that he wasn't a threat. He tried to treat it like any other dangerous, wild animal. No loud noises or sudden movements. It was all futile now that the gun was broken. Not to mention he was starting to realize that this creature had an intelligence beyond that of a mere forest beast. "Look, see? I just wanna go home to my family and I'll stay away, I swear." With a hand motion the creature released Albert. The roots crept back in the ground and the boughs and trees spaced out in an instant. The initial relief he felt vanished when he felt a terrible hand around his throat. It lifted him two feet from the ground and brought him eye-level with the devil. He grabbed its coarse, fur-coated arm and struggled to no avail.

"Wh-what do you want?" he managed to ask, choking. It pulled him closer to its thin, grave face. It kept looking at him with those unsettling goat eyes. He could see it had hooves to match, but more of a human-looking torso. It had jet black skin and its dark fur was thinner there.

"BRING ME A CHILD AND KEEP YOUR LIFE. REFUSE AND YOU WILL DIE A SLOW AND PAINFUL DEATH." Its horrible noises were even worse up close, feeling them creep up from the deep reaches of its abominable chest and coming out in a humming growl. The dour look in its eye, unfaltering, made it known to him that there would be no negotiating. It dragged its middle three fingers deep into the ground. Albert heard it whispering something he could not begin to comprehend. It took one finger and impaled him in the left leg. Another finger went into his right shoulder blade. The last incised into the right side of his neck. It put its mouth up to his ear. "...STRAWBERRY." It spread demonic bat wings that must have spanned ten feet or more. Twisted laughter spewed from its mouth that shook the trees. It threw Albert to the ground and took off. He lay there in bewilderment and pain. After laboring his neck for a while he got up and grabbed his gun. When he felt his neck he realized there was no exit wound from where that evil bastard had impaled him. He checked his leg and felt his shoulder. Nothing. It was just sore and a little red. *Did any of that actually just happen?* he wondered.

"What did you do to me!?" he yelled into the darkness. The languorous forest responded with silence. He began walking back to his truck, looking over his shoulder and up in the trees nonstop with a new paranoia. It was a new feeling he loathed. The serene place he felt safe and powerful in was ripped away and made into a haunted, fearsome space by what he thought was just a fable–just something to scare the kids with. He almost didn't even want to shine his flashlight around. The sounds of the forest weren't back besides the brushing of leaves and branches in the wind. *Maybe the critters are as spooked as I am,* he thought. Once he got to his truck he packed up his things and got in and sat inside. Just sat there. Staring at the steering wheel. Thinking about what happened. What it told him. He drove home. It was late.

CHAPTER 5

Lily had some friends over that night. They all enjoyed playing board and trivia games and had bonded over it since high school. She was sitting in a circle between her friends Brad and Ashlee playing a tense social deduction game where a team had to figure out who in their group was the spy. The spy had to figure out where they were before they got caught. They could only speak in questions. Lily was about to ask Brad, a guy she had a thing for in high school, a question when Albert came through the front door.

"Oh, hey guys," he said in a low voice before darting to the bedroom. They looked at each other.

"Hey Albert. Been holding it in, huh?" one joked. They all laughed, but Lily's chuckle was filled with concern. Why was Al acting so weird? He would usually grab a drink and socialize with them, even if it was only for a brief amount of time. He didn't find out, did he? How would he? The trepidation that accompanied a guilty conscience made her uneasy. She was filled with anxiety and blanked out while the rest of her friends awaited her turn in the game.

"Nature calls, right? But when you're in nature and she's callin,' I think it's pretty clear what's gotta be done!" another commented. They laughed some more and Lily apologized and excused herself to go check on him. She walked down the hall and was thinking about what she would ask next for the game. A shirtless Albert was off to the left in their bathroom. He was flummoxed, looking at himself in the mirror, inspecting his leg, shoulder, and neck. Light, curious footsteps approached him from behind.

"Hey babe. You alright? What's wrong? You know, I found a whole bunch of dead blackbirds in our backyard today, it's really creeping me out. That's like some bad omen shit you see in a horror movie. I got rid of them before the kids could see," she paused, then sighed. "Christ. You think it's just some sick prank or something?"

"Weird. Weren't there when I left this morning," Albert said with a blank, frightened stare, looking down at the floor.

"You're not mad at me for anything, are you?" she asked, tense and waiting for a response. She got to the bathroom doorway and was relieved. She didn't need a response anymore. "Jesus, Albert! Is this why you were home so late? What happened?" She got some supplies from the cabinet and started cleaning the wound on his head. "Do you have a concussion?"

"I don't think so." He splashed some water on his face.

"Please try not to move while I finish cleaning this, hun. You look like you've seen a ghost. Or the devil. Sheesh!"

A blank stare on his face accompanied a grave silence that concerned Lily. This was very much unlike Albert.

"I think I did see the devil," he said under his breath. It wasn't loud enough for Lily to hear.

"What was that? Are you sure you don't have a concussion? Please, would you tell me what happened?"

Albert realized he didn't want to raise any more suspicion and snapped out of it. He didn't want to worry his wife anymore than he already had, and if his children saw him like this they would be worried too. He tried to act normal and play it off. He looked at her in the reflection of the mirror and started with a little laugh to lighten the mood.

"I guess I'm just getting a bit clumsy, babe. Wanna know what happened?" He raised his eyebrows and put on a smile. "I was almost done climbing down my tree and slipped and fell! Right on my ass, but I hit my head on the way down too. Must've scraped it on a branch or stump. Laid there for a bit, trying to come to my senses. Took me a while to collect some of the things I dropped. I will be honest, it dazed me a bit because I went the wrong way trying to get back to my truck! Sorry if I spooked you by being late. Thanks for cleanin' me up." He started itching his left leg. "Damn, must've gotten a bug bite or two on my leg."

Now they were both hiding something from each other. They knew how to mask things up enough to be believable, although a hint of suspicion still existed in the backs of both of their minds.

"Al, you really need to be careful. You had me worried sick. You sure something didn't scare you out there?"

Albert turned around and gave her a hug.

"You kiddin' me? I got a gun and my superior human intelligence out there. Nothing can scare me!"

"Hmm. Yeah, I'd like to see more of this 'superior human intelligence' you speak of." They both laughed and held each other.

"By the way, why would I be mad at you?" Albert asked.

"Oh, what? Oh well, I don't know. You seemed dismissive when you came in. I wasn't sure if I told you I had invited some friends over tonight or not. You know we can get a bit loud for the kids. Especially if drinks are involved." Lily improvised the response well and figured it was enough to stave off any further suspicion. Especially with Brad still there.

"No, silly, I don't mind at all. Just don't bet on any of the games you're not good at!" He laughed and she gave out a nervous, yet relieved chuckle. "Go on now, get back to your fun night. I'm fine. They probably think we forgot they were here and started doin' something dirty by now."

"Oh, please!" She smiled, and gave him a kiss on the lips. "Maybe later," she said as she walked out of the door with a smirk on her face. Albert wore an expression on his face that said 'I wouldn't mind that at all!' He thought about Lily and her way of making him feel like everything would be alright. She was great at making him forget all the bullshit in his life. Then he started to itch his leg again. He had an enormous pile of bullshit to deal with now. One he couldn't ignore. A mental stench that would grow more vile by the hour. Its words echoed in his mind. It's like they were trapped inside, bouncing around. He took a shower and tried to clear his head. *There's no way I'm bringing any child back there to that ugly bastard. Who knows what it would do to them? Fuck him.* He itched his leg some more and it was becoming even more red and sore; it stung in the shower. The pain pissed him off. *He did do something to me though, didn't he?* He sent his hunting buddy Clint a text asking to meet up sometime soon. If there was anybody Albert could confide in with a story like this, it would be him. While Clint *would* listen, was there any possibility that he would believe everything? Albert had his doubts. But if Clint believed him, maybe they could come up with a plan and score the biggest kill of their lives. Maybe they could hunt down and kill the New Jersey Devil.

CHAPTER 6

Hunter Lawless was adjusting well to the 6th grade. He was a smart kid and when something piqued his interest he was all for it. He found himself not all that engaged most of the time in class, though. Gym was fun, at least. The biggest challenge was always dealing with new teachers. His math teacher was stern and a lot of his classmates didn't like her, but he knew you just had to behave and be on her good side. His history teacher was loud, but fun. Unfortunately, the loads of work in that class canceled out the fun. The gym teachers were usually all cool. They always favored the athletes, though. It was shaping up to be a pretty OK year of middle school overall. One curveball was thrown into the equation, however. There was a brand new 6th grade Language Arts teacher at Park Ridge Middle School. Hunter took comfort in knowing she was new. New teachers are pushovers. It's always an easier time having them. He was hoping they would read and study something that held his interest. And that he could goof off a little more with his friends than usual. Language arts class was always a hit or miss.

Lola Santos felt like she had a solid start to her first year of teaching thus far. The rapport she had already grown with her students helped her continue to build a positive classroom environment. She was afraid she wouldn't be able to connect with them, being younger and all, but that was not the case most of the time. She found it amusing when they would rabbit trail off of a lesson and chat about things. She learned more about them that way–by letting them talk. Sometimes it would go too far and she would have to reel them back in; time was always of the essence. She was a language arts teacher after all, some of the only teachers expected to teach not one, but two core skills that are very different from each other–reading and writing. It was an arduous task.

This year's 6th grade class was notorious for their bad behavior. Things could get out of hand quickly, especially if certain kids had the same class together. A class could have chemistry in a good way–producing a sweet, flowing nectar of knowledge and growth–or in a bad way–a chaotic concoction of disrespect and apathy. Every class Ms. Santos had besides one was the latter. It was already wearing her down. Imposter syndrome was starting to set in. It teased at her confidence and her abilities, trying to wear her thin. November was flying by and she was already behind on her pacing for her lessons. It was a new week though, and she was trying to take it one day at a time per the advice of her mentor teacher. It was helping. Most of the teachers in her grade would arrive early and have little chats out in the hall before the tsunami of students rushed in. Lola felt othered by the majority of her coworkers–jaded veteran teachers that never matured from their clique phase in high school, and carried all parts, toxic and unprofessional, with them. Their endless gossiping was exhausting. There were a good few who weren't like that which Lola was thankful for, however.

"Hey Lola. How was your weekend?" asked her mentor and fellow language arts teacher, Amanda Thomas. Ms. Thomas was an organizational machine and handled bad student behavior well. She came from a background of early childhood education and those skills carried over nicely into the middle school environment. Lola had massive respect for her. She would often work on the weekends, not getting paid any extra, just because she cared about the quality of her students' education. Lola couldn't imagine sacrificing the only free time she had. At some point you have to prioritize yourself. Lola valued her time more than gold.

"It was nice! I was able to watch a few movies I had been wanting to watch for a while. I also cooked some pretty yummy teriyaki chicken. I bought a new wok recently and it's been so fun to use. How was yours?"

"It was good. My husband and I took our kids to the park for a bike ride. It was a nice break from trying to rework all of this new B.S. curriculum they handed to us this year," she said with slight indignation and even more fatigue in her voice. "At least the book we're reading right now is a good one. It's just all the lessons and shit they try to make us cram into our block–we only have an hour and a half in our block!"

"Yeah, that really baffled me. They hand us lessons based on a three hour class!? I *wish* I had that much time, but that's not the reality, is it?"

"Absolutely not. And they do nothing to help," Amanda replied. By "they," she meant their supervisors. The ones that were always late and rescheduling meetings and whatnot, which made the teachers, who already had a million things to do, have to adjust and replan one *more* thing.

"It's infuriating. And *how* much more are they making than us? For being so incompetent and helping just a teensy little bit? I'm already stressed out as it is and they aren't really helping to alleviate it much."

Amanda rolled her eyes.

"Too damn much. And oh, your stress alleviation? 'Here, take some free candy, on us!' What a joke."

Lola laughed.

"Well, let's remember–take a deep breath and take it one day at a time. These kids need us." She was trying to settle Amanda down. The Monday dread was seeping from every pore of her body.

"You're right. We'll get through it. Sometimes taking your own advice is the most difficult thing." The bell intruded with a loud, jarring buzz. Youthful chatter began to fill the hallways.

"We will, Amanda, we will. Have a good class!"

"Thanks, you too."

CHAPTER 7

"Alright. Good morning class! Please work on your warmup and prepare yourself for *two* new units today: one being vocabulary, the other being," she put her hands up, moved her fingers around, and gave her students a comically fake, scary look, "foooooolkloooore!" She oo'd like a ghost. "I meant to do this unit in October, y'know, the spooky month, but I figured November isn't too far away." Her class was intrigued. A student had her hand raised.

"Ms. Santos?"

"Yes?"

"Is folklore scary? Like horror?"

"Well, not all the time."

"Then why were you making ghost noises?"

"I just like to be dramatic sometimes. Believe me, guys, you ain't seen the last of Ms. Santos being dramaaaaatic!" She stretched her words and pantomimed various emotions. Some of her students mocked her and others looked at her like she was crazy, but she paid no heed to any of it.

"Alright, so–" Ms. Santos was interrupted by two rude students chattering in the back. "Katie, Grace, *up here*."

Grace acquiesced, but Katie wasn't giving up so easily. With a harrumphing sigh, making it clear to the entire class that she was annoyed that her important conversation had been disrupted by the teacher, she posed Ms. Santos a question.

"Why do we have to learn about this stuff? It's not like we're going to use it in real life."

"You like stories, don't you?" Ms. Santos replied.

"Only some. None like this."

"Do you know why folklore was commonly taught in a startling way to children?" She walked closer to Katie.

"No, why?" she asked with an annoyed look on her face.

"Because kids are more likely to *listen* when they are scared. It doesn't just go in one ear and out the other. I imagine you're a pro at that, though. You're never going to learn with that mindset, Katie. I am disappointed that you would be so quick to dismiss a lesson your teacher is trying to give you, especially after working hard on it. I try to make things fun and interesting when I can, you know."

Katie was not used to being talked to like the child she was. She expected everyone to answer to her. She didn't feel the need to explain herself, even towards the adults whom she should respect. Lola could already see cases of the entitled brats in her classes, but this girl was up there. She tried to approach their arrogance in a professional way that encouraged them to be better people. She had to keep her anger and frustration in check, as she knew these kids were just products of their environments–parents especially. During back-to-school night she could see it. The parents who made a little bit more money than the other parents. About half of them supercilious and insufferable. The kids pick up on that stuff fast. Other times it was a lack of parenting–a desperate cry for attention. They resorted to the internet for their parenting, personality, and attention. A sad, shallow lifestyle encouraged by society, being driven into their developing brains at a critical, fragile young age. A malicious influence. A soulless, unforgiving factory churning out apathy with impunity. True evil. And Lola had to fight against it every day. This dawned upon her two months into the job. Was it too late to change careers? This was the question itching in the back of her mind. Her priority was to survive the school year first and foremost. With a deep breath and an understanding that Katie was speechless, she continued.

"So let me ask you a question before I give you a quick example: What would be the lesson behind this little piece of folklore? You guys like to play outside, right? And when you're having fun, time really does just fly on by. Suddenly it's nighttime. Oops! Too much fun was had. Well things are a lot different at nighttime. Your surroundings can quickly become unfamiliar. You get lost. You fall and get injured or trapped. Or a stranger kidnaps you." She could feel the tense and unsettling air in the classroom. "I know, guys–it's scary. But now you're listening. So now you're out in the dark and may not know your way home and may find yourself in a dangerous situation. It would happen a lot and children your age *would* get lost. So a piece of folklore was told around a small town in Canada. And they spread the story of the Finger Eater to all of their families and children."

"Finger Eater!? What the-"

"Yes, Jason. You like your fingers, right?"

"Uh, yeah I guess so."

"You use them for a lot of things, right?" Some students chuckled.

"I mean, yeah."

"So you wouldn't want some creepy woman to come up and start crunching on your fingers with her old, rotten, stained teeth, now would you?" Sounds of repulsion were heard throughout the class.

"No ma'am. I ain't sticking my fingers in any old lady's mouth!" More laughter.

"Exactly, so–" A hand shot up and Ms. Santos noticed. She called on him. "Hunter! Yes?"

"So in order to get the kids to stop staying out so late, they made the folklore of this lady?"

"Exactly! That was the answer I was looking for. Great job! Stories can be devices. Just like the phones I know some of you have, even though you're *way* too young to need them. And when I say device I mean they are used for something. In this case, it is used for teaching children a lesson that they shouldn't stay out too late because it could get dangerous and worry parents to death!"

"I like creepy stories, but I'm not sure if I've ever learned a lesson from them before. I just like the blood and gore and monsters," shouted out another problematic student who went by the name J. They loved to overshare and did not have a filter.

"Well I suggest you think more deeply about the stories you read then, J. I am a fan of horror myself and I can safely say there are lessons to be learned. Like if a big scary killer is standing in front of you with a knife, don't just stand there and look at him–run away!" Her delivery was playful enough for most of her students to laugh a little at it. J was amused.

"Alright, Ms. Santos. I'll try just for you next time. I'm a real deep thinker."

"Let's just hope that's reflected in the papers you write for me this year!" Ms. Santos said. J decided not to push it further. The lesson continued with Ms. Santos using examples from Native American cultures, talking about how a large majority of them were verbal and didn't write things down. This resulted in a ton of interesting folklore, like the creation of the Earth, the destruction caused by a great flood, and so on. She got into a good groove and was already having fun with the unit. She was engaged and she felt as if most of her students were as well. That was a victory in her book, especially for *that* class. It was her most disruptive by far. She powered through the rest of the day and sighed a breath of relief that she made it through while feeling productive. It was one of those days where the beautiful, curious feeling of students learning was in the air, almost palpable. She drove home and made some fajitas for herself. Afterwards she celebrated the day by playing a new video game with her favorite ice cream by her side–peanut butter vanilla. She passed out in her bed by 10:30PM with a book about Greek Mythology on her lap.

CHAPTER 8

The itching was getting worse. Albert Lawless had a ton of things to do, and scratching his leg every couple of minutes was annoying him. It felt so good, though, even if some blood trickled down his leg while he did it. Lily urged him to go to the doctor, thinking he had psoriasis. He didn't consider her comments or advice, however. His preoccupation came off to his family as cold and terse. His mind raced with how he was going to manage work, what he was going to say to Clint, and how he was going to plan tricking the devil himself. Was it even possible? He was starting to fall behind at his job, forcing his employees to pick up on the slack. Lawless Landscaping was fairly successful in New Jersey. Albert was a handyman who had a good eye for design. He was also a reasonable, fair, and diligent boss most of the time. He had the respect of his employees and knew them well. They knew something was amiss. As did his family. It was now four days after the nightmare confrontation in the pine barrens, and he wasn't hiding his itch anymore. Lily kept theorizing as to what it could be–a nervous tick? Poison ivy? He *was* out in the woods the night he got it, after all. Lily got home a little early that night and made a delicious cheese-stuffed meatloaf with a side of mashed potatoes and peas. They were eating dinner in near silence. Decapitated deer heads mounted above them watched with fake, sable eyes. The TV was on in the background. Lily tried to spark some conversation.

"So the weather looks like it's going to be pretty nice this weekend."

"Really? Dad, maybe we could go fishing at that lake we went to before where I caught that cool-looking rainbow perch. And that turtle that tried to bite my lure! I know we've been talking about wanting to go back for a while now," Hunter said. He had a gleam of excitement and hope in his eyes. Like when he was younger and asked if he could grab a candy bar at the convenience store. Albert was staying quiet for too long.

"Hun? How about it?" Lily chimed in.

"What? Oh. This weekend won't work for me," Albert said, detached from the conversation. They missed the snarky, interested father who usually sat down at the dinner table, asking questions and cracking jokes whenever he could. The gleam in Hunter's eyes faded in an instant as he was shot down for no good reason. Albert knew there was a good reason, but he wasn't going to drop that on his family.

"Oh…ok," Hunter managed, hurt. Another awkward silence.

"Hey, Hannah, how about you tell Daddy about your recent grade for Language Arts?" Lily asked, trying to pump air into the dead lungs of the conversation.

"Daddy, I got a 100 on my spelling test this week! Ask me how to spell, hmm, "passage" or, umm, "example"!"

"That's great, hun." Curt and cold. Albert was trying to make some mental effort to sound supportive for his family, but it was futile. His mind was tangled with stress and planning. Lily egged an enthusiastic Hannah on.

"P-A-S-S-A-"

Albert tuned out. The random letters being thrown around into the air by his daughter were background noise. Something on the TV hooked his attention instead. He got up, grabbed the remote, and turned up the volume. He sat back down and continued eating. Two news anchors shifted their tones from jovial (with the weatherman) to solemn in less than a second. It was a professional spectacle, seeing that switch they could flip on and off inside their heads–night and day. A heavy story was coming.

"As we get closer and closer to the end of the year, New Jersey *still* can't seem to break free from a disturbing and heartbreaking catastrophe plaguing the state, leaving many parents empty, confused, and in tears. Hundreds of new missing children cases stacked onto the already staggeringly high amount in the Garden State happened within the span of these ten and a half months, with no downward trend in sight. Investigators and law enforcement are at a loss, but they assure us they are trying as best as they can to fight it."

"That's just unthinkable. Truly tragic, Stacy," said the male news anchor.

"Would you turn that off, Al? I'm trying to eat here and I don't want to hear about that," said Lily. Albert kept it on. The anchors resumed their volley.

"I can't even begin to imagine losing my children and never knowing what happened to them or where they ended up. It's a nightmare," she replied, shaking her head.

"I agree, Stace," he turned to the camera. "Please, folks, do your best to keep your children safe. Know how to take proper precautions and be transparent with your children. I know it may be difficult talking to your young ones about this, but you *don't* want to come home one day knowing you'll never see them again."

"There's an article on our website going over things relevant to this situation and links with different techniques in teaching your kids public safety and to handle times when they may find themselves alone in a safe manner."

"Truly devastating."

"We're here now with Chief Investigator Campbell of the New Jersey State Police. Chief Campbell, many of us are asking ourselves, will this ever end?"

"We are working closely with the FBI to try and figure out what's–"

"I said, would you please *turn that off!?*" Lily grabbed the remote from the table and switched channels. She noticed that the news was scaring the kids and wanted to salvage whatever peace there was left at dinner. Albert sat there and connected the dots. His anxiety was through the roof. He got up from the table and went into the bedroom. He didn't finish his meatloaf. Albert always finished his meatloaf.

Lily and the kids finished dinner. After she cleaned up, they went into their rooms. She had had enough. She wanted things to be back to normal. She couldn't get the festering idea out of her head. It took place front and center. Poking and prodding her head. *But how? How does Albert know? Does she really look that much like him? He's never been this way. I have to come straight with it. Maybe he'll understand. Maybe I'm blowing it out of proportion.* She took a deep breath and headed towards their bedroom. Albert was sitting there typing notes into his phone. Or was it a thought-out message, addressed to her?

"Hey."

"Hey," Albert said. He was still cloudy and preoccupied. He itched his leg.

"Listen. What has been going on with you?" She took his phone from his hands and crossed her arms. "Look at me, Al! I'm trying to have a serious talk with you! What has been up with you lately? Not only is it affecting my mood and stressing me out, it's affecting the kids too."

"I…I wish I could explain it all. But I just can't."

Tears were forming in Lily's frustrated eyes. Albert wasn't budging.

"Babe. Why not?"

"I'm…afraid." It was hard for him to say. Albert Lawless was never afraid. The only time she had ever heard those words leave his mouth was when they were dating and getting serious. He admitted to Lily that he was afraid he would never find anyone again. After his wife died. But there he was. With her.

"What are you afraid of? Listen, whatever was said, whatever happened, we can fix things. We can get back to a normal, happy life."

"I wish it were that simple," he paused and itched his leg again. "It's just something I think would put our family in danger." Danger. Lily was almost at her breaking point. Would Albert really rather keep quiet about it? No…

"It'll *never* get better that way. You know, don't you? Somehow you put two and two together, you heard something from someone. I can see it in your eyes–god–I can practically *feel* it oozing off of you! You found out who Hannah's father is." Boom. And just like that it was off of her chest. It was all out in the air. Now she could finally begin to try and help herself and her family heal.

"Wait, what?"

"Oh, come on, Albert, don't play dumb now. I know it's a pretty shitty situation, but just come on. Do you not want me to involve him in anything anymore? Just say the word."

"Involve who? Lily, your husband died years ago."

"What? No…you know that's not true. How else could I have followed up? After you opened up to me about your wife dying, what, was I gonna say 'Yeah, I still hang out with my baby daddy from time to time?' For chrissakes, Brad was never even my husband to begin with!" All the beans were spilled. Albert's continued expression of confusion and bafflement was making her grow antsy and upset. A seed of doubt grew deep inside of her. She felt a weight drop in the pit of her stomach. Was she wrong? *Was* she overthinking things? Did Albert get into some sort of serious trouble he couldn't talk about? Either way there was a cathartic rush that came over her; it at least felt better to get that off of her chest after years of holding it in.

"Brad is Hannah's dad? The Brad that I saw this past Saturday night? God, Lily, no. I didn't know any of that." And for some reason, he didn't care. He didn't feel a thing from that confession. He knew he should be at least a little upset. It was, after all, a fairly nasty secret that Lily kept for years. But when you have an appointment with the devil, it puts things into perspective. He didn't have the time nor the mental capacity to deal with much else. He saw the toll it was taking on his family and he hated it. He found himself taking his first smoldering step down into hell. It would take everything away from him–his family, his peace of mind, his own self. He thought about it for a bit. Just sat there. Something cold from the innermost parts of his mind reached out. It spoke to him. It tried to detach him from Hannah. It taunted him and bartered with him, encroaching on his sanity. What was it? Survival instinct kicking in? No. It was much more sinister. Even if the devil was out of sight, he wasn't out of mind. *She's not even your daughter. Why should you care? Save yourself. Bring her there. You know you hate her. She looks like him. Every time you see her face you'll see him from now on. And he'll act like everything is fine. And so will she. They both still*

28

think about sleeping with each other. Hit them where it hurts. Why should you take care of his child? And he has the audacity to still come into your house? You should kill him, too. In front of her. And then kill her while she's screaming. Set an example for Hunter. Show him what a true predator looks like. But first, bring the child here. The foreign, intrusive thoughts whirred and hissed in his head like a cyclone of snakes. Albert was itching his leg hard and without any response to pain like a drug addict. He shook his head violently and wanted to scream, but what came out was more like a desperate hum. Lily hated it. She hated all of it. She started crying.

"I'm sorry. I'm so sorry I've lied to you for so long. I love you. I don't know, Al. Brad is such a big part of my friend group and it would just split us all apart if some nasty drama happened. I didn't want to lose any of you. I'm sorry."

"I can't do this right now, Lily. We'll talk about this another time." His head was buzzing. He felt bad for Lily. She had no idea. And he still wasn't going to tell her. He anticipated her next question.

"Al, at least tell me what is going on then? What is so bad that has happened to you that it's got you like this? Please tell me. Please!"

"I can't involve you, Lily. I'm sorry. Maybe one day when it's all over and done with I'll tell you. But I've got a long road ahead of me. Just know you guys are safe and I wanna keep it that way. I'm gonna get a shower. Please try and calm down."

Lily made no attempt to pry further, but she was scared. Calm down? Like that was a possibility. Any attempt to occupy her mind with something else would fail. Millions of different situations shot through her head of what messes Albert could be in. None of them would satisfy her. She was going to have a hard time accepting that she wouldn't know. Albert tried to prepare himself for what was coming. He knew what little sleep he was going to manage to get would make him sloppy. He had to be on edge; he was dealing with a malevolent and fearsome force. He elected to sleep on the couch so that Lily could get some sleep. That night he tossed and turned, itching his leg almost nonstop. He was bleeding again.

It was 3AM when he heard something strange. A metallic squeak caused by the wind? No. The sound was coming from the window. It was sporadic. Albert traversed his dark living room, stumbling around, confused. He got close to the window and what he heard shook him. It was laughter. Dreadful and inhuman, changing pitches on a whim. He didn't want to peek behind the blinds. He backed up and went into the kitchen. Not wanting to go back into the bedroom or down to the basement for a gun, he opted for a kitchen knife. He unlocked the kitchen side door and peeked out of the glass screen door. It was dark. He turned on the side porch light. He could see his driveway, garage, truck, and the back of his wife's car, nearest to him. The laughter was more distant now, and shrouded by the sounds of the vibrant night, but he couldn't shake the feeling of being watched. Similar to how he felt in the barrens last Saturday. He looked around and hesitated to go out front and see what the laughing was. He was glad he didn't. On his final scan of what he could see, his eye caught something. He pretended to keep scanning, not wanting to look directly at it. His heart started racing. It was looking through the back windshield of Lily's car. Its head was twisted sideways and it stared right at him. It had hair in odd places. A piercing, empty gaze came from impossible dark holes where eyes should have been. Accompanying the eyes was a large, gaping hole resembling what could only be its mouth. He needed to see it again. He couldn't believe it was really there. He shot a quick glance and sure enough, there it was. Stricken with fear, he slammed the door shut, locked it, and retreated back onto the couch in the living room. He had to be careful because he was clutching the knife. The laughing continued for another hour, then faded away. He wanted to warn Lily about something being in her car, but didn't want her to think he was crazy. They were just hallucinations, after all. Auditory and visual from a lack of sleep. That's all it was. He itched his leg and rested. He managed to get a smidgen of sleep.

CHAPTER 9

A pale gray morning reflected Hunter's mood. He could hear his mom and dad arguing about something last night. It didn't sound good. He didn't want to lose either of them. Since Albert's strange change in mood, Hunter couldn't help but feel he was somehow the problem. The mindset spawned from his protection over his little sister and the fact that he was the older child, and everything was always the older child's fault. How, though? He always tried his best in school and the results were exceptional. He played the sports his dad wanted him to play, he helped with things around the house, he didn't do anything rebellious…so what was it? He stared out the window on the bus ride to school. At least he had Ms. Santos' class to look forward to. Entering her classroom was like entering a different world, free of any outside issues and problems. She was interesting and lenient. Hunter did good in her class while still being able to chat with his friends and goof around a little bit. Before he knew it it was time for language arts class. He wasn't used to having it so early, as today was a half day for the district. For the students at least. The lucky teachers had to stay a full day for professional development.

Lola Santos stood in front of her class holding a sheet of paper. She held it out in front of her so that all of her students could see it.

"This piece of paper is red."

All of her students had confused and amused looks on their faces.

"This piece of paper is red," she repeated. The inflection in her voice convinced everyone in the room she believed the paper was red. Hunter raised his hand.

"Yes, Hunter?"

"Ms. Santos, umm, the paper is blue." Hunter was confident that he was one-hundred percent correct on this one and was starting to question his teacher's sanity. Ms. Santos just stood there looking at the paper held out in front of her with a new, confused look on her face.

"What are you, colorblind? It's clearly red," she said, unconvinced. More of her students started laughing and yelling out that it was blue. It was easy to rile up this particular class, and before they could start an amused uproar, she spoke up again with a chuckle in her voice.

"Guys, you must be pranking me right now. I'm looking at the paper and it's red, see?" She turned the paper around, and sure enough, it was red. Red on one side and blue on the other. Her students started to laugh.

"Okay, Ms. Santos, you got us with that one."

"Yeah, good joke. Aren't we supposed to be reading or something?"

They were curious as to where she was going with this. She walked around the room, flipping the paper around. It got quiet. She got back up to the front.

"One, single, important word. Perspective. You see, class, I wasn't lying about the color of the paper, was I? And in turn, neither were any of you. Well, besides Kenny over here saying it was yellow. You might wanna get your eyes checked there, bud. Don't you play baseball, too?" They chuckled at the banter. She continued, "The paper experiment here was all a matter of perspective. What is perspective?"

"Like a third person perspective in a book?" shouted out a student.

"We're getting somewhere, but please don't call out. But yes, kinda like that. That's called what? A third person what? They can be omniscient or limited. Yes, Bella?"

"A narrator! Right?"

"Correct! And narrators do what?"

"They tell the story."

"Exactly. It's their telling of the story. *My* story was that the paper was red, whereas yours was that it was blue. We had different perspectives. But the important thing is, guys, that we were both right. Not all the time are things always black and white. It's not just one side or the other, there's often a lot more that goes into it. The gray in the middle. Y'know, you mix black and white together and get gray? Anyways, we need to consider different perspectives when dealing with topics and stories. It is so important to see more than one side of things, right?"

"Yeah, or else we would've been arguing 'til the end of class," chimed in a student. Ms. Santos laughed.

"You're right. Us adults get caught up in that a lot more than you'd think. We argue over a topic we think is black and white, ignoring the gray in the middle. Because that requires us to think more critically. Well, guess what, guys? This is language arts class, and we are all critical thinkers here. I challenge you today to at the very least consider an opposite perspective of an old folktale that probably most of you know: *Little Red Riding Hood*. We are going to read this version of it from the perspective of the wolf." That caught their attention. Some were eager to hear it. Others were questioning why they should hear his story, he was the bad guy after all. Ms. Santos responded by saying that maybe we could still learn something from the bad guy. To keep an open mind. It was an interesting read and a fantastic lesson. Hunter was engaged and enjoyed it. He never thought school could be such an escape.

After the lesson Ms. Santos introduced a group project on folklore. There were some groans of disbelief in the room. She ignored them.

"So you guys are going to pick a piece of folklore from North America, it could be from somewhere close to home, or somewhere far away. Then you are going to do your project on it. It could be a powerpoint presentation, an art project, a movie project–I always want to give you guys options for things like this. Here is what I expect from your groups." She went over the syllabus. "Boom. If your project contains everything from that syllabus, you're going to get a good grade. And for all of you who like to take initiative, if you get done early and would also like to present early, you are free to." Ms. Santos knew project-presenting could make some students anxious, and didn't want that anxiety building up in them. There was no use in any of them waiting if they were ready and wanting to get it over with. Anticipation lingered around the room. She knew what they were all thinking. She was not going to be generous about it. "I have already assigned your groups and will read them out loud in a second. Each group does their own, unique piece of folklore. Right now, I would like to go over some examples of North American folklore with you. One is right in our backyard, shocking enough! I'm sure some of you have heard of the Jersey Devil?" Some knew, some didn't. There was a mixture of nervousness and curiosity about the room, although both of those feelings are very close to each other, aren't they? Of course, there were a few kids that didn't care, always disinterested in anything anyone had to say if it wasn't themselves. Nevertheless, Lola was satisfied enough with the apparent interest from the majority of her class. She wanted to make a fun project with different options for her students to collaborate and create something neat. "Another example would be from my neck of the woods way south of here and across some water in Puerto Rico–El Chupacabra! It's no devil, but it is some sort of strange creature. Reptilian and alien."

A student had her shy hand raised. Ms. Santos noticed and called on her.

"Ms. Santos, is there really a devil in New Jersey?"

"Well, there have been 'sightings' of it for years, which have turned into New Jersey's own little piece of folklore. It's supposed to be this big, weird beast-thing with horns and wings and hooves. As for reliable pictures and proof of it? I wouldn't let it keep you up at night, dear. It's just folklore, after all. There *is* an interesting poem about him, though. I know we're running low on time, but I can read it for you guys real quick. Here it goes:

Devil devil in the woods,
See Him, run away you should.
Trust your instincts, trust your fear,
Or it's you who'll disappear.

Pretty spooky, huh?"

Disappear. The word rang in Hunter's ears. Where did he recently hear about things disappearing? Two people were talking about it somewhere. That's it! The news channel his dad had turned up at dinner last night.

"There's also a saying that has been used for a while relating to the Jersey Devil: 'Don't stare into the woods.'"

"What does that mean?" asked an apprehensive student.

"Well, according to legend, the pine barrens and surrounding woods have a very dark and ominous aura about them. Like, bad energy, right? The Jersey Devil's existence alone within the barrens is enough to affect the people who live around it. If you even *stare* into the woods for too long, as the saying goes, it can make you go 'crazy.' Start seeing and hearing things. I finger quote the word, 'crazy,' because I think it has to deal with how we as humans tend to psych ourselves out if we look at something for too long. The whole 'I gazed into the abyss and it gazed back' thing. That's probably not the actual quote. It's from a guy named Nietzsche, you may or may not learn about him one day. Not in middle school, though! Anyways, our brains automatically try to recognize patterns and faces, so if a couple of twigs and leaves line up just right, or if a pattern on the tree bark looks similar enough to a face, we'll see them. Also, on a more basic level, to simply keep children from wandering and getting lost in the woods." As the kids processed this information, some were creeped out. Others were already saying the phrase in a ghostly tone, trying to scare their peers.

"Sometimes I go into the woods and I hear a deep humming sound. It tells me things."

"...What sorts of things?"

"It tells me to do things."

Things were getting out of hand.

"*Enough!* Alright, everyone, settle down now, and please return to your seats. I did *not* say that you could just get up and walk over to your friends and start chit- chatting. That's strike one. If I have to talk to you guys about this next time, it'll be strike two and I'll have to take away something fun we do." She gave herself leverage by taking those exciting things away if classroom behavior continued to decline. The disruptive behavior had the potential to derail and ruin a lesson, and was exhausting for her to deal with. It didn't seem like enough, as one girl ran up to her desk and paused, looking at her with big eyes.

"Alexis, what did I just say? What-"

"Ms. Santos…" Alexis said in a whisper. Lola noticed that she looked very distressed, as if on the verge of tears.

"What's wrong, dear?"

"What the others are saying, it's scaring me."

"Don't worry about what they're saying. It's all nonsense and I'll make sure they speak no more of it."

"But…I've heard things too."

"What? What things?"

"Well, sometimes I'll hear singing coming from the woods. It sounds nice and I want to see who it is. But I never go. Cus other times I hear screaming. And my mom pulls me back before I go see what the faces are looking at in the trees."

"I'm sure it's just your imagination, dear. It's ok. Just stay inside and don't worry about any of that, ok?" Lola sent Alexis back to her seat and collected herself.

"Ahem. With what time we have left I will call out your project groups." Hunter twiddled around eager fingers. He hoped he wouldn't get stuck with kids who couldn't care less about the project, who ultimately forced him to pick up their slack because that's just how he was.

"…Group C – Hunter, Brooke, J, Caleb." *Huh. An interesting group,* he thought. It could've been worse. He was glad he at least had J, a decent friend, in the group. He didn't really know Brooke, and Caleb was a weird kid. Quiet most of the time. They got together and started thinking about what they wanted to do their project on.

"Hey guys," Hunter said.

"Hunter! What's up? Hi Brooke, hey Caleb," J said.

"Hey," said Brooke.

Caleb sat there and gave them all a head nod before resting his head back down on the desk.

"So, what do we think we want to do our project on?" asked Brooke.

"I'm not sure, maybe we should research some North American folklore some more and see what we find," said Hunter. Caleb leaned forward and looked at them.

"No need to research. We're doing the Jersey Devil. Hurry up and go tell the teacher before someone else takes it." The other three did not expect Caleb to say much, but none of them wanted to butt heads with him. The Jersey Devil was interesting enough, anyways. It was bound to be a popular pick. J sprung up and jogged to Ms. Santos (and promptly got yelled at). They came back to their table and said they were good to do their project on it.

"Alright, sweet. Maybe we could all meet up at my house and work on it? I'll ask my mom if it's okay," said Hunter. They were all okay with that. Brooke seemed relieved. The bell rang.

"Alright guys, that concludes today's class. Have a good rest of your day, and remember–don't stare into the woods!"

The rest of the day went by, uneventful, and Hunter was on his way home.

Hunter got off the bus and headed down his driveway. He lifted up the rug to grab the key and went inside his house. He was always the first one home on the weekdays, and was even earlier than usual today. His sister would be home soon, which was nice. He felt better having his dear younger sister with him in the house. Since he was home so early, he was looking forward to more time spent playing video games, but there was work to be done. Hunter knew that his computer was a distraction, so he often elected to do his homework outside on the patio. Today was nice enough to go out and finish his vocabulary and math work that was due the next day. It wouldn't take too long. He tried his best to chip away at his homework during the downtimes of some of his classes at school. As he was working, he would look up at the backyard. Fields of corn swayed off to the right, playing their dry, calming music in the wind. The field was bordered by woods off to the left that led back a distance, but came out to more housing on the other side.

"Don't stare into the woods."

What was that? Did he just mutter it himself, or was he just hearing things? It almost felt like a gentle whisper, but he was alone on the patio. The words repeated in his head. Don't stare into the woods. *But they're right there in front of me. What if I just take a peek? I've looked at 'em before. They're far away, anyways.* He picked up his homework folder and peeked out from the top. Trees on their way to die for the winter, giving everyone a colorful show on their way out. Dark oranges and browns scattered the ground. Some were still on the trees, but sparse. He looked at the lines and knots in their bark, his brain already trying to form faces within them. He put the folder back up in front of his eyes. What did he see? Nothing out of the ordinary. Was he really that scared? He looked again. The wind was moving around branches and shrubs. Wait. What was that? Just another branch in the wind. Nothing. Of course it was nothing. He wanted to stop wasting time and finish his homework, so he got back to it. Ten minutes passed and he had made some progress. The vocabulary words were conquered, syllable by syllable. Now to tackle the math homework. There was a huge difference between math homework and language arts homework. It was not your average beast, with its mean, angled expression. Adding and subtracting the different ways it wants to divide up your brain before it multiplies into more pestering, imaginary numbers; planning out calculated strikes against you, making you grow exponentially more afraid.

A sound in the woods snapped Hunter's concentration. A crinkling of leaves? He looked up, but made sure not to stare too long. He saw nothing unusual and chalked it up to a frantic squirrel preparing to bury its plunder of nuts in a good spot in the ground. He couldn't shake the feeling that as soon as he looked away, something was watching him and appearing in the corner of his eye. A peripheral invader. He looked up again. Nothing. He started working on his math again and was shocked to hear a voice call out to him. There was someone standing at the edge of the woods. How long were they there for? Hunter hadn't noticed any movement or sounds, and that sent a cold chill down his spine. Now he knew he was being looked at.

"Hey. Come here," said the figure. They were gesturing to him to come closer. It looked like they were wearing all black. The white skin on their head contrasted with the rest of them. A bald head. Sunken, dark eyes pinpointed Hunter's anxious heart and started making it beat faster. It stepped closer to him.

"Who are you?" Hunter asked.

"Come on. Come here."

"Why? What do you want?" Hunter picked up his folder and started planning his retreat back into his house. The figure didn't come any closer. It just kept gesturing, like it was trying to get a dog to come up to it with a waving hand. Hunter had had enough and ran back inside, sliding shut the glass door and locking it. He dashed to grab the phone, returned to the window, and there was no one there anymore. He decided not to call his mom, as he didn't want to worry her since it was gone now. He went into his room, locked the door, and sat there. Unable to do anything.

CHAPTER 10

Albert left work early that day. He had things he needed to do. He went to get gas for his truck and filled up a gas can as well, then went searching for a couple of specific things. He drove twenty minutes north to a shopping district and pulled into the parking lot of a crafts and decorations store. The fall decorations were lined up in the windows of the store–orange and red leaves hanging from above, spider webs creeping in the corners, pumpkins of all sizes, scarecrows with hay sticking out of them, witches' cauldrons, and assortments of lights. A giant inflatable turkey was sitting down and wearing a hat out in front of the store. Albert looked at it. It was gaudy, but comical. He chuckled through his nose, itched his leg, and continued into the store. The itching was getting worse. Streaks of white appeared within the redness of his leg where he was itching. It was infected and that made it hurt a lot more. Soon he would be limping from the pain. For now, he had the willpower to dismiss it and focus on the bigger picture. He walked fast, searching for a particular sign, and it did not take him long to find what he was looking for. In an aisle paired with a display in front was the "Fall Decorations for the House" seasonal section. A scarecrow the size of a small child was sitting on a rocking chair. He grabbed it by its head and went to the checkout line. One thing down. Out in the parking lot, he saw a woman loading her trunk with a baby in a baby stroller behind her. The inflatable turkey watched him with lifeless eyes. The dark, intrusive thoughts violated his mind again. *Take her baby. You know where to bring it. The itching will stop. It would be so easy to just snatch it right up. I bet it'll even smile at you when you do it. It doesn't know what's going on. C'mon. She's not even looking.* He snapped out of it, disgusted he would ever consider stealing someone's child in broad daylight. He made a labored leap into his truck and headed to a beauty store.

Albert perused the beauty store for a moment, then headed to where he knew he wanted to go–the wigs. He stuck out like a pregnant pole vaulter, and the store associates eyed him with a playful curiosity.

"Ten bucks he's a drag queen."

"That's good, but I'm thinking his wife has cancer."

"Could be. What's he got? Medium length, blonde? Boring. It's definitely cancer. Bet's off. Here he comes. You can ring him up."

Albert was quick and dismissive. He had no time for conversation. He bought the wig and headed home.

"Poor guy."

"Yeah."

Once Albert was home, he went to the shed, grabbed something, and put it in his truck. A curiosity kept bugging him and he decided to go to the window where he had heard that awful laughter from the previous night. He stepped up onto the front deck of the house and peered into the living room. This was the window. No scratch marks on the screen. No dried up marks of saliva on the glass. He looked down. Black hair. Not a lot of it, but enough to lock him into place, stunned, just staring at it. He got upset, puffed at it like the big bad wolf, and stepped down from the deck. The logical part of his mind, clinging onto his psyche by a thread of skin, chalked it up to it just being a black cat snooping around. He knew that wasn't the case, though. After going back to his truck and taking a few bags out of the back seat, he trotted up to the house with his new purchases in hand. Noticing Hunter and Hannah were home before they should be, he rushed into the master bedroom and stuffed the scarecrow and wig underneath his bed. He knocked on their doors.

"Hunter? Hannah? You guys sick or somethin'?"

"No, Dad. We had a half day." Hunter wasn't expecting either of his parents to be home this early, and after what had just happened, was pinned up against his door with a tense grip on a baseball bat. His grip loosened and he leaned the baseball bat against a wall corner.

"Oh. Of course. That makes sense. Hannah?"

"Yes, Daddy?"

"Since I'm home early, *if* you promise not to tell Mommy, do you wanna go get some ice cream?"

"Oh wow, really? Sure! Ice cream!" Hunter listened with jealous ears. *What's with the sudden mood change, Dad? Did I really do something wrong? What the hell? He doesn't even bother to ask me. Like I just don't exist.*

"Go get in the truck, hun. I'll be out in just a second."

"Okay!" Hannah put on her shoes and, with a jovial skip, headed out to the truck.

Albert snuck into Hannah's bedroom after he had heard the front door close. He rifled through her drawers and took one of her shirts and a pair of her jeans. Luck was on his side, as an angered Hunter already had his headphones in, booting up a game to play on his computer. If he had not been so hurt, he might have asked if he could come with them. Albert went back into his room, put Hannah's clothes in the bag with the scarecrow and wig, and started walking out to the truck.

Good. You have her alone. Ice cream, huh? Smart! Gonna actually get her some before you bring her? A little last meal, like death row. Haha! Albert tried to shake the thoughts out of his mind, but they persisted like a certain bad itch. *Don't try to fight it. She's not even YOUR child. What does she really mean to you? Are you happy you're raising another man's child, you cuck? Bring her. The itching will stop. Bring her.*

Albert got into the truck and started it. He started itching his leg again. It hurt. He resorted to rub-itching it through his pants.

"Daddy, what's wrong with your leg?"

"Bug bites."

"Like mosquitoes?"

"Yeah."

"I don't like mosquitoes."

"Me neither."

A twenty minute drive to Dipper's. He loved their famous strawberry banana custard. It was a sugar cone kind of day, too. Classic rock played on the radio, filling the silence for the remainder of the ride. Albert's mind was buzzing; he was in no condition to hold a conversation with anyone. They arrived at Dipper's and got their ice cream. Albert got the strawberry banana custard, and Hannah got a chocolate vanilla twist. The sweet, creamy taste topped off a delightful surprise of a day for Hannah. First a half day at school she wasn't aware of, and now this? And it was only quarter past one–plenty of time for more surprises. They sat down at a picnic table beside the store and enjoyed their ice cream. Albert watched her, thinking about the voices in his head. She was so happy. His mind buzzed hard. Ravenous itches bombarded his leg. It had to be bleeding again, but it felt so good to itch it. The pain came after, but in the moment the temporary ecstasy of the relieving itch felt worth it.

"Daddy? Daaaddy? Your ice cream!" Hannah pointed at his hand with a laugh. He sat there, staring at her, as melted ice cream dripped down the cone onto his hand. He snapped out of it.

"Oh, shoot. Good thing you got some napkins, sweetie! I'm a mess sometimes, ain't I?"

"Sometimes," Hannah nodded.

"Well, can't let this go to waste," Albert said as he started licking the melted ice cream from his hand. He got a laugh out of Hannah, who was starting to eat down the cone. He wiped around his hand and on the table to clean up what he could and then finished his cone like a hungry dog.

"Ready? You're almost done so you can finish it in my truck, c'mon."

"Okay!"

They hopped into the truck and were on their way home. Or so Hannah thought. At the intersection of Cherry Road and Sunset Avenue, where home was right, Albert swallowed hard and made a left turn instead. Hannah didn't notice right away, but when she did, she was confused.

"Daddy, why is it taking so long to get home? Are we almost there?"

"Not yet, dear. I wanted to show you something else before we got home."

Another surprise! That's three in a row. Hannah was excited to see where her dad was going to take her now. Was it the zoo? Or maybe the mall? Fifteen more minutes passed. Albert's hand was gripped hard on the steering wheel. Almost there. They were surrounded by trees. Albert pulled into a small, open area on the side of the road. He got out and walked over to the other door and opened it.

"Come here, Hannah. Hop out," he said. He was trying to stay calm and speak with a friendly tone, but it was lined with an awkward coldness.

"Where are we?" Hannah asked. Being out in the middle of nowhere did not thrill her. She was becoming impatient and wanted to go home and enjoy the rest of her half day off.

"This is where Daddy hunts," Albert said.

"Are we going hunting?"

Silence filled the air. The sky was becoming gray and cloudy. A cold wind picked up.

"No." He took her hand and began walking towards the woods. Hannah didn't fight, but she was confused. She stumbled over branches as she was looking up at the tall pines. It was an endless gray and brown world. She had never gone far into the woods before and was feeling overwhelmed. She stopped looking around and watched her footsteps, hoping that when she looked up again, they would be back at the truck.

Albert's heart raced. His hand was getting sweaty holding Hannah's. His anxious eyes darted around every direction, searching for the lurking devil. They were still about a seven minute walk away from where his hunting stand was. From where he first encountered it. A dark aura surrounded Albert. He was sweating and his steps were becoming more and more timid, unsure, and afraid. He lowered his line of sight to his footsteps, unbeknownst to him mimicking Hannah. He didn't dare to look back at her. His anxiety spiked and he had to stop. It was abrupt and Hannah bumped into the back of him. She watched him bend down and start itching his leg hard. He pulled up his jeans a little and looked at it. It looked terrible. He tried to breathe deep and somehow calm down.

"Dad?"

He ignored her. From his downward gaze something popped into the corner of his eye. He turned his head and looked toward it. He let go of Hannah's hand and put his hand on her back, encouraging her to walk in front of him. He pointed down at the ground; there was something about eight feet away. Hannah directed her eyes to where her father was pointing. She smiled and almost tripped jogging over to what she saw–a beautiful, celestial purple sprouted from the muted brown ground.

"Wow, what are these?" She was mesmerized by the flowers in front of her. Albert, with a sudden relief falling over him, had a small smile on his face too. His mouth was slightly open with bewilderment. Had nature come to help bail him out?

"Looks like we found some pine barrens gentians," Albert said. "Strange. Didn't think they'd be bloomin' in November."

"Jen-shins? What is that?"

"Gentians. G-E-N-T-I-A-N-S. Like the beginning of 'gentlemen' and the end of 'martians.' Smack 'em together and say it without thinking too hard. Gentians."

"Gent-shins," Hannah said, stressing the 't' sound too much.

"Almost!"

"Gent-shins. Gentians. Gentians! I got it! What does it mean, Daddy?"

"Well, I can't say I'm entirely sure. Flowers have weird names sometimes. The important thing is that they're pretty, aren't they?"

"Super pretty! I love purple!"

"And look in the middle of the flower, there. The yellow-white pops out, huh?"

"Yeah!" She pointed at different parts of it. "This is the stigma, that's a stamen, and these are its petals. I forget what these are."

"Wow, good job. Can't say I remember all of my plant anatomy. I *do* know what a gentian was used for. Maybe still is, I don't know. Wanna know?"

"Yeah!"

"Well, the roots of this specific flower were used to treat aches and swelling. It had medicinal use. Medicinal, like medicine. I'm guessing it still could help. Cool, huh?"

"Wow, is all medicine made of flowers?"

"Not all," Albert said with a chuckle.

"I'm gonna pick one. I wanna show Mommy!"

"Pick another for your brother. I'm sure he'd like it."

"Okay!" Hannah picked two of the flowers, stood up, then bent back down and picked a third. "And one for Daddy! Is this what you brought me here for? How'd you know where the gentians were?"

"Well...," he started. The questions caught him off guard. He smiled at her, but a chill of fear shot up his back. He looked around and thought he saw a dark figure moving through the pines. He took her hand and started walking quickly.

Hannah, surprised by his urgency, asked, "Daddy? What's wrong?" Albert attempted to improvise something so that she wouldn't become frightened.

"I forgot I had to do something for your mom for dinner tonight! We gotta get home fast. We should be good if we walk fast, alright? Hold onto your flowers."

"Okay. I got 'em."

They picked up the pace even more. Spooked squirrels skittered by, but Albert was more spooked by their small footsteps than they were his. Every sound and every color became the devil in his mind. His focus on the path turned into tunnel vision. Hannah did well keeping up with her dad's frantic actions. Albert felt something creeping up behind them. It was gaining ground. Closer and closer. He thought he felt it breathing on his neck. The truck was in sight, and he almost started to run. Hannah was not wearing the proper footwear for traversing the forest, and ended up tripping. Albert didn't want to go back, but he had to. He picked her up and sprinted to the truck. She bounced up and down in his arms; her hair flailed around. She was half afraid and half amused. Albert opened the door and set her down. He swung around the other side, got in, and locked the doors. He never started a vehicle and whipped out of a place faster than he did then. Labored breathing filled the silence of the truck. Albert's eyes focused on his rearview mirror. Whether it was his mind playing tricks on him or not, he thought he saw dark roots receding back into the woods.

"Are you scared Mommy is gonna be mad? You look scared, Daddy."

"Yeah." He stepped on the gas and they were home before they knew it.

CHAPTER 11

Albert fiddled around in the kitchen so as to not arouse any suspicion from Hannah before stomping down the hall into the master bedroom. He reached under the bed and grabbed the bag he had stashed there. Albert's day was far from over, but he was already starting to feel exhausted. He shot Clint a text and headed out. In 25 minutes he was at their favorite place to eat, River Point Diner. Clint was already sitting in a booth near the front of the diner, sipping on coffee and watching for Albert to pull in. Clint had been a state police officer for seven years now, and had taken a day off per the request of his good friend. Something was up with Al. He sure as hell wasn't acting normal. He watched Albert walk up the stairs and into the diner. Albert greeted the hostess and had a brief chat before looking around and seeing Clint with a waving hand.

"Over here, champ."

Albert half-limped over and sat in the empty booth seat across from Clint. It was a quarter to three on a Thursday and the diner only had a few customers. The air smelled of coffee, pancakes, and potatoes.

"Hey man," Albert said. The waitress came over and Clint was surprised when Albert only asked her for water. If you asked Albert, River Point had the best damn home fries in the world. Your order came with a lot of them, and they were crispy and seasoned to perfection. Sometimes he felt bad adding ketchup on top of an already-immaculate specimen of food. Sounds of small talk and occasional metal cutlery clinking against plates and tables filled the air.

"How you been? How's the wife and kids?" asked Clint.

"Eh, I've been better, man. Family's doin' fine."

Clint took a sip of his coffee, but kept his eyes on Albert. Tiny drops of coffee got in his mustache as he pulled his cup away. He sat there, silent, still observing. There were dark circles around Albert's eyes. His hair was disheveled. A rough, unkept beard. He kept bending down to scratch his left leg. Clint needed no more signs to convince him that something was up.

"I'm gonna be honest with you, Al. You look like shit."

Albert rubbed his hand hard on one side of his face and let out a deep sigh.

"Yeah, I know." The waitress brought him his water and they told her that that would be all for now. He took a sip and continued. "Listen, Clint. You and I been huntin' for years now. We've seen our fair share of shit out there. But have you ever seen somethin' you couldn't explain? Whether it was a feeling, something you thought you saw or heard?" Albert looked deep into Clint's eyes with a serious face. He was about to confide in him something he thought most people would think was unbelievable. His desperate eyes searched for a glint of validation on Clint's face. Clint took another sip of coffee and looked out the window, then back to Albert.

"I suppose so. Something happened that's been bothering you?" He took a bite of a blueberry muffin he had ordered.

Albert, on the verge of tears simply because of a good friend's willingness to listen, continued.

"Just this past Saturday. I went over a ways up on a back road off Sunset Avenue."

"What's that, Rabbit Hole Road? Near where Jimmy hunts?" The food was still in his throat, but it came out in a muffle Albert could understand.

"Yeah, Rabbit Hole. Jimmy told me he had seen some ten-pointers around there and said he talked with the guy who owns the property, gave me the go ahead for settin' up a stand back there. So I did."

"Jimmy and his stories," Clint scoffed.

"Yeah, well anyways, I had set up a stand that was maybe a ten minute walk from where I park my truck on the side of the road. Just a usual morning. I don't see much, maybe a doe or two. After a while I start gettin' hungry and figure I'll throw in the towel. Spend some time with the family by getting home a little bit earlier than usual. Well I was climbing down and one of my screw steps was bent down and wet from rain the night before and I fell about five or six feet down. Landed and hit my head."

"Christ, man, you alright?"

"Yeah, Lily checked it out already and I'm not concussed or anything, but it hurt, that's for sure."

"Ok, good."

"It's what happened after that's got me shaken up, Clint."

"What happened?"

"I woke up and felt dizzy. It was already dark and I got up and started walking to my truck. Then a feeling hit me like I was bein' stalked. I felt so out of place, man. Like I shouldn't be there. I felt dread, like I knew I was being watched. I could hear my breath and heartbeat so loudly I thought I was going insane, but turns out the whole damn forest was dead quiet, like it just fuckin' shut off! Next thing I know there's roots and thorns growing up trying to snatch my legs and the trees are boxing me in like a trapped mouse. I felt like one, too. Because…Clint, you gotta believe me…"

"Alright," Clint said with a raised eyebrow.

"I swear to all that is holy the mother fucking Jersey Devil appeared right in front of me. Grabbed me by the throat. God, it must've been around eight feet tall. It breathed on me, and get this, it fucking spoke to me. And what I heard wasn't what entered my head either, it's got some telepathy bullshit going on, because I didn't understand the language it spoke out loud. And yet I still understood what it was saying." Albert took a long pause. Clint was sitting back in the booth now, with an expression of bewildered fear on his face. Albert continued, "And you know what that fucking thing said to me? It told me to bring it a fucking kid or else it would kill me. And then," he started shaking. He drank some water to try and calm down. "It called me *strawberry*. Fuckin' strawberry! Then it laughed and flew off with its huge devil wings."

Clint gave out a short spurt of laughter. It just sounded so comical coming from Albert. Truth was, he didn't want to believe it, but he had reason to. There were some things he was confused about, but he wasn't all that unfamiliar with coming close to what he thought was something out of legend. He decided he would inquire about the devil first and foremost.

"Strawberry? Why in the world would the Jersey Devil come out of the woods and call you something like that?"

"I thought about that for a long time. One of the more confusing things that kept me up at night. And then I remembered the chaotic morning I had with those goddamn blackbirds and, well, I have a ritual in the morning, right? I mean, we all do to a certain extent. I use different kinds of jams to spread on my toast depending on what hunting season it is. Well let's just say it somehow knew I had strawberry jam that morning."

"What the hell? Smell it on your breath or somethin'?"

"Maybe, I dunno. It had been a damn while since breakfast. God…gives me the creeps."

"Jeez. What did it look like?"

"Well, like I said, tall. Wings, sorta like a bat's. Jet black skin and fur. Pretty hairy. A goat's head with matching horns and eyes, but one of its horns was twisted and poking into the side of its head. Body was more human-like, but reverted back to being a goat at the bottom with hooves. Some kinda tail." Albert took a sip of water. "Just describin' it makes my fuckin' skin crawl. The look it gave me, man."

"Holy shit. Not too far off from some old sketches of alleged sightings I've seen. Did it hurt you?" Clint asked. He backtracked, embarrassed, after remembering a part of Albert's story, "...besides it gripping your neck?"

"It pierced me in three places with its claws, but left no exit wound. None at all, but I know for damn sure it did. I saw those black nails dig into my skin. First on my left leg, then my right shoulder, and then the left side of my neck. And I think it's poisoned those areas of my body. My left leg's been almost non-stop itching since. It's driving me fuckin' crazy, Clint. I mean, look!" Albert lifted up his pant leg. Clint peeked down under the booth table and grimaced at the sight of the awful state his leg was in.

"This itch ain't just on my skin, either. It's in my veins. In my *bones*. I'm like a rabid dog with this itching, man, it's like it cursed me or something. No use in going to a doctor, I've thought about it. You gotta believe me! This shit's been driving me up the walls so much that I almost caved in and took my own goddamn daughter into the barrens to make it stop! My own daughter! But I love her, even if...it's not her fault, y'know? She doesn't even know! And Lily, she's–"

"Whoa whoa whoa, calm down, Al. You're losin' me. What about your daughter?"

"Never mind, Clint. Listen. Y'know when you get a stray hair on your face, right on the ridge of your nose, and it just tickles and itches you like crazy? And when you get it off and scratch it it's just the best damn feeling?" Clint took off his hat and shrugged. His bald head glistened well enough in the warm diner light.

"Definitely a foreign feeling to me, but I can imagine it." He managed a small smile out of Albert.

"Yeah, well, shit is crawling in my skin, man. It's like there's little guys with feathers ticklin' my blood vessels."

"Like a fresh tattoo after a couple of days."

"Huh?"

"They itch like hell."

"Oh. Well then, yeah, exactly. I've gotten real good at ignoring it, but even still it drives me nuts. Comes to a point where it's a primal urge, y'know, I can't *not* itch it. This shit is probably infected. And my family is starting to think I'm nuts, too. I can't talk to them about it. Lily knows something's up and she's been stressed to hell. She's picking up more shifts at the hospital in order to be somewhere else, for chrissakes. You gotta believe me. Every word I've said is true, Clint. Hell, if *you* don't believe me...I don't know. I can feel my mind slipping, man. I've already been seeing some weird shit that I don't even know is real. It's fuckin' me up mentally too, like another unscratchable itch, but in my brain, that bastard!"

Clint took a deep sigh, looked down at the table, and rubbed his forehead. He slid his hand down his face, ending with an inquisitive brushing of his mustache. Albert stared at him in anticipation, all but holding his breath.

"There's two reasons I'm inclined to believe you, Al. This county, hell, this whole damn state has been plagued with missing persons cases. Predominantly missing children. It's been keeping a shit ton of families up at night. I'm sure you've seen it on the news by now. Most of, if not all of these cases have been going cold, and that's making everyone, and I mean *everyone* frustrated. Been gettin' national attention now. Well, I figured it was only a matter of time before I experienced one of these cases firsthand, as grim as that may be." Clint finished his coffee with another stare out the diner window and continued. "Well, it was just about two months or so ago. About half-past six at night. I passed some asshole as they were dumping out their nasty cigarette butts they had collected in a cup in their car. Y'know, so the little bunnies and squirrels would have a nice last meal before they suffered a slow death from accidentally eatin' 'em. Really respecting our collective big rock of a home. And then as I pull around to run his plates and see who he is and slap him with a nice juicy littering fine, he decides to throw the cup out too. Like the former just wasn't enough. He speeds up, must've noticed me, and I lose him for a bit as he goes down a hill and out of sight. Next thing I know I'm pulling up to his car smashed to hell into an electric pole on the side of the road. Well, I call for EMS and get out of the car to see the damage, and, get this, Al, there's no one in the goddamn car."

"Well, where the hell did they go? Wasn't that long after it happened that you pulled up, right?"

"Maybe a minute, probably less. I found a hole in the passenger-side of the windshield. It was an old, shitty AMC Gremlin."

"Christ, really? A Gremlin?"

"Yep. Whoever his passenger was must've flown right out the front windshield. Don't see too many survivors making holes like that at the speed he was going. We get in contact with his girlfriend and she tells us he was out with their daughter. Bastard let his nine-year-old daughter ride without her seatbelt on. Awful stuff, Al."

"Jesus. Tragic," Albert said, shaking his head. He thought about Hannah.

"It doesn't stop there. It gets worse."

"Worse?"

"Mhm. Driver's side window is completely broken. I walk my way towards the woods off the side of the road, trying to calculate the angle of trajectory from this poor girl, dreading what the body would look like. But there's no body to be found. We even had a small search party going with flashlights since it was gettin' dark and we still found nothin'. Another child just *poof*. Gone. Where the hell could she have gone, Al? The fuckin' moon?"

"You said it crashed near the woods?"

"Yep. Right on the side of the road there down on Maple."

"Yeah I think I know where that is." Albert was trying to piece it together. Part of him thought it was too crazy, that the dots were way too far apart to connect. He looked at Clint, and Clint tensed up and leaned in. He wasn't done.

"We found the guy. I walked off a bit to the left about two, three minutes into the woods, and there he was. No skin on his entire body, save his head. No teeth, either. Just a bloody mess, looked like one of those anatomical figures you see in a health book, but with a rubber halloween mask on."

"What? No way-how in the hell? You serious?"

"The breathing he made before he died is gonna haunt me the rest of my life. Blood was spitting from his mouth and he was clearly in shock. Died fast. No human could've done something like that, Al. And he sure as hell didn't do it to himself. I've heard stories of some people ripping off a hangnail from their finger and they can't tear it off, so it just keeps going up their hand and down their arm. Shit's weird, I know, but it was still a far cry from this."

"That sure is weird. My god. Just horrible to even think about." Albert sat there and hesitated to say what was on his mind, but he started to muster up the words. "Clint, you don't think-"

"I'm more inclined to think it. I asked myself what sort of human could do this to someone else, but now, well, wasn't a human who did it in the first place, was it?"

Albert was grimly ecstatic. He had all the confirmation he needed now to not feel crazy about what had happened to him. Not only that, but now he had another person who he could talk about all of it with comfortably.

"Clint, I think I've got a plan," Albert said. He was getting ahead of himself, but the faster this was all a thing of the past, the better.

"Do tell," Clint responded.

"It wants a kid? We'll bring it a 'kid'. It'll be a little decoy straw guy I bought at the store. From a distance it'll look like one, because it'll have a wig on and be in kid's clothes." Albert stopped and looked at the waitress and hostess, who were giving him and Clint the eye and whispering to each other. He was speaking too loud now. "Listen. Let's finish up and continue this outside." He eyed towards the two ladies and Clint gave him an understanding nod. He put more than enough cash on the table and they left. Clint followed Albert to his truck in the parking lot.

"Alright, a decoy. But...dontcha think this thing is gonna smell me coming from a mile away?"

"I was in the woods for a while before it noticed me. I feel like it's got some sort of range on its scent. Buy some women's deodorant and maybe a little perfume or a flowery body wash. Yeah that'll probably work. If you smell like a little girl, it won't bat an eye–or nostril in this case."

"Well goddamn, Albert," laughed Clint. "I guess I've done worse for you than smell like a girl for a night. Let's keep that between us though. People'll definitely get the wrong idea if you go tellin' 'em *that*." Clint was entertaining these ideas so far, but was on the fence about helping to this extent.

"Of course, man," Albert said. Clint got him to smile again. "I know this is all just batshit crazy, but look." He opened the back passenger door of his truck. Inside was the decoy straw girl with a wig and some small, pink clothing thrown on the floor. Sitting on the seat was a super soaker. "I borrowed this from Hunter. See, if you bring a gun, and I got a super soaker filled with," he pointed to the bed of his truck, "gasoline, we should be able to set that fucker ablaze." He started itching his leg through his pants again.

"My god, Albert. How close are you gonna get to this thing? Listen, I said I believe you, but I didn't know it was gonna be like this. We should at least try to stake this thing out to observe it first before we go in haphazardly, y'know?"

"I don't got the time or the patience. Nor do I wanna think about what happens to me or my family if I don't meet with it." He leaned in close enough to count the crumbs in Clint's mustache. "I've been so close that it breathed on my face." Clint didn't seem convinced. "Look, it's just a beast after all, right? It's gotta be afraid of fire. Weak to it. I ain't gonna stop 'til this thing's head is on my wall. No one threatens my family. Not even the devil. And I ain't never found anything that survives a couple 12-gauge slugs blasted through 'em."

"Hold on a second, Al. If this thing really is terrorizing our beautiful state of New Jersey and causing children to go missing, we need to analyze your story and prepare for what we're up against. I mean, shit, dude, you talked about it controlling roots and moving trees! Shouldn't there be some way to lure it out in the open?"

"I thought a lot about that, but it demanded I bring something back into the pines. It wasn't a negotiation. Assuming it has some intelligence, it might be onto us if we try to change anything like that."

Clint stood there, thinking long and hard. His time in the force had been as tame as it could be, being stationed in a smaller, more remote town of NJ. He had a hankering for action, though, and the reckless side of himself was fighting to make the decisions. Albert knew he was thinking hard about it, so he let him think. After some time Clint let out a sigh.

"I'm gonna be disappointed if this is some crazy elaborate prank you're pulling on me," he smiled and shook his head, rubbing his brow. "But, what the hell. Along with my gun I'm gonna bring a nice, sharp machete in case it tries to tie me up with any roots. I recommend you do too."

"Good idea, I will. We do this Saturday. I can't stand to wait any longer. Wear full camo too."

"Alright, man," Clint put a firm, caring hand on Albert's shoulder. "You just hang in there until then. Try and be there for your family as much as possible." Clint started walking to his car. Albert gave him a solemn head nod.

"I'll try," he said in a weak whisper.

Back home at the Lawless residence, once Hannah had returned from her ice cream surprise day, she knocked on her big brother's door with a freshly-picked gentian in her hand. Hunter, still upset that he wasn't invited, heard her, but did not bother getting up. Another knock.

"What do you want?" he said through the door. She could hear him talking trash online playing some game. "No, YOUR mom! My mom is a nice lady. She works hard. Hey! That's not nice—"

"I got something for you! Open up!" Hannah said with a smile, ready to surprise her brother. She was unaware of the bitter mood he was in, however. She stood there, holding out the flower.

"Just leave me alone. I don't want to talk to anyone right now. Especially not daddy's favorite." Hunter's words confused Hannah. The smile on her face vanished after she realized his tone was serious and upset. A small "Oh, okay," is all that came out of her mouth. She set the flower down at his doorstep and went into her room.

CHAPTER 12

"Happy Friday! I hope you guys have fun plans this weekend. Or if not, I hope they're at least nice and relaxing." Lola and her students felt it. There's always something in the air on a Friday at school. Everyone is in a better mood. Yes, that even includes the meanest teachers. There's the weekend to look forward to, there's (usually, fingers crossed) no homework, plans are being made, the teachers' lessons seem more fun, hell, even the shitty cafeteria food tastes better. This aura of positive anticipation also came with a tangible fog of impatience. It was an uphill battle for the teachers who needed to cover material or get anything done with their students. Lola was prepared. She had been researching appropriate-rated movies that related to their unit of folklore. She got approval for one and had an easy worksheet to go along with it. She felt icky doing it, but understood now. When she was a student, she detested teachers who assigned worksheets on movies they watched. In reality, it's an easy way to justify putting on a movie, having something undemanding to put into the gradebook, and helping the rising crowd of visual learners apply their lessons and readings to something on the big screen. It has its value.

She let her students sit where they wanted to and regretted it within the first five minutes of the movie. If they were to learn, they needed to at least pay attention. J gathered up the folklore project group and they quickly became part of the chatter.

"What are you guys doing this weekend?" asked J.

"Nothing," replied Brooke. She looked at Hunter. "Ooh, going to give that to a lucky lady or something, Hunter?" She pointed at a purple flower he had in a side pocket of his bookbag.

"Oh…no. Shut up, Brooke, it's nothing like that," he replied with an annoyed half-smile and a shake of his head. "Anyways, how about you, Caleb? Doin' anything this weekend?"

Caleb shrugged.

"Well then, how about you, J?" asked Hunter. He was curious and hoping J had something in mind. His fingers were crossed in hopes of there being a perfect opportunity to get away from his family, even if it was just for a day.

"Well…we're doing our project on the Jersey Devil, right? Why don't we get together tomorrow and go out into the woods? Maybe even where there have been sightings."

Caleb's eyes glowed up. An interested smile crept onto his face.

"What? That sounds kind of scary, J. I mean, aren't there a lot of kids going missing right now?" Brooke asked. The concern in her voice stifled some of the excitement Hunter was feeling in his chest. She was right. But most of him didn't care enough. He snuffed out the light of whatever was left of his caution.

"True, but it could be fun. And it'll help us with our project, right? And think about it, who is really gonna come out in the middle of the woods where we live and snatch us up?" Hunter said.

"I don't know, Hunter, ask all the missing kids 'who'," replied Brooke. "I don't know about you guys, but my momma is very protective of me. Chances are she's not gonna let me go."

"You could just tell her you're going to a friend's house to work on the project. It's not like it's a full lie, just a little white one. We can all *go* to J's house first, *then* explore the woods. J and I do live the closest to where I think would be best to explore," Caleb said.

"Caleb, you never talk, but it seems like when you do, it's always trouble. You're telling me to lie to my mom? She'd kill me if she found out!"

"She won't find out. None of us will say anything to her. And, again, it's just a little white lie. Nothing terrible. Nothing to feel guilty about."

"It's so easy for you to say that, isn't it? I bet if you actually had parents who cared about you, you'd think otherwise." Brooke's words came out hard and unexpected. Caleb was taken aback, but shrugged it off with a scoff and an eye roll.

"Whoa whoa, now, chill guys! Jeez. We need to work as a group, not fight with each other. I just thought if we took my mom's camera, we could take some pictures and write down our adventures in a journal or notebook. It's a lot easier than writing a boring paper or copy and pasting info onto slides. It won't even feel like a project!" J had some good ideas. They all thought that. Apprehension and hesitation could still be felt around the table, but before they could discuss it anymore, Ms. Santos had paused the movie and gotten everyone's attention. She didn't even have to say anything. All she had to do was stand up and look around, giving that stern teacher glare to all of her students, staring daggers at those being especially disruptive.

"You know, guys, I don't have to put a movie on. We can do boring, quiet work on a Friday. I don't know about you, but that's not how I'd want my Friday to go. Let's focus and pay attention here. It's honestly not a bad movie. Because I had to pause, I will be assigning you an open-ended response on what the movie was about after we watch it." She got looks and groans, but she needed to put her foot down. "And I'm sorry to those who were watching attentively and not being disruptive, but we need to keep each other accountable here and understand that our actions may have negative effects on others if we don't follow the classroom rules. Understand?" Some nodded. Others just kept giving her a look. "I'm gonna unpause it now. Think about what we've been discussing in class about folklore and how it relates to the movie." She sat back down at her almighty teacher's desk and continued grading some papers while looking up and scanning her class here and there. From then on out, Hunter's group operated no louder than a whisper, keeping their heads pointed towards the movie.

"I could even bring my hunting rifle if you guys want," muttered Hunter.

"I still don't know. I'll think about it," Brooke said to J.

"Oh, c'mon! When do we have projects where we can do something cool like this?" J wouldn't back down. They had been looking forward to it ever since they started brainstorming unique project ideas once Ms. Santos assigned it.

"Brooke, you're the only one dragging us down now. It's just a day of exploring the woods. My dad has been hunting forever, even if we *did* manage to get lost or something, he would totally find us. I know my way around from what he's taught me." "Whoa, really?" Caleb asked with an amused curiosity.

"Ok ok ok. I'll go. You don't have to bring your gun, Hunter. We'd all get in so much trouble if they found us and you had that on you. My mom would *actually* kill me. You'd never see me again." They chuckled. Tensions were down now, and they were all looking forward to tomorrow.

"Listen," Caleb gestured to all of them to get closer so they could hear his whisper. After a quick glance at Ms. Santos pounding away at her keyboard, he continued, "my big bro is going to a usual spot tomorrow with some of his friends–"

"Wait, you have a big brother? I thought you were just a big booger that got picked out of someone's nose and grew big and gained sentence." J's joke got them all cracking up. Even Caleb couldn't help but crack a smile.

"First off, asshole, it's sentience. Maybe pay more attention to Ms. Santos' vocab lessons."

"Alright, whatever, English nerd!" J made a face at Caleb and Caleb reciprocated.

"Second, yes, I have a brother. His name is Jake. He goes to the high school right down the road. He's a junior. They hang out around this big pond. It's like, pure blue, really cool. Not like the usual lakes you see around here. It's got a lot of sand around it. Really neat at night. Maybe after we're done exploring we can prank them! How about that to end a fun day?"

"Will you really know how to get there?" asked Brooke.

"Yeah, he's taken me once. And other times I've snuck behind and followed them."

"Ok, stalker," said J.

"Ok, loser," said Caleb. "Are you guys down?"

Caleb had a certain charm to him. Once a mysterious and rather antisocial classmate, he had now shown a bit more of himself to his project partners. Hunter and Brooke were surprised by how he carried himself–he was cool and funny and was someone they wanted to get to know better. He seemed witty and had a persuasive way with words. J rode on the same bus as Caleb; they were almost neighbors. They sat close enough to each other on the bus that it led to socializing here and there and a young friendship was the result. J had also felt the captivating aura that surrounded Caleb. Caleb was also an opportunity to break out of the norm for Hunter and Brooke. He was a gateway into rebellion. It all starts with "just a day out in the woods, maybe pranking his older brother." He wasn't someone whom either of their parents would want them hanging around. Nevertheless, they would, because they wanted to. Because they were good enough liars that their parents would be, for the most part, none the wiser. Because they were kids with their own lives and own volitions, and at the ripe age of twelve, the rebellious fires of defiance building up inside of them were ready to rage up into an inferno. An inferno with no set path, bellowing up ashes of worried parents throughout the air.

"I'm in."

"Yeah, I'm down."

"Sounds fun."

"Tomorrow. Saturday. Noon. My place. Be there or be balled up into the pile of other missing kids," said Caleb.

J was so excited that they had to let Ms. Santos in on their little adventure for their project, so promptly after the bell rang, Ms. Santos looked up to a smiling J.

"Guess what we're doing tomorrow for our project." An excited student? For a project!? Lola was pleasantly surprised. Amidst all of the groans and inevitable, hastily turned-in procrastination projects (if you'd even consider them "projects"), hearing this was a breath of fresh air.

"Ooh! What?" she responded with a big smile.

"We're going exploring. For research!"

"Oh yeah? Where are you guys gonna explore?"

"Some spots in the woods where there may have been sightings of the Jersey Devil. And if we see it we're gonna take a picture and run away as fast as we can!"

"That sounds fun, but you guys need to be safe. Don't get lost and give your parents heart attacks, okay? Especially with all the horrible things going on. Maybe you can make a collage and talk about some of the historical background behind the folklore of the Jersey Devil. If you don't snap any flattering pictures of him, you can at least give us a sense of atmosphere and journal any findings. Remember, the biggest portion of this grade is the writing part. Source any information you use, be descriptive, focus on the main pieces of info you want us to learn."

"Don't worry, we'll be fine. And yeah, we were planning on doing something like that. Can't wait to show you once we're done!"

"Well I can't wait to see it, J. Now you better get going, don't wanna be late!"

Lola watched J leave and the door close behind them. She undid her hair tie and let her dark-rooted rose pink hair fall on and around her shoulders. She sat there and thought about if she had just encouraged a group of children to put themselves in potential danger. Although she was young, struggling within the dating scene, and had no children of her own, she thought about if *her* hypothetical child's teacher were to encourage them to go wherever for a project. *Well, at the end of the day, they're the parents' responsibilities. And it's not like I didn't warn them to be safe.* She sat there staring at her laptop screen, and snorted with a sardonic smile. *Half of these fucking parents aren't very responsible from the get-go. Why even have children at that point? Just to hand little shitling demons off to the underpaid teachers?* She was starting to make herself upset and took a deep breath. *Whatever. You're overthinking it, Lola. Some things are just outta your power.* Thankfully, the rest of her day was lunch and prep. It felt weird to end the day that way, but she relished in the silence. It helped her get everything done she needed to do so that she wasn't taking work home with her. If that involved working while eating lunch, then so be it.

"Boom!" She gave a victorious final click on her lesson plan submission for next week. "I've got all of lunch to read my new modern American folklore book!" Lola tried to pair a more advanced book to read on her own time that correlated with what she was teaching to provide her students with interesting supplemental information. She also saw it as an opportunity to introduce some advanced topics to her more erudite students. Prep time was almost over, so she got up to go see Mrs. Thomas. Every Friday she liked to go over her lesson plans with her mentor teacher before the end of the day. Teachers had an unspoken open door policy during lunch and prep. Going over things helped her feel prepared come Monday. She always had to fight the Monday grogginess, and looked after her future self in any way she could in that regard.

Unbeknownst to Lola, Mrs. Thomas was already chatting with someone in her room. It was Julie Lemming, one of the 8th grade Language Arts teachers. She was someone whom Lola hadn't met, but rather someone she had just walked past here and there. Every smile or "good morning" Lola had attempted to give her was returned with no acknowledgement whatsoever. She walked up to the door and heard chatter, and decided to listen in on it briefly before making her decision to enter or not. If it was their supervisor or another teacher she knew, she would be more inclined to enter in what was going on. Lola didn't recognize the other voice and was about to leave before she picked up on what was being said.

"I know she's new, but why are they letting someone like her teach English? Go teach Spanish or something instead," said Mrs. Thomas.

"Does she even do her job now?"

"Yeah, she's a hard worker. You know them, they're all hard workers."

"True. I feel like there were better-qualified people who applied, though. I can't believe they didn't go with your recommendation."

"I know. Ridiculous. I've been working in the district for what? Fifteen years?"

"Listen, Amanda, don't let it get to you. Just another diversity hire."

"Julie, those kinds of hires are ruining education. Education starts with the best teachers available. I just don't get it."

"Don't worry about it. It could be worse, y'know? Anyways, I gotta go a bit early for the kids' soccer games. Thanks for going over the book club plans, I'm looking forward to it. Have a nice weekend!"

"Of course, no problem! You too, see you later!"

Lola was heartbroken upon hearing this. It's not how she was expecting to end her Friday. There went any respect she had for Amanda, as well as any hopes she had for participating in the book club (which she had already been researching some great books and planning some fun things for). She went back into her room and grabbed her bag and keys with a few tears in her eyes before leaving. She was determined to not let it ruin her entire weekend, but that would be hard.

Once she got home she decided to try and clear her head by going for a walk in a beautiful state park nearby. She put on some comfier clothes to walk in and wore her nice sneakers, grabbed her water and a multigrain bar and drove five minutes down the road to the park. She was happy she lived so close to one–and one with such historic value! The park was scattered with older buildings from decades past. Old logging villages, mills, churches, etc. Most of them couldn't be seen on any of the walking trails. They were only for the knowledgeable and adventurous to wander off of the beaten path and find. The park rangers did *not* encourage it. There were signs and markers to help people stay on the paths. Lola was one of those daring explorers who would take a map and wander off the trail (with ample equipment, of course) to bask in the historic glory of said derelict ruins, but she wasn't in the mood for any escapades today.

She began her trek and the fresh autumn air filled her lungs, immediately having a positive effect on her. Calm solitude. She could feel the initial dark cloudy haze start to clear up in her head, but she couldn't help but wonder as she walked–how could someone who seemed so nice and had been fairly helpful up to that point be so two-faced and rotten? Could a veteran teacher not have a shred of empathy for a new teacher in her situation?

Lola considered: I am resented due to administration going against Amanda's recommendation.

She also considered something her mother used to tell her: You will meet people who just have that hate in their heart. You are labeled far in advance of getting to know someone, as we all have our prejudices. Didn't matter what you did or didn't do, in fact, you could do everything flawlessly and be perfect and helpful and great and beautiful, and certain people will still hate you. They've harbored and kept that hate so close to them for such a long time that it's nigh inseparable. But you can't let that get you down. You just have to acknowledge that that hate will always exist within this world and keep doing your own thing. Try to encourage a change in their hearts by showing love. After all, who could look at my perfect little angel and not smile?

Lola remembered those conversations with her mother. She was incredible and radiated so much love and positivity, even in the hardest, lowest times. Even through pancreatic cancer, which took her too soon. Lola let out a tiny laugh filled with longing. Memories of her mother never failed to make her smile.

How long had it been? It felt like her trek had just started, but she noticed she was almost halfway through the trail already. The trail wrapped around a big lake and some campsites and playgrounds were scattered throughout the perimeter. Being submerged and lost in thought, she found herself walking on autopilot. Feeling better, she looked towards the lake. The trail had a few bridges, and they were her favorite points in the walk. She stopped and looked at the water trickling through stones and dead leaves. It was picturesque. She continued on for some time and decided to heed her mother's words; she was going to act like she heard nothing from Amanda and try her hardest to be the best teacher she could be in hopes her mentor teacher would notice that it didn't matter who she was or where she came from, she should be respected and seen as a human being who cares. The whole situation still bothered her deep down, but she had to be there for her students and not let things get to her. She doubted going to the higher-ups would be effective at all. In fact, it would probably be a huge waste of time, as Amanda could just deny saying any of it, causing bitter tension between the two afterwards. This was an unnecessary outcome to Lola. No need to add any more stress to her life. After making up her mind, she found that peaceful place in her head again. She was looking forward to going home and starting her weekend.

She didn't know what it was. Whether it was a chill wind hitting her face the wrong way, or the snap of a branch out in the woods, or a scurrying squirrel scattering around dried leaves, but whatever it was, it snatched her out of her tranquility. She had a shortness of breath and felt her heart beat a bit harder and a bit faster. She took a deep breath to compensate and calm herself down, which worked, but she couldn't shake off an unsettling feeling that had come upon her. She felt as if she was being watched, which was a feeling she knew well. Was some creep behind her? She turned around and saw no one. She stopped and listened. It was quieter than usual, but nothing to be concerned about. She turned back around and continued walking, opening up her snack and taking a bite of it. She washed it down with some water and noticed something just off-color enough in the woods to her right that made her doubletake. She was shocked by what she thought she saw—a huge black goat standing up, smiling at her with quivering, drooling lips. It had the body and arms of a human, but its height was abnormally tall. Were those wings, too? She couldn't tell. The piercing white of its eyes is what initially grabbed her attention. She couldn't believe what she saw, blinked hard, squinted, and found nothing unusual in the spot where she had thought she saw it. Was her mind playing tricks on her? She was an imaginative person, but this was strange. She picked up the pace. Something caused her to be put back in a negative state of mind, and intrusive thoughts began swirling about like rogue waves crashing down upon the sides of her brain. *Amanda Thomas. What a racist bitch.*

Miserable too, I bet. Put her out of her misery. Go into her room on Monday and take some scissors from her desk and stab her right in the throat. It'd be so satisfying to watch her bleed and choke on her own blood. Who cares what child sees it happen? They watch worse things on TV and online anyways. Bring them here afterwards. They could use some fresh air to clear their heads!

As images of this dark, intrusive fantasy popped up into her mind, she shook her head, trying to get them out.

"Get a hold of yourself, Lola, what the fuck? That's some dark shit you're *not* gonna do," she said under her breath, surprised at herself for even thinking of such things. At this point she wanted to be done. She tried to appreciate what was left of her walk. She did, ignorant to the fact that the Jersey Devil was watching her from behind surreptitiously, a grin still on its face.

She got in her car and headed home. It was 3:30PM and she was looking forward to prepping for dinner. Cooking was another way in which she could calm down. About halfway through her drive something black ran out in front of her car. A distressed foot slammed on the brakes. She had hoped her reaction speed was enough to avoid a collision as she held her breath and clenched her teeth. She pulled over to the side, fearing the worst. She looked out of her passenger side mirror and saw something black and fuzzy, motionless on the side of the road.

"No no no, please no," Lola said, hoping she hadn't just killed something innocent and adorable. She got out of her car and raced towards it. Kneeling down, she poked its scraggly, yet soft fur, unable to tell if the body was moving up and down from breathing. To her relief, it was very alive, and very scared. Pissed off, too. Hisses came at her in flurries as she leaned in closer to examine a cute little black kitten.

"Aww, are you okay, baby?" No collar. Male cat, maybe the runt of the litter. "Pobrecito." It being someone's pet seemed unlikely, as the only houses around were further down the road. She squatted down closer to it, considering the possibilities: rescue it, leave it, take it home.

"You know, little guy, I think we're both in need of a friend," Lola said. It replied with more hisses and a few swipes of its tiny, vicious paw towards Lola's extended hand. Although she had always been a bit more partial to dogs, her decision was final and she took it home after a last search for any signs of its family. The little kitten was perplexed by being put in a car. It breathed heavily, still scared. It mewed in short successions.

"Aw, I know, baby. Almost home, don't worry, ok? Looks like my plans have changed a little tonight. Not like I was gonna be doing much anyways, now I have an excuse to go out. Wait til my friends hear about how I met such a handsome little dude today, huh? ¡Un hombrecito guapo!" A couple more minutes passed and she pulled into her driveway. She turned off the car and looked at the kitten, sitting in the passenger seat, mewing still.

"Alright…you need a name, huh?" She went to pet it and it batted at her weakly. "I guess I deserve it, I almost hit you, querido. Crashed right into you. That wouldn't have been good at all. But you're still here. Crash…yeah, I like it. From now on, you're Crash Santos! Welcome to the family, little guy," Lola said with a big smile on her face. She picked him up and brought him inside. "Make yourself at home, little one! You can *crash* at my place as long as you'd like," Lola chucked to herself. Crash was wary of being inside a house. Lola assumed it was his first time inside, so she decided to push back anything on any shelves, pick up any hazards on the floor, and shut all of the doors for now. He was investigating anything and everything, sniffing about here and there. She figured he would be okay alone for no more than an hour while she drove to pick up some small food specifically for kittens, litter box supplies, and a few toys for him to play with. She was almost at the register when she doubled back and bought some soft-chew cat treats for him as well. Who else did she have to spoil, anyways?

She got back to her house and set everything up. It would take some time for Crash to adjust, but he felt warm and comfortable in Lola's house. She brought him over to where she set up his food and water, and after scarfing down a good amount, followed Lola to her bedroom. At this point she didn't feel like cooking much of anything, so just heated up some leftovers and sat down at her computer. She plopped Crash down on her bed and attempted to pet him. He gave in fast, his fierce look changing into one of pleasure in an instant as the chin scritches began.

"What a serendipitous little encounter, us two," Lola said. Their bond was growing already. She noticed how he had a little white spot on his chest and some more on his feet. She thought he looked like he was wearing a tuxedo and little socks. As cute as he was, she could still see that wild side in him. He had a sage look in his eyes for such a young cat, as if possessing some sort of arcane knowledge. She respected that, feeling as if in the presence of something that deserved it. It's almost like she knew it would come to her aid one day, in need of help from something dangerous. With a little yawn, he closed his eyes and was off to sleep. He already filled in a good chunk of the void of loneliness Lola had been in. She had more to look forward to. Something to come home to. And that made her happy.

CHAPTER 13

Another blaring alarm buzzing on a Saturday. The horror! The injustice! This time it was in Clint's room. His alarm was across the room and set to max volume. He forced himself to get out of bed to turn it off, otherwise he would hit the snooze button with better timing and intensity than a kid trying to win a circus prize for a girl he liked. He was really getting up for this shit. How could Albert have gotten himself in such a situation? Guess the man just has some bad luck. Clint was energized and ready to go. He took a shower using some feminine products he had purchased a night ago. He got out and was surprised at how good he thought he smelled. As if he could feel the masculinity slipping away from him, he decided to go get his guns ready. He ran to his gun locker like a child running to the tree on Christmas morning and took out his 9mm pistol and 12-gauge pump shotgun, along with ample ammo for the job. He checked over them, giving them a decent clean and oil, testing the slide and the pump. He took a machete from his garage and made sure it was sharp. Ready as ever.

"Undercover today as a little girl. Who woulda ever thought?" said Clint with an amused grin. He put on body spray and deodorant he imagined an elementary schooler would wear. The scents made him choke a bit, but he got used to it. He was running over things in his head as he thought they would play out today. The meetup. Albert dousing it in gasoline. Him blasting a nice-sized hole in this abomination's chest as it's on fire. Boom, job done. Then bringing it back and showing the world what had caused over 500 children in one state to go missing. They would be heroes. Modern day knights of the roundtable. *Hell, maybe I'll get a promotion. Maybe I could just retire then and there,* Clint thought. His blood was flowing with a foolhardy energy. He packed up his car and called Albert. They were going to meet up at the diner at noon and go over things one more time.

Albert packed up his devil-hunting kit as discreetly as he could while playing up the facade that he and Clint were gonna go do some hunting stuff. He didn't wake up as early as Lily thought he would. He tossed and turned a lot in his sleep again, and she wondered if he had gotten any sleep at all. She joined him out in the kitchen as he got off the phone.

"Hey," Lily said.

"Hey."

"You okay?" Lily saw Albert's bloodshot eyes and wondered no more about his quality of sleep. She let out a frustrated sigh, a caring one.

"Yep, just gonna maybe set up a new stand and put out some bait with Clint today. Shouldn't be too long," Albert said. Even with his tired demeanor, he was beaming. Lily noticed, but what she didn't know was that it was hope. Hope that things would get better. That things would be normal again. He itched his leg through his pants, not attempting to hide the strain on his face.

"If you're going out, let me at least take a look at your leg again. I can clean and wrap it for you."

"Alright," Albert didn't protest and nodded. It was hindering his ability to walk, and in case he needed to run today, it would help. Lily grimaced at the wound. It was getting worse, and if she didn't see any signs of it healing soon, she was going to tell him he needed to set aside his pride and see a doctor. She started talking about plans for the day as she dressed it.

"So Hunter is going to go work on his project with his group at his friend J's house with two others. Could you drop him off on your way to your hangout with Clint?"

"I'm about to leave, Lily. He's probably not even up yet, and–"

"I'm up. And I'm ready. Waiting on you," Hunter said, annoyed. He could hear them from his room.

"Perfect! Hi honey, have a productive day today, alright? Dad or I will pick you up around four or five, okay?" Lily was glad she didn't have to compromise with Albert today. Her extra shifts were getting to her and she was pooped. Using work as a catalyst to detach herself from the recent events was taking its toll. She needed this Saturday. It was a holy, sacred day for Lily. Absolutely *nothing* could disrupt it, lest the whole world be smitten by the angriest, most disgruntled nurse to ever set foot on this god forsaken planet. Albert acquiesced. They got in the truck and started off. J's house wasn't too much of a deviation from the diner, so Albert was still in good spirits. He attempted to make conversation with his teenage son during the ride, a daunting task indeed.

"So whatcha guys doing your project on?"

"It's on folklore for ELA."

"Oh okay, like stories passed down and all that. See, even your father paid attention in school. Sometimes...when he wasn't chasin' after girls." He managed to get a chuckle out of Hunter. "Don't tell your mother that, though." A momentary burst of laughter from the both of them. They shared a few minutes of silence before Hunter asked his dad a question.

"Have you heard of the Jersey Devil?"

Albert's eyes shot open and he couldn't seem to breathe. His leg felt itchier than usual. He held onto the steering wheel with stiff arms.

"...Dad?"

"Yeah? Oh, yeah, him. Stay away from that stuff, Hunter. Just Satanic nonsense."

"Oh. Well it was the folklore we picked for our project, that's all. We thought it'd be cool since it was a local legend," said a disappointed Hunter. Thoughts shot off into Albert's head, quickly trying to change the subject.

"Ah, okay. Look, I know you've been wanting to go out fishing before it gets too cold, so maybe on a warmer day we'll go. How about that?"

"Oh, really? Sure, sounds good," said Hunter. He sounded less excited than he had originally been when the subject came up earlier in the week. Albert understood why, and before he knew it they were at J's.

"Alright, buddy, have fun. See you later tonight."

"See you, Dad."

Albert, running a bit late, met Clint inside at one of their usual booths. The River Point Diner was as busy as it normally gets on a Saturday around noon. It smelled of fresh coffee, hot pancakes, bacon, and maple syrup. Their Saturday special was pumpkin pancakes with two eggs, home fries, and a choice of breakfast meat. Albert had this particular diner ranked so high due in part to their crispy home fries. None of that "soft, flimsy shit," as he would say. They both figured it'd be good to have some caffeine in their system and got coffee. After perusing the menu for longer than usual, Albert ordered the special with bacon and a side of grits. Clint was allergic to pumpkins, and elected for the Belgian waffle instead.

"So let's go over the plan again. I'm already smellin' like a girl for you. You brought everything you need?"

"Yep. All in my truck."

"So we get there, I'll follow near you, should I stay out of sight?"

"Out of sight, huh? Hopefully our camo is effective, but I'm not sure if there is such a thing as 'out of sight' for the bastard. Once you're in his territory, there's no tellin' whether he can sense you in one way or another. I still say be light on your feet. You're supposed to be in fourth grade, after all."

"Christ, alright." Clint took a sip of coffee. His incessant, tapping fingers were gripped around the cup, two through the handle. "You know, I can get a deputy or two to stay posted nearby in case anything happens. I can lie about why I'm there with you."

"Might be a good idea, but you sure lying like that won't get you in some big trouble?"

"Not after they see whose head we bring out of there."

"Well then, alright. Keep 'em a ways away from us, though. It's gonna expect shit like that, we can't have the cavalry ready to save us right up our asses. In fact, how far is the station from there?"

"Hell, I don't know, gotta be at least twenty minutes."

"That's fine."

"You sure?"

"Yeah," Albert said. He itched his leg. He was becoming anxious, and Clint picked up on it fast.

"Can't wait to see this thing on fire. I got my 12-gauge and my 9mm. You wanna hang onto the pistol?"

"Nah, you might need to empty everything you got into it."

Clint swallowed hard. He couldn't fathom anything being able to take more than one or two shotgun blasts and still be standing. Before his mind could dwell on it more, their food came in all of its glorious New Jersey diner goodness. They spread soft, golf ball-sized globs of butter onto their warm pancakes and waffles, which immediately melted down, being soaked up into the nooks and crannies of the food. Maple syrup was poured on top, gooey and delicious. Clint could still feel the uneasiness coming off of the both of them, however.

"Listen, Al. This isn't some last supper for us, got it?"

"Yeah...can't deny it would be a helluva good final meal, though."

"Ain't gonna argue with you there." They both laughed and finished and paid for their meals. The intrepid duo was off.

The first problem occurred as they were arriving at the trail where Albert parks his truck to go into the woods. Clint knew he wanted to have one or two guys in closer proximity to them just in case. Twenty minutes away was too far, and he planned on having them stationed in a church parking lot about eight minutes away instead. He tried to call one of the deputies he knew was working today, one he could trust, but he wasn't answering his personal phone. This wasn't something he was about to radio in, either.

"Shit!" He slammed his phone into his passenger seat. They were there, and after three full buzzes of the deputy's phone, he got nothing. They both got out of their vehicles and retrieved their gear. Albert looked ridiculous, holding a straw man with a wig and girl's clothes on in one hand, and a water gun filled with gasoline in the other. Clint thought about how badass he must've looked with his shotgun slung on him, pistol holstered at his hip, and machete strapped to his back. Albert noticed Clint's machete and realized he forgot his in the shed at home. He opened up his truck's toolbox and took out a large survival knife, feeling good that he was prepared.

"Here, put this under your camo. I already got one on," said Clint. Albert took the kevlar vest Clint had handed out in front of him.

"Kevlar, huh? That's some smart thinking. Thanks, man."

"Don't mention it."

"How's our backup lookin'?" asked Albert. Clint wished he hadn't.

"Deputy isn't picking up his goddamn phone," Clint answered with a frustrated sigh.

"Damn. Welp…just us then."

"Just us then."

They started off into the pine barrens. They felt it almost immediately. The gravity of a presence around them. An ungodly omniscience. Clint was tip-toeing as lightly as he could. Albert took his time walking to where his stand was. To where it all first began. Or had it begun there? What about those damn birds that morning…

"Al," Clint said in a whisper-shout.

"What?" an agitated Albert replied back. He'd rather them remain quiet. An agitated, impatient clench of Albert's jaw pulsed on his face as Clint abandoned his post to approach.

"I never told you the other reason why I believed your story–all of this–in the first place."

"Oh yeah? Well what's that, Clint? Cus, to be honest, I'm not in the mood for another gorey cop story."

"No, it's not that. Listen. I got the same feeling now as when I did in Montana when we went years back." They stopped walking and he turned to Albert. "You remember that massive albino elk you were obsessed with putting up on your wall?"

"Yeah?"

"Well, how do I explain this, it had a similar aura to it. Like a living legend. I saw it that morning you slept late, Al. Even took a shot at it. But guess what? That thing *knew* I was there before I even took a shot. Its antlers lit up as my bullet ricocheted off of them and then it just stared at me. Directly at me! I got up and ran, Al. I didn't dare look back. We might be fuckin' around with the same kind of force, here. Feels even darker."

"Real funny, asshole. Like an elk's antlers would just light up, like a goddamn Rudolph Christmas decoration out in my front yard," Albert said, knowing Clint had a penchant for joking around. "You even took a shot at it, huh?"

"Oh and a walking-fucking-human-goat devil in the pines is as normal as butter on toast now, is it!? *Think*, Al! I have no reason to lie. In fact, I was trying to reassure you."

Albert considered for a couple of seconds. Clint was right, but his mind had been so focused on the task at hand it clouded his head.

"Are you for real? What in the world, Clint? ...I never would've imagined. But I'll tell you somethin', that doesn't exactly comfort me."

"All I'm sayin' is let's be extra careful." With that, Clint made his way back a good distance away from Albert. They picked up the pace a little. Albert's thoughts were now running wild with the elk in Montana and what he was about to come face-to-face with. He stopped intermittently to itch his leg, but at least it wasn't hurting him as much at the moment. Clint was inside his own head too much, too, trying to shake a feeling he'd had for a while. He was turning more paranoid by the second, as the woods around him toyed with his psyche. He didn't *feel* as if he was being watched anymore. He felt he *knew* he was being watched. He tried to keep his cool. Every step was deliberate. *Tread lightly like Hannah would. It's expecting two pairs of footsteps, but not two grown men's.* He had to stick to the plan and be ready. He gripped his shotgun tighter. It was a fair day for November. Some would consider it warm for it being autumn. New Jersey tends to have its warm days, even well into the winter. Sweat formed on both of their temples. They approached Albert's hunting stand–they could see it up in the tree.

That was when they realized how exposed they were. How could you hide behind a tree when you didn't even know which angle it would come at? Regardless, Clint stood posted behind a tree to Albert's right, about fifteen-or-so feet away. They stood there for a while, waiting for something to happen. How would it make its entrance? Their eyes beamed around the barrens, hearts pumping fast, bodies tingling in anticipation. It was taking longer and longer. Had it seen through their trick? Had it not even wanted to entertain them with its physical presence? Albert was growing impatient. Time felt slow. At least five minutes had passed by now, and it was dead silent. *Dead silent.* Albert breathed hard, knowing what it meant when the natural sounds of the forest halted. They were both looking around, up in the trees, off in the distance. Was that the shape of something odd off to the left? Was there an unnatural discoloration way back there next to that tree? A twig snapped to Albert's right, breaking the silence. He looked over and saw Clint. He held his shotgun at the ready and motioned a shrug over to Albert. Albert shook his head back with a similar shrug. The minutes felt like hours. Albert thought it was getting darker already. He couldn't take it anymore. He couldn't afford to go back to a life derailed and cut short, hurting and confusing the ones he loved.

"WHERE ARE YOU!? I GOT WHAT YOU ASKED FOR. COME ON OUT, YOU UGLY BASTARD!" Albert held onto the fake Hannah, held it close, tried to sell it as best as he could. He bent down and held it by its stiff shoulders.

"It's gonna be alright, baby, don't worry," he said in a sad tone. His sadness was true. For a moment he saw the real Hannah there. Such a nascent little girl. He saw her life flash by before him. Her life without her father there. The joys of sharing her triumphs and the woes of sharing her failures stripped away from them. She morphed back into the straw man. Then he imagined his life without her. His entire family helplessly falling apart, now without the bright, teeming life she brought to all of them. They were both outcomes he would not and could not accept.

The water gun was hidden behind his shirt, tucked behind his back. It was uncomfortable, but it was concealed. He stood back up from holding the chic scarecrow. A shadow surged above them. A quick, black blur dropped straight down a distance away in front of them, straight into the ground. It was gone. But after a moment, a wave of leaves and twigs headed straight towards Albert with a frightening speed, throwing and tossing away any branch, bush, or beast in its way. It cut through the earth as easily and determined as a blood-starved shark in open water. It stopped just short of him as he shielded his eyes from tossed-up dirt and dust. He thought it was going to overtake him. Consume him. That it was already over. Such an insidious and powerful force would never let it be over that quickly, however. Silence came again and it was getting even darker, as if the shadow from before was eclipsing the sun.

Now Albert and Clint were both hearing faint noises from all around them: scattering leaves, broken twigs, grinding bark, branches collapsing, heavy breathing, children screaming. They both kept scanning around themselves, waiting for it to appear. Albert felt the earth beneath his feet vibrate. A deep growling was in the ground beneath him. He looked down slowly, first with his eyes, then with his head. Two large, white bulbs appeared from where the vibrations were coming from. They had black, horizontal designs in their center. He didn't notice any sort of strange mushroom or flower at his feet before now, so he took a closer look. That's when they blinked. Albert recoiled back as the creature emerged from right beneath his feet. It let out a growl, and as it got more intense, became an awful bleating. The straw decoy fell to the ground, but the beast quickly had it in its grasp. Clint was peeking out from behind his tree, getting a good look at it. Adrenaline was coursing through his veins. It was as Albert had described it. It had a mean expression on its face with a natural furrowed brow. Frozen and permanent in anger. He looked on in shock and awe, becoming a spectator, fully captivated by such a fearsome sight. The Jersey Devil examined the dressed-up straw man and threw it to the ground.

"NOT TOO CONVINCING UP CLOSE, STRAWBERRY. YOUR PERFIDY IS SHALLOW AND INSULTING. AN AUDACIOUS FAILURE," it said in its peculiar, foreign language. Clint marveled at how Albert described its speech, able to enter into his head in a language he understood, even though the sounds coming from its mouth were not of any language he knew. Then he snapped out of it. He was trembling, but ready.

Albert, not letting his nerves get to him, acted fast.

"You really think I was going to give up my precious little angel to a nasty monster like you!?" He grabbed the water gun from behind his back. "Leave me and my family alone!!" He doused the creature as much as he could, pulling the plastic trigger so hard it hurt, pumping as quickly as possible. He managed to get some on its face, and it screamed, eyes burning from the gasoline. "Now, Clint!"

"I KNEW I SMELLED A COWARD, EVEN BENEATH THOSE PUTRID SCENTS."

"This thing needs to be sent back down to hell! Burn, you ugly son of a bitch!!"

Clint aimed with shaky arms, but delivered two blasts to its body: A direct hit to the side of its head, most of the pellets hitting its inward-twisted horn, and another shot hit its left shoulder.

The second problem for Albert and Clint occurred when the devil didn't catch on fire. Unlike the action movies they had seen, regular ammunition alone was almost never hot enough to ignite gasoline. They had also severely underestimated this thing's resilience and reaction time. After Clint's second shot, he found his ankles ensnared in roots. He looked over and saw Albert already tangled up, cutting away at the roots with his survival knife. He pulled out his machete and made quick work of the roots around one leg, but it rushed over to him before he could free the other. It swiped at him and he dodged, but was thrown off balance. It ripped a vertical slice through the middle of his chest, but it barely reached his skin.

"It cut through my goddamn kevlar! Al, help!" Clint took the machete and swung at the creature. He hit it in the thigh, it yowled and backed up slightly. It pulled the machete out of its leg and thrust it aside in anger. As Clint drew his pistol it rushed in on him, shielding itself with its wings. The bullets didn't penetrate. It approached fast and pushed him down on his side, against the direction his leg was bound. The roots didn't give way. He heard his leg snap as his full weight fell down onto it and screamed in agony. He threw the pistol towards Albert's direction. Albert's fight or flight kicked in, and he was in full-on fight mode. He sprawled over to grab the pistol, but as he did, the devil came over and crushed it with one of its hooves, centimeters away from destroying Albert's hand. Albert looked up and without hesitation balled his fist. His knuckles were white with rage. He gave it an uppercut right in its hairy black jaw. It was stunned for a moment and Albert saw his opening.

"You *SICK. TWISTED. FUCK!*" He punched between each word, landing three right hooks onto its face and inward-twisted horn. He saw it bleeding pretty bad from its shoulder and left side of its face. Its horn and skull on that side took so much damage that the force of the shots and blows pushed the horn further into its skull, beginning to pop out its eye. It recovered from being stunned and stopped Albert's arm from delivering another blow.

"I HAVE HAD *ENOUGH* OF THIS!" it growled. "IT SEEMS YOUR FATE HAS BEEN SEALED."

It grabbed him by the neck and thrust its wings upwards, and into the sky they flew. Albert struggled hard. He knew it intended to make the rest of his life a long, tortuous hell and fought as much as he could to avoid that. If it meant dying, then so be it. The force of flying upwards had pushed the creature's eye even more out of its socket, and Albert noticed, but it was holding him by his left arm, dangling him away from its head. Exhausted, he struggled to no avail. He then reached up and bit it in the arm. It was fed up with him. The devil was also exhausted. It had damage to its vision and was laboring its left shoulder as thick, maroon blood that looked black seeped out of its wounds. Not wanting to kill Albert, it lifted him up in front of its face, planning on headbutting him until he was unconscious. Albert, however, saw his opening and swung his arm, using up what was left of his energy to hit its warped horn as much as he could. His body felt like it was on fire as he fought and flailed. He took a hit to the face and was dazed, but a raw, seething hate fueled every punch he threw. He broke some knuckles, but kept punching and managed to lodge its eye right out of its socket, now dangling down its face. It let out a vehement cry and dropped Albert, but in a last bid of hope, he grabbed onto something wet and fibrous. It was the dangling optic nerve connecting the beast's eye to its brain. It bellowed so loud that it rendered Albert's ears useless; he could only hear ringing now. It was frothing at the mouth from the extreme pain–a pain so intense it had never felt anything like before. Throbbing agony shot through its head like millions of red hot pinballs, like shifting barbed wire tangled throughout its sinuses and brain. The devil acted fast, out of instinct and hatred, and sliced off Albert's wrist with its sharp, thick claws. Albert plunged back down to the earth. As he fell he watched it fly away and saw its eye disconnect from its body, also now headed down towards the gray and brown abyss of dead trees and leaves. A weak smile appeared on his face, knowing how much pain he had caused it, hoping it would go die in a cold, dark hole.

CHAPTER 14

Hunter hopped out of his dad's truck and headed down J's driveway. Albert didn't care to pull in, and was off the moment Hunter was out. Hunter's body was tingling with excitement. It felt like forever since he hung out and went adventuring with friends. He breathed in the fresh air and found himself amused with J's property as he walked. The house had an unkempt look, with various decorations in the front yard, such as garden gnomes, a lawn flamingo, and a small fountain with a happy, dapper-looking frog in the center. It smiled straight at Hunter as he approached J's front door. Everyone else was already there hanging out in the kitchen. Hunter noticed the smell, and then the random trash strewn about the house. He stepped on a styrofoam cup and a cockroach skittered out. Looking up, he saw Caleb wearing a backpack and J with their camera.

"There he is!" said Caleb.

"Hey Hunter," said Brooke.

"Finally, let's go," said an upset J. Hunter gave Caleb and Brooke a look, and Brooke whispered over to him that she would explain later. J barged out the door and they all followed, beginning their short walk over to Caleb's house. Brooke couldn't get out of the house quicker. The part of town they lived in was lacking, as it was where many lower-income families lived. Brooke had her prejudices, and once she found out that J was poor, she was off-put by them. Hunter, on the contrary, didn't mind it at all, as he had always felt a certain charm to it. He had visited J numerous times after their family moved into that house. He thought elegant, upstanding developments with strict HOAs and picket fences could be cookie-cutter and drab anyways. The trailer park near them intimidated Brooke, and the sheltered girl walked on the opposite side of everyone, distancing herself as much as she could from it. She never heard good stories from her mom about trailer parks. Once they got to Caleb's house, Brooke noticed some similarities between his and J's.

"Are *all* the houses dirty around here?" Brooke asked. She didn't hide her appalled face too well.

"What is wrong with you? Y'know, I could tell you were uncomfortable in my house, but it's not my fault things are the way they are," replied J.

"Same…" Caleb added.

"*You* try living out of a motel for most of elementary school. *You* try stealing things for your parents so you don't get kicked out. When my mom left my druggy dad and decided to move in with my grandma, it was a huge upgrade for us. So *sorry* if my house is a little dirty. It's the best we can do right now!" J had tears coming from their eyes. Things had been bottled up in their head for quite a while and Brooke's comment was enough for the cork to pop right off. "Y-you're lucky you get to see your mom so much. Mine works two jobs and is so tired when she gets home I barely get to do *anything* with her! I'm left to deal with my grandma! So maybe next time you open your mouth, think about what other people might be going through-" Before J could say another word, Hunter cut in.

"Alright, alright! Let's calm down for a second. Listen, I'm sure Brooke didn't mean to be rude or look down on you, right Brooke?" Hunter eyeballed at Brooke, his hand on J's shoulder. Caleb was staring off into the distance, full of thought.

"No…no J. I didn't mean to be rude. I'm just not used to being in the poor part of town," Brooke said with brutal honesty. This didn't make J feel too much better, but they didn't want the day to be completely ruined before it even started, so they wiped the remaining tears from their face and gave Brooke a weak smile.

"It's ok. I'm just in a bad mood from yesterday. My grandma is just crazy. I thought moving would make things better, and I guess they are in some ways, but it still sucks, y'know?"

"I'm sorry, I hope things get better." Brooke thought about it and realized she wished she saw her mom more, too. At least her grandmother wasn't crazy.

"Thanks."

"You guys gonna kiss now? Or are we gonna go prank my brother?" Caleb said, snapping out of his daydream.

"*And* explore for our project," chimed in J, holding up their camera.

"Yes, and explore for our stupid project," Caleb agreed, his eyes rolled towards the sky.

"Hey, before we go, can I use your bathroom, Caleb?" asked J.

"Sure, just be quiet…you know why," Caleb said.

"Yep, be right back."

J trotted up the wooden stairs of the small front porch of Caleb's house and went through the door with a careful, quiet step.

"Ok, so…what's up with J?"

"Well…you heard about how their grandma is kinda cuckoo, right? Well she had some sort of weird episode and got angry at J for one reason or another. Makes 'em get in the car, drives off into the middle of nowhere like five minutes away and tells them to get out. Starts *screaming* at J to get out. And just leaves 'em there," said Caleb.

"What the hell? J must've been scared to death! Did they hitchhike or walk back?" asked Hunter.

"Walked back. Apparently not the first time it's happened. And she used to do it to J's mom as well when she was younger as a way to punish her rebellious kid. Super weird," said Brooke.

"Super abusive…," said Caleb in a low voice, shaking his head.

"Well let's have a fun, positive time exploring today then. I'm sure J needs this," said Hunter.

"Yeah, well *somebody* already messed that up," Caleb said, looking at Brooke. Brooke gave him a mean look back.

"Listen. We're starting over as of now. Good vibes only, ok? Here they come," said Hunter, who has been ready to head into the woods. J regrouped and Caleb pointed towards a small, beaten path down a ways from his backyard. It comforted Brooke, who liked knowing they all had a path to stick to. They walked for a while, enjoying the nice, warm-enough day for it being November. Hunter told a funny hunting story he had heard from his dad. J was telling the group about how they had talked to Ms. Santos about their plans to adventure and how she gave them some good ideas on what to do for the project. They brainstormed some ideas for the paper and solidified their roles for the project. Caleb chimed in with a few outrageously creative things he could contribute towards the project. The mood was light and positive. Caleb decided to change the subject and told them the plan on how they were gonna prank his brother. He stopped, opened up his backpack, and pulled out four masks. They were of surprisingly good quality, earning "whoas," "oo's," and "aa's" from his friends.

"Look at these–I carved them out of wood. It took a while, but I think they'll do nicely for spooking my brother and his friends."

"Wow, you even put straps on the back and made them all look different, huh?" said an impressed J.

"Yep! It took me a while to find cool enough looking bark and twigs to glue onto some of them. I tried to make this one look like it had antlers, and this one look like it had spikes around the edges."

"Impressive, but they look…weird. Caleb, you're weird," said Brooke.

"Why, thank you," replied Caleb, bowing and taking it as a compliment. "You three get to pick which one you want. I already call dibs on this one." He pointed to a mask that was smiling with a mean look and had two antlers sticking out. J reached out a quick hand and took the mask with horizontal slits for both its eyes and mouth, adorned with wooden spikes around the edges. Brooke took an eerie mask that had no mouth hole. Hunter was left with a mask that resembled a distressed Melpomene mask. It wasn't the one he preferred, but he decided he would pick last so that his friends would be happy.

"Sweet. So cool!" J put on their mask and raised up their arms, practicing their scare tactics on everyone. Hunter put on his mask for a second to make sure it fit, then took it off. Brooke held hers and examined it, not interested in putting it on yet.

"Nice. So we're gonna split up when we get to the lake. He's gonna be there with, like, four of his other friends so we gotta come at them from all angles. We'll lurk around at first, behind the trees and stuff, stalking our prey. Maybe one catches a glimpse of one of us, rubs their eyes, next thing they know, we're gone. Mess with their heads a little, right? And as Jake gets closer to the lake, we'll all rush him, hopefully scaring him into the water. Whether he has his bathing suit on or not, it'll be great!" Caleb was cracking up at the thought already. They all seemed amused by this plan.

"It'll be like we're part of the monsters who scare people on the haunted walks!" said an enthusiastic J.

"Oh my god, you're right," said Hunter.

"Hmm. Okay, I'm down. Sounds like a good plan, but weren't we going to explore *first* and *then* scare Jake?" asked Brooke.

"Yeah, well I heard they weren't planning on staying for too long today. I guess they have other plans later in the day. It's no problem, we can explore afterwards, right?" They all looked at Caleb and pondered.

"Well, I guess so, as long as it doesn't take too long," said Brooke.

"Awesome! Well then let's keep going, we still have a ways to walk," said Caleb.

Jake and his friends were having a nice time at the lake. They ran around, balancing on branches and throwing pine cones at each other. It was always a fun time away from the world. There was a secret competition going on, however. Jake and his "friend" Aaron were both interested in the same girl–a pretty blonde with a bit of a tomboy personality. Ava was her name. Other than Aaron and Ava, his best friend Ronnie was there with his girlfriend Meg. Jake didn't really like Aaron in the first place, and their vying for the same girl made it much worse. But Aaron was Ronnie's good friend, and Jake respected that, so he acquiesced whenever Ronnie invited Aaron to hang out. Ava was a smart girl. She knew they both had a thing for her. She had favored Aaron over Jake. Aaron was, after all, the more athletic of the two. And his family had a fair amount of money. She didn't *dislike* Jake, though, but he was a lanky foster kid. He *was* much funnier than Aaron, which she enjoyed. She wasn't a big fan of commitment, so she played with the two, helplessly wrapped around her fingers.

Jake never liked swimming. He rarely ever swam with the rest of the group when they would go out to the lake. They all sat down in foldable chairs around an impromptu fire pit they had made in the past. Ronnie rolled up a joint, took a hit, and passed it around.

"So, you're all coming to my party tonight, right?" asked Aaron. "Remember we gotta get heading back in a couple hours. Still gotta set most of it up."

"Hell yeah, man. Meg and I will help you set up!" said Ronnie.

"Yeah, probably, if I don't have other things going on," said Jake. Aaron didn't care. He had actually *hoped* Jake had something going on.

"Ava?" Aaron asked.

"Hmm. We'll see. Depends on if I feel like being social later. I might just wanna ride my four wheeler for a bit before it gets too dark."

"I gotcha. That's cool, that's cool. Well you're more than welcome. It's gonna be a ton of fun," said Aaron. They all sat there and shared the silence. A slight breeze drifted through the trees. They were down on a small beach by the water.

"Isn't it nice? Just being out here. No parents blabbering your ears off. No homework. Just the autumn breeze," Meg said.

"Jeez. When can I buy your debut poetry book, Meg?" Jake said. Everyone chuckled.

"You know what I mean!" said Meg with a smile.

"Of course, the forest always has a cool, free vibe to it," replied Jake.

"Until you're never seen again. Just another missing persons case tragically plaguing our beautiful state of New Jersey," said Ronnie with a facetious tone. They all laughed, but couldn't deny a small chill run down each of their spines. "Well, it's a pretty nice day, we're gonna go for a little swim."

"Oh, are we?" asked Meg. Ronnie took her hand and they walked down to the shoreline. They stripped down to their bathing suits and slowly made their way into the water.

"Goddamn! This shit is *cold*! We're doin' a fuckin' polar plunge here, fellas!" exclaimed Ronnie.

"It's not too bad once you get used to it. It'll make the fire pit feel so much nicer once we're out!" said Meg. Jake went to get more kindling for the fire pit. It didn't take him long, but when he got back he saw that Aaron and Ava were in the lake too, flirting here and there with an innocuous splash to the face. Ava noticed Jake return and got out of the water to talk to him.

"Hey, Jakey! Gonna come swim with us?"

"Eh, I dunno…"

"Oh come on! It'd be more fun with you. Pleeease?" Ava gave him cute puppy eyes. Her words were convincing. And so was her bathing suit.

"Alright alright, Ava, gimme a sec, ok?"

"Ok! Thanks for getting more wood for the fire pit," Ava said, walking back to the water. Aaron watched them talk from the lake, acting like he didn't care. He definitely did.

Clandestine footsteps approached the group. Four sets. They were spread out, coming at different strategic angles. They closed in as Jake was beginning to take his shirt off. One of the masked stalkers noticed their opportunity, and started rushing in. The other three noticed and followed suit. Jake, with his head still inside of his shirt as he was taking it off, heard something approaching and panicked.

"What the hell is that!?" he yelled, running, unable to see in front of him. The others noticed Jake's frantic movements and began laughing at the sight of a headless Jake, arms sticking out in odd ways and his face imprinted into his shirt, running towards them. Their laughter ceased when they saw four masked stalkers rushing towards the lake.

"Run, Jake, run!" Ronnie was starting to panic as well. Jake tripped in the sand, falling face-first. He managed to take his shirt off and jumped into the water. The initial cold shocked him, but he managed to swim out to the group. They weren't too far out, thankfully. The four masked menaces were screaming, and their shouts soon transitioned into laughter as they watched Jake's panic unfold. They took off their masks.

"C-Caleb!? You little asshole!!" said Jake, spitting out a few grains of sand from his mouth. At this point everyone was laughing at him. J couldn't give up such a chance, so they snapped a quick picture of it all happening. Ava swam up to Jake and put her arm around his shoulder. He felt even more embarrassed by this.

A dark figure watched from the other side of the lake.

"Aw, it's okay, Jakey-poo. Looks like you got pranked good," Ava said. Aaron was behind all of them laughing his ass off. He laughed so hard that when he gasped for air, he caught some water in his lungs. The tears from his laughter blurred his vision and he lost control. He grabbed his neck, coughing hard and loud. He was stricken with fear, as he drifted off further from the group. He regained his composure and started swimming back closer to the group. *Phew, close one*, he thought. But as he swam back, something took his ankle and pulled back with a violent tug. He swam harder, starting to cramp, mind racing in confused alarm of what in the hell just touched him underwater, but got pulled back again. Then he realized he couldn't feel the bottom of the lake anymore. Aaron tried his best to tread water, but was not breathing right. The water got colder as he began to sink. So much colder now. His friends were all amused with the four masked menaces and the prank they had just pulled, and they thought Aaron was still having a laugh and a swim in the background. They chatted with Caleb and company a bit more before Brooke noticed Aaron was further away from the group and really struggling. She pointed it out and they turned around. The mood changed immediately. All they could see were a pair of desperate arms for a moment, grabbing for anything solid to hold on to. His head surfaced for a split second, but went back under. He wouldn't breathe a fresh breath of air ever again. The water was slightly swelling from where Aaron had been. Distraught bubbles surfaced.

"AARON! Oh my god, someone help him!!" cried Meg. Jake watched, not feeling compelled to help at all. Ronnie tried to swim over to Aaron, but felt the steep dropoff of the lake and how cold it was. He still tried and dived down to see Aaron sinking. He tried to swim down and pull him up, but he was too weak. They would've both drowned if he exerted himself anymore. Instinct prevented him from trying any harder and he swam up to the surface, freezing. Caleb, Hunter, J, and Brooke watched on in disbelief.

"Aaron, no!! *NO!!*" Ronnie cried as Meg grabbed him and pulled him closer to shore. Jake was expressionless as he made his way back to the beach with Ava. Ronnie and Meg's crying wails filled the soft silence of the woods. Everyone else was muttering under their breath in denial and shock. The cold gripped Aaron tight, paralyzing him. Then he felt nothing. With the last bit of sight he had, he thought he saw more bodies, bloated and purple, suspended in the water, reaching up in desperation, but something like a root was wrapped around their ankle, coming up like evil, jagged tendrils from the gelid abyss. His numb body twitched and sunk slowly down into darkness.

Ava just stared at the lake. The enchanting blue hole where they all had so much fun was now turned into a cursed place of death, wiping away any and all good memories. She kept muttering "no" and "what the fuck" under her breath, eyes wide open still looking at the lake. Jake did his best to console her. They were both shaking. Jake and Caleb looked at each other with stunned, morose eyes.

"We need to leave *now*. Jake, let's go. You guys, stay away from the lake. I suggest you wrap up your little fucked up adventure for the day, too," Ronnie said through tears, grabbing Meg's hand. The four of them started running back to contact the authorities.

"It...it wasn't our fault, right?" asked J. Silence. "Right!?"

"There's no way. No. That didn't happen 'cus of us. There's no way," replied Hunter. Brooke sat down, curled up, and started to cry. J went to go comfort her. The collective guilt they felt washed over them like a hot, suffocating blanket. Caleb, much like Ava, couldn't help but stare at the lake. Moments ago it was a lively place with a group of friends having fun. He looked at the exact spot Aaron was just minutes before in the lake. The lake was indeed something out of a fairytale. It was a blue he'd only thought water could be in movies and video games. He was expecting a knight to come prancing by on his horse or a Lady of the Lake to come out of the water, Aaron in hand, perfectly fine and alive. He would smile and tell everyone everything was alright. They would get invited back to the castle and live there. They wo-

"C'mon guys. We can't stay here. Let's at least snap some pictures for our project. Who knows when we'll be able to do anything like this again now?" said Hunter, breaking the silence that had fallen over them all.

"Someone just *died* in front of us because of a prank *we* pulled. How can we just move along like nothin' happened!?" said an upset Brooke.

"He's right," said Caleb. "Maybe a walk in the woods will be a good thing. Exploring is still fun, right? We won't be around anybody else. Let's get all of our feelings out there."

"And what use is there going home now? We'd have to tell our parents everything and that'll be stressful anyways," said J. "Might have to talk to the police too."

"C'mon, Brooke. It's not our fault. We had no intention for that to happen! We couldn't have possibly known..." said Hunter.

"Ok," replied Brooke. She got up slowly and kept her head down, not wanting to look at the water at all. J wrapped an arm around Brooke.

"Hey, listen. We're just four middle schoolers. Nobody expects us to be heroes in a situation like that. What if you were at the beach and a lifeguard failed to save someone from drowning in the ocean? It sucks. It's horrible and unfortunate, but would you really blame yourself for what happened?"

"I get it, I get it. Thanks, J. Let's go," Brooke said, still processing everything. Some time passed.

"I wonder what it's like. To drown," said J.

"It's probably awful. You ever drink water and it goes down the wrong pipe?" said Caleb.

"I can't even imagine…" said Hunter.

It would take them all a while to process it. They walked away from the lake, all in silent agreement to get as far away from it as they could. It was in a different, offshoot direction from where they came. None of them remembered how far they had been walking before something foreign broke the silence: gunshots. Two of them. They were distant, but it was a familiar sound for Hunter.

"Were those–"

"Mhm. Definitely gunshots. Didn't sound like they were from something small, either," Hunter said. He noticed concern in his friends' faces. "Although it is sorta hard to tell…they were definitely a long distance away. No need to worry. Some hunters probably, that's all."

"Hunter's a hunter. Who would've guessed?" Caleb laughed. He managed at least a small smirk from Brooke and J. This wasn't the first or last time Hunter would hear a joke at the expense of his name.

"Ha ha. Yeah, Caleb. We get it," said Hunter. They continued on and heard more, smaller pops coming from the same direction.

"Huh…smaller caliber than before. What the…?" Hunter wondered.

"Umm, should we just head back?" asked Brooke.

"If we hear any more like that, then yes. Keep an ear out," replied Hunter.

They continued on and heard nothing more besides the wail of some animal. None of them thought much of it. J stopped to take some scenic shots of the woods. J's passion for photography was a beacon for the group. They explained certain theories they had learned, as well as how their camera worked. It sparked some idle chatter and they used the project as a way to distract themselves from the tragedy they had witnessed. Caleb picked up sticks as they walked, breaking them into smaller and smaller pieces. Hunter was always on the lookout for the next point of interest or any wildlife. Brooke would look around and feel like no matter which direction she looked, it was all the same, so she instead decided to look down at her feet or at her friends. The group stumbled upon large stone rubble further into their walk. They pondered what it could've been. J took some pictures and told them that maybe Ms. Santos would know. Regardless, it was more content they had for the project. Along they went, trampling over leaves in gloomy glides, getting pricked by sticker bushes here and there. Their energy was coming back, slow as it may be, and when Brooke's mind was a bit clearer, she spoke up.

"Hey guys…do we even know where we are right now?" They all wound up turning to Caleb. He hadn't taken note of the direction they took from the lake, as his mind was buzzing about what would transpire once home to his brother and foster father.

"Um, yeah, I'm not too sure," Caleb said.

"So you're telling us we're lost?" asked Brooke. She began to panic. "No way. We need to get back home. My mom is gonna freak. It's gonna get dark and we won't know where we're going and it's going to get cold and we'll all get hungry…oh my god someone please tell me they know where we are becau–"

"Brooke!" Hunter shushed at her. "Listen, it'll be fine. I have a good sense of direction in the woods. It might not be the fastest way back, but the most reliable way would be to retrace our steps and go back from where we came from." As Hunter said it, all of them thought the same thing: *we'll have to go back to the lake, then.* They were anxious about it. Brooke thought about the police being there, pulling Aaron's body from the water. But it was the best way to not be lost anymore.

"We still have a fair amount of daylight. We've probably been walking and exploring for a little over an hour. That makes it about 2ish, maybe? We left around noon so that's my guess. Don't worry. We'll be home before dark."

"Alright, then let's start heading back," said Brooke.

"Hold on. You see up ahead there a ways? It looks like an old cabin or something. Let's go to that and then take some pictures and then we can head back," said Caleb. They all looked in the direction he pointed and saw what looked to be an old, rotting, wooden structure.

"I'm down. Whaddya say?" asked Hunter, looking at J and Brooke.

"The more pictures the better. But then, yeah, after that I wanna go home," said J.

"Fine," sighed Brooke. She took a look back from where they came and made gestures, pointing at things that she could remember so they wouldn't get more lost.

They approached the ramshackle building with curiosity. It wasn't big at this point, but the other areas around what was left standing of the cabin made it seem like it could have been part of a larger building years ago. Hunter thought it looked neat, like something he would see as a desktop background on his computer. Caleb sprung ahead, striding over small stumps and sticks. The leaves were thicker around the cabin. J followed in a hurried walk, while Hunter and Brooke took their time. Caleb put his hand to the side of the cabin, feeling its damp, rotting wood. It left a residue on his hand that had a pleasant earthy smell. He noticed moss growing in patches here and there, giving it some color, as well as the little bugs and fungi that had made it their home. He turned the corner, out of sight of his friends, and looked at where the doorway was. No front door anymore. There were barely any remnants of a floor in most places, too. He was thinking of a pose to make for J's camera, not having much desire to try and unearth any hidden treasures or curios. That was when he listened closely to a noise that he previously had thought were his friends' footsteps. It grew louder inside of a section of the cabin that must've been a larger room, perhaps a master bedroom at one point in time, long ago. No, it wasn't footsteps on dead leaves, but some sort of labored breathing. He stepped closer. It was dimly lit, but there was enough sunlight pushing through the patchy, dilapidated roof to reveal something moving up and down, inhaling, then exhaling, with occasional shaking to mess up the natural rhythm. Caleb stepped even closer, his pupils larger, greedily sucking up all the light it could to satiate his curiosity of whatever this was. He was so concentrated on carefully moving closer that he jumped when J said "hey" behind him.

"God. You scared the shit out of me, J!" Caleb said in a whisper-shout. He motioned a finger to his lips to let J know to be quiet. J nodded.

"Ok, what's going on?" the whispering continued.

"Whoa, this is pretty cool!" Hunter said on the other side of a rotten, hole-ridden wall that was barely standing. J went to grab him and Brooke.

"Guys, come here, quietly! Caleb found something."

"Huh? What is it?"

"I don't know yet. C'mon."

They entered the area with caution and all heard the serene silence of the forest interrupted by an odd breathing.

"Look," Caleb pointed in the corner. Black fur and horns. It lay sideways, with its body leaning against the wall and the ground.

"What is that? A goat? What the heck is a goat doing all the way out here?" asked Brooke.

"Shh! Brooke, a little quieter. You might scare it. I think it's hurt," replied Caleb. Hunter walked up to Caleb and they both inched forward, examining it. Brooke stayed back with J, who turned the camera's flash on and was primed to get some great pictures.

"You're right. Listen to its breathing. It's like, shaking sometimes," said Hunter.

Then, as Caleb saw more of it, he saw that it was not a goat. Or at least no ordinary goat. Its limbs seemed longer than usual. Its face seemed bigger, longer, with more expression. J took a picture and the flash revealed something that shocked them all. They all looked at each other, questioning whether they all saw what they thought they did.

"Guys…does that goat have…hands?"

"What *is* that thing!?"

Caleb moved even closer to it. His eyes were adjusted and could see it enough.

"It's bleeding," he said.

"It's a freakin' monster, Caleb! Or some mutant or demon, I don't know, I don't wanna know, we need to get back home *now*," said Brooke, fear and panic starting to rise in her chest. "I'm gonna need to go to church after this. Lord please keep us safe," she said under her breath. She was in the very back now, away from the rest of them. Hunter was so interested in this creature he decided to stay close and marveled at it. He almost felt pity for it. It was like that one time when he realized that a deer he had shot and tracked down wasn't dead yet, as he had missed its vitals. It just lay there, breathing, dying.

But Caleb did not see a creature, demon, or mutant lying there. He saw something that reminded him of himself. He saw pain. He saw the struggle to stay alive. He saw a helpless, vulnerable, living thing with nothing there to take care of it. There was no monster before him, no matter how abnormal it was. And Caleb, caught up in this fiery, painful compassion, knelt down next to it. He reached out his hand and caressed its head. He couldn't hear any of his friends asking what he was doing. Tears started to fall from his eyes.

"I know what it's like to be hurt…with no one there to help you feel better," Caleb said in a whisper through his tears. And there sat two beings, whose lives had been devoid of love, and yet who both carried a will to keep living. Neither of them knew why, but neither could deny such a will existed deep within themselves. There was a resonance. An unspoken connection. Hunter, J, and Brooke looked on in astonishment. J took another picture and they saw it more clearly in the flash again. Its shoulder and head were bleeding. A large, white orb appeared in the darkness accompanied with a grunt. It had a horizontal pupil inside of it. The three standing backed up further, frightened, not knowing what they were dealing with. Caleb decided not to touch it further and stood up, mouth agape. He wiped his eyes and backed up as the creature awoke and started to stand up. It stretched and blew air from its nostrils. It towered over them, with its head almost touching part of the decayed roof. As it stretched, two large, black, bat-like wings pushed out from the back. That was when they knew. All of them knew exactly what they had stumbled upon.

"Th…the Jer…"

"Th-th-that's…"

"It's the Jersey Devil…"

"Wh-whoa…"

They all gave each other a glance, and before they could start running away, a voice entered their heads. Its telepathic ability confused and shocked them after hearing it speak an unrecognizable language aloud.

"A NAME I HAVE CARRIED FOR A LONG TIME. TELL ME, CHILDREN, WHY I SMELL FEAR ON ALL OF YOU BESIDES ONE? THIS IS UNFAMILIAR."

"Guys, *RUN*!!" screamed Brooke. They all shot for the entrance besides Caleb, who took his time timidly backing away from the devil. Their escape was short-lived. It had enough energy still to get up and make a gesture with its hands and arms, summoning a wall of thorny, thick roots blocking any exit from the ruined building. The devil touched its face and noticed its thick, dark blood still fairly fresh and slowly seeping out. It looked at the four children, completely defenseless, and the helplessness was so apparent on their faces it tempted and urged the beast to take their soft little skulls and crush them into each other, squeezing their bones, brains, eyes, and blood into a splattered mess that would feel good passing through its fingers. With a closed eye and a deep breath, as the four children stood there, knowing they were trapped, paralyzed, it turned around. As it walked away its tail dragged behind it like a triangle-headed snake slithering on the ground. It moved its injured shoulder and gave a deep wince, then sat back down, leaning its back against the wall.

"IT IS USUALLY I WHO GO AFTER THE LIKES OF YOU. AND YET HERE FOUR OF YOU ARE, RIGHT AT MY DOORSTEP. CURIOUS," it said, pointing at each of them. Its pointing finger remained on Caleb. "YOUR STENCH…I SMELL IT UPON MY BODY."

"You're hurt," Caleb managed to muster up the courage to speak. "What happened?"

"IS THAT COMPASSION I HEAR IN YOUR VOICE?"The Jersey Devil laughed. "SYMPATHY FOR A DEVIL LIKE ME? FROM A CHILD, NONETHELESS. WHAT AN AWFUL, CHAOTIC, SURPRISING DAY." It grunted as it reached into an old, rotting drawer and took out a pestle and mortar, along with various plants. It started to grind up the plants into a paste. The pain it was suffering had put it in a sour mood.

"Mr. Jersey Devil, sir, w-we don't want any trouble. And seeing how you're…hurt and all, c-c-could you just let us go?" asked J. They were contemplating taking another picture. The temptation was too great, and J snapped one at their hip, hoping they got a good shot. The devil recoiled a bit and gave J a snarl.

"Please let us out of here. I want to go home!!" cried Brooke.

Hunter studied it, trying to think of a way to convince it to let them leave. He looked at Caleb, too, unsure of what he was going to say or do next. He felt as if he were in a fairytale. The gruesome kind, where the children usually don't make it out alive. It was like Ms. Santos said: those kids' lives were warnings. Hunter watched as the devil applied the paste it had been making onto its wounds. This was a creature with so much intelligence that he no longer considered it some beast or goat-thing.

"FOUR LEAVES OF A CLOVER FALL INTO MY LAP. LUCK IS NOT DISCRIMINATING BETWEEN US TODAY IT SEEMS. I MAY LET YOU ALL GO, BUT FOR NOW, ENJOY THIS DEVIL'S COMPANY. PERHAPS WE CAN MAKE A DEAL?" It kept carefully applying the salve, breathing harder every time it touched one of its fresh wounds on its face. As it touched its shoulder, it started picking out shotgun pellets with its long nails before applying more. Hunter motioned to his friends and the four kids grouped up away from it, watching in an amazed horror as this thing treated itself. They sat down huddled on the floor and whispered to each other. Brooke was curled into a ball with her head down still crying, muttering to herself how none of this is real and that she'll wake up any second now. They all consoled her, with J rubbing her back.

"Brooke, we're all here in this together, okay?" said J.

"Yeah, we're gonna make it home. Don't worry," added Hunter

"It doesn't want to kill us," Caleb said.

"Oh yeah? And how do you know that?" asked J.

"Because we'd already be dead by now if it really wanted to," said Hunter. The creature sounded like it scoffed in the background. They paid little mind to it.

"Exactly. We have to see what it wants," continued Caleb. Brooke had lifted her head up.

"You some kind of devil whisperer? Huh, Caleb? You freakin' weirdo. *YOU* woke it up. Why would you even *touch* that thing? I didn't see a sign that said Hell's Petting Zoo out front! God, why did you have to be in our group? I knew you were a freak as soon as you opened your mouth in class. I never heard you talk before that, and I wish I never had," said Brooke.

"Well at least when I open my mouth I'm helpful. Especially right now. Unlike you, who has been an annoying asshole for most of today!

God, I can't believe J still wants to be friendly with you. So how about you shut up now?" replied Caleb.

"No, I don't think I *will* shut up. *YOU* shut up!" An already stressed out Brooke was becoming very upset.

"Guys, *guys!!* You both need to cut this out, *now*," said Hunter.

"Okay, Ms. Santos, how about yo-," as Brooke was replying to Hunter, she saw him pointing at J, who was beginning to cry.

"This...isn't helping. Please. We need to be a group. We need to be friends," J managed through their light tears.

"She started it," Caleb said under his breath.

"*Enough*," Hunter doubled down, giving Caleb a vicious glare. Another scoff from the devil. Or was it a grunt from it tending to its wounds? They were all silent for a few moments. Then Hunter spoke up.

"Okay. If it wants to make a deal with us, it obviously doesn't want to expend any more energy trying to fight us. It's hurt...we can make it out of here alive. We have to be prepared for whatever it's going to throw at us."

"It's right, y'know. Ever since I first saw it in the corner there, I wasn't afraid of it. It can sense how we feel. We are dealing with something with powers...like in an anime or comic book. We have to keep our cool," added Caleb.

"Well it's not like we can go anywhere," said Brooke.

"Let's go talk to it then," said J. They all stood up from their huddle and walked up to it.

"SIT," said the devil. Even as it sat, it looked at them at eye-level, but when they sat down it could look down upon them, and this pleased it. "SOMETHING HAPPENED AT THE LAKE TODAY, DIDN'T IT?" It smiled, showing its big, menacing teeth.

"...are you the reason why so many people have been disappearing?" asked J.

"And especially...k-" Hunter gulped, even though he was trying to play it cool. It embarrassed him, "...kids?"

"OUR ENCOUNTER TODAY HAS LED ME TO BELIEVE THERE IS A DIFFERENT APPROACH I CAN TAKE."

"A different approach to what?" asked Caleb.

"MY EARLIEST MEMORY IS OF THIS PLACE. I CONSIDER THE PINE BARRENS AND MYSELF TO BE ONE. IF I STRAY TOO FAR AWAY FROM THEM, I START TO FEEL MORE AND MORE LIKE A RABID BEAST. THE ENTIRETY OF MY SOUL EXPANDS AS FAR AND AS DEEP AS THE EXPANSE AND DEPTHS OF THIS FOREST. BUT THERE EXISTS ONE AREA OF IT THAT HAUNTS MY EVERY WAKING AND DREAMING MOMENT. I CANNOT

ESCAPE ITS TORMENT. IT IS ENOUGH TO DRIVE A DEVIL, AS YOU CALL ME, MAD. ABOUT TWO THOUSAND PACES NORTHEAST FROM HERE YOU WILL FIND A CLEARING WITH A LARGE WHITE OAK TREE. THAT IS THE AREA I SPEAK OF. FIND OUT WHAT SORTS OF DARK SPECTERS HAUNT THIS AREA. FIND OUT WHAT HAPPENED THERE. I MUST KNOW. MY DOMAIN IS TARNISHED BECAUSE OF IT AND IT MUST BE CLEANSED. I WILL GIVE YOU ONE MONTH TO DO SO WHILE I HEAL. IF YOU FAIL, I WILL INSTEAD TAKE THIS ENCOUNTER AS A WASTE OF MY TIME AND YOU WILL END UP LIKE THE REST."

It took them a while to take it all in. They were talking to a legendary monster about its problems. And now they were the device for it to fix its biggest problem? They were just four twelve year-olds! What abilities could they possess to solve some sort of ancient forest curse? Did they have a choice? Maybe a counteroffer? How could it really expect them to figure this out? The anxious thoughts and questions swarmed their heads. They just wanted to go home. They had had enough of exploring in the woods for one day. For the rest of their days. All of them except for Caleb, who looked forward to this deal. J was the first to speak up.

"You really hate kids, don't you? What did any of them ever do to *you*, huh? We're just trying to live and play and have fun, and you have to take us and do god-knows-what to us. Well, we know *one* thing you do to them now. You drown them. Do you really think they aren't going to find bodies? They will burn down your entire forest before letting you get away with *any* of this!!" J was trembling, not entirely sure where this bravery and feeling of indignation came from. The devil let out a sigh, its natural, furrowed brow making it look upset.

"Yeah, and are you ever going to tell us what happened to you? You know you're missing an eye, right? Did your horn poke it out?" asked a curious Hunter.

"IS THE MANNER OF YOUR SPEECH IMPUDENCE, OR JUST DELUSIONAL BRAVERY? YOU BEST CHOOSE YOUR WORDS CAREFULLY, AS EACH ONE YOU SPEW OUT OF YOUR WRETCHED MOUTHS THINS DOWN MY PATIENCE THAT MUCH MORE."

They all looked at each other with big eyes. None of them spoke a word.

"REGARDLESS OF WHAT YOU MAY THINK OF ME OR WHAT HAPPENED TO ME, I WILL SPEAK NOT OF IT. IT IS EXHAUSTING ENOUGH KEEPING YOU TRAPPED HERE WITH THORNS. I MUST REST," it said. It pointed to Caleb. "YOU. CALEB,

YES?" Caleb's eyes shined with a timid awe. He nodded. "I HAVE BEEN WATCHING YOU MAKE MASKS OUT OF WOOD. PRESENT THEM TO ME." They all took out their masks. "ONE FOR EACH OF YOU. PERFECT. I WILL ADORN EACH WITH MY BLOOD. THIS SEALS OUR CONTRACT." The Jersey Devil twisted its finger into its injured shoulder and smeared its blood on all of their masks. They all inspected the new red marks on their masks. Hunter smelled its blood. Caleb touched it. J took a picture of theirs. Brooke was repulsed and wanted nothing to do with any of it.

"And what if we don't want to be your little detectives? What if we just wanna go home and enjoy our childhood?" asked Brooke.

"I AM AFRAID THERE IS NOT MUCH OF A CHOICE FOR YOU FOUR. IF THAT IS WHAT YOU TRULY DESIRE, YOU HAVE A MONTH TO PROVE IT."

"You have to hold up some part of the deal, right? You're the devil. At least offer something in return," said Caleb.

"Yeah, you know, while you were sleeping we could've just caved your head in with a rock or something," added Hunter. The devil exhaled with an impatient, soft growl.

"IT IS BEST YOU DO NOT UNDERESTIMATE ME." It sniffed, then clenched its jaw. "ESPECIALLY *YOU*, SMALL HUNTER. LITTLE STRAWBERRY."

"...ok? Is it going delirious from blood loss or something?" Much like his father, Hunter carried a boldness that could get him into trouble. But this time, it was helping alleviate the stress his group had pent up inside of them. "Isn't time kinda precious right now? You gonna tell us what your end of the deal is or not?" The devil got up. It was in no mood for games. But it looked at Caleb again and remembered his gesture of sympathy. It stifled the bitter anger welling up inside of it and calmed down, thinking of something to offer in return if they held up their part of the deal. It let out low, menacing "hmms," deep in thought.

"IF MY BLOOD IS MIXED WITH CERTAIN INGREDIENTS FOUND IN THIS FOREST, I CAN MAKE VARIOUS CONCOCTIONS. FOR EXAMPLE, SOME RESULTING IN DIABOLICAL HARM, AND OTHERS OF REJUVENATING HEALTH. IF YOUR EFFORTS RID ME OF THIS PAINFUL CURSE, I WILL GIVE EACH OF YOU A CHOICE: A VIAL OF LIFE OR A VIAL OF DEATH. THE FIRST WILL EXTEND YOUR LIFE APPROXIMATELY 100 YEARS AND LET YOUR BODY HEAL MUCH FASTER THAN USUAL. THE LATTER WILL KILL ANY LIVING THING IF INGESTED. IT HAS NO TASTE, SCENT, AND IS UNTRACEABLE. THEIR DEATH WILL BE SLOW AND

AGONIZING. THIS IS JUST A SMALL DISPLAY OF MY POWER, AND I EXTEND IT TO YOU ALL TO HONOR THIS DEAL." The Jersey Devil hid its morbid curiosity well. It wondered who would pick what, and for what purpose they would use it for. Upon hearing this, the four kids all seemed satisfied, minds already buzzing with the possibilities. Brooke's eyes lit up, and her willingness to work with Hunter, Caleb, and J came shooting back. They all gave each other a knowing look and nodded.

"Ok. Deal," said Hunter.

"PERFECT. WHEN YOU HAVE FOUND SOMETHING OUT, COME BACK HERE. I WILL SENSE YOU," said the devil. It released a clenching hand and waved it, and the wall of thorns regressed into the ground. "YOU ARE RELEASED. REMEMBER: IN ONE MONTH I WILL KNOW WHERE YOU ARE. THERE IS NO HIDING FROM ME. YOU CAN TRY AND HIDE UNDER YOUR BED SHEETS. YOU CAN TRY TO SLIP INTO THE CRACKS OF AN OLD BUILDING. THESE ACTIONS WOULD BE FUTILE. EVEN IF YOU PLUNGE YOURSELF INTO THE DEEPEST ABYSS ON EARTH, I WILL BE RIGHT BEHIND YOU, READY TO DRAG YOU OUT AND DELIVER UNTO YOU YOUR FATE FOR FAILING ME. NOW LEAVE ME TO REST." As they left, Caleb gave it an awkward wave goodbye. They made their way back home.

"What. Just. Happened? Like, is this for real? What did we just get ourselves into? Guys?" asked J. They didn't get a response for a while. "W-we're all gonna die, aren't we? I'll never get to take any more photos after a month from now. We'll never graduate. Never be able to eat pizza again."

"No. Don't think like that. Some of us are good at researching. Like for history and English class, right? Maybe we can find out what happened there. I don't think it has access to the internet like we do," Hunter said, thinking about how silly it sounded. "But who knew...something like the Jersey Devil was actually real...and *can talk*."

"God must really be testing us or something. That's Satan. Like *actually* Satan. Y'know. The *Devil*," said Brooke.

"Yeah, and it's not really a test we can fail, is it?" asked Caleb.

"Guess not," Brooke replied with an unenthused scoff.

"I just can't believe it. Today was like some dream," said J.

"More like a nightmare," said Brooke.

They kept walking and Hunter's strategy paired with his good memory was guiding them back in the right direction. They reached the lake, keeping their distance from it, as the authorities were just getting there, setting up a scene. They saw a man putting diving gear on. None of them said anything, and they all walked past it at a quicker pace. Once it was well enough behind them they started talking again.

"So...we're keeping this between us, right?" asked Caleb.

"I guess so. It's not like anyone would believe us anyways," said Brooke.

"Y'know, we could have some fun with it. I was thinking about one of Caleb's silly ideas he had for the project. Like how about we start a "fake" cult as part of our project? We could scare some of our annoying classmates," suggested J, hoping to change the mood. They had a big grin on their face. "I've seen when people are close to dying they try to go out and do fun things before they pass. Maybe we could at least have some fun...if it came down to, y'know, us not...making it."

"What? No, that's just weird," replied Brooke.

"Finally, one of my brilliant ideas gets acknowledged! C'mon Brooke, you don't have any bullies you wouldn't mind messing with a little?" asked Caleb. Brooke thought about it. She did, indeed, have some bullies.

"Y'know what? It's still weird, but you bring up a good point, Caleb," Brooke was grinning now.

"Sounds fun to me, too. We already have these cool masks. Maybe we could wear them to *really* scare 'em," said Hunter, gesturing with his mask and making noises.

"We're gonna act like we know the Jersey Devil. And no one is gonna even know it's not a lie. No one would even know, dude!" Caleb was getting more and more excited.

"Ok, another question–what would you guys pick and do with the mixture it gives each of us?" asked J.

"Don't you mean, 'CONCOCTION'?" mocked Caleb. They all laughed. None of them knew why, but in hindsight, their meeting with the Jersey Devil felt ridiculous. They almost viewed him as some sort of evil cartoon character that was the comical relief. It was a sort of twisted game to them. Deep down they might have been terrified, but they tried very hard not to show it. It did them no good to be scared right now. And being scared was no fun, anyways. Today had been an overload of emotions and astonishing events. They dealt with the trauma together. Shared it. Were forever connected by it. Such a staggering experience had already started to change many parts of them. They were in a race for their lives, but they didn't seem to worry about it too much.

"My grandma is old and sick. She's always been there for my mom and I. I'm gonna give her the vial of life. I don't know what I'd do without her. She's taught me a lot of things and been there while my mom worked for us," said Brooke. Her sincere tone almost made no one else want to chime in.

"Wow. That's really nice, Brooke," replied J. "For me...well, I think I might just drink the life vial for myself. That way I can build up a huge catalog of photography over a whole century. I'd be legendary."

"You already are, J. You have pictures of the Jersey Devil," said Hunter.

"Yeah...yeah! I guess you're right! How about we look over all of today's pictures after school some time next week? With all that has happened today I think we should all just kinda go home for now."

"Alright. That's fine," Caleb sighed. He was disappointed.

"So Caleb, how about you? What will you do with the devil's reward?" asked Hunter.

"Not sure yet," Caleb shrugged. He knew exactly what he was going to do. "That's *if* we lift this curse or whatever. On the day we get together again we need to come up with a plan."

"You're right. Not to mention we still have this project to do," said Brooke. "Are we...are we gonna use all of the pictures from today? Y'know...*all* of them?"

"Maybe. I could scan them onto my computer. Think about it. We could have the best project in our class. No, the best project the school has ever seen," said J. "Imagine the look on Ms. Santos' face!" They laughed thinking about it.

"Wait. But then we wouldn't be keeping any of this between us," said Brooke.

"Well, we would play it off like it's just all some sort of joke. And the pictures? We'd say we got some of those from the internet. That's where everyone else is gonna get their pictures, anyways," said Caleb.

"Hmm. Ok, makes sense."

"Yeah. The details of what *really* happened and our deal with it? That stays a secret."

"Y'know guys...there's no turning back now," Hunter said, the seriousness of their situation hitting him again like a truck. "Our lives are actually on the line. There's a chance we'll all just disappear in a month. No one will ever see us again."

"Yeah...there really is no going back. It's like trying to reheat french fries. No matter how you try to do it, it's never the same again," said J. It was quiet for a while before Caleb spoke up.

"Then we won't fail. That's it."

They found their way back to where the rough, beaten trail started from behind Caleb's house and all let out a sigh of relief. It was 3:30 PM. They heard more police sirens close to Caleb and J's houses. The mood shifted when they were reminded of Aaron. They all planned to keep it to themselves unless they were asked. Another secret.

"Well, whaddya guys say after school next Friday? Big sleepover at Hunters? Y'know, Hunter, you *did* volunteer to host the project group," said J.

"Yeah, sure. I'll ask my parents. Should be fine. I'll give you both my address," he said to Caleb and Brooke.

"No need, I'll be going with J," replied Caleb.

"Alright. Well, Brooke, I'll make sure to get it to you, ok?"

"Ok," replied a half-listening Brooke. She was on the phone with her mom telling her she was ready to be picked up. This reminded Hunter to do the same. He called his dad first, but got no answer. Another call. Then another. No answer. *What's he so busy with?* Hunter thought with a sigh. Then he tried his home phone and finally his mom's, but no one was answering. Brooke noticed he was growing upset getting no answer and told him her mom probably wouldn't mind dropping him off. J and Caleb said their goodbyes and they eventually all got home safe.

CHAPTER 15

"Safe" was a word neither Caleb nor Jake had ever associated with home. They had stuck together their whole lives, being the only positive constant either of them had. They both fought hard not to be empty husks of humans, as life had its way of draining any sense of joy and purpose from them. Every day it seemed like it got harder to feel anything, yet something kept them going, be it their indomitable human spirit or a hateful spite for the world.

Jake and his friends did the right thing in reporting the drowning of Aaron right away, but this brought authorities up to their doorstep. After Jake was questioned and the police left, he was confronted by Will Tate, their foster father. Will Tate had been in a construction accident, leaving him unable to work. He fell into a deep depression and abused substances as a coping mechanism. This led to his divorce. Tate, not content with the disability money, decided to become a foster parent. He had little compassion and didn't have the right intentions from the start, and the boys suffered because of this. His aggression was almost constant. Caleb heard him and got up to see what was going on.

"The fuck they want?" Will asked.

"Some kid drowned in the lake back in the woods," said Jake. He tried to be vague. He never liked to share anything with Will. But Will wasn't quite as dumb as he looked.

"And they asked only *you* things? You were there, weren't you? With those fuckin' no-good friends of yours. Always hanging out god-knows-where; bad things were bound to happen, Jake!" He turned around and pointed at Caleb. "And *you*! Where the fuck were you at, huh? Haven't seen you all day."

"I had to work on a project," said Caleb. His voice was low and he refused to make eye contact.

"Huh? Speak up, boy! Get over here," Will gestured and Caleb traipsed over to him.

"I said I was working on a project," repeated Caleb.

"Don't get snappy with me, little shithead," Will got up in his face. His breath reeked of alcohol. He belched and let out a mocking laugh. "Caleb doing schoolwork, huh? Outside? Whaddya pickin' leaves or some shit?" He got no response. It always pissed him off when they were silent and it happened often. "Listen. You two shitstains better not do anything else to have the police coming around here."

"Why? Because you're a drunk, abusive, good-for-nothing *FUCK*!?" snapped Jake.

Will threw an almost-empty bottle of beer on the floor and it shattered.

"The *fuck* you just say to me, you little punk? I am your *father* and you will show me some *respect*!" He slurred some of his words as he approached Jake with a clenched fist. Caleb knew what was coming and spoke up.

"You're not our father. You're just a sorry excuse for a man." Will recoiled at the comment, turning around to assert his drunken self in Caleb's face.

"What would *you* know about being a man, you little *maggot*!"

It was Caleb and Jake's dangerous game of monkey in the middle. Only the monkey was an abusive drunk asshole. And it never ended well. Regardless, the brothers had each other's backs, and Jake, seeing Will about to grab Caleb, yelled.

"We'd both rather be maggots than a sad, pathetic leech who can't support anyone!" Will turned around again at Jake.

"You two never learn how to shut the fuck up, huh? Oh, I'll teach you," Will said through gritted teeth, spittle coming out in strands going down his chin.

"Jake's right. No wonder your wife divorced your sorry ass!" said Caleb.

"That's it, you little motherfucker. C'mere!!" This was the tipping point. They both knew it was futile to insult him anymore. It was going to get physical. Will grabbed Caleb's neck and squeezed hard. Caleb's face quickly turned red, and Jake ran over and started hitting Will's back.

"Let *GO* of him!!"

Will didn't stop, so Jake swung around and bit Will's arm like a rabid animal. He broke skin and Will screamed and let go. Caleb wheezed on the floor while Jake spat out Will's blood from his mouth–he didn't want that filth inside any part of him. Even though Will was on disability, he was still able to beat up a couple of kids he was supposed to look after. He recovered and started hitting Jake. Jake knew how to take the blows.

"Yeah, big fucking man beating up a couple of kids, *huh*!?" Jake said in between blows, trying to shield himself. He was bleeding from his nose.

"You gotta learn. Oh you're gonna learn. You're gonna fuckin' learn," Will said. He backed off and went to go grab something. That's when Jake and Caleb knew to run. Caleb was still on the floor and Jake picked him up and they ran into their room, locking the door and sliding their dresser over it. A belligerent Will Tate pounded on the door, clenching a broken beer bottle in his hands. He gave up after a while, muttering obscenities to himself, exhausted.

Alcohol. It had been the enemy of the bereaved brothers their entire lives. They had lost their parents when they were struck by a drunk driver speeding on the wrong side of the highway. They had hired a babysitter that evening and went on a date night to celebrate their anniversary. Caleb was barely one year old; Jake was five. They didn't have any family to take them, and so off they went, tragically thrust into the cold machine that is the American foster care system. Their lives were nomadic, going from group home to group home. Once they finally got a foster parent, their eyes lit up with the hope of living a normal life.

"I hate this. I can't take it anymore, Jake. I can't," Caleb said through tears. Jake was checking for bruises and had a tissue to his nose.

"He doesn't usually get *that* bad. Fuck," Jake winced at the pain.

"I swear it won't have to be like this anymore. We can't keep living like this. He would've *killed* us if we kept trying to fight. This has to stop. It has to," said Caleb.

"Yeah…and he really *will* kill us if we go to the police. Just keep being strong, little bro. It'll be okay," Jake went over to Caleb and gave him a hug. He teared up, wishing he could do more to help out his little brother.

"It will be, Jake. Just give it a month or so. I think a change is coming. Thanks for always being there for me. I couldn't have asked for a better big brother."

"We've been through a lot together. We'll always have each others' backs." They sat there in a light embrace, some tears trickling down each of their faces. Caleb's stomach growled. He felt ashamed. Jake noticed.

"Hey, hey. It's ok. I'll go out and see if he's passed out again. I think there might be some cereal left to eat for dinner."

CHAPTER 16

Albert Lawless woke up to his phone ringing. He was dazed and in pain. But he was alive. And that surprised him. He opened his eyes and looked at the branches above. They helped break his fall, along with the mass of leaves he landed in. He tried to get up and pain shot through his upper right back. He had fractured his right scapula. That was the least of his concerns when he realized he couldn't feel his right hand. He looked at it and it was bleeding from the stump. He screamed in a mixture of agony and rage. It was the first time a beast had bested him, and in its victory it had taken something very precious from him.

"*Goddammit*! I hope you're *dead*!! I hope you writhed in pain for hours all alone, you bitch! My fuckin' hand!!"

Thanks to a clean cut from that big ugly bitch, the bleeding wasn't as bad as it could've been. He applied pressure and figured he had about fifteen minutes to live. That was, unless some miracle happened.

Albert's miracle came in the form of a distressed Clint, who also woke up from passing out due to the pain from his snapped leg. All he remembered was Albert going head-to-head with the Jersey Devil and then it grabbed him and flew away. It took what felt to him like forever to get his injured leg out of those tangled roots. He immediately phoned in an urgent emergency, and since there was recently a report of a kid drowning near the same area, authorities were close enough to respond in time. He notified rescuers of Albert most-likely being north; he thought extra hard about the direction he thought he saw them fly off in. Albert's phone rang again. Hunter had called him a handful of times to be picked up, unknowingly saving his life as rescuers heard the ringtone as they were searching. They found him in a bad state. Hypovolemic shock set in and they rushed him back to the ambulance hoping none of his organs would shut down. They dressed his wounds and gave him a saline drip. Then they tried their hardest to manage his blood pressure. He had to get more blood in his body before he perished. It was all a blur to Albert.

Clint shuddered at the sight of his leg bending in all the wrong ways, limp as a boiled noodle. He was put on a stretcher and they held his leg in place. They were both off to the hospital. It would take some time before anyone was able to visit either of them. They were both treated and the skilled doctors did all they could to ease the pain and help Albert and Clint begin their recoveries. They mentioned to Albert that they might have been able to reattach his hand by first grafting it to his leg, had they found it. It wasn't before long that various men in suits came to question them. Given their proximity to the drowning of Aaron and their injuries paired with the mass disappearances going on, investigators had to see if any of it was related. Albert told all of them he couldn't remember much. Clint, being the one who called it in, also claimed his memory was hazy, but mentioned some wild animal attacking them. Investigators weren't happy with those answers, but after some time, it seemed that's all they would be getting out of them.

Lily had gotten the news the night that it had happened, but was told they wouldn't be able to visit for a couple of days. She sat down Hannah and Hunter after school Monday and let them know Daddy had been in an accident. As soon as they could, they visited the hospital. The story stayed the same. Lily, still not getting answers about why her husband had been acting so differently as of late, grew further saddened and frustrated, still thinking he had got himself tied up in some sort of drug ring. Clint being there only deepened her theory of it all. Hannah was confused and very upset. It was the first time she ever saw her father in such a state. For Hannah, and for many other children, she thought of her father as invincible–a superhero, capable of doing anything. Even Hunter still carried this mindset to an extent, and it hurt them both to see him like this. The thought of their parents' mortality frightened them. It was something neither of them had thought about before.

CHAPTER 17

Crash the kitten was growing fast. He sat on the couch and with a casual lick of the paw and subsequent washing of the face, listened to Lola after she got home from another enervating week of teaching. Even though she vented to him, having a cute little fuzzball like Crash to come home to helped lighten her mood.

"Y'know, I thought you were rambunctious, but some of the kids I teach? Dios mio, so *wild*. I mean what the hell gets into them sometimes?" Lola took out various ingredients from her pantry to prepare for cooking dinner later. "I mean, besides the usual talking over me when I'm trying to teach, bringing in masks and talking about needing a sacrifice? They didn't prepare me for this. If it happens again maybe I'll have to write them up," she let out a sigh as she placed down a box of pasta. "...But at the same time, wouldn't it look bad on me? I did kinda encourage them with the project." Crash paused and gave an affirming look at Lola, then continued to wash his face.

The suspects were, indeed, Caleb, J, Hunter, and Brooke. Moreso the first two than the latter. Caleb and J had been terrorizing some of their fellow classmates in school about being in a Jersey Devil cult, and went so far as to talk about being in need of a "sacrifice." The more fear and discomfort they saw in some of their peers and bullies' eyes, the greater their delusional passion for their made-up cult was. Caleb and J even picked on a kid they sat close to on the bus. Chester was a normal kid, more on the quiet side. He kept to himself for the most part and was a bit of a nerd. He wasn't used to people coming up and talking to him. He very much didn't like feeling his anxiety grow more and more as Caleb and J teased him with their twisted antics. They pointed out of the bus window into the woods, claiming to have spotted the Jersey Devil. "There, there! See it? In the back behind that tree. Oh my God I saw him!" they would say. It got bad as the days went by, telling Chester it required a sacrifice. Hunter attempted his own shenanigans for a day, but became unenthused and disinterested after feeling embarrassed about putting on a mask in school. He was afraid of it being taken away, and was also not in the right headspace with his father being in the hospital. Brooke had fun with it for a bit. She didn't care if she was seen as weird as long as she could scare some of the rotten bullies. The most amusing part to all of them, however, was how a handful of their classmates went along with it, asking to join the cult. Some of them also started claiming to see glimpses of the Jersey Devil here and there, maybe out of a window at school or in the backyard of their neighbor's house. Unfortunately for Lola, it had been spreading fast, a lot of the kids involved being her students. Many of her fellow coworkers judged her quietly while putting up a front that they were shocked, yet amused by what had been happening. Mrs. Thomas was one of the most crucial of her coworkers, talking behind Lola's back whenever she could. Lola could sense it and it only added to her increasing embarrassment and imposter syndrome. In reality, the kids were growing to like her more and more and genuinely enjoyed her class. It didn't stop them from acting up, but at least they were on her side. That didn't give her much comfort, but it made her feel like they at least looked forward to her lessons. It was such a wonderful, fulfilling feeling as a teacher when she looked into her students' eyes and saw that glint of yearning–that thirst for knowledge. Being the purveyor of something so crucial to these young, nascent lives was all that kept her going sometimes.

The kitchen was all prepped for dinner so Lola decided to sit down next to Crash and turn on the TV. He was dreaming about something as he twitched his whiskers and paws in his sleep. Lola thought it was cute, but hoped it was a good dream. She got cozy and didn't pay much attention to the TV as she was also on her phone, but something on the news caught her eye. She had been following the New Jersey kidnapping situation closely. Her concern was intensified due to her job field paired with a genuine interest in unsolved crime. Even if, day by day, her job was starting to make her dislike for children grow, she still wanted them to be safe and have an opportunity to live a fulfilling, successful life.

The news was about to cover safety hazards of the "blue hole" lakes found scattered about the pine barrens. She had gotten an email about Aaron's death because he attended the high school in the same district she worked at. It was awful to read. It was even more awful when she heard about how he had died. When a child dies, the entire school district develops this tangible, cloudy aura throughout the halls. It's one of sadness, confusion, tragedy, and indignation. No one was the same for a while, thinking about how terrible it is for a life to be cut too short.

She could only imagine the helpless, crying friends watching him drown. The grief and trauma would most likely be a permanent mental scar they would have to deal with for the rest of their lives. Lola shook her head thinking about it and watched on.

"Concerned New Jersey residents, many of them also parents, are calling for authorities to drag the lake where they found Aaron Cunningham's body last Saturday. This particular lake being located back in the woods behind Cains Hollow Road, and is about a three mile hike. Many are seeking answers as to just where so many children have been disappearing. Could the answer lie within the depths of these lakes? At this point in time, authorities have not responded. Over to you, Jim."

"Thanks, Vanessa. We do know that the particular kind of lake in which the drowning took place is much more dangerous than meets the eye. Its pure blue color may be nice to look at, but we have an officer on standby to let us know what these 'blue holes' really are. Officer Kennedy?"

"Hi Jim."

"Good afternoon. Now, many concerned parents are watching, and we all want to know more about these surreal 'blue hole' lakes. Could you fill us in a bit and talk about the safety hazards to be aware of and precautions to take?"

"Of course. Well, first off, the best precaution to take is to just not swim in these lakes at all. This doesn't matter how good of a swimmer you may be. I mean, even if you're Michael Phelps, I wouldn't recommend it. These are not normal lakes, as many have very abrupt and extremely deep drop-offs. This is because they were originally quarries, long since abandoned now, and they've filled up with water over the years. The loose sand can also act as a sort of quicksand which is another deadly factor to these lakes."

"Wow, quicksand? That's not something you think about when you go out for a swim at the lake."

"You're exactly right, Jim, and that makes it all the more dangerous, because it'll catch you off-guard. And, listen, these drop-offs can be *feet* away from shore. The water gets very cold, very fast. If anyone is going to go to the blue holes, please appreciate them from afar. And children need to be under strict and direct supervision the entire time."

"Oh my god, *I* didn't even know that…and I've hiked around near there before," said Lola. She was thankful for tuning in, as she had thought about going for a swim in one of the blue hole lakes as something fun to do during the summer. She thought about how there was no way over 500-and-counting children had disappeared all into lakes. Unless there were serial kidnappers all with the same idea, but that seemed way too far-fetched. No. Was it a coincidence? It had to be. It didn't make sense in her head. Part of her wanted to go out and investigate it herself. She dismissed the thought, already drained of enough energy for the day, hell, maybe even the whole weekend. She wondered about the news story with Albert Lawless and Clint Morris as well. It was already a shame enough that one of her student's fathers was found in such a critical condition. She had noticed Hunter's change in mood. It was sad seeing a kid go through something like that. But them being in such a close proximity–was that also a coincidence? What the hell actually happened with Hunter's dad? The vague story they gave didn't reflect the fear she noticed in their eyes. Nevertheless, she was glad to see them both alive and on the path to recovery. Lola got up and went to her room to continue progressing through a game on her PC. Crash gave out the cutest little grunt as he stretched, then followed her in.

CHAPTER 18

It had almost been a week since the Jersey Devil project group was thrown into a bizarre chain of tragic and otherworldly events. They were taking it in stride, however, finding pleasure in the rush of being in their own little cult and scaring the daylights out of their fellow classmates. They had all made it to Hunter's house after school that Friday afternoon on the basis of working on their folklore project. Lily had taken the day off and didn't mind Hunter having some friends over, whether it was to work on something for school or not. It was a nice little distraction from all that was going on with Albert. She was hoping he'd be discharged from the hospital soon. Ever since Albert had his accident in the woods, Lily felt as if a dark shadow loomed over her. She felt as if she couldn't shake it off, either, but was able to distract herself enough to bear it. The project group were all in Hunter's room. Hannah kept to herself in her room, as she was timid around older kids who weren't her brother.

"So I've been working on the powerpoint for our project," said Hunter with a slight ounce of pride in his voice. "Check it out."

The others were relieved and impressed at how the project was coming along. The powerpoint looked nice, with a cool, dark theme and neat transitions. Some of the writing Brooke and Caleb had been doing was on the slides. J's pictures and research were the only things missing, and they had already emailed the pictures over that day.

"All that's left is to put in the pics and info J sent me today and I think we'll be able to present early. Maybe even Monday if we all feel like it?" They all agreed. None of them had much anxiety about public speaking; that fear was stifled by their excitement and confidence for their project.

"This is actually sweet," Caleb chuckled as he thought about what he said. "I never thought I'd say *that* about a school project." They surprised themselves with how far they had come, wishing more school projects gave them the same feeling.

"Haha, I know, right?" said J. "*And* I brought all of the pictures from last week by the way. Wanna have a looksee?"

"Sure!"

J had a stack of photos in their hand. There were various pictures taken of the group having fun, doing poses, smiling all the way. Once they had gotten more into the woods, J had taken many pictures of nature–some pointing up towards the sky with towering trees, others down at their footsteps trampling on leaves–and J couldn't hide a big smile as their group remarked how nice some of them were. There were pictures of the masks, of them wearing the masks, and them at the blue lake. A couple of hilarious shots of Jake panicking, tangled up in his shirt from being pranked. They couldn't help but laugh, but the giggling was short-lived. The air grew heavy when they saw the photos of Jake's friend group enjoying themselves at the lake.

"Th...those are probably the last pictures of Aaron that exist," said Caleb.

"Yeah..." said J. They continued flipping through. One picture showed Aaron seeming to struggle in the lake. Behind them in the treeline Brooke noticed something. It was taller and darker than usual. It looked just different enough from a tree that she pointed it out.

"You don't think that's..."

"Huh? Oh, wow. It just might be. I think I remember it hinting towards being responsible," said Hunter. The picture terrified them, but Hunter's words relieved them of much of the guilt they had been bearing from the incident at the lake. J continued flipping through. There were pictures of old, torn down structures. Any remaining pictures of their friends were drastically different from the ones taken at the beginning of the day. Somber, serious, and sad faces were all they would find in the remaining pictures. Then there it was–the old, rotting building where they had found that legendary, vile, despicable, intimidating creature. J had taken only three pictures of it, and all of them were frightening. None of them said anything. J got back to the beginning of the pile.

"So yeah, that was it."

"You're a great photographer, J. Thanks again for sending me some for the project," said Hunter, breaking the silence that had come upon them.

"Thanks. And no probs," replied J.

"Maybe keep some of those photos put away in a box for a while. You know which ones I'm talkin' about," said Brooke.

"I was actually wondering if I could...uh...have one or two. Just as a keepsake, y'know?" said Caleb. J handed him the stack and he picked out a couple and put them in his pocket. "Thanks, J. And to think, it all happened because of the project topic Ms. Santos assigned us."

"It's still definitely not a topic I'd say I'm too thrilled about, but I can't deny it has been...interesting up to this point. And y'know, just a *little* terrifying," said Brooke.

"Speaking of terrifying, let's start planning out what we're gonna do. J, you've already done some research. Learn anything helpful?" asked Hunter. The three of them looked at J with hopeful eyes.

"Ok. So admittedly…," J closed their eyes, trying to remember. "I kinda skimmed over things and didn't get *too* far in the research. But…I remember reading that the story originated around the 1700s. I think that's like, kind of around the Revolutionary War time?"

"Yeah. Revolutionary was late 1700s," said Brooke.

"Ok. So it could've been even before that all happened 'cus I think I remember it being early. Like 1710 or 20. Anyways, there was this *really* big family. They had thirteen kids," J saw the baffled expression on their friends' faces.

"Sheesh! If I had that many siblings we'd be gettin' in fights all the time I bet," said an amused Brooke.

"Yeah, I know. An absolutely ginormous family. But apparently the number 13 is unlucky. And so when the mom had her 13th kid, it was like cursed or something. Or at least they thought it was. And it turned into the Jersey Devil."

"Okay. So is that the curse it was talking about? Do we just go wake it up and tell it that?" Brooke asked.

"Well, no. Remember it talked about a specific area that drove it nuts. Like it didn't belong there. So I was thinking we should go there first and see where it's at and what it looks like," said Caleb.

"Yeah, then we can compare it to where that 13th kid was born! Maybe its birthplace is making it feel crazy or something," said Hunter.

"Ooh, that's good. That's a good start. Okay, so when are we going to go back into the woods?" J's question sent a surge of anxiety down each of their spines. Were any of them prepared to go back into the pine barrens? To return to where so much had happened to them already?

"Y-yeah. Um…"

"We can meet at my place and go from the trail we took before and retrace our steps," said Caleb. They all considered it and came to the realization they didn't have much of a choice but to do what he suggested. "How about tomorrow?"

They nodded in agreement. Lily ordered pizza for everyone and they enjoyed a big sleepover playing games and chatting the night away. Even Hannah hung out with the bigger kids for a bit.

CHAPTER 19

The next day came fast. The group woke up from their sleepover groggy, so they took some time to refresh and eat to prepare for another journey into the woods. Lily let Hunter know she'd pick him up around dinner time. They got dropped off at Caleb's house and embarked into the forest, each of them putting on their masks as they entered. J was equipped with their camera, ready for any opportunity to snap a cool shot of something in the woods. Caleb had his backpack on again, holding onto the straps as he walked down the beaten path. A church bell rang a deep, solemn chime in the distance. They passed the time with some idle chatter about school and what TV shows they'd been watching recently. During a lull in the conversation, they could hear a small whistling sound. Hunter, Brooke, and J looked at each other with questioning eyes while Caleb walked on straight ahead. He had one hand up to his mouth.

"Caleb, are you making that whistling noise?" Brooke asked, putting a hand on his shoulder so he could turn around.

"Yeah, hah. Look." Caleb held out his pointer finger. It was bruised and there was a hole in the nail. He proceeded to blow into his fingernail and out came the faint whistling sound. "My hand got slammed in the door last Sunday and I was playing with my finger and found out I could whistle through it. Pretty cool, huh?"

"Um, ouch?" said J. "You ok?"

"Yeah, it really hurt, but I'm alright now."

"You might need to keep a bandaid on that or somethin.' That's wild. I can't even whistle normally," said Brooke. She continued to look goofy as she blew air out of pursed lips, her lack of whistling skills on full display. Hunter chuckled.

"My dad taught me to whistle when I was younger. I was always amazed watching baseball games on TV and being able to hear people whistle from the broadcast," said Hunter. He proceeded to let out an ear-buzzing whistle using his fingers.

"Jeez, Hunter! That hurt. Please don't do it again," J said, half laughing.

"Whoa, you gotta teach me how to do that!" said Brooke.

"Well I can't go *that* loud, but I did kinda learn to whistle by myself." This time J let out a whistle, albeit a dissonant one. It had room for improvement.

"I feel like Caleb's fingernail whistle sounds better than yours," Brooke chuckled.

"You're one to criticize!" replied J. They all had a nice laugh, which they needed. They walked a bit longer and got to the lake. It was a chilly day, but one look at that deadly, azure body of water had all of them feeling sweaty. They walked by it faster and Caleb tried to make conversation to distract everyone.

"So...what's something you guys like to do for fun?" A frigid, gentle wind rustled and danced through the trees.

"I try to hang out with friends whenever I can. Some of my other friends have four wheelers and we ride around their big property. They're neighbors with farm owners and sometimes we'll see cows and pigs," said J.

"Aww," remarked Hunter.

"I know! So cute. It's nice riding out there, the wind in your hair, surrounded by nature and friends. Kinda like right now." Their comment was received with affirming nods and it helped the others think of a response to the question.

"You're the only friends I really hang out with outside of school. I like being around and doing stuff with my sister, but she's younger so it's different, y'know? Going to the beach with my family is fun, but I guess it's not something we do regularly," said Hunter.

"Hunter, you're rambling!" J said with a smile.

"Yeah I guess you're right, umm. Well I play games on my computer. I have some online friends, so yeah. That."

"Nice. For me, I like to spend time with my mom whenever I can. It's always a blast when she has time to sit down and watch a movie with me. I help my grandma cook sometimes too. Other than that, reading in my bed."

"Sweet, what do you read?" asked Caleb.

"Umm, I dunno. Usually manga and some other fiction books."

"I wanna get more into manga. Is it hard to read from right to left?"

"Nah. I mean it's a little confusing at first, but you get used to it pretty quick." They walked further and their conversation helped them forget about the lake. Caleb thought about what Hunter and J had said. *Friends*. It was quiet for another brief moment before Hunter returned the question.

"So Caleb, how about you? What do you like to do for fun?"

"Eh. I dunno," Caleb replied.

"What? C'mon, you asked first. You gotta do *something* for fun."

"After hearing you guys..." Caleb hesitated. "I don't know, man. You guys are gonna think I'm weird."

"Caleb, we already *know* you're weird!" said J. That got a laugh out of all of them, even the sheepish Caleb.

"Alright alright. Well, like J, I like to get out of the house too. I'll hang out with Jake and we'll take a walk down to that big lot across the tire place. It's like where they tow cars that were in accidents. We'll sneak in and sit there or walk around and play a game."

"What kind of game?"

"We try and guess whether the person or people in the car died in the crash or not."

"...Wow. I don't know what I was expecting, but it certainly wasn't that," said Brooke.

"Jeez, that's kinda dark," replied J.

"...Yeah. I know," Caleb said with a sigh. Before this exchange could get any more morose, Hunter pointed out in front of them.

"Look. It's the devil's cabin. We're almost there."

"You're right..."

"Shh. I wonder if it's sleeping," J said in a whisper. As they approached the rotting structure it felt like time had stopped. The wind died. Any sounds from insects or fauna ceased. No rustling in the trees or on the ground. Four isolated pairs of footsteps approached with apprehension.

"Guys, I really don't think we should bother it. Especially if we haven't made any progress on this whole curse situation," said Brooke. They walk around it, trying to peek into the dark and dilapidated cabin. Caleb fought the urge to see if it was still okay. None of them could see clear enough inside to know if the Jersey Devil lay there, resting, or if it was out and about doing whatever it did. Neither of those possibilities gave any of them much comfort.

"Agreed. Let's go," replied Hunter. Small chills trickled down his spine as he moved along, the devil's cabin now at his back. Once they made some distance Caleb stopped. Then the rest of them stopped one by one.

"It was a thousand steps northwest, right? That's what he said?" asked Caleb. As Caleb's question sunk in, fear saw its opportunity to creep through the cracks of their psyche and appear on each of their faces like hideous wrinkles. A deep pit grew in each of their stomachs. They had forgotten what it told them. Without this piece of crucial information they were lost. They were as good as dead. "Right? Guys?"

"Wait. None of us remember where it said for us to go?" asked Brooke in response. "Oh no. Oh no no no no no! You gotta be kiddin' me right now." She paced back and forth in short, fretful steps. With her hands clamped up to her temples like a vice, she continued muttering "no no no" under her breath. The trees felt taller and more encompassing than usual. Every second mattered and they knew it, but all they could do was stall there, digging through their memories like downtrodden hostages, desperately looking for a key to escape their captor. None of them could shake the feeling of being watched. Was he in the shadows, peeking out of a window in that old, beaten-down cabin? The many dark knots on the trees surrounding them turned into eyes, and each of them beamed a twisted scrutiny towards them so menacing and confining they found themselves unable to look anywhere but the ground. Caleb was able to shake it off, having a sliver of confidence in what he thought he remembered.

"Listen guys, I know for a *fact* it said north-something. Whether it was northwest or northeast, if we just keep continuing north, we can adjust from there. C'mon." He knew the pervasive anxiety would only spread and become heavier if they continued to sit there. His words did give them a glimmer of hope. Better yet, they had aided in jogging Hunter's memory.

"He's right. I remember the words 'north' and 'thousand' as well. So if we go at least a thousand steps north we'll sorta be on the right track."

"'Sorta'? We gotta do better than 'sorta'!" said Brooke. She took off her mask in frustration, and the rest followed.

"I know, but it's a start! Brooke, you need to calm down, you're freaking the rest of us out. We haven't eve-"

"Calm down? *Calm down*!? If we don't even know where this place is we're done for! We'll be thrown on top of the already-high pile of corpses that *dumb*, *ugly THING* has made for god-knows-why! God…you know, I never asked for *any* of this. I was perfectly fine living a normal, boring life. You guys can go be weird hanging out in crashed car lots and living in dirty, dysfunctional homes, but *I* just wanna go back to my *normal* life. And have one ahead of me worth *living*!"

"Oh, and here goes high and mighty Brooke showing her true face again! Why do you have to say stuff like that? God, you're so annoying!!" said J.

"Look. We're *trying* here. Like usual, you have contributed *nothing* to our situation besides making fun of our lives. Lives of which, by the way, we can't *FUCKING* control! So you should get your head out of your ass and start walking north, or els,-" Caleb was cut off by Hunter.

"Guys, *GUYS!!* Fighting won't get us *anywhere*. Let's-"

"*No*. Shut up, Hunter. I'm sick of you always being the mediator. Let Brooke speak for herself or shut her mouth and start walking with us. Or go curl up in a ball and cry like a big baby," said J. The comments being thrown at Brooke made her more and more upset. Her anger was growing at an alarming rate.

"Psh. Yeah. Fuckin' *crybaby*. *Waah waah waah*!! Every time. I'm *sick* of it," said Caleb.

"You learn those filthy words from your filthy parents, too, don'tchu?" said Brooke.

"Okay. Gonna keep being like that? God, I'm so tired of your shit. Let's go guys," J motioned to Caleb and Hunter.

Brooke stepped up, tears in her eyes. Her tears were not tears of sadness, however, but tears of unhinged, pre-teen rage.

"I'm tired of *YOU*!" Brooke said through gritted teeth as she put almost all of her weight into pushing J's chest. J wasn't braced for such a violent push and flew back, falling about four feet, dropping their camera in the process. They barely caught themself as they hit the ground. Although J had managed to protect much of their body, their hands braced down forcefully onto a sticker bush scattered about ground. Thorns pierced through J's palms and fingers with ease, causing them to bleed immediately. They were slow to get up because along with their hands taking much of the impact, so did their bottom. The impact damage stung them in a different way than the thorns, but hurt just as much. They started to cry. It was not only the physical pain, but the mental pain as well that culminated into a breakdown. They thought they had reconciled with Brooke and become friends on their first journey about a week ago. They *wanted* to be friends. But as they held their hands up to their face and watched the blood trickle down, they thought, with an ugly frown, that now they could never be friends.

"Yeah, who's the crybaby now? Who's cryin' now, huh!?" said Brooke, still filled with rage. It was dissipating fast, but there was still a lot of anger to blow off. Caleb continued to not help.

"What the hell is your problem, Brooke!? You're just gonna push down your group member now? Look at them! They're bleeding! You're a *bully*, Brooke. A bully!" Caleb clenched his jaw and marched towards Brooke, but the tenseness in his muscles betrayed him and wavered after he realized he was outclassed in both weight and height. He paused, knowing it probably wasn't a fight he would win. It was a familiar feeling that made him angry and unhappy at his strength and inability. He took it as a defeat, and it left a bitter taste in his mouth. Brooke was raring to go, but her aggression died down as Caleb's words echoed in her head. She stared at J on the ground. Hunter was helping them now, examining their wounds and looking for their camera.

"You know, Brooke," J said as they started to get up, ass still stinging, hands still bleeding, "you talk about your mom a lot. And even your grandma. But what's your dad like?"

"My dad? My dad...he's, well, he-"

"He's not there, is he?"

"Well, no. He hasn't been around since I was two."

"And you think you have a normal family?"

"They're just divorced."

"*Just* divorced?" J scoffed in disbelief.

"Unbelievable. Brooke, you-"

"*Shut up,* Caleb. Brooke and I are talking right now," J turned back to Brooke. "It doesn't matter, Brooke. It's all the same."

"It's *not* the same, though. A lot of people's parents are divorced. I still live in a normal house with a nice family. My mom doesn't do drugs or-"

"You really don't get it, huh? Divorce isn't 'normal' or the 'standard'. It *sucks*. Just as much. Being passed around or not being able to see one of your own parents, who's responsible for you? What a good feeling, right? They should *care* about your life more than anyone else." J paused, picked up a stick, broke it, threw one piece at Brooke's feet, and the other out into the woods. Brooke stared at the ground where the distant stick landed. "It doesn't matter! Don't you get it? Your family is fucked up just like ours." J stepped closer to Brooke. Caleb let out a morose scoff and side-eyed the other way, getting lost in thought. "Well, except for Hunter. Hunter, you bastard! You're not fucked up like us!" J tried to be humorous to lighten the mood a little. Hunter smiled, shaking his head and looking down. He didn't want to interrupt. In fact, he was trying to distract himself from the drama, not being a fan of confrontation. He picked up a stick and drew little lines in the dirt as the conversation went on. He was thinking about what the Jersey Devil had told them, running it over and over in his head, and figured that their current plan was still the best course of action. The crestfallen crew's conversation continued.

"No...my mom cares about me. And so does my grandma. That's still two people in my life there to support me. I'm...I'm not like y'all." Brooke's eyes started to well up. J moved even closer.

"You are. And it's okay. It's not like it's your fault, y'know?" J's lip quivered as tears now started forming in their eyes. "We're not all lucky. Think about how better your life would be if your dad was there all the time too. All the memories you could make with him. Memories that aren't seeing him yell at your mom in the hotel room you were living out of. Memories that aren't seeing him in the bathroom, overdosed when you're nine years old, confused, not knowing what's going on. Not knowing why your mom had to take you and leave him and move in with your crazy grandma. It's not easy when you think about what could have been."

"No…it's different."

"It's okay," J said, hugging Brooke. Blood from J's hand smeared on the back of Brooke's denim jacket in small blotches. "It's alright. You don't have to be embarrassed. We make the most out of it, y'know?" Brooke hugged back and they both cried. After some time their reconciling embrace ended and they wiped the remaining tears from their eyes. "Right now, more than *ever*, we need to be a team, right?" Hunter gave a nod in reply.

"Hey, J? Brooke asked.

"Yeah?"

"Thanks."

"Team?"

"Team. Are you okay, by the way?" Brooke pointed at J's hands.

"I'll be fine. Caleb, how about you? Caleb?"

Caleb wiped something away from his eyes as his distant gaze came back to the project group.

"…yeah. All good." He held out something in his hands. He motioned for his group to come closer. "If one of us fails, we all fail," he looked at J. "Your pain is mine." He poked the palm of his left hand with thorns from part of a sticker bush he held. He squeezed his palm and watched blood droplets fall into the soil. He handed out the thorn-riddled stem to Brooke. She looked at it, then up at Caleb, then at J, then Hunter. She took it and hesitated for a moment, but then pierced her palm with one of the thorns. She gave it to Hunter. Hunter did the same to his palm in an instant, not even wincing. J felt a deep, prideful energy in their chest. It compelled them to hold their hand up to their forehead in a fist, poking out their pointer finger and pinky. With their pinky curled, they extended their arm out. The group all mimicked the gesture, and their hands met in the middle, connecting their pointer fingers and pinkies together in a circle.

"Jersey Devil Squad," J said, breaking formation. It got a smirk out of Caleb, and a couple of bewildered chuckles out of Hunter and Brooke.

"C'mon. Let's go," Caleb said, putting his mask back on, and one by one the other three did the same.

Hunter had approximated about a thousand steps before he told the group they needed to start going west. They all decided that if they didn't see any sort of large clearing with a huge oak tree in the middle, they'd double back east. They were walking for a few minutes when they saw something ahead, but it wasn't a clearing with a big tree.

"Whoa, look! A deer!" said Brooke.

"Ooh, gonna take a picture of it!"

Hunter knew straight away something was off with the deer. Caleb noticed Hunter's quiet, disturbed reaction as he observed the deer.

"What is it?" Caleb asked.

"We're loud. It should've run away. It's actually not even moving right. It's going around in circles." Upon hearing this, Caleb couldn't contain his curiosity and tiptoed forward. Hunter followed him. J managed to get a few pictures, but was upset it wouldn't stop moving. As they got closer it ran and startled them. But instead of running away, it ran headfirst into a tree.

"Ooh, Hunter, don't they do this when they shed their antlers?" asked J.

"Not exactly...it just hit its actual head into the tree. Not its antlers." They were perplexed, inching towards it. Another jolted smash into a different tree. They heard a crack. It turned around and just stood there. They could hear it breathing. Raspy inhales and exhales pulsed foam and saliva from its mouth and nose. Thick strands of it were hanging from its mouth. The group was close enough now to reach out and touch it when all of them recoiled in shock and disgust. Two dead, yellow yolks of eyes stared off into nothingness. Its teeth were bared a bit and it didn't have a lower jaw. Its tongue was drooping down and moving about. But the most shocking part was-

"Are those its *brains*!?" Brooke asked in terror. She had little experience with gore.

"H-how is it moving?" asked J.

"Wow, it must've caved its own skull in. It's possessed or something I bet."

"No. I think I remember hearing about this. It's something that makes the deer pretty much a zombie," said Hunter.

"We're standing in front of a zombie deer? It sure looks like one," said Brooke, waving her hand in front of her. The stench penetrated straight through her wooden mask.

"Like some sort of parasite?" asked Caleb.

"Hmm. Could be, but I think it was more of a disease. It's just been standing there now. Jesus," said Hunter.

"Ok, this is freaking me out, let's go back northeast now. I don't think we're going the right way," said J. They started to back away from the deer.

"Wait," said Caleb. Something was brewing inside of his head. "Don't you guys feel bad for it? We should put it out of its misery, right?"

"I just kinda wanna get away from it. It looks like it's gonna die soon, right?" asked Brooke. J took one more shot of it as it stood there with its off-putting, blank expression.

"Not necessarily," said Hunter, pulling out his survival knife. It was big enough to do the job. He knew where he needed to stick it.

"Whoa, you're really gonna do it?" asked J.

"Caleb's right. It's probably really suffering. Poor thing," he walked up close to it. "Doesn't even have a jaw. Beautiful buck too, a 13-pointer. Jeez." He petted its neck in sympathy and lined up where its heart would be. One thrust and it was over. J covered their face, but watched, squinting through the cracks in their fingers. Brooke turned away, and winced at the sound of the knife piercing its body. Caleb watched on in fascination as the deer dropped down on the ground, giving out one final deathrattle before passing on. Hunter rubbed it on its side as its blood poured down its body. "It was the right thing to do. He's not suffering anymore." They were all saddened by it, but understood why it had to happen. It was an intimate thing, being so close to death. Something they all feared, and yet, in this moment, it was peaceful. Fitting. Natural. Caleb didn't reflect too much on the topic, still near the deer, opening up his backpack. He had something in a cup, but emptied it into the backpack. Cup in hand, he knelt down next to the deer carcass and held the cup to its body, catching as much blood as he could.

"What are you doing?" asked Hunter, turning around after he noticed Caleb wasn't walking back with them.

"Just getting something I need for a plan I have in mind." He pressed on its body, hoping more blood would come out.

"When did we ever talk about a plan involving deer blood?" asked Brooke.

"It's suffered enough, Caleb. C'mon, let it rest in peace now," said J.

"Alright, hold on, almost got a decent amount." Hunter turned to J and Brooke and confused chatter was all a focused Caleb heard in the background. It had surprised him how it had worked out up until now. He got up, holding the cup close to him, being extra careful not to drop it. The metallic smell of blood wafted up and into his nose. They walked back and made their way northeast.

"So...gonna tell us what this plan of yours is? Because I'm dying to know," asked Hunter. He couldn't think of any use this poor deer's blood could have.

"Good question!" said Brooke.

"For real," said J.

"Jake and I…we still talk to our parents."

"Wait…I thought your parents died when you were little?" said J. Brooke had a comically startled look on her face upon hearing this. Hunter had his eyebrow raised in curiosity.

"Well, yeah. But we saw this movie about the paranormal. They contacted the dead. We both thought, wouldn't it be neat to talk to them? To let them know how life is without them? To get to know them more? To tell them how much we miss them?" A sullen, indignant tone was starting to form in his voice. He paused, collected himself, and then continued. "And so at first we bought a ouija board and talked to them for a bit."

"Those things work?"

"Mhm. Our parents contacted us through it and they told us they wanted to see us. I swear it moved on its own. Jake and I were both barely touching it. They could hear us but they couldn't see us."

"Did you end up seeing them?"

"Well, Jake looked up how we'd be able to. Did you know that movie was based on a true story? They did something called a 'seance'. It's basically a way to summon the dead. We did see them. Like, their souls at least."

"Uhhhh-"

"…souls?"

"Why do you want to summon the dead out here?"

"Think about it. The Jersey Devil has been killing kids for a while, right? What if their angry souls are the ones cursing him? Maybe we can contact some of them and find out."

"Yoo what the hell, Caleb? You're wild. I would've never thought of that," said J, half-impressed, half-spooked.

"That's some Satanic stuff, Caleb…" said Brooke. She swallowed hard and decided not to discuss it further.

"Let's just get there first, then we'll see what we should do," said Hunter. He masked an unsettling feeling he'd had well, trying to keep a cool, collected outward demeanor. In all honesty, he had no idea what they were gonna do when they got there besides look up info on the location later. He wasn't too keen on the whole seance thing, though. That much he knew.

They were in the thick of the barrens now. Not much wildlife was around. The desolation was tangible. They all felt it, and in an unspoken act, all picked up the pace. It wasn't before long Hunter's intuition ended up being right, and as they came upon a large opening in the woods with a rather large oak tree in the center, he breathed a sigh of relief.

"This has to be it, right?" asked J.

"Oh yeah. Can't you sense it?" Caleb closed his eyes and took in a deep breath. "Smells like a curse to me."

"Shut up," J chuckled.

"No, but for real, this place does feel, I don't know...*off*," said Brooke.

"Yeah, I don't like it. I've got a feeling whatever that oversized goat wants us to investigate ain't something neat or fun. Something bad happened here," said Hunter.

They all looked up and noticed they weren't alone. The trees were spotted with black. Dozens of blackbirds perched up high with watchful eyes. Some were rustling their feathers, others hopping around from branch to branch. They didn't make much noise, which only added to the strange aura of the area.

"Jeez...that's a lotta birds," said Brooke.

"I wonder what they're doing out here. Been a while since I've seen much of anything," said J.

Caleb looked around with fascinated eyes.

"Only time I've ever seen birds like this is out in the fields near my backyard. Only around this time of year I'm pretty sure. Maybe they're resting or something," said Hunter.

"Well, we might as well start looking for clues. Like stuff buried in the leaves maybe?" said J. "Looks like there's a pile of 'em right near the tree."

"Good idea, but for now, let's split up. Then we'll all meet up in the center at the big tree in five minutes, okay? We'll make that the last place we look," said Hunter.

They spread out around the area, aimlessly rummaging through the leaves and flipping over rocks, investigating the perimeter. After five minutes were up, they all met up at the tree in the middle. They stood there and stared at it for a second. Thick roots shot from the base of the tree and they had to be careful not to trip. It almost felt out of place, easily outclassing the rest of the surrounding trees in size. But where's a more fitting place for a tree to be?

"Anything?" asked Hunter. A resounding "no," besides Caleb showing them a cool-shaped stick he found. "Welp, last place." Hunter pointed at the tree.

"Does anyone else smell something weird?" asked Brooke.

"Yeah..." J said, staring at the mound of leaves on the ground. They knelt down closer. "Oh my god."

"What?"

"What is it?"

They all looked down and saw that the leaves were hiding corpses well into decay on top of a pile of various bones.

"Wait. Doesn't that kinda look like one of the kids that went missing?" asked Brooke as she pinched her nose.

"Yeah. I saw them on a poster in the grocery store a while ago," said Hunter. Caleb stared at the tree.

"We-we're gonna end up like them, aren't we? Just more lifeless bodies added to the pile…" J said, falling back.

"It's just playing another sick, twisted game, isn't it?" said Brooke.

"An actual monster…" said Hunter.

Caleb circled the tree, examining its ancient bark, softly swaying branches hiding secrets above them.

"Wait. Look," he said, pointing at the tree. They got up and went over to him. They noticed some unusual, darker spots in random places on the bark, but were unsure what it could've been. "What an odd tree…"

Brooke stopped, squinted and got closer to look at something that caught her eye. The abrupt stop made J bump into Brooke's shoulder and startled them as they were hyper-focused on the tree.

"Oof. What is it?" asked J. Hunter and Caleb hurried over.

"You see something?"

"Yeah. Look," Brooke pointed to a carving on the tree. It had stood the test of time, being carved thick and deep into the wood. A commemorative scar from a stranger.

"'JL - a loving mother.'"

"Initials. We found initials. Guys, we found something!!"

"Oh my god. This is great!"

"Wow."

A glimmer of hope was all they needed. Their spirits shot up as they believed they had found something important.

"This is perfect," Caleb said under his breath as he rushed away from the group. He set down his backpack and excited hands took out five flat, moderate-sized rocks along with five black candles. He placed the rocks in a meticulous manner, making sure to get it right. He balanced the candles on top of them with ease.

"Oh god, he's really doing it…"

"Caleb, do we *have* to do this?" asked Hunter.

"We can contact J.L. here and find out who she is," said Caleb. "There's no time to waste!"

"Or we can just, y'know, search for it online?" said J.

"Yeah? You really think we can pinpoint who exactly this is based on searching 'J.L. pine barrens New Jersey' on the internet? For all we know, this could've been carved over a hundred years ago!" All Caleb got were looks in return. "Listen. The seance works, trust me! But we all have to channel our energy," he said while getting ready to pour the deer's blood in the shape of a pentagram, the candle-adorned rocks being each of the five points. He was adamant. Brooke looked on in terrified bewilderment.

"Guys, I-I don't know if I can do this. I think I'm fine not being all up in dead people's business," she said, half-knowing that there was no getting out of this. Caleb ignored her and made sure not to waste any of the blood, finishing the pentagram up to the last drops.

"Wow…look at this. You were totally prepared weren't you?" asked J.

"Like I said, done it before."

"Well, there are four of us this time, so if you had enough energy to do it with two, I can sit this out, right?" asked Brooke. Hunter raised his eyebrows, thinking about opting out as well to equalize things.

"No, we need you. Who knows how many spirits may be out here? A seance is like a beacon in the darkness. It might attract more than we bargain for, but as long as we can find J.L. it'll be fine."

"Do you really think this J.L. person is here though?" asked J.

"We need to summon her by repeating what we know: she was a loving mother and her initials are J.L." Caleb got more looks and was growing impatient. "I'm going to light these candles. Once I do there's no turning back. We will each stand at one of the points with a candle and link hands. The point at the bottom will be empty since there's only four of us." Without waiting for a response he started to light the candles. Three pairs of apprehensive feet stepped up to a different candle. Caleb lit the final one and they all linked hands, palms already sweating. Caleb began.

"Spirits of this forest clearing, we come to you today. We wish to speak with J.L., who was a loving mother." He urged the rest of his group to join in now in a whisper-shout. "C'mon guys. J.L., a loving mother, are you here?"

"J.L., LOVING MOTHER, ARE YOU HERE?" Their voices blended in unison.

"J.L., loving mother, we would like to have an audience with you."

"J.L., LOVING MOTHER, WE WOULD LIKE TO HAVE AN AUDIENCE WITH YOU." Some of their voices were shaking, but they spoke louder. A light wind twisted and turned at their ankles. It shifted the flames on the candles, but they endured. The group continued their chant around the pentagram, and Caleb decided to invoke, what he felt was, the missing party.

"The Jersey Devil joins us in spirit on this day as the fifth point on the ritual circle. May his energy aid us!"

And with this, the birds in the trees shuffled around. The gentle breeze winding between their ankles stopped, and now a quiet fog crept in from below. Before long they couldn't see their feet, just the faint, orange glow of the candles. The rest of them weren't too happy that Caleb decided to change the script on them so abruptly.

"Guys, what's happening?"

"Shh!"

Whispers started shooting up and around them like small, paranormal fireworks.

"Do you hear that?"

"J.L., are you with us?" Caleb gave a light tug on the arms of the two group members he was joined with.

"J.L. ARE YOU WITH US?" they all said.

The whispers grew louder and the fog rose higher. Small trails cut through the fog that accompanied the whispers. The trails got bigger as the fog enveloped them. They turned into elongated faces, whisps shooting up in the air around them. It was difficult to make out what they were saying until the whispers turned into hundreds of haunting cries. *ARE YOU MY CHILD? WHERE ARE THEY? I MISS YOU SO MUCH. WHAT IS HAPPENING?   KILL HER. WE MUST LEAVE! PLEASE DON'T. LET GO OF ME! HELP ME!! WHAT ARE YOU!? MOMMY!* The random voices continued whizzing up and about their ears. They looked down and saw the faint glow of the candles, but the more noticeable glow was the blood pentagram. The sinister shine illuminated the fog, giving it an oppressive, red tinge. It swirled around them faster and faster. Before they knew it the fog turned into a vortex of souls spinning around them. It was getting hard for them to see each other. They held onto each other with sweaty, iron grips, their hair whipping around every which way, feeling as if at any moment they could be swept away into the chaos, flying through an endless maelstrom of tormented screaming. All of them were shaking besides Caleb, who had his eyes closed and his head pointed up. He was listening. Trying to pinpoint clues or a voice in the torrent of spinning souls that continued buzzing and whooshing around. He was able to tune them out and found that many kept screaming about the tree. His concentration broke as he felt something strange scrape against his leg.

"Are you my baby? Where have you been, child?" Caleb looked down and could make out a decayed, elongated face looking up at him. It had tears coming from empty eye sockets and held onto him with ancient, brittle arms. They were also rotting and some of the bones were exposed. It wailed at him, holding his leg in a desperate embrace. He felt tension and panic in his group members' hands as they held on. There were more reaching at the others' feet as well. An urgency moved through them.

"MOVE TO THE TREE!!" Caleb screamed with all of his might.

"TO THE TREE!"

"OK! HEAD FOR THE TREE!"

Hearing each others' voices gave them confidence and helped their minds stay grounded. They began moving away from the ritual circle in a frantic tandem, almost losing grip. But losing grip now was not an option. Who knew what ocean of awful spirits they'd get lost in, what abyss of agonizing distress they'd be thrust into? They didn't even feel like they existed in the real world anymore, but still they pushed towards the tree, holding onto each other with such strength that it hurt, but even pain felt different right now. Closer and closer they got to the tree, still linked up, but bunched up so they could see one another. It became calmer the nearer they got. The chaos had fizzled and the fog lingered low again. They stood in front of the tree and looked around. It got very quiet, but the stillness was not pleasant. They could all hear a constant sound from above. A rope swaying. Looking up, they saw a figure hanging on a noose from a large branch of the tree. It swung back and forth, limp and lifeless.

"Do you think that's-"

"J.L., loving mother?"

"What the..."

"Guys, oh my god, it moved. I swear it twitched!"

Another twitch of the foot. It was a skeleton, somehow connected and still possessing its hair, which was draped over most of its face. It cracked and contorted before stopping again. Then it moved its hanging head up ever so slowly. A grunting came from it. It fixated on the four kids standing there with all of their flesh still on them. The stare from those deep, empty eye sockets pierced through them. It was an image that would stay burned into their heads, along with the sound that came from its skeletal grin next. As its jaw opened it let out such a horrible, rage-filled shriek that it rang the whole group's ears, putting them in a temporary daze. None of them knew how it was able to move or make any noise, but they were stunned. It started twisting in odd fashions on the rope again.

They had just about reached their threshold of how much weird shit they could experience in one day (an already-high threshold, mind you). Unfortunately, that's when the smell hit them. It came on strong and sudden, invading their nostrils and instantly triggering their gag reflex.

The foul, repugnant smell was enveloping them, a boa constrictor slowly constricting their senses. J ripped off their mask and stuck the bottom half of their face into their shirt. Upon seeing J dealing with the smell a tad bit easier, the rest of the group followed suit. Then they heard something else fall from the tree; a headless corpse of a child suddenly fell at their feet. A contorted, smashed face of another pushed through the tree's bark like it was breaking through plastic wrap. The soil was loose beneath their feet, and looking down, to their horror, they found themselves on top of a pile of corpses, many of them children. The ones who still had intact, recognizable faces wore terrified visages that made the whole group scream, but as they opened their mouths to scream, the smell of hundreds of rotting corpses flew into their mouths, making them gag even more. What came out instead was a small yelp followed by gagging and coughing. Another limb fell from above. The tree seeped a thick, maroon sap. Echoing wails came from the mouths of the corpses. Other wheezes, clicks, and gasps were heard from twisted necks and disembodied heads. They could even hear odd rattles from the bloodied stumps of where heads should have been, with chests expanding and contracting from rotten lungs, desperately screaming and yelling and pleading for help, for justice, for anything. Their stinking, putrid, impossible breath added to the stench. The incorporeal clamor and tumult shook them to their core. The stunned group fought with all of the strength they had to break free of the otherworldly distress that held them. Their consternation and fright had turned their legs into Jell-O, and cold, dead hands, some without fingers, others with broken and bent back nails, grabbed at their feet to pull them down into their mire of misery and decay. But as the group linked together once again, their determination returned, and they rushed back towards the light of Caleb's makeshift pentagram. It wasn't far away, but it sure as hell felt like it. The corpses, upset, combined their energy together and became a twitching mass of flesh, which slithered after them.

"Ahh!! Oh god, oh god, keep running!" The corpse pile pursued, hundreds of different screams coming out of it. They had to lose it, but it seemed impossible. They had to double back around the seance circle, but were running out of breath.

"Keep going, guys, I," Brooke panted, "I can't anymore." She began to cry. She turned to face the corpse monster. Limbs stuck out from it everywhere. It spewed blood and other unknown liquids from different places.

"I'm," she kept panting, then took in a deep breath, "I'M SORRY!!" The monster stopped for a second at the unexpected volume of her words. "I'm sorry so many of you got killed. It's not fair! We know that.

We're-we're trying to fix that, somehow, maybe, but we're trying! Please, let us try to end it all so no more kids suffer. So that you can move on! *Please!*" Brooke began wailing, falling to her knees. The corpse pile got close and wailed too. The eyes on and within the pile, some dislodged and others on smashed- in and decapitated heads, shed tears, clear and bloody. It screamed and cried right in her face, and she reciprocated with her own. The three others watched, baffled, but it had bought them enough time.

Once they got there they knew what they had to do. Arriving at the circle, they broke up and put out the flames of the candles in any way they could. They hollered at Brooke to come as fast as she could.

Brooke gave it one last look. "I'm sorry."

She ran over and they broke the formation of the pentagram. With great relief, they noticed they could hear nothing but themselves. The nightmare they were in faded, and they had successfully returned to their own living world.

Brooke fell to the ground and began to cry (she wondered if she had ever stopped). Hunter stood there, panting, staring blankly at the ground. Caleb looked at the tree. Normal. J walked up to Caleb after consoling Brooke.

"Caleb, are you sure that was a seance? Because to me, it seemed like we opened up a freaking portal to hell!" They paused. Caleb sat down and put his head in his hands. "I mean, *seriously*, what just *happened*!?"

"I don't know. It wasn't like that when I did it before," Caleb said.

"Let's just go home," said Hunter. In silent agreement they all got up and followed him. They had had enough of the barrens for one day. Knocked over candles and smeared deer blood lay scattered in the clearing.

It was only a few minutes into their walk out of the woods that they had noticed a small group of larger black birds, perhaps buzzards, bickering over something on the ground near them. They were not startled by the kids, even though they were close to their path. The kids looked on at the birds, reminded of how many there were earlier near the clearing. They were all curious as to what they were fighting over, as they were really causing a ruckus. Caleb was the first to get close enough to see what it was they were picking away at.

"Oh my god, is that a hand? Is that someone's hand!?" asked Brooke.

"What? No way," said Hunter.

"It is...well at least what's left of one," said Caleb.

J squatted down to take a picture of the birds and the hand, disgusted, yet interested. The birds continued to pierce and peck away at the flesh, ripping it off with an awful snapping sound. They tore away blue veins and any meat they could get from the hand after much of the skin was off. An image of Hunter's dad in a hospital bed with a wrapped up stump for a right hand flashed through his mind. His heart started beating faster.

"There's no way…" Hunter muttered under his breath. He hadn't told his friends the details of what happened to his father yet, just that he was in the hospital.

"Hey, you okay?" J asked Hunter, noticing the intense trance he had been in, looking at the buzzards.

"Whose hand do you think it is? Looks pretty big," asked Caleb.

"Ew, Caleb, c'mon. I don't wanna think about that. It's weird that it's out here in the first place," said Brooke.

"Doesn't feel *that* weird after, y'know, what just happened and all…" said Caleb.

"They could've brought it out here from somewhere else. Who knows?" said J.

Hunter got closer and knelt down to look at the hand. The buzzards whooshed their wings and let out some deep squawks in irritation, but he didn't care. He looked at it closer and his mind filled up with thoughts of confusion and uncertain anger. He fought back the tears that were beginning to well up in his eyes as he heard his friends muttering things behind him. He shook out of it and walked back to them.

"I know I already asked this, but Hunter, you good?" asked J.

"Y-yeah. Let's keep going."

The rest of their journey home was uneventful. They were glad about that.

CHAPTER 20

It was Wednesday, which sucked. Lola felt as if the week was dragging along, but something that didn't suck was that it was "Bring Your Child to Work Day." And while she was single, she still very much considered herself to have a son: her cat! Crash had grown on her quickly and her love for him parallel to that. With this in mind, she saw no reason why she couldn't bring him into her classroom for this little occasion. Of course, she had brought in a small animal cage for him to stay in throughout the day, which had food, water, a mouse toy, and a cat bed for him to lay on. It was a lot to bring in, but it was worth it to Lola, even if she had to come in a little early to set it all up. She got to show off something she loved, and that made her ecstatic.

On the bus ride to school that Wednesday morning, Caleb was up to no good yet again. It was about to be Chester's stop, Caleb's main target. He thought it was funny how flustered he would always get.

"Look! I think I saw him back in the woods! Near that tree!"

"Ooh, really? Where? Oh, I think I see him too!" J said, enabling Caleb, as per usual.

Some other kids on the bus looked out too, playing into Caleb's mind games. A few believed they saw it, too, while others took a quick glance before disregarding it. Chester got on the bus and sat down, already red-faced. Chester had sat down for a bit, but the bus still hadn't started moving again. Noticing this, Caleb looked up the aisle and saw the bus driver talking to someone. They soon came onto the bus. He was an older man. Didn't look too happy. The bus driver pointed out where Chester sat, and the man walked up to him and Caleb.

"You stay away from my son, you hear me!?" the man said, pointing straight at Caleb. At first Caleb sat there, dumbfounded with a smile on his face, but it faded as he realized that it was Chester's father. J was spooked and didn't interfere, not wanting him to know they had been pestering Chester with Caleb. "I don't want you talking to him anymore. No more of this *nonsense* you've been telling him."

"O-ok."

"You little shit," he said, getting in Caleb's face. "I mean it! Stay *away* from him." He charged off past the bus driver as they had been looking on. Chester still sat there, staring at the dull gray seat in front of him. Caleb thought about saying something to Chester, but decided not to. The anger and conviction in the dad's voice had stunned him, even if he laughed it off on the outside. Something *did* watch them, though. From the fringe of where the woods met the field. It was a silent bus ride the rest of the way to the school.

Caleb would continue having an abnormal day as his morning Language Arts class with Ms. Santos came to an end. The entire class was amused at Ms. Santos bringing in Crash, and to keep them on the right track, she said that they could come up to his cage and pet him at the end of class if they acted good. Only two students, who were friends and some of the most disrespectful, misbehaving kids she had that year, didn't get to see Crash. They moped at a desk in the back while the others got to see the cute kitten. Crash was an affable and affectionate little animal, and was just as amused by all of the attention he was getting. He enjoyed the pets, oohs, and awws he was getting, but as Caleb walked up to him, his mood quickly changed. Caleb's extended hand was met with bent-back ears, clawed swipes, and mean hisses. All of his classmates found it funny, pointing and laughing at Caleb. Lola found it very strange, and concerned with Caleb's safety, ended the interaction. She tried to calm down Crash, but he kept looking at Caleb, frozen in an aggressive position, still bending back his ears. Caleb was put off by this, but more so by the treatment his classmates were giving him. For the rest of the day they pestered him about the whole ordeal.

After class was over, Lola walked around to tidy up her classroom when she found the words "FUCK MS. SANTOS" written in heavy graphite on a desk in the back. She knew who did it. She took a picture and went to the office on her lunch break, explaining the situation. She went through the process of writing them up, which was annoying to begin with, and proceeded to call the parents. To her astonishment, they were on their kids' sides. They questioned if Lola had actually *seen* when they did it, why she didn't stop them immediately, etc. They denied that their child would ever do such a thing. They complained how she couldn't manage and control her class. It turned into a shitstorm that made Lola irate. Her useless administration dropped the write ups, and Lola was less surprised by this when she found out that one of the kid's moms was prominent in the community. Nice, big, comfy job. Arrogant. And very vocal. Lola was disgusted at the carbon copy her child was of her. The last thing administration wanted was an uproar from this kind of person.

Lola felt like she needed to get the ridiculousness of the situation off of her chest, so she confided in the veteran history teacher, Mr. Blake.

"I mean, can you believe that? They can just get away with any kind of disrespect nowadays. God, y'know, if my mom heard from my teacher that I had done something like that, she would believe the *teacher* and I would get *disciplined*. They are just awful nowadays, all of them!" She smiled and scoffed, having a realization. "I'm only twenty-five and I sound like an old lady."

"I would say that's unbelievable, but sadly I believe it. Mm, it's unfortunate, but, yeah, it's bad. There's only so much you can do anymore. God, I remember back in Catholic school if I was just a *little* out of line, they'd get me with a ruler, y'know?" Mr. Blake said, mimicking an old nun swinging a ruler. He had a way of lightening up the mood.

"Hah, yeah, right? I mean, *that* might be taking it too far, but I dunno. It's just shocking to me. We're a little over two months in and I've already had to address bullying multiple times, inappropriate notes, drawings, and comments, ugh."

"Oh, believe me, we've all been dealing with it. Doesn't help that this class in particular has a bad reputation."

"Yeah and what does admin do about it? Nothing! Where are the consequences? Because if these children go into the real world thinking they can act way outta line and however they want and not face any consequences? Whew, they are in for a *rude* awakening."

"Believe me, I share your frustration. And speaking of admin, don't forget we have a meeting today. I'm sure you're excited for that, huh?"

"Oh great. I totally forgot. Well, thanks for letting me vent a bit. As a new teacher, I don't know, it's just so eye-opening."

"No, I getcha. That's why a nice bottle of wine helps me after a long day!"

"Enjoy your lunch!"

"You too."

They both laughed and went their separate ways. Lola thought about how depressing it was to think about relying on alcohol to take the edge off of a job she had a ton of passion for. Then she cursed under her breath after realizing there's no way she could get out of going to the meeting at the end of the day.

Hunter, Caleb, J, and Brooke had made it an objective to get together during 7th period and sneak to the computers in the library to look up the secrets behind their seance. They all had to conveniently "use the bathroom" at the same set time and found themselves sitting down at a computer in the library. The school didn't have a librarian that year, rotating teachers in and out throughout the day instead. Cheap bastards.

This made it easy for them to go mostly unnoticed, feigning working on a research project (which was a good alias for them anyways).

"Heyo."

"Yo yo, we all made it."

"Sweet. Let's start."

"Ok, so what exactly should we search?" asked J who was at the helm, controlling the mouse and keyboard.

"J.L. mother 1700s hanging pine barrens New Jersey?" They all thought about this suggestion from Hunter. No one disagreed, so J typed it in. Promising results popped up fast.

"Ooh! Click that one!" Brooke said, pointing at the second link. It read "Jane Leeds and the New Jersey Devil." It led to a site about New Jersey's history. The entire group's mouths were agape as J read aloud the info in astonishment.

"Jane Leeds was said to have thirteen children. The thirteenth child ended up turning into what we now call the 'Jersey Devil' or 'Leeds Devil'. It is fabled to possess features of a horse, goat, and bat. It has shown up in New Jersey legend since the 1700s, terrorizing various peoples and towns, including Napoleon Bonaparte's brother, Joseph Bonaparte, who claimed to have seen the Jersey Devil while hunting on Bordentown Estate. It is also notorious for killing livestock. Occasional sightings are still rumored to this very day."

"No way…"

"Jane Leeds."

"Do you think she was…"

"Hanged?"

"…yeah."

"Holy crap, holy crap, you know what this means, right?"

"What?"

"We get to *live*!!"

"Ok. Ok ok ok. Soo, what do we tell it? That the clearing is cursed because that's where its mom was hanged?"

"For giving birth to him. That has to be it, right?"

"Wow, that's actually kinda…sad."

"We got it. We did it, guys!!"

"Heck. Yes."

"Alright, let's get back to class before our teachers get mad."

"Okay, but listen. Saturday. My place. Noon like before."

"Sounds good. Let's put an end to this."

It wasn't before long that the school day came to an end. Another grueling Wednesday vanquished. The final bell rang and the kids emptied the school. Lola packed up her things and gave out a big sigh.

She was glad that at least her last class went well. She walked down with Amanda and a couple of other teachers, all of them expressing their desire for the day to be over with. The staff meetings that administration ran were held in the cafeteria, which Lola hated. It smelled. They had to sit on these small, shitty lunch table chairs with no back support. It began and, oh boy, big surprise, another fucking meeting that could have been an email. She was already itching to leave, expressing this, whether she was aware of it or not, by bouncing one leg up and down over and over. It was a complete waste of an hour. *Just introduce another vapid acronym or abbreviation I have to cram in my head and let me leave.* Due to recent events, she was feeling a little extra bitter towards them. She sat there and thought about Crash's aggression towards Caleb earlier in the day. It was only towards him, no other person Crash interacted with had a bad experience. It was strange, but that whole project group seemed to get stranger by the day. The meeting felt like it took forever to end, and after a disgruntled back stretch, Lola was one of the first to leave.

CHAPTER 21

"Happy to be home?"

"Damn right I am. You know I'm not the biggest fan of hospitals."

"Well I'm sure Hunter and Hannah will be excited to see you back home too."

"I've missed 'em a bunch. Missed being their father, y'know?" Albert let out a shameful sigh. "Almost all my damn vacation days are used up for next year already, though. The guy who is doing my job right now doesn't have the experience. The company can't sustain itself without me, so I wanna go back to work as soon as I can."

"I get it, hun, but you need to focus on recovering first. Things will work out, okay? Just take it a day at a time. The business will still be there. Trust your guys for now."

"Yeah…I know."

"Before we go in, though–is what you told me true? About you and Clint and this 'creature' out in the woods? You think it's the *cause* of the kidnappings and it's also what took your hand? I'm sorry, Al, I've been trying to make sense of it all and believe you, but it just sounds like…it sounds so damn surreal."

"It's all true. I wouldn't make up such a ridiculous lie. You think I'm creative enough for that?" Albert got a chuckle out of Lily.

"It's just-it blew my theories of you being caught up in some drug crime ring out of the water. That at least made *some* sense to me." She paused. "It's gonna take me a while to process all of this."

"Believe me, I know it will. I made some mistakes out there, but I'll be sure that thing never messes with us again. I promise." They got out of the car and walked to the house. It was a rainy Thursday morning. Lily had taken the day off work to care for Albert and make sure he adjusted well to being back home.

"Y'know, Thanksgiving is coming up. Next weekend I think."

"Well that's some good news. Can't wait to gorge myself like a pig and watch some football."

"Hah! You'll fall asleep before halftime."

"Hey, if that means I ate good, then so be it."

"Well, glad my food makes you feel so nice! I was wondering, have you heard from Clint? He got out earlier than you."

"Yeah, that lucky bastard," Albert laughed, then thought about it. "I think he mentioned taking some time off. Maybe going somewhere away from here like a Florida beach. But that was when we were both still in the hospital. Haven't heard anything since, now that I think about it."

"Huh, well I hope he recovers well. Man. The beach. I'd kill to go too. Can't wait for the warm weather to come!"

"Yep. Be here before we know it."

They settled down inside. Lily didn't want Albert being too active, but as the day went on, he was getting antsy. He was tired of sitting around. It felt like that's all he'd been doing for a while now. He figured he'd go out into the garage and maybe tidy up a bit. Something to keep him busy. Lily didn't want him to at first, but gave in after she knew how stubborn her husband could get. She put on her stern voice when telling him not to exert himself, however.

The garage hadn't changed much. Albert didn't know what he was expecting to be different. Same old dust, same old cobwebs, same old tools sitting on the bench. He breathed in the musty, oily aroma of the garage, picking up a broom and brushing some dirt out, making sure not to go too fast per his wife's instructions. That was when the itching picked up again. It came on strong; it was an itch that made him stop everything else he was doing to scratch it. He had to take off some bandages on his leg and he scratched away.

He was going wild, a boar with an almost insatiable urge. Nothing could stop the single mission his brain put him on: get rid of that itch. His eyes darted around the garage as he scratched. They fixated on a metal brush and he went up and took it. He began rubbing the spot on his leg with the steel brush. It felt good, but it wasn't enough. Just a little bit more pressure. He pressed down and it began to irritate his skin, making it red. Before he knew it he couldn't stop. He rubbed harder and faster, the metal hairs of the brush scraping away his skin and flesh. A mixture of blood and puss poured down his leg, but he didn't care. He kept going, eyes closed, alleviating the itch, feeling the pleasant pain. High pitch noises came through his gritted teeth. He did this until he had made a sizable, pink hole in his leg. He had ground his flesh down to the bone, and could see small hairs of metal brush in there as well. None of that mattered to him when he saw what was attached to the bone: a black, writhing mass with prickly tendrils that vibrated and tickled around the meat and bone. The culprit for what had been driving him insane.

"That's one spot where that bastard impaled me," he said. In a rage he barreled around his garage, looking for the first tool he could find that would be able to detach this thing from him. He threw things around his workbench, making a mess. His blood kept pouring down his leg, into his socks and shoes and onto the floor. He grabbed a large pair of pliers, and with all of his anger-filled might, pulled it out with a few good tugs, surprised at the resistance it put up. He threw it in a bucket and looked down at his leg, surprised he could still stand. The adrenaline would wear off soon, and he rushed into the house to get Lily's help.

"Jesus Christ, Albert! What did you do!?" she said. "Oh my god. Ok. Umm, this is *awful*. Here, come to the bathroom. Quick!" She helped him get there, not wanting him to put any weight on the leg.

"Listen, I'm not crazy. I dug somethin' out of me, Lily. I put it in a bucket, I swear. I'll show you," he said through labored breaths, wincing.

"What?" Lily said, half listening. She was too concentrated on the wound. "Christ, Albert! Are there pieces of *metal* in here!? Shit, we're gonna have to go back to the hospital. Great, and after you had just come home!" Lily did as much as she could and they drove to the hospital.

"Listen, Lily. When you get home, look in the bucket on the floor in the garage. That thing in there was attached to the bone in my leg. I *swear*," Albert said on the car ride there.

"You're not making sense, Albert. What 'attached' to the bone inside of your leg?"

"That creature in the woods, it infected me with something. Some parasite."

"What *the* fuck, Albert!?"

As they pulled up to the hospital, he itched his left shoulder. He stared ahead as a pit dropped in his stomach. It dawned on him that there were two more of these things inside of him. He remembered–it got him in the left shoulder and in the neck as well. To dig the one out in his neck would mean certain death.

CHAPTER 22

They were getting used to the walk, even though the masks which they wore skewed their peripheral vision. The path was set in their heads, as some of the trees and landmarks along the way got committed to memory. Hunter was confident that he could find the old cabin and cursed clearing without the help of Caleb by now. They ventured forth towards where the Jersey Devil had been resting and kept going over what they were going to say to it, hoping it was enough "help" for it to not kill all four of them.

It knew they were approaching, could sense them long before they got to the cabin. It wondered whether it would have to kill them or not, because if they had failed, maybe their efforts would at least make them deserving of a swift and painless death. The thought of not getting any closer to knowing why that cursed land still existed in its domain frustrated it. It wanted nothing more than to purge it of whatever was there disturbing its solace. The devil was especially disquieted by all of the feelings that stirred inside of it as it neared the tree in the clearing. Something knew how to get into his head, and he took that as a great threat. Those feelings were hard to translate, as it didn't feel much in the first place. It had only felt joy in toying with others' minds, and the rest of the time, besides brief moments of calm and peace, all it felt was wrath and bitterness. Maybe those feelings were the result of observing the world or other people as they went about their day. It didn't quite know. What it hated the most was confusion and not knowing things it wished to know. Besides the curse, confusion also came as to why it gave any amount of consideration towards these four children.

The four kids got within sight of the cabin and the air grew heavier. It was a feeling they had felt before–the isolating silence creeping up on them, the world above them growing unnaturally darker. This time, however, they did not lose the confidence in their step and were prepared for what would transpire. Fear was not completely absent from their minds, but with familiarity came comfort. They approached the musty dwelling of the creature, smelling of moss and rotten wood.

"YOU ARE EARLY. DO YOU NOT VALUE THE TIME I HAVE GIVEN YOU? OR ARE YOU CONFIDENT IN WHAT YOU HAVE

FOUND REGARDING THE CURSE?" The Jersey Devil was standing in the corner of the main room, much healthier than the last time they saw him.

"Your wounds are almost healed," said Caleb.

"Y-YES. NEVER MIND THAT. WHAT HAVE YOU FOUND?"

They looked at each other. The creature looked at them with a single, impatient eye. They had forgotten how terrifying its gaze was.

"Alright. So, uh, so we found out…" The anxiety was rising in J's chest, but they fought it back down. "The clearing with the big oak tree is cursed because someone was hanged there, like 300 years ago." The Jersey Devil let out a thoughtful, deep "hmm".

"Yeah and, um, apparently that person was The Jersey Devil's mother. *Your* mother. Her name was Jane Leeds," said Brooke, backing up J.

"M…MOTHER? HOW DID YOU COME ABOUT THIS INFORMATION IF IT HAPPENED SOME 300 YEARS AGO?" The kids stood there, thoughts racing on how to answer. "SPEAK!"

"Well, you see, we can look up information like that on the internet. It's like this huge database that we can access," said J.

"INTER-NET? WHAT? YOU ARE MAKING THIS UP. I HAVE NO MEMORY OF A MOTHER." It clenched its head in a spike of mental pain.

"We're not! It's like a library. We took information from records and books and put it into a machine that can store it," said Caleb.

"A…MACHINE LIBRARY," the Jersey Devil pondered. "AND YOU HAVE ACCESS TO THIS MACHINE?"

"Yeah. At school. Y'know, where we learn…and get an education," said Brooke.

"YES. I HAVE SEEN YOU LITTLE ONES CONGREGATE INTO ONE BUILDING MULTIPLE TIMES, TRANSPORTED BY THOSE LARGE YELLOW MACHINES." The beast took a pause. "YOU KNOW, IT IS IMPRESSIVE. I HAVE SEEN HOW YOU FOUR ARE TREATED–ALL OF YOU A BURDEN, AN INCONVENIENCE. YOU ARE CALLED UGLY, MADE TO FEEL UNWANTED, AND YET YOU SET ASIDE YOUR DIFFERENCES, SURROUNDING YOURSELVES WITH THOSE WHO CARE ABOUT YOU. YOU STILL YEARN TO LIVE DESPITE ALL THAT THE WORLD HAS ALREADY PUT YOU THROUGH."

"Umm…"

"Yeah, the world sucks. But that's why you have to keep going. Fuck the world, y'know?"

"MMM." The devil stood there with its arms crossed. "PLEASE CONTINUE. THIS INTERNET MACHINE LIBRARY."

"Oh, yeah, well, the internet is a tool we use. And it contains a lot of information. Including things written about *you* and your origins. And your mother, Jane Leeds," said Hunter. He hesitated saying what he wanted to say next, because he was now sure it would upset the beast. "We believe she was wrongly hanged on that tree because her village saw your birth as unlucky. A bad omen."

"H-HOW COULD I BE BORN FROM ONE OF YOUR KIND? MY MOTHER IS THE WILDERNESS. SHE EMBRACES ME. TEACHES ME. PROVIDES FOR ME ALL THAT I NEED." The devil breathed faster as it processed what the four children had found out about the curse that had concerned him for so long. A single tear fell from its lone eye, perplexing it. The beast let out a great cry. The group covered their ears and started to back away from the creature. It grabbed its head again and fell back, breaking the rotten wood behind it with ease.

The kids fled outside the entrance of the cabin and could see it inside, sitting down with its eye closed, still breathing heavily, but not as fast.

"...Are we gonna leave now? Doesn't seem like that put him in the best mood," said J.

"Hold on a sec. How do we know it's going to hold up its end of the deal?" asked Brooke.

"Should that really be our concern right now?" replied J.

"Well, yeah, I don't wanna just randomly die one day next week," said Brooke. "Oh yeah, and I *definitely* did *not* go through that crazy Satan seance Caleb set up for nothin'!!"

"True...and there's, that, y'know, potion or whatever it said it would make each of us," said Hunter.

"Wait here," said Caleb, going back inside.

He looked at it on the floor, still intimidating, but having some sort of crisis. He noticed its twisted horn poking out of its empty eye socket further than the last time he saw it. He walked closer to it and sat down next to it. His friends watched on in amazement. They couldn't make out what he was saying, as he talked in a soft voice.

"My mom died too. People said she was really nice. I never knew her. I was only one when it happened."

It opened its eye and turned its head towards Caleb. It looked at him with its furrowed brows. Caleb watched as it slowly reached out its arm towards him. Then he felt cold, hard hands around his neck, as it pulled him closer to its face. His friends watched on in horror, hoping Caleb wasn't about to get his head and neck popped like a grape.

"DO NOT ASSUME I FEEL THE SAME AS YOU, CHILD." And with that, it let Caleb go. He was stunned for a second, then backed out of the cabin. It wasn't before long that the beast was out with them. "LEAVE ME. I HAVE MUCH TO THINK ABOUT NOW."

"B-but, what about our deal?"

"OUR DEAL...YES. THE MIXTURES WILL BE DONE SOON. YOU WILL KNOW WHEN TO COME BACK AND CHOOSE ONE."

"Ugh, seriously? *Again*!? I gotta come out *here* again?" Brooke said, waving her arms in frustration. The Jersey Devil looked at her, and then scanned its eye over all of them and let out a low growl that they could feel in their chests. It watched them walk about thirteen feet away before pointing at Hunter.

"WAIT! YOU. COME HERE."

"Me?" Hunter gulped, not wanting to take any steps back near it, but he had no choice. The devil nodded its head. Once Hunter walked up to him, they turned away from the group and it spoke briefly with Hunter. Caleb looked on, a jealous glint in his eye. *Why him?* he thought. Hunter came back to the group, a serious expression plastered on his face. No matter how many times the group asked him, he didn't tell them what was said. It felt like it took forever to get out of the pine barrens that day, but the huge weight of imminent death lifted off their shoulders put them at ease.

The group faded from the Jersey Devil's sight and it decided not to channel its energy to surveil them any further. He stood there, a poignant yearning falling over him. What was it? His mind was already swirling with the newfound knowledge about the curse, but this was different. He was disgusted that he envied something, and was even more angered that he couldn't figure out what. He opened up his wings and flew up, away from there.

CHAPTER 23

Out of all of them, Caleb was the most excited to present their folklore project. Lola still couldn't get over *any* group wanting to present their projects early, but there they were, Hunter Lawless, Jesse O'leary, Caleb Kane, and Brooke Simpson, raring to go. None of their academic records stood out besides Hunter's. She saw potential in Hunter, but wasn't sure what he was passionate about. Taking a step back, she had to realize and understand that these kids had fun with a project and were proud of their work. The negative cloud that she let form above her head over the past three months had warped her views, making her think that every student hated every assignment. The joy she lacked became the joy her students lacked, but these four reminded her what the reality was: sometimes school can be fun. Really fun. Whether you're a teacher or a student. And as they got through their warm-up assignment and these thoughts germinated in her mind, she grew happier and her smile didn't seem to leave her face. She felt like she was almost as excited to see the group's presentation as they were to present it.

It woke up in an instant. Something was missing. No, worse. Something was taken from it. It searched around just to make sure, but it knew. It flew off, set to claim back what was theirs, not knowing if it was prepared to tread in such unfamiliar territory.

"Alright, class! There's a project group who is already finished and would like to present their folklore research to us a bit early! Please be respectful and quiet as Hunter, J, Caleb, and Brooke present to us a rather close-to-home piece of folklore." Ms. Santos gestured at the four and they got up in front of the class. Hunter got the technology situated and had their powerpoint on the projector screen for the entire class to behold.

"Since the 1700s there's been many sightings of a strange flying creature in the skies of New Jersey."

"Even during war times, at Landover Mill Works where they inspected cannonballs, they saw it flying and shot at it, but it had no effect."

"During these hundreds of years there have been many reports of unexplained livestock killings, strange tracks, and terrifying screams in the otherwise beautiful forests of New Jersey, *especially* the New Jersey Pine Barrens."

"It's no surprise that the legend and folklore of the New Jersey Devil has been passed down from generation to generation. There have even been rewards for its killing or capture!"

"People even wanted to trap it alive and put it in a private zoo!"

"There have been multiple accounts of an attack from this creature, including it attacking a trolley car in 1909 in Maddon Heights."

"But why is the Jersey Devil folklore important? Well, for one, it could be a lesson to teach children to not wander off in the woods, because it can be dangerous and you could get lost. Or it could also be used as a fun campfire story to tell your friends."

"In conclusion, the folklore of the New Jersey Devil is a fascinating, dark piece of New Jersey's culture that was fun to learn about."

The class applauded.

Ms. Santos was very satisfied with the information they presented alongside some not half-bad shots from the novice photographer J. She could tell that each of them put in effort as they took turns speaking to the class. Caleb's excitement had in turn exposed a side of his personality not many had seen before, and half of the class was in awe that weird, quiet Caleb spoke out loud and clear. What was odd, however, was how at the end of their presentation, after their Work Cited slide, they had put a couple more slides of uncanny pictures with no text or explanation. One was a dark, hairy figure in some old, rotting building. The other was a closeup of what Ms. Santos thought was some sort of art piece, perhaps a video game character of some angry-looking goatman with one eye that resembled descriptions of the Jersey Devil. *Crazy what kinds of pictures middle schoolers could find on the internet nowadays.*

Ms. Santos wanted the audience to participate as well, so she opened the floor for any questions or comments.

"Did you guys really go out into the woods for those pictures?"

"Yep! That's where we took all of them."

"Nice job, I never knew we had something like that around here."

"We talked about it less than a month ago!"

"Oh, did we? Well…I forgot."

"Overall this was a good presentation. Thumbs up from me. I'm gonna ask my parents if they know about this!"

"Did you guys see the Jersey Devil? Those weird pictures at the end got me spooked, not gonna lie."

"Yeah," said Caleb. "And I think the Jersey Devil requires a sacrifice."

"Ugh, *Caleb. Please,*" Ms. Santos said in a stern voice.

"Oh, he does? Well maybe we can sacrifice Ms. Santos," said one of her worst problem students. "Sacrifice Ms. Santos! Sacrifice Ms. Santos!" They gestured to the class and chanted, getting most of the class to chant along.

"SACRIFICE MS. SANTOS! SACRIFICE MS. SANTOS!"

"You need to *stop this*, *NOW!!*" Lola was not amused. J, Hunter, and Brooke stood up there, embarrassed, deciding not to join in on the chant. Brooke was so embarrassed standing up there still that she wished something would happen so that she could go home. With a hard, draining effort, Lola eventually regained control over the class. After a stern talking and banishment of fun classroom incentives for a month, it became quiet and remained quiet. All up until Caleb spoke up, still with his group in front of the class.

"Ms. Santos? I-I also brought something related to our project. It's pretty cool. Can I show it to everybody?"

This caught Lola off guard, but she figured it was okay. After all, the presentation was fairly thorough, especially for four middle school kids handing it in early.

"Sure, go right on ahead. Everyone hear that? Caleb has a little show and tell for us that goes along with their project." Hunter, J, and Brooke gave each other looks. They had no idea what Caleb was doing.

That morning at the middle school, one of the main office secretaries heard something odd on the main door intercom.

"Help me. Help me please!"

It was the voice of a child. (It knew that line well, and could mimic it near-perfectly).

"Hello? Honey, are you okay? What's your name? Are you late, do you go here?"

"Please, please let me IN!" The secretary noticed a weird shift in the tone of voice on that last word. It almost didn't sound human.

"Stay calm, dear. We'll have our security guard come check on you, okay?" she said over the intercom, and then, to herself, "Poor thing. Out in the rain all alone. I hope the rain has let up a little bit, or they'll be soaked."

The security guard was notified and went to check on the stray student at the main doors. He put the hood up on his red windbreaker "SECURITY" jacket; it was raining hard. He glanced around the doors and out into the front area. Nothing. He tried to listen for a child's voice, focusing hard to make sure the sound of rainfall wasn't masking anything. Nothing. He came back inside and walked up to the secretary in the main office. Something caught the door before it could close.

"Um, Karen, you sure you heard something on the intercom? I didn't see or hear anyone out there. And believe me, I woulda noticed a kid in the rain."

"Wh-what? Of course I heard something! We're pretty far away from April Fools, Tim! I'm not gonna waste your time faking something serious like this."

"Listen, I get it, but I swear, there was nothin-"

A loud thump and crash. Proceeding the racket came a somewhat panicked, grinding growl. A blur of black was seen shooting by the glass office windows.

"Ok, so while we were out in the woods, we found this old, messed up cabin, but it was still, like, standing. So we went inside and explored and I found something on the ground underneath the remains of some wooden dresser or something. It was hard to tell, being all rotted away and whatnot. Anyways, look." Caleb took a plastic bag out of his pocket. Inside it was a large, white eyeball, its fleshy, thick optic nerve still attached. Caleb took it out of the bag before Ms. Santos could say anything and held it out. Many "oohs," "huhs," and "whoas" accompanied the entire class piling up to get a closer look.

"What is that from, Caleb?"

"Yooo, are you for real!?"

"Oh my god, I think I'm going to puke."

"That. Is. Disgusting."

"Why does it look like that!?"

Ms. Santos made no effort hiding an incredulous (and according to her class, hilarious) look on her face.

"Caleb, you need to put that away. You can't just bring some rotting eyeball from a corpse to class! What were you thinking?"

"But, Ms. Santos, the cool thing is, I've had it for days now, and it hasn't smelled or rotted one bit. It's a little slimy, but yeah!" said Caleb. The exhilarating delight in his voice disturbed Lola. She stepped closer to take a look at the eyeball. She could see red and blue veins like worms throughout it. It was quite massive and she wondered what animal it could be from. Then she noticed the pupil. A black, horizontal strip laid over a yellow-brown iris. *Horizontal*, she thought. *A goat?* She studied it, looking down at it, wondering how big goats can grow. Then, in a jolt, it looked up at her. She recoiled back.

"What the fu-...Caleb?" she started to say.

"It *moved*!"

"Whaaat? No way, I didn't see!"

"Yo, oh my god, it just moved!!"

"It looked up at Ms. Santos!"

"Caleb, what *is* that thing!?"

A dumbfounded shock appeared on Hunter, J, and Brooke's faces, wishing they had their masks to put on right now. They all had the revelation as to what Caleb had in his hands simultaneously. They looked at each other, asking the question they all wished to know with their faces: *How did he get the Jersey Devil's eye!?* This was bad. If it had moved, they had no doubt it was able to see or at least sense around itself. The class was in a baffled uproar. Next door, Mrs. Thomas' class was taking a test, but Ms. Santos' class was so loud that she got up from her desk and opened the neighboring door to see what all the commotion was, upset that her class was being disturbed by the brouhaha.

"What in the world is going on here!?" said Mrs. Thomas. Ms. Santos had no control over her children anymore. She felt helpless, embarrassed, furious, and ashamed all at once. And before anyone could say anything else, the Jersey Devil found its way to where its stolen eye was.

The beast was in unfamiliar territory. It was frightened; there were too many things surrounding it which it could not comprehend. But it was on a mission: claim back what was theirs. And it was dead set on fulfilling that mission. Mustering up all of the focus it had left, it arrived at a door. The door led to a loud room. That's where it was, though. It had to go in. It was barely aware that it had trampled a school employee and three students in the halls on its way to the door. It kicked the door down with one of its mighty hooves. Before it a room full of children and two adults, various colorful things around them with chairs and desks forming small tables.

"What is *that*!?" Amanda said, turning around at the sudden sound of the door blasting open.

With a swipe of the arm it sent Amanda flying into a supply closet, her body going straight through the wooden door. The children were screaming and some started running around. Lola tried to direct them towards a back exit door her classroom had. Caleb, Hunter, J, and Brooke stood there motionless, their mouths wide open in terror. Even they could tell how different the Jersey Devil seemed to be acting. Many children made their way out of the exit door, but other children from neighboring classrooms surrounded the entrance, effectively trapping the beast inside Lola Santos' classroom with small bodies. Teachers and other faculty were yelling through the chaos in the hallways. The chatty Katie was the next in its way, frozen screaming as she looked up at it. The beast's ears quivered in response to the screaming, and it was driven further mad by a boundless voice from the heavens.

"EVACUATION. EVACUATION. THIS IS NOT A DRILL," said the voice. Although it seemed godlike to the beast, it was shaky and stricken with fear.

Katie's brother was next to her, and in a childlike act of fight-or-flight, stabbed its leg with a pencil. It grabbed both children in one swoop of its hand.

"I WILL WEAR YOUR SKIN, PESTS."

It let out a piercing bleat, its one eye closed, shaking its head around in a frenzy. The two children kept screaming in its hand, and it squeezed until the screaming stopped. More screaming surrounded it, driving it further from its mind. Its eye was dead set on Caleb. It looked at him with disdain, rushing up to him, squeezing his wrist until his hand was fully open. It grabbed its eye, and just as it was about to slice off Caleb's head, a chair hit it in the shoulder. Lola, having gotten most of her students out of the classroom (even though more lingered at the entrance, watching the dreadful situation ensue) noticed the four from the project group still inside, not moving. She threw the chair with surprising force and stunned it. They were all lucky. It had retrieved what it came there for, and wanted nothing more than to be away from all of the intense lights and sounds. It looked around and rushed out the back entrance, and further out a side entrance of the school. The children and faculty who were already evacuated watched in astonishment as a giant, black beast propelled itself through the air with its enormous, menacing wings.

"What *is* that thing!?"

"Wait, is it holding something?"

"Oh my God, does it have two children in its hand?"

"We need to take a roll call, *now*."

Students, teachers, and administration were all in a panic. Many in tears. Many talking to each other about what was happening.

Dumbfounded. Traumatized. Awestruck. Dismayed. It was almost an impossible task to establish order and get everything under control. Lola blanked out within the chaos, outside now with her class. It dawned on her that the photos J had taken for their project were real. She swallowed hard and muttered "what the fuck?" under her breath. Authorities arrived and taped off the school. It took everyone a while to communicate that the threat was gone. It would take them a considerably longer amount of time to establish what the threat *was*.

After an overwhelming amount of first-hand accounts and descriptions of what happened, local authorities, in disbelief, realized they needed to contact the higher-ups. The FBI was on the premises shortly after. Upon hearing the truth of what happened, they started a cover-up operation. No one outside of the event was to ever know what truly happened at Park Ridge Middle School. It would be insulting to say such a fantastical creature was now the reason behind two more children gone. This wasn't some Grimm Tale, it was real life. Hundreds of children had been missing, most presumed dead. The public would be in that much more of an outrage. They wouldn't stand for such an explanation. But those who witnessed it…they knew. Somewhere deep down in them, they felt it. The true cause. It could swoop down and grab two kids in one hand, then fly off into the deep forest. Many witnesses were so terrified of what they felt like was the truth, they didn't dare bring it up. If they came out to the public about it, there would be people working behind the scenes to make sure everyone thought they were crazy. But they knew.

On the news later that night, authorities would "come to the conclusion that" there had been a school shooting. The autopsies of the dead would not be publicly disclosed. There was no explanation at this time for two missing students who happened to be siblings. NDAs were signed. The "shooter" had been "apprehended" as well. There were only so many holes the cover-up story would fill, and it wasn't long before the "Park Ridge Middle School Shooting" gained national attention. Many conspired as to what happened. The further they researched the details of the situation, the more confused they were. Some pictures of a giant black beast flying far away in the sky over the trees surfaced on various websites throughout the internet. Many were taken down, others were said to be faked.

Lola drove home after hours of questioning. The shock would take a while to wear off. She was machine-like as she got home, doing everything almost automatically. Even when petting her cat, it was with cold, distant hands. Crash noticed and tried his best to bring her back down to earth. She couldn't stop running it through over and over in her head, like a particular scene in a movie that sticks to your memory like a thick paste.

CHAPTER 24

In the midst of tragedy, life goes on. That was the conclusion Lola Santos came to at first after being shocked at the email she received from the district: the school would be back open in three weeks. Was that really enough time for *anyone*? Would it be taboo to speak of it, a lingering, dark cloud over the school, or would it be the talk of the district for years to come? Countless thoughts swarmed through her head. She could only imagine what everyone else had on their minds, and for the sake of their sanity, hoped those thoughts didn't carry into their dreams. To cope with the tragedy that befell the school and her classroom, she leaned hard into the morbid fascination she had for it all. It consumed her. It wasn't before long she was neck deep into research, theories, and photos all on and about the New Jersey Devil. A living mythological creature. She threw a fucking chair at it! Her obsession became planning. She needed to talk to Caleb or, hell, anyone else she could reach in that project group. The burning question on her mind: how did he come into possession of its eye? She wanted to go out into the barrens and see what she could find, so she pulled out maps and marked potential routes that matched up with historical records of old colonies, villages, mills, and more. During her research she had found articles about something strange that happened to a very old logging village. Apparently more and more people went missing until there was no one left. Not even the animals. Lola hoped that she could uncover more about this when she was ready to go out and explore. She also found out where Caleb lived via her teacher-student information and planned to thoroughly explore all back around that area; she noticed it happened to be around where the notorious blue hole was as well.

She wanted to start off with a short trek first, and after a couple of days of preparation, she felt ready. She cursed as she looked at the time upon waking up. She wanted to leave for her first small route early, but it was already half past one. She scrambled to put on some clothes and ate a quick meal. The local state park had a couple of trails that led deeper into the woods and she arrived there around two o'clock. The fresh air felt so nice she didn't mind its cold bite at her face. As she made her way further into the trail, she pulled out a map and knew where she would want to stray from the path. She felt awkward walking deeper into the forest with no trail to guide her, and kept looking behind her hoping no one noticed. Of course, very few people walked these trails during the cold season–especially at this time of day in the middle of the week.

About fifteen minutes into the unguided trek she came across some old train tracks. It was nice to see something different. She found a large branch that had snapped off and fallen to the ground and leaned it up against a tree to mark the start of her new path. She followed the tracks going right, entertaining herself by attempting to balance on one side of the rails. She got quite good at it. As she trampled and slipped from the rusted, metal rails to their rotted wooden supports, and then on top of the dead, orange and brown pine nettles, she noticed how the barrens could get surprisingly dense on a whim. Anything could be hiding in those parts. A small pond peeked through the trees and down. She smiled and stopped at it, then investigated some rubble nearby, but to no avail; she wasn't expecting to find anything on her first, shorter adventure anyways. Although, it wasn't beginning to feel so short, as she lost track of time following the tracks. *At least I have something to guide me back*, she thought, looking down at the old rails.

Lola Santos didn't consider herself nyctophobic, but the creeping darkness still freaked her out enough for her to pick up the pace. She looked at the time on her phone: *quarter to five already!?* The gray-blue sky was beginning to bleed pinks, reds, and oranges. The crescent moon was a cut of ice in the sky, the waking eye of heaven.

"Thank god," she said as she saw the branch she had stood up earlier. She made her way back towards the trail, looking down to focus on the disturbed ground she had treaded not too long ago to stay in the right direction. Looking down also helped because she was starting to see things. They were shadows, figures, always right there in the distance when she looked up. One stood out among the rest; she thought she saw a lanky, horned creature wearing the skin of two children. One eye with the rotting flesh draped around it pierced through the barrens at her. It had to be a mental thing, right? But no matter if she looked one direction or the exact opposite, something was there. And it crept ever-so closer along with the darkness. The orange sky's generosity was running out, but she found the park's trail and jogged back to her car, looking straight ahead of herself the entire time.

This was an issue in Lola's mind. As she drove back she was disappointed in herself, as she had planned to take some longer trips into the more remote, historical sites in and around the barrens that would surely go into the night. She got home and made herself dinner, chewing slowly in thought. She made up her mind, and after dinner, slid open her back sliding-glass door. She turned on the light and looked out, the woods in her backyard twenty feet away. She stepped out and into the night, solidifying her choice of exposing herself to it all. To explore and uncover the mysteries of the legend that haunted her and so many others, this had to be done; she didn't care how vulnerable she felt; her obsession drove her past her normal limits. But then she turned around and went back inside the house. She flicked the outside light switch off, and then made her way back out and to the edge of the woods. She couldn't see the edge of it, but she could sense all of its vastness in front of her. That creature…it had been three feet in front of her, it even stared into her eyes! She had to know more. She must journey out into the unknown. She shivered.

What was so frightening about the darkness? It's always just two shut eyes away. Lola stood there at the edge of the woods, lost in thought. Everything was still and her breath came out in slow plumes. The cold air stung her lungs, no longer as refreshing as earlier. *I've seen it hundreds of times. I know what's there*, she thought. But when it's covered by darkness, it's different, isn't it? And she stood there and felt her skin crawl. Like she couldn't see something staring back at her. Part of her told her it was just trees and bushes, maybe the wind moving them a bit. But a larger, more vocal part was screaming at her, going, "RUN. WHAT ARE YOU DOING JUST STANDING THERE!?" But she failed to see the urgency. She closed her eyes. Not that much of a difference. But she *felt* it. And if she turned around now, something would tear the skin off of her back, ripping it from her body and then she'd be dragged by her loose flesh into some unknown part of the woods. And dirt and insects and dead leaves would stick to her fleshy, red, exposed dermis, stinging and infecting to no end. Dragged along further and further. Maybe to where there's a deep, dark, suffocating hole that leads to hell. And she stood there and thought, *is this all rational? Why would I have such strong, fearful feelings if it weren't?* And as she tried to ground herself back into her reality, she was reminded that her reality now included something thought only to be a myth. As the fear and anxiety gripped their way up her back, she fended them off with the obsessive fascination that brought her there in the first place. *But it spoke. If I could locate its dwelling and find it, would it speak to me?* She *had* to get in touch with Caleb, but she knew his living situation. And as her thoughts drifted further away from the horrors that lurked within the darkness, the more at ease she felt with it. And as she turned around to go back inside, out of a mixture of respect and anticipation, she experienced small chills run down her spine.

Crash watched Lola from the open sliding glass door with curious eyes. He was a creature well-acquainted to the night, and had no issue with vision in the dark. When Lola made her way back to her house, Crash stood still with his head and ears down, eyes big and black. Frozen in concentration, he made sure whatever he saw in the dark didn't make any threatening moves. Lola noticed Crash's strange behavior and took a look back to where he kept his gaze. She knew what was out there now and did not allow her mind to fill in the empty darkness with horrors. She bent down, smiled, and petted Crash.

"You're a brave little kitty. Thanks for having my back, but the thing that's out there? It's a bit bigger than you. C'mon."

She picked him up and shut the door, locking it and closing the blinds. There was much to be done in these next handful of days, so she showered, read for a bit, and went to sleep.

CHAPTER 25

Lola Santos wasn't the only busy person when it came to dealing with the New Jersey Devil. Thursday came fast, and Hunter, J, Brooke, and Caleb had planned to meet up today and get their end of the deal from the horror in the woods. They had all gotten good with slipping out, making excuses, and telling white lies in order to meet up. Lily was off to pick up Albert from the hospital again, and Hunter saw his time to act. But there was something he had to do first. He knocked on Hannah's door after he watched Lily leave the driveway.

"Hey, Hannah."

"Yeah?"

"Wanna come on an adventure with me and my friends?"

"Adventure? Ooh, with who?"

"My friends who all slept over a few weeks ago!"

"Oh yeah! They were nice. Where are we going?"

"To one of their houses. Wanna tag along?"

"Hmm. Maybe. We'll see."

"Well we have to leave now. They asked about you and if you were coming. Sounds like they really wanna see you."

"Alright, let me finish something!"

With a burst of energy Hannah shut her door and Hunter sighed a breath of relief. She came out soon after and they left the house. Hunter took out his bike and made Hannah hold him from behind while she stood on the pegs he had on the wheels. She was having a blast already. They arrived at J's house and saw Brooke and J come out the front door, Brooke doing her best to hide a repulsed face from the disorder and clutter in and around J's house.

"I can't believe you just…cut cockroaches in half with scissors."

"It works, doesn't it? Oh, hey Hunter!"

"Hey J."

"Heya," Brooke looked down at Hannah. "What is she doing here?"

Hannah was confused, and before she became upset, Hunter spoke up.

"Oh, don't you remember? You guys wanted Hannah to tag along to adventure with us this time! Right? *Riiight?*" The inflection in his voice was enough for them to catch on.

"Ohhh yeah! I remember! Um, yeah. We have a ton of fun. Do you like exploring in the woods, Hannah?"

"Yeah. My daddy and I do that sometimes."

"Hunter, you *sure* our, um, *friend* that we meet up with in the woods will, uh-" said Brooke.

"It'll be fine, don't worry," replied Hunter. He took Brooke and J to the side for a moment. "It was *his* request. He said I needed to bring my sister if I wanted my reward."

"What the-? Really? How did he know-"

"Listen, how does he know *all* the crap that he knows?" Hunter got worked up for a second. "Just keep going along with it, okay?"

"Alright."

They formed again with Hannah.

"What friend?" asked Hannah.

"Oh you'll see. They're…different from anyone you've met before," said J.

"Oh…okay," replied Hannah. She was a smart kid, but didn't catch on too fast to things and was laid back enough to roll with it. They all started to walk over to Caleb's house.

"So, Hannah, what are your other friends like?" asked J. "We're a bit older than them I bet."

"Yeah. They're okay." She paused. "I only have one friend from school."

"That's okay," said Brooke, looking at J. "You'll make more."

They walked up to Caleb's driveway and he came out of the door, slamming it shut. They could all hear yelling and profanities coming from inside the house. Caleb, a bit embarrassed, and a bit surprised from the sight of Hannah, let out a weak "Hey guys," and received greetings in return. He looked at Hannah, then at Hunter, then back at Hannah. He squatted down, facing her.

"Hannah, right? I remember you from the sleepover," he said. He extended his fist out and got a timid fist bump in return. "Let's go," he said, taking a deep breath. Hannah smiled.

"The D-, um, our *friend*, he's, like, definitely gonna be mad at you, right?" J asked Caleb.

"Yeah. But I think we'll be okay if he is true to his word. And I think he is."

His response gave no solace to the worried bunch, but they marched forward into the pine barrens once again. A glimmer of hope resided inside most of them, wanting so bad for it to be the last time they'd be making this awful trip.

"So…how did you get it?" asked Brooke. It was the first time they were all together since the incident at the school.

"Seriously, Caleb. What the hell was going through your head?" said J.

"You guys think he's scary, but there's more to him than that. I wanted a keepsake," replied Caleb.

"Huh?" said Hunter.

"I don't wanna talk about it," said Caleb, exhaling sharply and shaking his head.

"I bet I know where you got it, though. Last time we were here. You were in the cabin," said J. Caleb didn't respond.

"Can't believe he came into the school, though…" said Brooke.

"Is your friend from a different school? What happened?" asked Hannah.

"Yeah, you could say that. It's complicated," said Hunter. Hannah gave no bother to question more, staring off in different directions looking for more flowers. It was December now, so she would have no luck. Not until she met the "friend" they had been talking about. The Jersey Devil wasn't at the rotten, broken down cabin, but off to the side about 100 feet away. It was down a bit and they still saw him clearly. They walked up to him and realized they were on the edge of a boggy swamp.

"OUT HERE, THE FLOWERS BLOOM WHEN I TELL THEM TO." The beast held some dead flower buds in its hand, and all of a sudden fresh yellows and stunning pinks emerged from the now-alive flowers. Hannah had to lean back with her head all the way up in order to see its face. He was intimidating, yet had a fantastical nature about him. She stood there, distressed, mouth agape. The beast came closer, reached out its long arm and placed a Bog Asphodel and a Swamp Pink in her hair on either side of her head. He stepped back and she felt the flowers in her hair, closed her mouth and looked to the side. Then she mustered up the courage to speak.

"I'm Hannah. Wh-what's your name?"

"MY NAME?" The question took it off guard for a second. "I DO NOT KNOW MY TRUE NAME, ALTHOUGH I HAVE MANY NICKNAMES. LET ONE OF YOUR GROUP HERE TELL YOU MY NAME."

They all looked at each other and decided to say nothing, but Hannah pestered at them to tell her.

"His name is Blackhorn. Cool, huh?" said Hunter, improvising.

"I guess. Thank you, Blackhorn. You're scary," said Hannah.

"COME." He motioned for them to follow him back to the cabin. "WE HAVE MATTERS TO DISCUSS. FIRST AND FOREMOST, MY END OF THE DEAL." It handed Hunter, Brooke, and J their vials, promising to hold an elixir inside to extend the consumer's lifespan twofold. It then turned to Caleb. "CONSIDER YOU STILL BEING ALIVE ENOUGH PAYMENT FOR YOUR TRANSGRESSION AGAINST ME. WHEN YOU SEE YOUR TEACHER AGAIN, THANK HER FOR SAVING YOUR LIFE IN THE FIRST PLACE."

Caleb wanted to reply, but choked on his words. He nodded and looked down at his feet. The devil pointed at Brooke and J.

"YOU TWO ARE FREE TO GO. I HAVE MATTERS TO DISCUSS WITH THE OTHER THREE. GOODBYE."

"Oh, uh, okay. B-bye guys," said J. Brooke wasn't expecting this and looked at Hunter, Hannah, and Caleb, worried. She stood there with her mouth open, releasing a quiet "uhh" from under her breath. The devil did not avert his gaze. It was his way of making sure they knew he wanted them to leave promptly. They turned around and were off. It felt different not going back with everyone else.

"Wait. Do you know how to get back? Cus I don't think I 100% know how to," said Brooke.

"Yeah, don't worry," said J, fighting the urge to look over their shoulder. As they walked back they both marveled at the liquid in the vials they were given, talking about their futures.

The Jersey Devil turned to Hunter and Hannah, pointing towards the old cabin.

"WAIT IN THERE."

Hunter held Hannah's hand and they acquiesced, making their way inside, watching their step on the rotting floor.

"YOU." The creature got up close to Caleb's face, clenching its jaw. "I HAVE A TASK FOR YOU, AND IT WOULD BE UNWISE TO DECLINE IT."

"Oh. Ok," Caleb's eyes lit up.

"I HAVE DEVELOPED SOME PLANS AFTER BEING DEEP IN RUMINATION. BRING MORE TO THIS PLACE. FRIENDS. YOUTH. A SIZEABLE AMOUNT. YOU HAVE A WEEK. NOW BEGONE."

"Friends n' other kids. Here. Gotcha. You can count on me."

"WORDS OF TRUST MEAN LITTLE COMING FROM YOUR MOUTH. GO."

"Alright alright, jeez. See ya." And with that, Caleb was off. He was in a sour mood at the devil's cold manner towards him, but thankful he had another chance to prove himself. He wondered if he could catch up with the others if he was quick enough.

The Jersey Devil made its way into the cabin, slid an old dresser over, revealing a hatch. It tossed a vial to Hunter. Hunter almost didn't catch it.

"THIS IS YOURS. BUT YOU ARE NOT FREE YET." It opened the hatch and looked at the two siblings.

"YOU WILL BE STAYING DOWN HERE FOR NOW. IF YOU STRUGGLE IT WILL ONLY MAKE THINGS WORSE. I WILL PROVIDE WATER AND FOOD WHICH IS GRACIOUSLY GIVEN BY THE BARRENS, EVEN IN THESE COLD, DEAD DAYS."

"What, why? Why are you doing this?" Hunter said, an indignant shake in his voice. He quickly pocketed the vial. Hannah hid behind him.

"ONE DAY YOU MAY FIND OUT. GO IN."

Hunter was smart enough to know his position: there was no talking their way out of this and there was no chance of running away or fighting back. He held Hannah close and they entered the hidden cellar. The cellar entrance was big, but Hunter noticed that the beast itself would probably have a tough time trying to get down it. Something resembling a candle lit the dank room. It wasn't suffocatingly small, but it wasn't too spacey either. The creature threw somewhat of a blanket made from animal hides down to them. It shut the cellar door and punched a hole through it. Then it slid the dresser partially over it.

"YOU HAVE AIR AND WON'T FREEZE TO DEATH. YOU CAN SEE. SOON YOU WILL HAVE FOOD AND WATER."

Hunter went and picked up the hide blanket and wrapped them both around it. They sat close to the stairs. Hannah began weeping.

"What the hell...," said Hunter. His mind was racing, but he had to stay calm for his little sister. He felt responsible. And that made him feel awful. He held her close, telling her that everything would be okay.

Caleb, rushing back, did eventually catch up to Brooke and J about seven minutes later. He startled them for a second, causing sounds coming from behind them. They turned around in brief horror.

"Jesus, Caleb! What's the rush?" asked Brooke.

"Did something happen!?" asked J, noticing Hunter and Hannah weren't with him.

"No, not really," said Caleb, catching his breath, hunched over with his hands on top of his thighs.

"Well then where's Hunter and Hannah?" continued J.

"I'm not sure. Listen. He wants us to come back."

"Oh no no no. You're not bringing us into any more trouble with that thing. He can live out in the forest and I can go about my life without ever seeing him again," said Brooke.

"But–"

"But *nothin*'! He said J and I could go, then he said 'goodbye'. He ain't said nothin' about us doing anything else for him. And we're keepin' it that way."

"...yeah, Caleb. I'm kinda on Brooke's side with this one. It was fun and everything, but we coulda *died*. And I'm not doing another seance or experiencing anything like that ever again. After that I don't think I'll be the same. So, yeah. Sorry."

"Alright," said Caleb. He knew not to fight them or try to persuade them at this point. There was nothing he could say. And with that he started brainstorming how he would get thirteen more back there. After some time of silence, J spoke up.

"Are you sure we shouldn't go back for them?"

"They'll be fine. Remember, he said 'goodbye',' so I don't think he'd be too happy seeing us back so soon," said Caleb.

"Yeah, you're probably right," said J.

"I hope they're okay," said Brooke.

CHAPTER 26

"We're home! Happy Friday! Hunter, Hannah, your goofy dad's home *again*!" She looked at Albert, "And hopefully this time for a *lot* longer." They both smiled. They didn't expect Hunter and Hannah to come running up to welcome their dad home (well, maybe Hannah), but when neither of them even came out of their rooms to greet their dad and give him a hug, it struck them both as a bit odd.

"Guys, come on. You can at least come out and say hi," said Lily, walking towards the hallway where their rooms were. Albert just sighed. "Hunter? Hannah? Where are you guys? If this is a prank you need to cut it out and come out *now*." Lily was growing impatient and her heart rate was starting to increase.

"They're not in their rooms?" asked Albert.

"No, check outside."

Albert went outside and limped around, searching for them, but he didn't find anyone. It was silent and eerie. Like that morning. He came back inside, Lily stomping up the stairs, just having checked the basement.

"Nothing?"

"Nope."

"Where are our kids? *Where the FUCK are our kids*!?"

"Hold on. Let's check their rooms. Maybe they took some stuff and went over to a friend's house or something?" Per Albert's suggestion, they each checked a room, but found nothing that would imply his guess. Lily sat on her knees on Hannah's floor, a devastated hand to her head.

"I was looking forward to this. This was supposed to be a *good* day. I said goodbye to them just thirty minutes ago and now we get back and they just *disappear*!? We were going to be a normal family again. Things were going to start getting better!" Tears came running down Lily's face as she bent down to the floor. Albert, shaken, couldn't get a horrible thought out of his head. It pestered him like a fly on a hot day. It was as if Lily could read his mind as she managed to get up and look at him. "Where are they, Al? Where are they?" Albert hugged her tight and let her cry on his shoulders. Lily took his lack of a reaction as knowledge of something, and as she put two and two together, she reared back from him, holding him by the shoulders and looking deep into his eyes.

"No…you don't think…no, Al, *no no no*!! This fucking *thing* didn't take our children!"

"Hold on. There's one place we haven't checked," said Albert after thinking hard for a minute. He barreled out of the house and headed for the small storage shed they had. Lily followed. Albert opened up the door and saw something that gave him a shred of hope. "Look. Hunter's bike's gone. They must've gone somewhere, right?"

"Oh my god," Lily said, feeling slight relief. Even that slight relief felt like boulders of pressure off of her chest. "But where in the world would they have ridden off to? I don't get it…"

The pestering thoughts resurfaced in Albert's mind. He just couldn't shake them. When he squashed one fly off his brain, two more came from under his hand. It felt futile. He put his hand up on where his neck met his shoulder, rubbing it in thought.

"I don't know, maybe a friend's house?" He wondered more. And he felt good. Why? Why was he thinking about feeling good all of a sudden? Then he realized that the second spot that should be itching like all hell wasn't itching at all. His leg was even feeling a bit better. He grabbed at his shoulder. No itching. His neck. No itching. A pit in his chest dropped and he swallowed an unpleasant, dry gulp full of fear and anger. Lily was still trying to brainstorm, but noticed his change in mood.

"Al? What is it, Al?"

Albert, not knowing what to do, got his keys and hopped in his truck. Lily looked at him, confused, and yelled at him, the truck door still open.

"Where are you going? Talk to me, Al! Please. *Please*! I need you, we need to find our babies!"

"Listen, Lily. I'll be back. We'll cover more ground if we split up. If they're on a bike, they haven't made it *too* far yet. Stop by some of their friends' houses and ask. You can do this. Call me if you find anything. I'll do the same."

"O-Ok. Ok. We can do this. I'll head left towards the school, you go right and search around and down there."

"Sounds good to me, hun. Stay strong. They need us right now more than anything."

"I will. I love you."

"Love you too."

Truth was, Albert had no idea where he was headed. It was more of an instinctual thing to just get in his truck and start driving. And as he saw Lily beam left out of the driveway and race up the road, he went right. He looked around and saw nothing. There was little urgency in him, and he didn't even know if he believed in his search plan. He eventually found himself at a church. He pulled in and got out, walking straight up to the entrance. There was no service today, but he knocked anyway. *What am I doin'?* he thought. And as he was about to turn away, mad at himself, a priest who had been studying and working on his next sermon in an office near the church's entrance, opened the door. He looked at Albert with a warm suspicion, his eyebrow raised and his mouth slightly open.

"May I help you, sir?"

"Priest, uh, or Father, rather-"

"Father Henry."

"Right. Father Henry, could we talk?"

"Of course, come in. I was just in my office," Father Henry said, sensing distress in Albert's demeanor. They went into his office and sat down. Father Henry sat behind his desk which had various holy books on it along with his computer.

"I'm Albert Lawless. I used to come here with my wife sometimes, but I'm not here for small talk today. Father, listen. I know I haven't been to church in a while."

Father Henry knew it had been years since Albert came to a service, but did not speak up to shame or judge him for it. In fact, he almost didn't even recognize Albert in the first place.

"Y'know it's just…having kids, they don't wanna go, and those extra hours of sleep Sunday morning feel real nice. Don't normally think of sleep when it comes to temptation, I guess."

"Mm," Father Henry nodded, taking quick glances at Albert's stump of a right hand.

"You've heard about the disappearance of all these kids…"

"I have, and they have affected families within the congregation as well. These truly are trying times."

"Well, you may have had someone ask this question to you then, hell, you might've even asked it yourself: do you think this is some weird way of God punishing us?"

"Not everything bad that happens to us is some divine punishment. We as humans love to blame our misfortune on something, and a lot of times that blame lands on God. What if, instead of a punishment, it was more of a test?"

"A test of what, exactly? Cus' guess what, Father? Now it's my family on the chopping block. My kids just, *poof*, disappeared! Just like so many other kids in this god d- darn town. It's just gonna get lost in the pile of missing kids cases! I gotta do somethin', Father! I'm at a complete loss! I don't know what to do! It's despicable."

"Albert, are you familiar with the book of Job?"

"I might be," he shrugged in impatient frustration. "I don't know."

"In it, Job is tested. He has everything taken away from him. Family. Wealth. Health. But he did not lose faith, nor did he curse or deny or get angry with God. In the end he was rewarded."

"Why would God do that in the first place? What did Job do to upset him? Did he make a deal with the devil?"

"Job didn't make a deal with the devil. God did."

"I'm sorry, Father Henry, I gotta go." Albert wasn't sure he got any answers. He was upset, knowing his faith in God and mental fortitude couldn't ever be compared with Job's. He got up and was about to leave, but Father Henry stopped him in the doorway.

"Albert, wait."

"Yeah?"

"There's something you aren't telling me. I could be more of a help to you if you wished to share more about your situation." Father Henry had used this line time and time again, never once being wrong about the person he directed it towards. Deep inside he prided himself in that. He kept count. It was in the hundreds.

"Father," Albert began, then gave out a sardonic laugh. "You're gonna think I'm crazy if I share half of all the shit that's been going on in my life."

"Not the first time I've heard someone say something like that to me, although usually less vulgar..."

"Sorry, lotta bad things going on right now, an-"

"It's fine. I understand you're under much stress and must be feeling extremely anxious about your children. Continue. You would not believe some of the things that I have heard in my tenure."

Albert sat there looking down, rubbing his brow. He let out a sigh and thought about how if he were to confide a story about the devil with anyone, a priest would be a fitting person to tell.

"Father, have you ever performed an exorcism?"

Father Henry leaned forward in his chair, and joined his fingers together just below his lips, his arms bent up on the arm rests of his chair.

"I may have assisted in an exorcism or two, but," he paused, "those were many years ago, but I *am* a priest, and therefore have the ability to perform major exorcisms."

"Then you might just be able to help get my kids back."

Father Henry, now beyond intrigued, already thought of the possibilities. Imagine: a head of the church, helping more than those useless police officers and investigators! His church would *at least* be in national news. He would be the savior of so many future children! Stopping the horrific plague that had lingered in New Jersey for far too long! Even if he didn't have much experience with exorcism at all...he was sure he could handle it. He *had* to. For the sake of transcending himself as a priest and his church as an organization.

"If the power God has invested in me can be utilized to save your children, and, consequently, many more, then rest assured that I will do all that is within my power to do so."

"Is it within your power to go head to head against a devil?"

"There isn't a day we go without taking on the devil head to head, whichever form he decides to take."

"Well, *this* form is especially bad. He's won every time against me."

"There is no shame in that, especially if it is a demon that is haunting you and can manifest to play tricks on your mind. Is it a case of possession? What are the conditions of your children?"

"No, not possessed. At least I don't think so. Kidnapped."

"...kidnapped?"

Albert grabbed a pen and a piece of paper from the Father's desk. He wrote down an address and slid it to him.

"Be here tomorrow at 4PM sharp. Bring everything that we'll need. Cus' I've seen the Devil, Father. And I can't beat him alone." And with that Albert got up and left, concerned that he had been there too long and wished to be with Lily again.

Father Henry watched him leave, both startled and peeved at Albert's message and abrupt exit. He sighed and began researching exorcism practices with serious conviction.

Lily found herself driving around near the trailer park where she remembered Hunter going to meet up with his project group. She stopped at J's house and knocked on the door. No answer. Feeling defeated, she walked back to her car when she saw a local kid, who she thought looked like was from the trailer park, riding on Hunter's bike. He was pedaling away fast, and turned down the road leading to the trailer park. She rushed to her car, yelling at the kid. She caught up to him and rolled down her window. He didn't stop, but looked in at her.

"Hey!! Where did you get that bike!?"

"It's my bike."

"That's my son's bike, you little *shit!* Where did you find it!?"

"My mom got me this bike! Leave me alone!" the kid said, giving her the finger.

Lily considered hitting the kid off the bike with her car. She wanted to stuff the kid in her trunk and take him to her basement, where no one would hear him scream as she squeezed every ounce of information out of him she could by any means necessary in order to find her son. She shook out of the dark fantasy and tried a different approach.

"Listen, please! My son is missing. Please!" She didn't try to hide the desperation in her voice. The kid sped up and into the trailer park, muttering something under his breath. Lily decided not to pursue him further as she saw some frightening individuals lingering around the trailers looking at her. She turned around and drove back up the street. She stopped on the side of the road.

"Fuck fuck fuck fuck *FUCK*!!!" she said, hitting her steering wheel harder every time. Her hand hurt, but she didn't care. She drove home, defeated.

Albert was home before her and was surprised Lily had found a kid riding Hunter's bike, although deep down he questioned whether it had actually been the right bike or not; she could just not be coping after all. He hated that he questioned it. They decided they would report them as missing tomorrow and try to muster up a search party around the area where she saw the kid on the bike. The rest of the day slagged on in pure, devastating misery. Lily didn't cook dinner that evening. She didn't eat at all. She didn't even think of eating or anything else for that matter. Albert tried to console her as much as possible, hoping with all of his heart that Father Henry and him could face the Jersey Devil the next day and get his kids back. He was tired of not being able to be there for his family. He was tired of the helpless feeling. Lily had cried so much that there were no more tears left. The house felt empty and lifeless. Neither of them slept at all that night.

CHAPTER 27

It was now Saturday. Lola had nine days left before school would resume. Her Friday was not as fruitful as she had wished, as neither J nor Caleb's parents answered the door when she had knocked. She had called it quits early and headed home, but as she was leaving, she saw some woman parked on the side of the road having a temper tantrum in her car. Lola was glad she wasn't having *that* bad of a day. Alas, today was a new day, and she had planned to make her way first to Hunter's house, and then Brooke's. She grabbed her keys, gave Crash some pets and made sure he had food and water, and was out the door.

Upon arriving at the Lawless residence, she felt a dark presence looming over the entire property. Black birds watched from the trees. Did others watch from the woods? It made her nervous to leave her car, but she got out and knocked on their door, peering out into their yard. A sleep-deprived Lily got up lightning-fast as soon as she heard the knocking, but when she opened the door and it wasn't her children there, the life was all but sucked out of her once again.

"Yes?" Lily said. Lola didn't need a microscope to see that Lily looked awful. She also looked familiar, but Lola had no time to pinpoint why. She was wondering what was wrong.

"Hi, my name is Lola Santos–Ms. Santos, your son's ELA teacher."

"What do you want?"

"I would like to sit down and discuss something with you, your husband, and your son."

"If this is about the shooting, there's nothing to talk about. This family's had to deal with enough tragedy already, and we *definitely* aren't in the mood to resurface any of the horrible *shit* that's been going on recently."

"I'm sorry, Lily, right? I understand how hard this must be. But, forgive me asking, what do you mean? Has something else happened?"

Lily dropped her head and sighed.

"I only ask because this is an important matter," Lola continued.

"Honey, who is it?" Albert asked from the living room. He got up to see for himself after he got no response. "Well, hello there."

"Hi, I'm Lola Santos. Hunter's ELA teacher. You must be Albert."

"That's me. What can we do for you?" Albert had Lily in one arm, who was so despondent she let Albert do the talking.

"I would like to talk to you and your son about something important."

"Oh. You don't know, do you? How would you, we just filed the report this morning," said Albert in a low voice.

"What? You don't mean-"

"Hunter and Hannah have gone missing. Lily drove to pick me up from the hospital and left the kids home for maybe twenty, thirty minutes tops. Came back and they were nowhere to be found. Hunter's bike was gone. Reported 'em missing just a little while ago."

"Oh my god, I'm so sorry to hear that. You guys must be going through so much, I didn't know, I don't want to bother you so I'll leave. I hope-"

"No, no, please, come in. If you wanted to talk to us about something important, we're all ears," Albert said, gesturing for Lola to enter their home. She hesitated for a moment, but went in. "You know, Hunter had been pretty quiet since the shooting...we tried to talk to him and help him out with things, you know, the trauma and all the things he must've been feeling at the time. I just can't believe children are going through such horrific, unspeakable things in, what should be, a safe and comfortable environment of *learning*, you know? Christ Almighty...you see it on the news sometimes, but you never expect to be *that* parent." Albert was starting to tear up, but Lola thought it was best for him to speak uninterrupted. "If we could've just been there...to help...somehow, a parent should be there to protect their kid. You know? I just don't get why someone would ever do such a hateful and horrendous act. To just take away a budding life! I-"

"We get it, *we get it*, Al! Enough! Please, just stop," Lily said. Until she had interrupted, Lola was sitting there nodding along with what Albert was saying, but she jumped at the fire in Lily's voice as she spoke up.

"Alright, I'm sorry, hun. Guess I just had to get some things out. And I thought a teacher of all people would understand more than anything." Pictures of Hannah and Hunter smiled at them in the living room.

"I do. I completely get it and I agree. I find myself alone in my room, just asking myself 'why?' and there's never a good answer. These kids are already growing up in a tough world, they don't need such heavy trauma from a tragedy like that. It's just too much to bear, y'know, for *children*."

"Yeah..." Albert nodded in complete agreement. After a moment of silence, he spoke up.

"So, Ms. Santos, you came to us to discuss something. What is it?"

"Ok, so," Lola took a deep breath, "I am going to preface this by telling you guys that I am not delusional, I have no history of insanity or anything like that. I am healthy and of sound mind. But, on the day of the shooting, it happened in *my* classroom, right before my eyes. Right before your son's eyes. And I'm not sure, maybe Hunter told yo-"

"Oh my god."

"...But listen. It *wasn't* a shooting," Lola lowered her voice to a surreptitious whisper. "That was just a coverup. Fabricated by the FBI after they had arrived."

Albert and Lily leaned in with baffled expressions.

"*What?*"

"The *FBI?*"

"I swear on the grave of mi abuela, what happened in my classroom on that day was something much different."

"Wh-what happened then!? What could've possibly happened that they ha-"

"Calm down, Al, let her speak."

"A large, black creature with one eye burst into the school with some sort of murderous intent. Everything happened so fast that I didn't realize what this thing was, but I have my suspicions that-" Lola stopped. She had never seen such shocked expressions before in her life. Albert and Lily looked at each other with open mouths, knowing exactly what it was. "Um, was it something I said?" She thought she began to understand their expressions. "Wait, do you guys already know? But how?"

"No, we didn't know about what happened in the school. But it's not the first time we've had a run in with that *bastard*."

"So it's true...other people *have* seen the Jersey Devil. ¡Ay, Dios! What is happening in our town?"

"Evil shit. That's what," said Albert. "Tell us more."

"We know you're not crazy, so don't worry about that," said Lily.

"Ok, wow. Um, ok. So, Hunter was part of the group that was doing their folklore project on the New Jersey Devil. And-"

"You? It was *you* who assigned that bullshit!? This is your fault then, isn't it?" Lily said, finding it difficult to control her anger, looking for someone to blame.

"No no, please understand-"

"Understand *what*!? Huh?"

"Lily, please-"

"*NO, Al,*" Lily said, glaring at her husband. She looked back at Lola. "*YOU* understand: our two babies are *missing*, and all the signs are pointing towards this fucking *demon* being the monstrosity that took them away! Who the hell knows what could be happening to them right now at this very moment!? How could you assign 6th graders such a horrible project!?"

"The *project* was on *folklore*, Mrs. Lawless. Please calm down. It was my students who *chose* what they did their project on. It must have appealed to Hunter and his group as interest grew over a very local piece of folklore."

"Ain't folklore *now,* is it?" said Albert, scoffing. He considered not saying what he was about to say next, but went against his better judgment. "That newfound fact won't bring their grade down, will it?"

Lola looked at him with confused amusement while Lily stared daggers at him.

"Listen. One of his group members, Caleb Kane, had brought in something for their presentation that day. It was a severed eye in a plastic bag. Shortly after, that *thing* came barging into my classroom and took it back before flying off with two of my other students in its hand!"

"Unbelievable..." Albert said.

"It's true!"

"No, I know. But...Lola, *I'm* the one who *gave* that fucker 20/0 vision. *I* severed its eye!"

"Por los clavos de Christo, ¿¡que está pesando!?" Lola said quickly, a raised eyebrow resting atop her serious face like the hook of a question mark. She tried hard to piece it all together in her head.

"It's-it's not letting up," said Albert.

"It holds a grudge, then?"

"Guess so."

"I thought you were going to handle it? How did it all end up like this?" Lily said, defeated.

"It's tougher than anything I've ever come face-to-face with in my life. I tried, Lily, I did. And I'm gonna keep trying. Trust me."

Lily didn't respond.

"Mr. Lawless, I have *so* many questions, but my main one is this: How did you come across the New Jersey Devil in the first place?"

"Well, I went hunting in the woods about a month ago," Albert started. He explained his first contact with the creature.

"Oh my god, it really has been taking kids," Lola said after she heard all of his story, flabbergasted. "There *must* be a reason, right?"

"Why should we assume this piece of shit has a reason?" asked Lily.

"Well, it speaks, communicates; I am under the assumption that it has the capacity for some sort of intelligence."

"Listen, we don't have time for this. We just want our kids back, and every second we sit here and talk is a second we could be searching for them. They must be cold and starving by now, oh god," Lily said, a few tears managing to squeeze out of her eyes.

"Speaking of searching, we need to get going. I've got something I gotta do soon and Lily has been getting a search party together," said Albert, getting up. "Ms. Santos, thank you for this eye-opening conversation, but now is the time to act. If you're not gonna join the search party, I'm going to ask you to let us get on with our day. I think Lily and I have both had enough of talking about all of this. I won't rest until that son of a bitch is dead and I get my kids back."

"Of course. But please, confirm just one more thing for me before I leave," Lola said, pulling out a map. "You said you first encountered the Jersey Devil here, yes?" She pointed to a spot on the map. Albert got closer and took a look.

"Hmm. No, it was more around here," he said, pointing down and a little to the right of Lola's original spot.

"Ah, I see…okay. Thank you again, both of you, for your time. I would join the search party, but I have things to do. I'm sorry and I hope you find your kids as soon as possible. Hunter–he's a good kid. And I'm sure Hannah is as well."

"Thank you, Lola. Take care."

"Goodbye."

They both saw Lola out. She backed out of the driveway and was on her way. Albert looked at Lily and gave her a long, tight hug. They both knew they had things to do, and were off shortly after.

It was nearing 4PM, and Albert was headed to the spot he told Father Henry about. Father Henry had packed various items related to performing an exorcism, took a deep breath, looking at himself in his rear-view mirror, and drove off to meet Albert. He was confused once he arrived, seeing no buildings anywhere. He saw Albert's truck and got out to see what the situation was. Albert got out as he watched Father Henry approach.

"So where is this exorcism taking place, Albert?"

"In the barrens."

"Ah, an older property in the woods, I presume?"

"Nope."

"Then…?"

"This is on a larger scale than what you're probably used to. Let's go."

Father Henry adjusted his collar, grabbed his things, and followed Albert back into the small dirt road that led deeper into the woods. The trail soon appeared and they were in the thick of it.

"So, what exactly haunted you out here? I know you mentioned it was a devil, but that term is quite vague. You know there are different types of spirits that linger and overlap into our physical realm."

"*The* devil. The *New Jersey* Devil."

"What? What is that?"

"You never heard of him?"

"I'm afraid not."

"Well you're about to become a believer, Father."

Father Henry stopped, set his bag down, and took out a crucifix. He held onto it tightly.

"I-I'm not sure one person can exorcise an entire forest, Albert. What happened here?"

"I wish I knew. It came up to me when I was hunting and told me I had a week to bring my daughter back to it. Like hell I would! So a buddy and I tried to trick it, but the plan kinda backfired and I've been haunted ever since."

"Do you have a gun on you, Albert?"

Albert laughed. "Believe me, a gun'll just piss it off. We're trying a different approach."

Father Henry had a concerned expression growing on his face, but he did not lose confidence in his faith that God was on his side. They were getting much deeper into the pine barrens. He was slightly annoyed that he was not dressed properly for a long walk in the woods, and obsessively checked his ankles for ticks. Albert figured they were almost around where he knew he had run into it before. They both stopped when they heard a strange voice accompanying broken branches and the rustling of dead nettles and leaves. Father Henry quickly glanced over to where he thought he heard it. A black blur. Albert knew it was time.

"You ready, Father? Looks like he ain't playin' no games today."

"Yes. I will prepare now."

"Better hurry."

Father Henry set down his bag and took out a container of holy salt, a bundle of pure incense, and a set of matches.

"Protect us, oh Holy Father, within this circle. Hallowed be thy name," he said, encircling both himself and Albert with the salt. He then lit the incense. "Let this frankincense ward off evil and purify the air around us, oh Lord." The bundle was clutched in his hands, releasing small, wisping billows of smoke that disappeared into the air around them. Albert noticed the earthy smell of it. It had slight, sweet undertones. An odd smell. It reminded him of- *THUD!* A loud crash followed by a gust of air...it was right before them. The smoke of the incense whirred around, disturbed by the gust.

"WELL LOOK WHO IT IS! STRAWBERRY, BRINGING YET ANOTHER POOR SOUL INTO MY DOMAIN. AND FOR THE SECOND TIME, *NOT* WHO I REQUESTED HE BRING." The creature gestured with its arms as it spoke. It twitched and rubbed its wings, waiting for a response.

"So, this is our devil, Albert?"

"Yes. Yes it is."

Father Henry noticed its strange language and manner of communication. His head felt vulnerable, his ears hearing an ancient, demonic language, yet his mind penetrated by words he could understand. The creature sniffed once, then more and more.

"AH! A PRIEST, ALBERT, REALLY? I WAS WONDERING WHAT THAT FOUL SMELL WAS." It coughed. "MY LUNGS RARELY FEEL LIKE THEY ARE BURNING. PUT THAT AWAY." With a forceful gust of wind from its mighty wings, it blew out the incense in one go. The salt scattered around, no longer a circle. Father Henry took out a book and a vial of holy water. He flipped through the pages of the book with a dexterous hand, still clutching the crucifix. Once he got to the page he wanted, he held out the crucifix and pointed it towards the devil. He was fixated on its face, with its missing eye, twisted horn, and mixed features of beast and man. It was truly an abominable chimera that needed to be purged from this world. He began the exorcistic prayers.

"YOU THINK SOME MUMBLING WILL DO ANYTHING? WHO ARE YOU, PRIEST?" The devil turned back to Albert, looking at his leg. "I COULD HEAR YOU LIMPING BEFORE I EVEN SAW YOU. POOR ALBERT, DOESN'T LOOK LIKE YOU'RE MUCH OF A *HUNTER* ANYMORE!"

"Goddamn you. *Goddamn you!* You fuckin' freak, give me back my kids!!" Albert clenched his fists, but knew it was a losing battle.

The Jersey Devil laughed. Father Henry continued, but spoke louder now.

"The Sacred Cross commands you, our most almighty and powerful Lord commands you, cunning serpent, leave this forest, leave this world."

"NO ONE COMMANDS ME," said the beast. It now stood in front of the crucifix being held by the priest.

"I call upon your name, oh great Lord, and pray to you and the angels, Most High, Michael the Archangel, aid my spirit, help me banish this evil! Oh Lord, who created man, deliver us, let us vanquish this beast. Le-"

"YOU BEGIN TO BORE ME, PRIEST. YOUR WORDS ARE MERELY HORSE FLIES BUZZING AROUND MY EARS, SO EASILY SWATTED AWAY."

"In the name of our Lord Jesus Christ, deliver us, shed down upon us the light of mercy, aid us in victory! Deign, oh Lord, grant us your power and protection, God of Heaven, bring us peace, drive away this beast! Hear our prayers, Heavenly Father, aid us, who are made in your image, and drive Satan out of this forest! Bring those who grieve and mourn their rightful justice, oh Lord! Most glorious Prince of Heavenly armies, defend us against this agent of darkness! We beseech Thee, hear us, Almighty God! In the name of the Father, the Son, and the Holy Ghost, AMEN!" Father Henry's delivery was an impressive thing to behold. He signed the cross over his body and then uncorked the holy water, and in a brief moment of hesitation, instead, as if guided by the hand of God, threw the entire vial at the devil with a grunt through gritted teeth. He threw it with such conviction that it broke and the liquid splashed all over its long, muscular torso. The dark hair wetted and grew ever darker, but only for a second, as the liquid started to steam. The beast looked down at its chest with slight surprise. The steam grew hotter, and Albert and Father Henry looked on as the monstrosity's chest lit on fire. The smell of burning hair filled the air and the devil let out an angry bleat.

"C'mon, burn. Burn faster. BURN, YOU FUCKER!" Albert said. Father Henry continued to utter another exorcistic prayer.

But the wishes of the two men would quickly die as the beast raised its head, filled up its large lungs, and blew out the fire on its chest before it spread.

"CONGRATULATIONS. YOU MANAGED TO TICKLE ME, PRIEST," the Jersey Devil spat on the ground.

"Stay back!" said the priest.

"TELL ME, FATHER, EITHER I WAS CREATED BY YOUR GOD, OR THE CREATION OF SOMEONE ELSE'S. DOES IT REPULSE YOU THAT SOMETHING LIKE ME WAS CREATED BY THE SAME THING THAT CREATED YOU?"

"Your evil ways are what repulses me! We are all created with free will. We choose to do evil or good! You are nothing but a spawn of the Devil!"

"I *AM* THE DEVIL."

"I *refuse* to believe your words, *serpent*! The Devil is in Hell, banished there for his transgressions against God!"

The Devil looked around and laughed. "YES, I AM IN HELL, AREN'T I?"

"Lord, lend me your strength!"

"YOU ALL LIVE IN YOUR BLACK AND WHITE FANTASIES. GOD IS GOOD, THE DEVIL IS BAD. NOTHING MORE TO IT, IGNORING THE MASSIVE GRAY SPACE TOWERING OVER YOUR MINDS LIKE A TYPHOON. YOU CALL ME THE DEVIL, AND YET I HAVE DONE THINGS YOU WOULD CONSIDER 'GOOD'. YOUR GOD IS GUILTY OF DOING WHAT YOU WOULD CONSIDER 'BAD' AS WELL—ALLOWING HELPLESS CHILDREN TO BE ABANDONED BY THEIR MOTHERS, DIE AS VICTIMS IN WAR, STARVE IN A SOCIETY THAT REFUSES TO HELP THE POOR. IT IS NOT I WHO ALLOW THAT. THEY DO NOT SUFFER UNDER MY HAND."

"You can try to justify your evil all you like, you will *never* enter the gates of heaven!"

"LOOK WITHIN YOURSELF, PRIEST, EVIL IS NOT SO FAR AWAY, IS IT? I SMELL IT ON YOU. I SEE IT WITHIN YOUR MIND. IN PURSUIT OF FAME? GLORY? DO YOU WISH TO BE A SAVIOR, HOPING TO END THE HORROR THAT HAS BEFALLEN THIS AREA'S CHILDREN? SACRILEGE! THE GREED OF MAN IS HIS UNDOING."

Father Henry was shaken–a tangible devil. Intelligent and strong. He almost fell to his knees, but felt Albert hold him up.

"C'mon, Father. It was worth a try, but we gotta get out of here. Have any more of that holy water?"

"O-One more vial in my bag."

Albert reached into the bag and felt for the vial. He grabbed it and handed it to the priest.

"I could never throw southpaw. Do your thing when the timing's right. And don't miss."

They began running away. The Jersey Devil, amused, wiped off its chest and pursued, flying low in chase.

"COME NOW, ALBERT, PRIEST! WE WERE JUST BEGINNING TO HAVE SOME FUN! WHERE ARE YOU GOING?"

Albert and Father Henry kept their distance only because the creature allowed them to. He sprouted a few roots in front of their feet and tripped them up a couple of times, stopping and laughing at them before continuing the chase. They ran as fast as they could and could see the edge of the barrens where the trail was that led back to their vehicles. Albert was surprised he had made it this far given the condition of his leg, but adrenaline was a hell of a thing. Father Henry tried to find the right time to throw the vial, and right before the edge of the woods, he turned around and threw it. The beast thrust upwards with its wings in anticipation and the vial shattered on its left thigh. It began to burn, so he wiped it off with his hand, but this time his hand also began to burn. He landed and shoved his hand down into the ground while blowing on his thigh, putting out both fires. It bought them enough time to make *real* distance this time, but that came to an end quickly as it was going faster than before now. Albert and Father Henry both noticed. It was just toying with them? Was this all really just a game to it? Albert made it to the trail and looked behind him. Father Henry was caught.

The Jersey Devil had its massive jaw clamped down onto the priest's skull near his chin. Albert looked on in horror. He was helpless again. All he could manage was a faint whimper, saying "no," in a voice he immediately hated hearing coming out of his mouth. Father Henry screamed, as all he could see was the black and pink gummy ridges of the top of the creature's mouth.

"AHH, YES. YOUR FAITH LEAVES YOUR SPIRIT WITH EVERY SCREAM. IT FEELS SO NICE TO INHALE IT DEEP INTO MY LUNGS. DELICIOUS." It laughed and snarled so loudly into Father Henry's head that his ears began to bleed. Thick, sticky saliva ran down the priest's head and face in foamy strands. The creature's black-pink tongue made its way into his ears, his nose, and his mouth, forcing him to gag as it went further down his throat. He grabbed at its face and flailed, trying to break free, but it was to no avail. Its thick teeth were a vise, clamping down ever-so carefully on the priest so as to not crush any of the bones in his skull. Father Henry tried his hardest to keep his eyes shut, but the creature's tongue still managed to slither and pry its way in, its saliva stinging and blurring his vision. He gained enough composure to reach into his back pocket and take out the crucifix that he had earlier, and with the rest of his strength, stabbed it into the beast's side. It let go of his head and yelped. The priest gasped for air and ran out of the woods, wiping his face with his garment. His hair was wet and flat. He stood up and instinctively backed away while continuing to wipe his eyes.

"Father! Over here! Keep coming this way!" yelled Albert.

The creature yanked the crucifix out and stood there, watching them both.

"ENJOY YOUR REMAINING YEARS IN THE CHURCH, FATHER. AND ENJOY YOUR TIME WITH YOUR WIFE, STRAWBERRY." With a final laugh, it flew off. Its laugh faded, echoing throughout the barrens, shaking the trees, startling the birds into flight, and scattering the insects about.

Albert ran up to the priest and guided him the rest of the way to their cars. Father Henry was stiff and had a thousand-yard stare. Dried blood and saliva were in streaks down the side of his head.

"I'm sorry, Father. I should've-" Albert stopped. The priest got into his car like a robot and drove away. Albert got in his truck and slumped over, propping his head up with his arm that rested on his center console. He half-expected the devil to open up the truck and hop in the passenger seat.

CHAPTER 28

Caleb woke up early, had cereal for breakfast, put on his backpack full of various things, and began roaming his neighborhood with one clear objective in his mind: convince a good amount of kids to take a nice little stroll deep back into the pine barrens. He started to walk down to a small development about a mile down the road, his hands in his hoodie pocket. This was the development Chester lived in, and upon getting there, Caleb noticed turkey buzzards perched on the roof of his house. They flew and circled high above as well. Caleb walked on past the tidy lawn and up the stairs to the front porch. One ring of the doorbell and soon Chester was at the door.

"...what do you want?"

"Hey Chester. Heh, I'm surprised your dad didn't answer and chase me off the porch. Listen, I g-"

"My dad's *dead*. He was sick for the past couple years."

"Oh. Wel-"

"Leave. Me. *ALONE*!!" Chester slammed the door.

Well, there go my chances for my first recruit, Caleb thought. He tried a few other houses where he knew there were kids who went to his school, but got no answer in return. He decided to head back towards his home and checked a section of a park that was near that had a couple of small baseball fields and some large pavilions with benches for outdoor events. It was fairly cold outside, but a group of kids had come out to play some two-hand touch football. As he was walking up to them, they stopped playing to take a breather, but then he saw two of the kids get circled around by the others. It seemed almost like some sort of planned fight to Caleb, lacking any loud ramp-up or spontaneity. He got closer to watch. The kids looked at him, then looked back at the fight. The two kids in the middle were both keeping their distance. A few punches were thrown, and then they backed off again. A few more punches were traded, but they didn't fully land. After a while the crowd stopped egging them on and started cracking up about how shitty of a fight it was. Caleb was confused, but kids have their trivial bullshit that they have to settle. The two fighters even shook hands afterwards.

"Who is that?"

"I think it's Caleb. Jake's lil' bro."

"Hey guys. Been playing for a while?"

"Yeah, wanna join? Always looking for more players."

Caleb recognized most of them, many being from the trailer park not too far away. They were almost all older than him, around Jake's age. He felt intimidation trying to crawl up and settle into his throat, but was too determined to let that happen.

"I was actually wondering if *you* guys wanted to join in on something." Caleb was taking a head count as he talked. Ten in total. Was that enough? What was a 'sizeable amount' to the Jersey Devil?

"Oh yeah? What's that?" They all seemed interested.

"I found this really weird thing in the woods. It's in a trap and I don't know what to do."

"Weird thing?"

"What is it?"

"Yoo, what?"

"What's it look like?"

"Well, it's like, this really tall animal, but it's part human. I don't know, it's hard to describe, you guys gotta come check this out," said Caleb, hoping the lie he had crafted piqued their interest enough for them to follow him into the barrens. If not, he had one last trick up his sleeve.

"The hell?"

"This lil' dude is nuts!"

"Yo, where's Jake at? I can't believe this."

"We gonna keep playin' or…?"

"Where at?"

"It's by a trail that starts behind my house," Caleb said, fingers crossed behind his back.

"I don't know, I think we just wanna play for a little longer then go have some lunch."

"But…it…*talked* to me."

"What?"

"Yoo, I'm going, I gotta see this shit!"

"Wait, what did it say?"

"Bro, what?"

"You don't live too far away, right?"

Caleb was ecstatic; the interest he had garnered made him feel powerful. He had a group of kids, either older or the same age as him, under his control just from his words.

"Yeah, I live down the street. And, well, it pleaded with me. It asked me to help it. Guys, I'm not sure what we should do," replied Caleb.

"Let's not make any decisions until we get there. C'mon, let's go."

"Hold on. You guys play for a little longer. I need to grab a couple of friends who want to come, then we'll come back and go together." An idea popped into Caleb's head. He wasn't finished yet. He could get more than this group. And maybe he could impress the Jersey Devil.

The group of kids looked at each other.

"Alright, same teams? *We* get first possession this time?"

No one disagreed.

"Come back soon, Caleb. Better not be bullshittin' us!"

"I'm not!" Caleb said, already starting to run down and to the trailer park. He had wished it hadn't come to this, but being pressed by time, he had to resort to something dreadful. Dreadful, but depending on what the devil wanted to do with this group of kids, could end up being sweet vengeance. He rushed down the street and made it to the trailer park in an impressive two minutes. He stopped to catch his breath, and then walked down the smaller road with trailers lined to the left and right of him. He knew which one it was. The trailer was a rusty red, three rows down and to the right. It had a whole bunch of random shit hanging from it and in the microscopic yard. He walked up to it and a small dog barked at him from the beaten-up screen door. He heard random yelling as he knocked on the door. One of them answered, saw who it was, and quickly got the other two. They rushed out to the tiny porch where Caleb was, crowding the area. Caleb backed off, not wanting to be cramped on the porch, and he almost fell going backwards down the couple of steps.

"Oh my god, don't fall, Caleb!"

"He's ok, he can handle himself."

"Hiii, Caleeebbb!"

The Midwell sisters. One looked like a toad (sounded like one too), one looked like a rat (also sounded like one), and one looked like she was kicked in the face by a horse (no, she didn't sound like a horse, but she *did* sound like a wailing seagull). The Toad picked her nose as she watched Caleb. They were all wondering why he would come up to their trailer, and awaited his next words with great anticipation. Caleb clenched his jaw and looked up. These three girls had been cause for great humiliation and agitation over the years for Caleb.

"Listen, I don't have much time to explain, but I'm gonna hang out with some friends back in the woods, wanna join? I found something pretty cool back there."

"Wooow. *Caleb*? Asking *us* to hang out with him?"

"Yeah, seems sudden, but…"

"What'd you find?"

"I'll explain as we walk. We kinda need to go. *Now*," Caleb was counting the seconds.

"Now hold on there, mister. You can't just ask three pretty little ladies like us to tag along and go with no questions asked. Do you *reeeally* want us to come?" asked the Rat. Caleb sighed.

"Yes."

"Yes, what?"

"Yeah I want you guys to come along. *Please* can we just get going now?"

"Hold on. Girls, c'mere." The Midwell sisters convened in a huddle, turned away from Caleb. After some whispering and giggling, they faced him again.

"Ok, Caleb. We'll come along. But fiiiirst, you gotta give each of us a kiss!"

Caleb put his hand to his head and let out an even deeper sigh. He looked around the area for anyone else that might seem like they'd come instead, but there was no one. He was about to sacrifice his first kiss, no, first *three* kisses, to the Midwell sisters. But he was compelled by his mission, so, with a gulp, agreed.

"Oh my god!"

"Yay yay yay!"

"I called dibs first!!"

"No way, *I* came up with the plan, first kiss is *mine*!"

They argued. It sounded like a fight had broken out in a private backwater zoo. It was mainly the Rat and Seagull screeching at each other back and forth while the Toad was now eating her boogers. Then she walked up to Caleb, and ol' Booger Breath held him by the face and gave him a big, wet smooch. The sound of the smooch shocked the other two sisters so much that they started slapping at the Toad. The Toad was laughing so much she didn't care.

Caleb grimaced and wiped his mouth with his sleeve. The Rat walked up to him and looked up at him, as she was much shorter. She got on her tippy-toes and Caleb flinched as her face drew closer to his. Her rancid breath invaded his nostrils; it came from a dead tooth he could see in the front of her mouth. She ever-so-slowly kissed his lips with a strong sucking motion that made him feel like he was kissing a fish. He recoiled, disgusted as it ended. One more. Just one more to go. Horse-kicked Face stood in front of him, confident. Her smirk bothered Caleb. She grabbed the side of his head near his ear and went for it. She gave him some tongue. Then a lot more tongue. Caleb didn't know what to do with his tongue, but when he started gagging he pushed her off.

"Alright, alright!!" He spat and wiped his face. "Can we *go* now!?"

The Midwell sisters laughed, agreed, and they started their walk to the park. Caleb tried to speed walk and influence their pace. He was hoping with all his might that the kids from the park were still there. Those three kisses felt like an eternity, but surely it had only been a minute or two tops.

"Caleb, you're a good kisser!"

"You think? I thought he could use some work."

"Hahaha!"

"So, Caleb, what's in the woods you wanna show everyone, huh?"

"You'll just have to see for yourself," Caleb said, smiling.

"Ooh, wow. Mysterious!"

They were almost at the park.

"So Caleb, I got a question for you: who do you think's prettiest outta us three?"

"Psh," Caleb shook his head and scoffed. There was no way he was going to answer that.

"He looked at me for a second! It's me! I knew it!" said the Rat.

"Nuh uh!"

"Shut up! No he didn't…right, Caleb?"

"Thank god," Caleb muttered under his breath as he saw the group of kids finishing up their game.

"Hah! Look at this stud!"

"Wow, Jake's little bro is a real lady's man, huh?"

"Damn, Caleb. You brought some real lookers."

The group gave Caleb a lot of shit. The Midwell sisters joined in on the fun.

"I bet he's a better kisser than all of you!" said the Toad.

"You kissed her!?"

"Not just her," the other two sisters said in unison. Caleb was red-faced. The group let out a cacophony of laughter.

"Are we *going* or not? You guys still wanna see?" Caleb said. He was getting fed up.

"Calm down, lil' bro. We just got done so, yeah, let's see this thing."

They followed Caleb to his house. Rain began to fall from the sky, at first in small intervals, making them feel like they could make out the sound of each individual drop. But it soon all became that beautiful, calming, one-note symphony many of us know and love. As the rain pattered onto the asphalt, it gave off the smell of childhood and wonder. Although it was cold, it was still light enough not to bother any of them. Once they arrived, Caleb told the group to wait a second and went inside his house. He zoomed into the bathroom, turned on the sink, and rinsed out his mouth in a chaotic fashion. After he was done he took a big swig of mouthwash and swished it around for a moment before spitting it all out. He spat more into the sink, shook his head, and then ran back out before his foster dad could start something with him.

"All good. Let's go."

It knew they were coming; they were easy to sense once they stepped into the barrens. Thirteen plus one. Perfect. And with time to spare. Things were finally coming together. It had been crafting a plan. The revelation those four children had given it changed everything. For once, it was not just existing anymore. It had a goal, a newfound feeling inside. *Something* inside. Truth is, it didn't know what it was, but it spoke to him. It compelled him.

Time was becoming an enemy for Hunter and Hannah. They were still down in that dark hole, captives of the creature. They didn't know what day it was. They were bored. They just wanted to go home. At night, they would both go up near the entrance because they had been hearing strange sounds. They weren't sure what exactly it was, but had reserved their theories. The creature slid over the drawer and opened up the trapdoor to give them more food and water. It was about to close the door again, but Hunter spoke up.

"Wait."

"HM?"

"You sleep here, don't you?"

"USUALLY. WHY?"

"You make noises in your sleep." Hunter looked at the scratch marks it had on its arms. "And maybe it goes past just making noises."

"Yeah, like our daddy! He has trouble sleeping. Real itchy too! Too many mosquitoes," Hannah said.

"MM. WHAT OF IT?"

"It's like...you're troubled. What's wrong?"

"OH? AND WHY ARE YOU CONCERNED?"

"Why are you keeping us here!?" Hunter couldn't keep it in anymore. "If you're gonna kill us, just do it already. I know we don't stand a chance against you. You rubbing it in that much more by keeping us here? Huh?"

"Hunter..." Hannah was getting upset. The beast sighed.

"THINGS ARE DEVELOPING FAST NOW. GREAT THINGS." It looked at them with that one awful eye for what felt like minutes. "I GUESS I'VE HAD MY FUN WITH YOU. I WILL CONSIDER LETTING YOU GO TONIGHT. MY PRIORITIES HAVE SHIFTED. THEY WILL BE HERE SOON. EAT. DRINK. KEEP YOUR EARS OPEN TONIGHT."

"What do you-" Hunter couldn't get his next question out before it left and slammed the door. The drawer slid over the entrance and a newfound hope surfaced in the siblings' hearts.

"We can leave soon then? Right, Hunter?"

"Yeah..."

They both looked down at the food and water. Minutes later they heard voices outside, but they were too muffled to make anything out.

"Whoa, I never knew there were, like, ruins and shit back here!"

"Right? Look at that old house!"

"Was a cabin or something, I bet."

"Duh. It's made outta wood, dumbass."

Laughter. Caleb's nerves were jumping and buzzing inside of him.

"It's here," he said.

"Wait, it's trapped in the old house?"

"Woow, romantic, Caleb," said the Rat.

A large, black hoof appeared from the darkness and stomped down on the earth beneath it.

"Th-that's-"

"I thought you said it was trapped!!"

It anticipated their fear. They were already sinking into a mucky mire. All of them struggled, but to no avail. One of the older kids dropped the football he was holding. The Jersey Devil came and picked it up, inspecting it.

"HMM. THE SKIN OF A PIG? INTERESTING..." it muttered.

The mud felt like it was sucking their strength away, because even when they tried their absolute hardest to pull themselves out, they only sank deeper. It fed off of their struggle. The devil would not let them perish, however, limiting the depth of the mire to come up to around their knees. Many flailed and screamed, flicking mud all over. Caleb stood there and accepted it, but the creature came over to him and pulled him out with one arm, placing him down and away from the thick mud. Caleb got a kick out of watching the Midwell sisters squirm and yell, helpless. The creature walked up in front of the thirteen kids and spread its wings, holding its arms out in grand fashion.

"I AM BOTH THE DESOLATION AND THE BEAUTY OF THE BARRENS. TEEMING WITH LIFE AND ROTTING WITH DECAY. BASKING IN THE RAYS OF LIGHT AND STALKING UNDER THE COVER OF DARKNESS. TODAY YOU WILL MAKE A FATEFUL DECISION: VOW TO JOIN ME, OR DIE SLOWLY AS MUD AND SLUDGE OVERTAKE YOUR BODY, FILLING UP YOUR MOUTH, STOMACH, AND LUNGS." It paused, giving them a moment to make their decision. All of them were quiet now, as fear, shock, and awe gripped them tight. They were paralyzed. But none of them wanted to die, so they all accepted the devil's most generous offer. "PERFECT. WE WILL BEGIN! COME."

The Jersey Devil solidified the ground and the kids wiggled their way out and followed it to the clearing with the large oak tree. Caleb noticed it was much more composed around that tree now. He walked beside the beast, shooting glances up at it, hoping, yearning for any gesture or word of approval. They stopped when they were all in the clearing near the tree. It stood in front of them, with Caleb still by its side.

"DESTINY HAS BROUGHT US ALL TOGETHER TODAY. YES, I CAN TELL BY YOUR FACES, I WILL CONFIRM THIS: I AM WHAT MANY CONSIDER 'THE JERSEY DEVIL'. MAYBE YOU HAVE LIVED YOUR YOUNG LIVES UP TO THIS POINT IN CONFUSION, UNABLE TO FIT IN OR FIND A PURPOSE. BUT TODAY THAT ALL CHANGES. YOUR PURPOSE IS A GREAT ONE. WIPE THE FEAR FROM YOUR FACES AND THE PERIL OUT OF YOUR EYES. DO NOT COWER, HUNCHED OVER, BUT INSTEAD STAND UP TALL. YOU ARE IN THE PRESENCE OF GREAT POWER, AND I WISH TO BESTOW SOME OF THAT POWER UNTO YOU ALL TODAY. ALL YOU MUST DO IS TRUST IN ME. DO I HAVE YOUR TRUST?"

The kids looked around at each other. They were still in shock, but the devil's words were surprisingly sweet, dancing around inside of their heads like a nice song. Its earlier ultimatum made them feel like they didn't have much of a choice, and they all acquiesced, nodding their heads.

"WONDERFUL. MY FAITHFUL SERVANT HERE WILL HAND OUT SOMETHING I HAVE PREPARED FOR YOU ALL." The devil motioned with his hands and thirteen branches came winding down around him and Caleb. The branches carried wooden masks that had one eye hole for the right eye. The spot where the left eye hole should have been instead had some of the devil's blood strewn in a messy streak going down the mask. He collected them all and set them beside Caleb. Caleb understood, and started handing out the masks one-by-one, exchanging awkward glances with the thirteen others. Once they were all passed out, the Jersey Devil looked at all of them. Its face was fierce and excited. The kids marveled at its one, big eye. They could see the red veins like rivers inside of it.

"THESE MASKS DISTRIBUTE MY ENERGY. YOU ARE ABOUT TO TASTE THE VIGOR AND POTENTIALITY OF A GOD. ALL OF YOU, PLACE YOUR MASK OVER YOUR FACE." They did as it told them, holding the mask against their face. There were no straps on these, however. "NOW I WILL TEACH YOU A PRINCIPAL RULE OF OUR WORLD: WITH GREAT POWER COMES GREAT SACRIFICE."

Caleb heard an odd sound before all of the thirteen kids wailed out in pain, holding both of their hands up to their masks. Some fell to their knees. Red trickled down the left side of their necks, dripping further down to their torsos. *Blood? But from where?* Caleb pondered. He then understood how the masks were staying on their faces without straps. They tried to pry the masks off of their faces, but couldn't manage to do so. He looked up at the creature, who had its eye closed in deep concentration. It was letting out a deep hum that Caleb could feel in his chest. Wind surged around the area and a red light emanated from the devil's eye hole. The muffled cries of pain came to a halt and were replaced with sighs of relief. The wind subsided and the sinister glow faded from the creature's face.

"YOU FEEL IT, DON'T YOU? LET MY POWER NOW FLOW THROUGH YOU ALL. YOU HAVE DONE WELL. IT WON'T BE LONG BEFORE YOU WILL BE ABLE TO WITNESS HOW GREAT IT IS. STAND ASIDE, PLEASE." The kids parted like a sea and the devil made a spreading motion with its arms. Then it held out its large hands and motioned with them again, intricate lines on its twisted horns glowing an immaculate green, and before them in the clearing came roots and all matters of leaves and ferns forming something large in the middle. It was miraculous. They witnessed an entire structure made from the earth be built before them. It resembled a large tent. The creature urged them to enter. They went inside and saw two columns of seven beds made out of comfortable-looking plant matter.

"THE PINE BARRENS WELCOME YOU."

They were happy. An excitement replaced any and all fear that had been inside of them. They felt good and chatted inside their new base. The beast took Caleb outside. Caleb almost couldn't stand it anymore, but was glad he now had its undivided attention.

"COME." They walked back to the old cabin, standing outside of it. "GOOD WORK. I AM BEGINNING TO TRUST YOU AGAIN. WE NOW HAVE A PROPER GROUP. I CAN SAFELY EXIT THE FOREST FOR A LONG AMOUNT OF TIME, AS THEY ARE ALL AN EXTENSION OF MYSELF NOW. WE WILL WREAK HAVOC. I HAVE HAD A CRAVING FOR CHAOS AND MISCHIEF FOR QUITE A WHILE NOW. I DO NOT KNOW WHERE IT HAS COME FROM, BUT I FIND IT IMPORTANT. WILL YOU LEAD THEM?"

"Y-yes. Yes I will. But…"

"BUT?"

"Why can't I have some of your power?"

"YOU ARE DIFFERENT, CALEB."

"O-oh. Okay, well what am I gonna do then? How will I lead them?"

"YOU WILL DECIDE WHAT WE DO FIRST. MY POWER IS AT YOUR DISPOSAL. TAKE IT AS A TOKEN OF GOOD FAITH. I CAN SEE IT IN YOUR EYES. THE PAIN. THE ANGER. NOW IS THE TIME TO CHANNEL THAT. THINK ABOUT IT. TOMORROW NIGHT WE WILL ACT. MAKE YOUR DECISION BY THEN."

Caleb sat there, dumbfounded. Then a few ideas popped into his mind.

"Thank you. We'll have some fun, don't worry about that. I gotta ask, you got the mask idea from me, didn't you?"

"AND IF I DID?"

Caleb laughed.

"Y'know, I have some other cool things, too. I've been wanting to show you. Sit down." It took a moment to consider and let its curiosity get the better of it. They both sat, propping up against trees near the old cabin. Caleb took off his backpack and opened it. The creature was curious.

"I *DO* HAVE MY OWN PLANS WITH THE OTHERS. I CANNOT IDLE FOR LONG."

"Oh yeah? What plans?" Caleb asked, rummaging through the bookbag.

"YOU WILL KNOW IN TIME. LET'S JUST SAY YOU AND YOUR THREE OTHER FRIENDS HAVE OPENED A DOOR TO A REALM I NEVER KNEW EXISTED."

"What, when we told you what the legend of the Jersey Devil was? I guess if it's true, it's some startling info if you weren't aware of it."

"MMMM..."

"Anyways, look. I brought a couple of cool things I wanted to see. As a kid in today's day and age, here are some things I like to do for fun."

The beast raised one of its furrowed brows. Caleb thought he looked funny. He took out a comic book, a handheld game console, a pack of chips, and a can of soda.

"First I'll show you a comic book. It's like a picture book, but with more action and cool characters from a whole made-up universe. This is the good guy and he's fighting the bad guy."

"I SEE. THE TIMELESS STRUGGLE OF POWER DISPLAYED IN A BOOK. WHO WINS THE FIGHT?"

"I'm not sure, it leaves off on a cliffhanger. You gotta buy the next volume to continue the story."

"...WHY NOT HAVE THE ENTIRE STORY IN ONE BOOK?"

"Um, I guess they want to keep selling comics so they do them in shorter volumes. It takes time to draw all of it too."

"I SEE."

"Next is one of my favorite things. My brother Jake and I worked a whole summer to get this. It's a GamePal. It lets you play video games anywhere."

"VIDEO GAMES? HOW IS THAT LITTLE MAN MOVING?"

"I'm controlling him with the buttons! You progress through levels by making it to the end of each one."

"YOU JUST DESTROYED THAT TINY MUSHROOM MAN."

"Yeah, there are enemies and obstacles you have to get past. Sometimes you get power ups too!"

"GET HIM TOO! CRUSH HIM UNDERNEATH YOUR FEET. YOU'RE EVEN BIGGER NOW, YOUR POWER GROWS!"

"Got him! End of the level, woo! And you get to retry the level again as long as you have enough lives. It's just a game, but digital."

"DIGITAL? HOW EXACTLY DO THESE MOVING PICTURES WORK?"

"Well. It's electronic. Energy from electricity, like lightning." The beast looked up towards the sky.

"LIGHTNING..."

"It has batteries. People code it on computers I think. I'm not smart enough to do it, but it's so fun. Wanna try?"

The creature took the GamePal in its massive hands and struggled, as it was pressing multiple buttons at once. The game company did not have legendary monsters in mind when creating their console. The video game character fell into a pit and died.

"...oh. Well that's ok. It's just too small for you."

"I WILL WATCH YOU PLAY A LITTLE LONGER."

"Ok!" Caleb opened a bag of chips and the can of soda.

"THOSE. I'VE SEEN MANY OF BOTH OF THOSE LITTERED IN AND AROUND MY DOMAIN."

"Oh. I'm sorry. I try not to litter. These are chips and this is a soda. They're snacks. You eat chips when you don't wanna eat a full meal. And soda tastes so good."

"I AM UNFAMILIAR WITH 'SNACKS'. I EAT AND USE EVERY PART OF ALL ANIMALS I KILL IN ORDER TO HONOR ITS SACRIFICE."

"Well try one then. They're crunchy," Caleb said, pointing the bag towards the beast. It reached two fingers in the bag and picked up a chip. It sniffed it and then put it in its mouth, chewing thoughtfully.

"MMM. MADE FROM A VEGETABLE? THIS IS WHAT I SENSE. NOT BAD, BUT I WOULD NOT WANT TO EAT TOO MANY."

"Yeah, potatoes. Potato chips. You can get 'em in different flavors. Want a sip of soda?" The beast smelled the can from Caleb's hand and squinted its eye.

"I'M NOT SO SURE…"

"Oh, c'mon. One sip won't kill you."

It took the can from Caleb's hand and took a swig. It winced and swallowed, shaking its head.

"WHAT IS THIS POISON? IT IS BURNING MY THROAT AND CHES-" it let out a large burp. Caleb couldn't help but laugh. "THE TASTE WAS ODD, BUT IF IT HARMS ME, MARK MY WORDS, YOU WILL SUFFER TOO."

"I'm not worried," Caleb said, still looking down at his GamePal. He beat a tough level.

"YOU ARE GOOD AT THESE GAMES. THANK YOU FOR SHOWING ME THESE. IT WAS MORE ENJOYABLE THAN I EXPECTED. I ASK THAT YOU RETURN TO THE CAMP NOW. DON'T FORGET–TOMORROW NIGHT WILL BE OUR FIRST VENTURE, AND IT WILL BE WHAT YOU WISH TO DO. KNOW WHAT THAT WILL BE BY THEN."

"Gotcha. I will, don't worry. Later!"

"GOODBYE." The Jersey Devil watched him leave and looked towards the cabin. After a moment of thought, he went in and opened up the trapdoor. Hunter and Hannah were already close to the entrance, listening as the creature had told them to.

"COME OUT." Its voice echoed into the cellar. They both hugged each other tight, crying, unable to hold in their excitement and relief. They walked up the stairs.

"Thank you. Thank you. We'll never say anything or come back, I swear," said Hunter.

"ARE YOU SURE YOU TWO DO NOT WISH TO BE A PART OF WHAT IS HAPPENING? YOU WILL BE AMONG FRIENDS. AND I ASSURE YOU, YOU WILL BE STRONGER THAN YOUR ENEMIES WITH MY POWER LENDED TO YOU."

"Friends? I knew I heard Caleb. What are-you know what? I don't even want to know what you guys're up to," Hunter said. He held up the vial and wiggled it between his fingers. "I got what I wanted days ago.

We're okay, right, Hannah?" Hannah nodded, timidly. They started making their way out.

"VERY WELL."

Hannah turned around one last time to look at him.

"Thank you again…f-for the flowers." She turned around and they were off.

CHAPTER 28

That night there was a knock on the door. It was shortly followed by a scream. The scream was followed by tears and an embrace. Hunter and Hannah had returned in one piece, and not in body bags. Albert and Lily were so overjoyed that the kids could barely enter the house.

"I appreciate the hugs and everything, but could we please step more inside?" asked Hunter. He missed home. After a cathartic Lawless family reunion, the questions came.

"Where did you go? We looked everywhere for you," asked Lily.

"We just went to hang out with some friends. The usual. I guess a celebration for getting our project done. Hannah asked to tag along so we went."

"But I didn-" Hannah couldn't finish.

"And then we took a walk in the woods to get some fresh air, an-"

"And we met their friend in the woods! He was big an-"

"Yeah, haha, um, Caleb is pretty tall. But anyways-"

"Son. Listen. I know," Albert said. Hunter was at a loss for words. Albert got up and gave Hunter another hug. "I know, I know...that *thing* had you, didn't it?" Hunter began to cry. On the TV behind them the news headline read: Thirteen More Missing Children in Hamberton Township.

"I'm just, I'm just glad it's over. The whole time we just wanted to be home. We didn't want to end up li-"

"Shh. It's okay. We're here, home, safe," Lily said, holding Hannah by her side. A short silence occurred before Hunter asked a question that gave Albert chills.

"Do you think it'll leave us alone?"

"I-well, I don't know." Crows cawed outside. They all shuttered at the sound. Such an awful sound, especially at night time. It felt like they were everywhere, cloaked within the black of night, their feathers indistinguishable from the darkness. Charcoal tally marks on a blackboard. Lily quickly changed the subject, asking them, even though it was late, if they wanted anything to eat.

"You both must be starving. I'll get some water."

"Actually, Hunter's friend gave us water and some weird food to eat. I didn't like it too much," said Hannah. Hunter wished she would keep her mouth shut.

"Maybe the bastard does have some kind of a conscience," said Albert, baffled. He gave out a few laughs as he sighed. While Hunter and Hannah were snacking, Albert went and got everyone's pillows and sheets and started making a pillow fort in the living room, which he found surprisingly difficult to do with only one hand. Everyone else noticed and started to help.

After they were done he put some cartoons on the TV and they all snuggled together, munching on popcorn. *Not gonna be out of reach tonight*, he thought, looking at his family. It wasn't before long they were all snoozing in the pillow fort, happy to be a family again.

The next morning Albert went outside and looked around.

"Motherfucker," he said with a sardonic smile. Bird shit was everywhere. All over the yard, the house, and his truck. He thought he could hear a deep laughter echoing from the woods in the distance. With the smile still on his face, he flipped up the middle finger out in the direction of the woods, then he went back inside.

CHAPTER 29

Lola's lips were dry from the cold. She had been out exploring for a while with nothing very interesting to show for it, but she was still enjoying the quiet day with Crash, who was in a cat backpack Lola had bought. He didn't seem to mind it, as his curious eyes peered out through the mesh windows. And thankfully he wasn't too heavy to carry around. It was just about four in the afternoon; she began just before noon and felt that she was making good time. She was surprised at how well she could read and follow a map. Lola expected the first half-or-so of her extensive trip out into the barrens to be uneventful–she was saving the bigger and more interesting-sounding points of interest for last. And now it was finally time to head towards the first one: the blue hole.

As she walked along, she wondered how many trees she had seen so far. How many pinecones, leaves, and nettles? Thousands? Tens of thousands? The forest made her feel small, but there was an appreciation in that. She hadn't felt a presence either. No feeling of being watched or anything of the sort. This disappointed her because the deep desire of seeing if she could come face-to-face with the urban legend itself once again burned within her. An ocean of thoughts ebbed and flowed within her mind, and she drifted through them, almost becoming unaware of the forest she was in. She felt like she was ready and hoped that feeling wasn't too audacious.

The blue hole was within sight. It really was as beautiful as she had thought it would be, but then she remembered what had happened not that long ago. Yellow crime scene tape tarnished the otherwise picture-perfect scene. The juxtaposition of ugly death with beautiful nature depressed her. She imagined one of her students drowning in the hole. A nascent, shining life full of possibilities taken away in the cold, quiet darkness. She shuddered. It was going to get dark soon. She took Crash out of the cat backpack, gave him some treats and held him close.

The air around them felt red from the sunset peeking behind the gentle storm clouds. If it rained, they were expecting blood. With their masks adorned and sitting around the Jersey Devil, they knew they were hours, minutes away from their first taste of pure chaos. Caleb had made his decision. They waited with a hungry patience. He stepped up before them, the beast motioning him to speak.

"Y'know, for as long as I remember the only one that was ever there for me was my brother. I'll never know why the world took away my parents before I could even get to know them, but I know the world had potential to help me still have a decent life. But I've never had a decent life. I've tried to get out my anger, but tonight will be the night I feel like I can truly get it all out," Caleb said. Nodding, understanding heads were the only response. He lifted up his shirt, revealing bruises and other marks. "You see these? Foster dad. After tonight, no more of these. I'm sick of them. They hurt. So let's make someone else hurt. Follow me to my house. He'll be there, and I bet he'll be drunk or passed out."

A chill wind gusted. They could all feel the energy they were all emanating. Teeming to test out the power of the creature that coursed through their veins, they ventured forth to Caleb's house. Along their way they chatted and shared their own stories akin to Caleb's, consoling each other and letting things out. Caleb felt a strange feeling inside of him. Was it pride, or something else?

Lola had taken in all of the conflicting emotions she could handle from the blue hole, which now wasn't blue at all. The sunset spilled out its magnificent oranges and purples on the water, and with one last look, she turned around to face the encroaching darkness. The map showed the 'lost village' area being roughly around where Albert Lawless had pointed out where he first met the devil. It was her number one interest, and it was time to go. She pulled out her flashlight, knowing she would need it soon. Northwest.

But she stopped. It hadn't even been five minutes. She heard a noise that, previously, only she had been making: footsteps. She hid behind the biggest tree in her proximity and watched. Children? And…a lot at that. They looked strange, but she couldn't make out too much. She did see a resemblance in all of their faces, their silhouettes cutting through the woods with the red sunset peeking through around them. Masks? It unsettled her further.

The creature sensed her. A familiar scent. It soared high above the group as they made their way through the woods. It was excited, paying no mind to Lola, not seeing her as a threat. Caleb and the thirteen others marched onward. Will Tate was indeed sleeping in his reclining chair with the TV still on. He had no idea he was as good as dead. The Jersey

Devil landed in the small backyard with a whoosh. Caleb's breathing accelerated, adrenaline already pumping through his veins. He stared at the front porch steps. The thirteen others quietly awaited his orders.

Will Tate found himself floating. Was it a dream? He felt like he might've been floating through the sky with angels, soaring through the clouds, and looking down at the world below. Or was it just the alcohol swaying his mind back and forth like a ship in rough seas? His mind sloshed through the different possibilities, questioning how grounded in reality he really was. When he thought he opened his eyes and saw that he was being carried out the back sliding-glass door by six-or-so bigger teenagers, he closed his eyes again, wondering where his alcohol-ridden mind would take him next. He smelled outside. He envisioned himself as a child with his dad at the park. Before his accident, when he was still happy. But even that world crumbled down before him as he managed to open his eyes again and saw some horrific black creature standing in front of him with kids in masks all around. He closed and opened his eyes once more, but this time nothing changed. No magical blink would take him away. Instead, he was now trapped in some sort of nightmare. Before he could think anymore, a voice entered his head that pulled him into the present like a loud alarm.

"WILL TATE. YOU HAVE VOLUNTEERED OF YOUR OWN WILL TO ACT AS A FATHER, AND NOT ONLY HAVE YOU FAILED, YOU HAVE WILLINGLY MADE THE LIVES OF THOSE YOU SWORE TO SUPPORT WORSE. DO YOU HAVE ANYTHING TO SAY FOR YOURSELF?"

Will looked around and struggled, but the grips of the teenagers holding onto him were abnormally strong. He kept flailing his limbs.

"What the fuck!? Let go of me! Let go of me right fuckin' now!!"

Caleb looked on with a frown that hinted that he was on the verge of tears. He clenched his jaw and gave them a nod. To get a better grasp on Will, two held onto each arm, two held onto each leg, one held onto his head, and two held his torso at either side. The remaining two were digging a hole in the backyard. He could see the veins popping from under the skin on their arms and necks and wondered if they were still human.

"What are you doing!? Stop!!" Will Tate's cries continued and elevated into shrieks of agony as they began to pull him apart. They were slow and thorough, and Caleb heard the ligaments and tendons snap. Will made a weird gargle-choking sound as his head was pulled away from his body. Then the flesh began to tear, making a sound Caleb could only relate to the sound of pulling apart a rotisserie chicken. His left arm went first, then his right leg. The other arm and leg followed at the same time as his head did, which made an even worse, incomprehensible tearing sound. Caleb did not avert his eyes. The blood was now spraying out in rhythmic, red streaks, covering everyone. Stringy, blue and red veins and vessels hung out of the fleshy stumps, continuing to spatter the blood everywhere. The Jersey Devil began to laugh, and the masked executioners mimicked it. Caleb just stared. Then he looked down at the blood on his clothes and felt an odd mixture of happiness and disgust. It was like when he had crushed a bird's skull to put it out of its misery after a neighborhood stray clawed its guts out.

"THIS IS JUST THE BEGINNING. DID YOU FEEL HOW EASY IT WAS TO REND THE FLESH OF SUCH A MAN? THIS IS HOW ALL SCUM SHOULD MEET THEIR END, AND WE WILL BE THE ARBITERS OF SUCH DEATH. KEEP THE ARMS AND LEGS. BURY THE REST. WE WILL RETURN TO OUR DWELLING NOW."

They threw the head and body into the hole and covered it up. The thirteen kids had never felt so alive and in control. They hungered for more bloodshed already. As they walked back, the beast and Caleb were in front.

"SO, CALEB, HOW DO YOU FEEL?" The beast was smiling in anticipation.

"It was…it was unlike anything I've seen or felt before," Caleb replied in a monotone voice.

During this time, Lola had made her way northwest. She had passed the area with the old cabin and the large tree in the clearing without ever knowing they were there. Her footsteps were quicker as darkness followed the sunset. Seeing those children with masks shook her and she began questioning whether they were all a part of her imagination or not. As she thought, she tripped over roots and bramble she couldn't see. Noticing some interesting stone formations at her feet, she took out her flashlight and shined it around. Among the dead leaves, nettles, and branches jutted out weathered stones. She pointed the light around. More of them, some more intact than others. An old, deteriorated angel statue judged her with mossed-over eyes. She had found herself in some sort of old cemetery. She went to some of the more intact headstones to try to read what was on them, but couldn't make out much until one of the last ones she planned on checking; she could make out "REBECCA LIVINGSTON 1690 - 1766".

"Wow, remnants of a cemetery dating back over 200 years? There's gotta be more around here..." Crash meowed in response. He was getting a bit antsy. "Aw, it's ok buddy. Hang in there."

She walked north from the cemetery and after about five minutes grew all the more excited. The ruins she found herself in front of were different–most consisted of wood, but some she could see had brick and stone. She looked around more and could make out where there used to be buildings. *Is this the village where everyone went missing?* she thought, but was frustrated, as there was no surefire way of knowing besides the accuracy of her map. She was thankful that there was more of a clearing around the old ruins, and shined her light all around. Up ahead looked like what she was hoping for–a building that was still standing enough for her to explore on the inside. She jogged over and to her pleasure saw the doorway into a dilapidated, worn-down building still intact. It looked shitty, but was still standing enough for her to want to know what was on the inside. The doorway, however, was obstructed by rubble. She went over to the side and saw a window, but shards of ancient glass threatened her entry. She went back to the entrance and tested the rubble with a kick. She stood back and examined it more with the flashlight.

"Hmm. I might be able to squeeze through here." She took off the cat backpack and set Crash down near the entrance, then tried to enter. She managed to get a good way in, but soon found herself stuck. The wood rubble scraped up against her and she quickly felt claustrophobic. She tried to play it off. "Damn, girl. I guess there are some downsides to being curvy." She sucked in all the breath she could and squeezed through the rest of the way, her hair catching on something behind her, yanking out a few strands. "Ouch!" She bent down, gripping her flashlight and pointing it towards Crash. He was barely within reach, but after a while, she wiggled him through at the bottom of the entrance, which had more leeway than the upper half. The rubble shifted slightly, then stopped. Lola was relieved; for some reason she didn't want to make a lot of noise right now. She almost felt like a burglar, and it gave her a rush.

The flashlight beamed around the room in Lola's eager hands. From the looks of it, it had once been a fairly large house, and this came as no surprise to her, as many families in the 1700s were bigger compared to the modern day. She had to watch her step, as the wood flooring had given out in many places. Crash gave out a few more meows.

"I know, gatito, I know. Once we search around here we'll head back. I bet you're just as cold and hungry as I am!" A couple more meows in response. The flashlight beam revealed a once open area to her left, but it was littered with debris and inaccessible as far as Lola was concerned, but a portion on the right side had held enough for her to see that there was a little hallway with two doorways on either side. The one on the right was up closer and littered with broken pieces of wood. The roof had caved in enough to let time destroy anything that could have been of interest to her. She sighed and walked down to the end of the hallway. A large spider web stood in the doorway to the next room, so she grabbed a nearby stick and cleared it out. To her surprise, this room had endured the test of time enough for her to discern most of the furniture.

"Whoa. Ok, where to start?" she muttered, teeming with excitement. First, she set down Crash in the corner of the room near the doorway. Her nose was dripping and she was losing feeling in her face, but she didn't care now. She decided to open up what looked like a wardrobe or large closet. As she opened one of the doors, it fell down with a crack and a crash, nearly landing on Lola. She jumped back and almost fell, but caught herself. "Holy shit, gotta be more careful. Whew!" She felt slight embarrassment from making a loud noise, but kept at it. There was nothing in the closet. After scrounging around the room more, she came across a dresser that had three drawers. There was a small keyhole in the top drawer. She opened the bottom first and found what was left of an old doll. It looked at her with one button-eye left that was barely hanging on. It was sad, withered and dirty. Setting it back down, she also noticed some small, wooden toys in the shapes of animals. She decided to pocket one that resembled a horse. The middle drawer contained vestiges from various fabrics, damp and dull. Top drawer time. The most mysterious one by far. She hoped it was unlocked, but it didn't give way, even with a hefty tug.

"C'mon, you bitch," she said, wiggling it more. She set down the flashlight and, using all of her force, managed to open it enough to see what was inside: some sort of book. She became dead set on getting her hands on that book, viciously wiggling the drawer, but it felt stuck, not sliding anymore. Her mind was completely filled with ways on how to get into this damn drawer. She settled on using the downward force of her body weight, trying to break it off. It bent down a bit, but didn't fully give out. She jumped up on the top of the drawer and stepped down with a determined foot. It was starting to give, and the wooden cracking sound was like music to her ears, urging her to step down harder. The drawer didn't need much more force to break, but Lola, ignorant to that fact, let all of her force down and crashed down with the drawer as it shattered. She fell down and backward with it, overextending her left leg and scraping her back on the edge of the drawer, hitting her head at the end of her fall.

"Ah! ¡*Puñeta!*" The pain writhed up her back, down her leg, and on the back of her head. "Ow...that's gonna leave a few bruises." Crash meowed in concern, standing up against the mesh window of the backpack, wanting to get out and run up to her. She got up slowly, rubbing the back of her head, old, rotted wood coming out of her hair. She stretched, grunting some more. "I'm okay, Crash. I think. Agh...hurts though." She picked up the flashlight and took the book out of the destroyed drawer. The pain became distant as she examined the book. "No way..."

Elizabeth Leeds - A Journal

9th of June, 1728

I grow tired of summer work. It bores me so I have started a journal. I do not know what it will be for, but it feels nice to jot down my thoughts. I don't see much good in sharing all my thoughts with anyone else. Being a middle child of twelve, not much I do or say gets noticed anyways. Working in the sun always makes me more tired, so I will retire to my bed for the night. Goodnight, journal.

22nd of August, 1728

I almost forgot I had started a journal. Things tend to get buried in my drawers. Regardless, I anticipate things becoming much busier around here. Father will be joining some others from the village on a journey south to spread the Good Word to the savages. Every native I've met has shown me kindness, so it confuses me why we must call them "savages". Nevertheless, I hope Father has a safe journey and won't be gone for too long. He tries to share his attention with everyone even after a busy day. I wish there was more time in the day. Maybe Mother wouldn't be so exhausted.

4th of September, 1728

Beautiful, warm summer is coming to an end so we will be preparing for autumn. I don't much care for autumn because that means winter is on its way. And oh, do I hate the cold. At least autumn brings some pretty colors. *Timmy and Tommy got in trouble at school today. I laughed at them and almost got in trouble myself!*

21st of September, 1728

I have been spending more time outside during the evening. I like to watch the bats at night. They swoop down near the lamplight, gobbling up all the bugs. The sounds of the evening are quite calming. Mother is stressed out so I asked her to just sit down with me for a little outside. I hope she does.

1st of October, 1728

We are growing corn and pumpkins this year! I love them both, so I don't mind when I have to tend to the crops. Much like ourselves, the Earth takes much tender care in order to grow beautifully. It's beginning to get colder.

20th of December, 1728

Sorry, journal, we have been so busy without Father, but he just came home today! We were all so excited, although he seems very tired. I gave him a hug and he didn't really hug back, but I understand. Thank the Lord he is home for Christmas!

25th of December, 1728

Father still doesn't have his energy back. He looks strange. Off. It's hard to say, but different. I hope he's not sick. He seemed very detached from our celebration and ate very fast. We are all becoming silently concerned. I still had a nice day. I got this gorgeous blue and white dress! Usually I don't get something as nice as that for Christmas.

7th of January, 1729

The winter has been awful. Mary and I heard something strange last night. It was way past our bedtime, but we were woken up by strange sounds coming from our parents' bedroom. We inched closer and heard Father yelling and grunting. Mother sounded like she was crying, but it was muffled. Mary and I looked at each other, confused. We had to tip-toe back quickly as we heard footsteps coming to the door.

20th of March, 1729

Spring is here and I got to wear my new dress today. I think some of the boys in school were looking at me. I don't care. I kinda like it. And even if no one noticed, I felt pretty and that's what matters. I am going to grow some flowers for Mother and Father. They don't seem to be getting along and none of us like it. We don't know what to do.

11th of July, 1729

Father yells at us now, even when we haven't done anything wrong. He also eats more of the food and leaves less for us. The light from Mother's eyes has dimmed, even though she has been with child. I wonder whether I will get another brother or sister. I am hoping for another sister because we are outnumbered seven-to-five. I fear for my journal. It's only a matter of time before Father starts rummaging through our belongings. I look at my big brothers' eyes and see fear. I don't like that. They've never been afraid of anything.

13th of October, 1729

Much has happened and we are all scared. Mother is in labor as I write this. Her pregnancy has gotten the entire town's attention. The men from the church are here, yelling at her because it doesn't sound like she wants the baby. Father is furious at her too. I have seen Mother pregnant before, but never like this. She looks so sick. I hate all of the commotion in and around our house. I have been trying to comfort my younger siblings. The doctor keeps saying that he needs to concentrate.

Hours have passed now, and Mother delivered the baby. The doctor said she is in critical condition. We are all so worried. I cried with my sisters while we prayed to God she would recover. I saw the baby and it seemed deformed. I will love my new brother no matter what, even if he has two little stubs on his head. Someone has entered the house.

The priests came again and many of the townspeople were outside the house. It is evening now and they just won't leave us alone! The older, uglier priest got in a fight with my father while he was holding the baby and he dropped the baby on the floor. He fell on the left side of his head. I hope and pray to God he is alright. They haven't given him a name yet. When will this terror end? I miss when we were a family.

19th of October, 1729

Writing helps me calm down from all of this stress. Things are just terrible. Mother keeps screaming "I don't want it, it's cursed. You're not my husband. Get away from me." Even though the doctor says she is still recovering, we are all glad to at least know she is gaining back her energy.

23rd of October, 1729

No one can find the baby. The entire town is blaming Mother, and my brother Joseph said he heard them talking about a lynching. I can't believe this. It all feels like such a nightmare. I just want to hug father and grow more pumpkins with mother.

I was trying to take a nap, but the entire outside of the house was glowing. Many of my siblings were peering out the windows, and I joined them. So many of the townspeople were holding torches and saying awful things about Mother. I ran back into my room so I could write this down. I can't handle this anymore. I can hardly sleep.

Oh my God, they just carried Mother out of the house! She was fighting them the whole time, and we were all trying to get their hands off of her. I grabbed onto one man's hands and he struck me in the face! It still stings. What do they think they are doing acting so savage inside of our house!?

4th of February, 1730

It has taken me much courage to open up this damned journal. This period of my life has been nothing but a nightmare. Our family is ruined. Tarnished. I worry for my siblings. The future scares me to death. I am sorry, journal, sorry for tainting these pages with such tragedy, but I must get things out...

They hung Mother. Up in the big oak tree in the clearing near the church. I can't even bear the thought. Imagining what she went through in her final moments, it horrifies me. It follows me into my dreams. She was a good mother. She worked hard for us. Bathed us when we were young, made sure we all had food at the table, taught us many skills like sewing and how to milk cows. She would even read to us when she had the chance. They painted her as a criminal. The only crime she committed was serving her husband! (I say husband because he feels less and less like a father as the days pass). Yes, she was indeed a good mother. I snuck out last night and carved something into that awful tree to commemorate her. They did not give her a marked grave. It saddens me so deeply that tears fall upon this very journal as I write. I hope with all of my heart my mother's tainted name will be wiped clean and she is brought the justice she deserves. It saddens me even deeper that I will never be able to achieve this of my own accord.

2nd of April, 1730

This whole town is cursed now. And good. To hell with them! They all deserve it. First it was the occasional disappearance of livestock. A horse vanished from the stables one night. Just this morning the Smith family had no idea where their goat went. But goats have been the least of many's concerns recently, as some families (including the priests') have had children go missing. No one has found any trace of them, even though many efforts searching for them have been made. I have been thinking about my poor little brother whom I never knew. But I do know that we will be reunited in heaven one day.

4th of June, 1730

The night brings strange sounds now. The pines are not what they used to be. Even the children have begun reciting strange nursery rhymes about a devil in the woods. Somehow being out at night feels comforting, however. It's as if the night itself can feel my sadness. But, it's strange...the darkness echoes back and I feel it inside my breast. The darker it feels out here, the darker my thoughts become. My thoughts reflect out into the wild wooden darkness and I start seeing and hearing things, strange things, unfamiliar things. The most frightening nights, however, are the rare ones where it's absolutely silent. As if I'm in school taking a test, under the scrutiny of Mrs. Livingston.

So much is happening with Father and our family that I must focus on our safety and the next steps in my life. I wish so badly to get away from it all, and I have my plans to do so now. I do not wish to simply abandon those that are left, so I will try my hardest to help them out before leaving for good. Nevertheless, this journal will not be coming with me, as it highlights the darkest times in my life. I must begin a new chapter in my life now. God Bless the Leeds family. -Elizabeth

Lola was speechless. As she read, her eyes soaked it all in, hungry for every next word. She had read almost the whole thing with an open mouth, shocked. She had hit a mythological gold mine of a primary source. She closed the journal and placed it inside the largest pocket of the cat backpack. There was only one objective in her mind now: get the hell home. She had the motherload and did not, under any circumstance, want to lose it. She picked up Crash in the backpack and headed out. As she walked down the hallway, Crash began yowling in an odd manner. He sounded threatened.

"What is it?"

A wicked gust stirred the trees outside. They both sensed it–an uncanny presence encircling the house. Windswept whispers slipped through the cracks and danced around their ears. Lola peered out, but didn't see much. She made her way to the doorway to leave and noticed outside near the front had a faint orange glow. She set Crash down and peered through the rubble, but couldn't make much out. When she heard an odd noise come from inside the house back around the room she had just been in, she jumped and forced herself through the tight doorway. She scraped herself and it hurt getting through, but the backpack got stuck. The whispers in the wind became clearer and sounded angry, and she thought she heard footsteps get closer, accompanied by the orange glow. She began to freak out and gave the backpack a good tug, but it didn't budge. She peered out into the pines, shining the flashlight around, and to her horror, saw ghastly figures making their way towards the old house. The whispers became angry, slurred gasps as they noticed Lola struggling on the ground. She turned around and pulled harder, hearing something rip. More viscous tugs and the backpack squeezed through. She was worried that Crash got hurt, but he started yowling and hissing more and more, sensing the evil presence coming for them. The figures, withered husks with sunken, incomprehensible faces, looked to be holding torches lit with a supernatural flame. They reached out at Lola, and Crash, with all his might, lunged out of the backpack through the mesh window that had been ripped getting through the old doorway. His instinct told him to defend his owner at all costs. To Lola's amazement, Crash was managing to repel them, but there were too many. She got up from the ground and was about to take off with Crash, but a force grabbed her shoulder, turned her around, and gripped at her throat. She stared into the dead, empty eyes of one of the ghosts. It screamed bone-chilling words at her.

"WHERE IS THE CHILD? FIND HIM! BRING HER TO THE TREE. WE WILL BEGIN THE EXECUTION SOON! WHERE IS THE CHIL-" The ghost's voice became low and distorted as Crash jumped up its back and began tearing away at its face. It let go of Lola and collapsed into dust on the ground. Lola got up and saw nooses shoot down from the dark above her. One hit her chin and snatched up just before she recoiled back away from it.

"Holy shit! Thank you, Crash. Let's get outta here!" Lola put Crash back in the backpack and weaved around the nooses and remaining lingering spirits, hoping to god her intuition was right and she was headed in the right direction. She ran and didn't stop, guiding the flashlight at her feet so she wouldn't trip up. After a while she stopped, took out her compass and looked at her map. Her hands were shaking. She had been running a little off-course, and after catching her breath, adjusted, running in the correct direction to get back to her car. She made it back after some time, and on her drive home, felt a slight disappointment that she didn't have a run-in with the New Jersey Devil. The specters she had run into, however, would haunt her memories for a long time, even if they felt less abnormal with the knowledge she had.

She got home and it was already nearing midnight. The pine barrens seemed to suck the time right out of life. The moans of the vengeful figures she had been attacked by echoed in her head. It was a struggle to shake it off. She looked up at the ceiling to make sure there were no nooses ready to drop down and slip around her neck, ready to break it as it snatched her up and away from everything she knew. Up and away into a dark void in the sky that felt more like a bottomless pit. Trying to calm down, she decided to watch something lighthearted. Crash jumped up on the bed with her.

"Hey there, baby boy! You were pretty badass today, y'know that?" she said as she scratched his chin. "I guess you'll get some extra treats tomorrow, huh?" Crash's limited knowledge of the English language didn't matter, because when he heard the word "treats", his ears pointed up and he became excited.

"*Tomorrow*, gatito, not now." As she lay there, watching her video, her mind shot around, trying to figure out what to do next. Should she go to an organization specializing in supernatural claims? What about other authorities, would her claims be taken seriously? No. What she *really* wanted had not yet been achieved: company with the Jersey Devil. The bridge between her and that fearsome creature stood out in her head, the missing piece of the puzzle: Caleb. She *had* to find him.

CHAPTER 30

The smell of coffee filled the morning air inside Lola's house. Days ago, she had scoped out Caleb's house in the morning and didn't see much of anything, so today she was going to stake out the house from 3PM until it got dark. It was a weird feeling, staking out an eleven year-old, but nothing was off the table in her new reality. She *needed* to see it again. With the journal she found she felt she had information that the creature would be interested in. She couldn't stop thinking about what she had read last night, studying the journal cover to cover. She empathized with Elizabeth Leeds, wondering if she ever got out of that town and lived a fulfilling life away from all of the terrible tragedy. Then her mind drew comparisons to Elizabeth and herself, wondering whether she would live a life that felt worth living. If she planned to come face-to-face with the Jersey Devil, would her life even last much longer? Regardless, she wouldn't know until it happened.

The pine barrens encampment was buzzing. Their terrorizing continued in subtle ways. They stood at the edge of the woods in different places, *wanting* to be seen, if only for just a moment, while they chanted something underneath their breath. A couple more people were reported missing. Posts appeared online about strange sightings of masked people. Conspiracies arose of cult activity which gained traction and didn't help the already bleak, desperate mood of the local area. At the camp, human limbs hung from dead branches like ornaments forgotten on Christmas trees. The Jersey Devil had been plotting and was ready to unveil its next plan.

"MY CHILDREN. COME." They all gathered around. Caleb had no idea where things were going to go from here, but he was curious. The lack of direction in his life had led him to an outlandish place that maybe he could call a home. He had no regard for the future, but this newfound feeling comforted him.

"WE RECENTLY GOT RID OF SCUM THAT HAD STAINED CALEB'S LIFE. MANY ARE AFRAID TO STEP FOOT OUTSIDE OF THEIR HOUSES OUT OF FEAR OF DISAPPEARING OR SEEING STRANGE THINGS. BUT I TELL YOU, IF LIFE IS A

POND, THEN YOU CAN'T SEE MUCH OF IT BECAUSE OF ALL OF THE SCUM THERE TRULY IS IN THIS WORLD." It paused, touching its shoulder. "I STALKED A POLICE OFFICER AFTER HE INJURED ME. SEE, CHILDREN, MY EYES AND EARS ARE MANY, AND I SEE AND HEAR EVERYTHING IN AND AROUND MY DOMAIN. I WATCH PEOPLE EVERY DAY UNBEKNOWNST TO THEM. AND IN MY RECONNAISSANCE, I FOUND A BIGGER PIECE OF SCUM, SO MUCH BIGGER THAT I FELT MY VENDETTA AND RAGE LEAVE FOR THE OFFICER WHO INJURED ME AND TRANSFER OVER TO THIS ONE." It paused again, with that same, mean look on its face. It lowered its head, kneeling to the ground, clutching a fist.

"NATURE IS INNOCENT, LIFE AND DEATH NATURAL. BUT WHAT IS NOT NATURAL IS THE WASTEFUL SLAUGHTER AND TORTURE OF LIFE. I WILL ONLY TELL YOU THE MOST RECENT ACCOUNT OF ATROCITIES THIS MAN HAS DONE, BUT KNOW MANY MORE HAVE BEEN COMMITTED BY HIS HAND. HE GOES BY THE TITLE 'OFFICER PEARSON'. DURING A TRAFFIC STOP, HE PULLED OVER A VEHICLE THAT CONTAINED A WOMAN AND HER TWO DOGS. SEEING AN OPPORTUNITY TO FULFILL HIS TWISTED DESIRES, HE PURPOSEFULLY ACTED LOUD AND AGGRESSIVE DURING THE ENTIRE STOP. HE DEMANDED THE DRIVER TO STEP OUT AND THE DOGS TROTTED OUT SOON AFTER, FEELING ANXIOUS. THEY SNIFFED AROUND THE FRINGE OF THE WOODS, POSING NO THREAT. NOT EVEN A BARK. BUT OFFICER PEARSON DREW HIS GUN AND SHOT BOTH AS THE DRIVER SCREAMED AT HIM. I WATCHED BOTH OF THE BEASTS LAY THERE ON THEIR SIDES, WHINING IN PAIN, TAKING THEIR LAST BREATHS." The devil stood up. Gasps and angry comments came from the group.

"THE ENTIRE PRECINCT WILL BURN. WE WILL TAKE OFFICER PEARSON ALIVE AND SHOW HIM THE WRATH OF NATURE. HE MAY THINK THERE ARE NO REPERCUSSIONS FOR SUCH ACTIONS, BUT HE IS WRONG. I HAVE KILLED SCUM LIKE HIM BEFORE, AND NOW WILL BE YOUR CHANCE." A resounding cheer. "CALEB?"

Caleb now knew why the creature had asked him to retrieve some extra clothes and bottles of alcohol his foster father had remaining in his home. They sat together, enjoying each others' conversation while making Molotov cocktails. The devil went over the details with them all and they were off before sunset. The children of the pines had no trouble traversing the woods and made it to the precinct in a little over an hour.

Police Chief Watkins had his legs kicked up on his desk and was reading accounts of new information regarding the recent missing children's cases in his town. He was lost in thought upon reading it through, and before he could try to come to any conclusions, one of the two officers there at the precinct came into his office.

"Sir? Y'know the missing kids from the park and trailer park? Well, there are thirteen kids outside the station right now–"

"This is great! We might finally have some answers, Wedgewood! Are they with Pearson?" asked Chief Watkins, springing up from his chair.

"Well, they're not inside yet…"

"Well why the hell not? Pearson!?" Watkins was ecstatic. Any evidence or story leading to finding any missing children alive was going to be massive. National news for sure. He made his way to the entrance of the station. Pearson was peering out the door.

"What the hell are you doing, Pearson? Let them in! Don't keep these poor kids outside," Watkins grabbed Pearson's shoulder.

"Sir, wait! They all have, uh, masks on. And they're standing all around the station," said Pearson.

"The fuck you talkin' about? What're they just pranksters or somethin'? I swear I'll have 'em all up to shit in community service hours if–did either of you even talk to them yet?" Officer Pearson and Wedgewood looked at each other. "Well!?" Still no response. Watkins was becoming irate. "Pearson, you've been standing there with your dick in your hands long enough. They're *kids!* Get the fuck out there and see who they are!!"

Pearson was red in the face, already plotting out in his head how he'd get back at Chief Watkins for the abasement. Sheepish, he opened the door and went outside. The thirteen masked children were surrounding the station in a circle, while Caleb and the beast watched from the woods not far off. Watkins and Wedgewood went over to watch from a window. They heard Officer Pearson yell out to the kids for a few moments before a long silence. They thought it was unusual that he hadn't come in yet, and checked all the windows, seeing that the children had indeed surrounded the police station. It was beginning to get dark.

"Pearson! Where did he go? Chief, what do we do?"

"Let's go out and see what the trouble is."

They looked around and saw thirteen flames light up, sudden and eerie.

"The hell they got in their hands? Fuckin' Molotovs!? Oh shit. Wedgewood! Get back inside!" They both bolted for the door.

"What are we gonna do?" asked Wedgewood, reaching down to his holster.

"Christ, *no*, we're not gonna shoot fuckin' *children!* Especially not ones that could be missing!" Watkins scrambled about, completely unprepared for such a bizarre situation. "Go get all the tasers we got. Shit, man. What the hell?" He peered out the window and found himself afraid. Their lack of movement and animation was unnerving to witness. Their masks were lit up by the Molotovs. The chief kept a steady mind, called for backup, and grabbed a fire extinguisher, meeting back up with Wedgewood.

"Only four…"

"And they're the single-shot ones, huh? Shit! Guess we gotta make 'em count."

"Chief, say we do incapacitate four of them, what's the plan for the other," Wedgewood counted on his fingers, "nine?"

"Guess I'll be on the offensive with the extinguisher. Help me get in close."

And with that, they ran out of the front door, calling for Pearson and telling the masked strangers to set the bottles down on the pavement of the parking lot. The strangers didn't comply, however, so Wedgewood fired the first taser shot. It was a hit on an easy, non-moving target, but the shock seemed to have little effect–they could hear the kid grunt, but their grip on the Molotov stayed strong.

"What the fuck!? These kids made outta stone or something?"

"This ain't right. None a' this is right…"

The creature, who now carried an unconscious Officer Pearson, ordered the thirteen to make the station burn nice and bright, seeing that Watkins and Wedgewood were on the offensive. The two stressed police officers ran around the station trying to handle all thirteen aggressors by themselves, but it was futile. Watkins managed to put out a couple of Molotovs with the extinguisher before the rest were thrown at the station and into its windows. Backup had arrived too late. Watkins looked on as the place he had worked at for over twenty years went up in flames. The masked strangers retreated into the woods and were gone just as abruptly as they had come. They had no idea where Pearson was.

It was dead of night and Officer Pearson woke up, bound by thorns upon a tree. Torchlight illuminated a horrific scene: masked weirdos all seeming to be looking at him through their singular eyeholes and a strange-looking creature was with them. His mind tried to make sense of it. Was he abducted by a cult? This large animal-human thing, was it some guy in a costume? He struggled and regretted it, as the thorns dug deeper into his skin.

"What the fuck!? Who are you guys? You know police backup will be here any minute," he gave out a nervous laugh, "yeah, and you're all gonna be shot on sight!"

"Shot on sight? Why? We ain't dogs," said a voice from the masked crowd. A mixture of chuckling and sighs followed.

"Wh-what?" Pearson asked. He watched as the large beast-human thing walked up to him. It looked so real. Then it spoke and he knew that it *was* real.

"THE SUFFERING YOU HAVE CAUSED WILL BE GIVEN BACK TO YOU TENFOLD, JOEL PEARSON."

"Who are you, talkin' like you know me? Let me down!!"

"OH I'VE SEEN ENOUGH TO KNOW THE LIKES OF YOU. MANY LIKE YOU START OUT SMALL. MAYBE TORTURING KITTENS AND FISH. KILLING BIRDS AND RABBITS. NO USE TO IT AT ALL. ENDING LIFE SIMPLY TO END IT. TO SEE IF YOU FEEL ANYTHING FROM IT. BUT YOU NEVER DO, DO YOU? WELL REST ASSURED, YOU *WILL* FEEL THINGS TONIGHT."

"Their lives don't mean anything. They're just animals that piss and shit everywhere."

"AND WHAT MEANING DOES *YOUR* LIFE HAVE? YOU DO THE SAME, BUT ON TOP OF THAT, YOU ALSO DEFILE LIFE. SUCH A BLATANT DISRESPECT FOR NATURE–THE VERY THING THAT LETS YOU LIVE YOUR PATHETIC LIFE IN THE FIRST PLACE. I LIKE TO HANG YOUR KIND FROM THE TREES, SKINNED ALIVE, AND LET THE BIRDS PICK AT YOUR FLESH LITTLE BY LITTLE, BUT YOU ARE A SPECIAL KIND OF SCUM. YOU HAVE SOMEHOW FOUND YOURSELF IN A POSITION OF PROTECTION IN THE WORLD, AND YET THIS IS YOUR TRUE SELF? DESPICABLE. ABHORRENT. THE VERY SIGHT OF YOU PUTS AN AWFUL TASTE IN MY MOUTH."

"Fuckin' pig!" came another voice from the small crowd.

"PIGS ARE INTELLIGENT. DO NOT DISRESPECT THEM SO."

"S-sorry…"

"You're all delusional. I'll kill *you* too. Just for fun. And I'll shit down your throat after I cut your fuckin' head off," said Pearson.

"IS THAT SO?"

"Yeah. I'll watch you rot and force your little freak cult to watch as I play with your corpse more and more," Joel Pearson went on, oblivious to his own situation.

"PUT ON THE GLOVES I GAVE YOU TODAY," the devil said, turning around to the fourteen others. Caleb was as ready as the rest of them. "COME GIVE THIS SCUM A GOOD STRIKE WHEREVER YOU SEE FIT. AND MAKE SURE TO SPIT ON HIM AFTERWARDS."

The masked kids lined up with a singular glove on which had jagged, pointy splinters glued on by sap. They each went up to Officer Pearson (who had no clothes on besides his underwear) and hit him wherever they wanted, embedding many splinters in his skin. They all spat on him afterwards. No one could hear his screams out in the barrens. The Jersey Devil made sure that any search teams around would never find them.

"Stop! Quit it!! You've had your fun, now let me go, you fuckin' freaks!!" Pearson yelled, spit dripping from his mouth.

"FINE. I'LL LET YOU DOWN," the devil said, releasing the thorny bindings. He dropped to the ground face first, many of the splinters lodging themselves further into his skin. He rolled over, crying in pain. Everyone else was laughing around him.

"YOU DUG THE HOLE I ASKED YOU TO?"

"Yes, we did."

"BRING HIM THERE."

Caleb watched as the masked kids took Pearson by the limbs and dropped him into a hole that was about three feet deep. He felt it too–the power that they had over a life. The collective lack of guilt. It was euphoric. He felt like he was finally getting back at…what? Who? Life? He didn't know. He sat there, watching Joel Pearson squirm as his legs and arms were bound again. They did not fill the hole. Not yet. The creature took them back to their camp and addressed them.

"WE WILL LET THE SCUM WRITHE FOR A BIT AND CELEBRATE A SUCCESSFUL NIGHT. I KNOW THE MUSHROOMS I PROVIDE AS YOUR MAIN SOURCE OF FOOD MAY BECOME DULL AFTER A WHILE, SO CALEB HAS BROUGHT SOMETHING DIFFERENT YOU CAN ALL ENJOY. CALEB?"

"Oh…well. Um, I knew we were gonna have fester-festivi-tivies, um, a party tonight, but I forgot the snacks. I can run and grab them and be back super fast, I promise!" Caleb looked down, hoping the Jersey Devil wasn't upset.

"NONSENSE! WE ARE IN NO RUSH. COME. WE WILL FLY THERE TOGETHER. PLEASE, TURN ON THE MUSIC BOX AND HAVE FUN WHILE YOU ALL WAIT." The others jammed out to some music from a battery-powered stereo Caleb had brought. They talked about how it felt to throw the Molotov cocktails. How it felt to cause something to burn down, watching it.

They were off, Caleb being held in one big, black arm. Above the cover of the forest, Caleb gaped his mouth in awe. The moonlight lit up the barrens and surrounding roads and buildings. It was a bit chilly so far up, but he didn't mind. He was up where no one could hurt him. Up on a dark cloud, cutting through the darkness above. They soon landed in the woods just before the edge where Caleb's house was.

"AS YOU KNOW, I DO NOT WISH TO STRAY TOO FAR FROM MY DOMAIN, NEVER MIND ENTERING AN UNFAMILIAR BUILDING AND FEELING TRAPPED. I WILL WAIT RIGHT HERE."

"Ok, be right back!"

Caleb ran up to his house. It was around eight o'clock. Lola was still staking out his house at the time and saw him run into the house. She sprung into action without hesitation, creeping her way up. Jake was home and had heard Caleb enter and came out to the kitchen where Caleb was stuffing snacks into his backpack.

"Hey," Jake said, scaring Caleb a little.

"Oh, hey."

"Have you seen Will go out or anything? I haven't seen him for a while now. We both know if he's not in the bathroom or drunk watching TV then something's up."

"Hah, true. That's weird, but I haven't seen him. Haven't really been home too much–been hanging out with friends. Maybe he finally went grocery shopping?"

"I dunno, maybe. I've been out too, but I was just kinda worried about you. You doing okay?"

"Yeah, uh, yeah I'm okay. It's just…thinking about the future scares me. So I've been trying to live more in the now, y'know?"

"I feel that. It'll be alright, little bro. Stay outta trouble, okay? We can talk more later. Maybe play some video games or something too."

"Yeah. That'd be fun, Jake. I gotta get going now, just wanted to pick up some snacks."

"Damn, you must be having a huge sleepover. That or you guys got black holes for stomachs!" They both chuckled. "Anyways, night Caleb."

"Night, Jake," Caleb said, leaving. Jake called back.

"Oh, real quick! You seen the stereo anywhere?"

"Umm, nope, sorry. I haven't."

"Damn. Aight, later!"

"Later!"

Caleb walked out of the house and by the time he had made it down the steps, the instinctual part of his brain gave him an odd feeling as if someone was somewhere close, watching him. Then he saw a figure cut out in the darkness, the faint light from his front porch highlighting the slightest outline of their face and color of their clothes. A girl? Wait, he knew her.

"Caleb!" Lola said in a whisper-shout.

"Ms-Ms. Santos? ...What are you doing here?" Caleb asked.

"Listen. I know this is strange, but I need to talk to you about what happened the day you presented."

"Um, sorry Ms. Santos, but I gotta get going."

"Caleb. Was that *really* the Jersey Devil? *How* did you come across its severed eye!?"

"It was. I know you're a big nerd for this stuff, but I don't have time right no-"

"*Please*, Caleb. I went back into the pines yesterday and I might've found something amazing. What do you know about him?"

"Do you...wanna meet him?" Caleb was curious. How would his teacher react? She *had* saved his life. The creature was only a walk away. He let her decide, finding the face she made after he spoke hilarious.

"Huh? What? Do you know where it is? I mean-I, um, well, I gue-"

"Ms. Santos. Do you wanna meet him or not?" He enjoyed having power over his teacher way too much. Lola's eyes darted around and her breathing quickened.

"Yes. I do."

"C'mon, follow me."

She followed Caleb to his backyard, walking over a small, loose dirt mound. It had an odd smell, but she paid no mind to it as her mind flooded with what she was going to say and how things were going to go. She wasn't ready. They got to the edge of the woods.

"I SEE YOU'VE BROUGHT A FRIEND," the devil stared at her.

"Yeah, she was teaching us about folklore and was the reason our project was about you."

"AH, THE TEACHER! INTERESTING...LUCKY FOR HER, SHE IS MORE THAN WELCOME ON A NIGHT LIKE TONIGHT. COME."

"H-hi?"

It held out its hand and Lola, stunned, put hers out slowly. It secured both in each arm and launched off towards the deep pines. Lola screamed and breathed hard, but the odd majestic feeling she got when she opened her eyes and saw the beauty of the moonlit night calmed her.

She felt like a little girl again, fantasizing about fairytales. But she was in no fairytale.

It was a fast trip–the creature's robust wings propelled them through the cold night air with ease. Both Caleb and Lola wished they could've stayed up there a little while longer. Upon landing, the thirteen others were still having a good time with the music. Caleb passed around snacks while the Jersey Devil addressed everyone.

"FOLLOWERS, CALEB HAS BROUGHT A FRIEND TO WITNESS THE BLIGHT UPON THE WORLD WE CAPTURED MEET HIS END TONIGHT. GIRL CAN THROW A CHAIR, I'LL TELL YOU THAT. EAT AND BE MERRY!" The creature took Lola to the side while some of the young strangers said hello. Their masks freaked her out.

"Wait, 'captured'? 'Meet his end'? What is happening out here?"

"I SUFFER FROM A CURSE, AND IT EXTENDS INTO MY DOMAIN. AND FOR THE LONGEST TIME I COULDN'T FIGURE OUT HOW TO LIFT IT, UNTIL RECENTLY. YOU HAVE COME AT AN INTERESTING TIME. NOW, TELL ME, WHAT DO YOU WISH TO ACCOMPLISH BY BEING HERE?" She was lost in its otherworldliness. The horns, one sticking into a boney eyehole, the wings, huge and bat-like, the fur, black and coarse, the hooves, commanding and intimidating, the tail, long and forked, the claws, fierce and sharp, and the body, goat-like yet humanoid–all of it was in front of her in its mythological glory.

"YOUR EYES, VORACIOUS WITH CURIOSITY WHERE I USUALLY FIND FEAR. WHAT IS IT YOU WANT?" Its words rung around inside of her head.

"Well, I…it's just, I've read and heard stories about you. Stories I had believed were fiction until you c-came into my classroom and-"

"YES, I UNDERSTAND YOUR INITIAL SHOCK. GO ON."

"I don't know, I guess I just wanted to see what you did out here. I wanted to know if it really was something supernatural causing the mass disappearances."

"YES, MOSTLY. I WILL NOT TAKE RESPONSIBILITY FOR ALL OF THEM, HOWEVER. NOT ALL MONSTERS LOOK LIKE ME, MANY MORE LOOK LIKE YOU."

"Don't try to justify or downplay it. You talk of suffering, but did you once think about all of the families suffering, knowing they'll never see their children again? It's immeasurable!"

"DEEP SUFFERING, WHAT DO *YOU* KNOW OF IT? DO YOU KNOW THE FEELING OF NEVER BEING WELCOMED INTO THE WORLD FROM BIRTH? THE FEELING OF NO ONE EVER

LOVING YOU? PEOPLE WANTING YOU ONLY FOR THEIR MORAL STANDING OR TWISTED DESIRES?"

"That's a selfish way of thinking! Why cause more suffering when you know how awful it is? It's all the same!"

"I DO NOT SEE HUMANS AS EQUALS, WOMAN, SO WATCH YOUR MOUTH. HUMANS CAUSE MORE UNNECESSARY SUFFERING ON THEIR OWN KIND THAN I EVER HAVE." The beast thrust out an angry arm and grabbed her by the torso. Its hand fully wrapped around her body. It squeezed and she couldn't breathe. It let her go after a few seconds and watched as she gasped for air.

"Cabrón," she said, coughing. Was it time? Would the information she had found help? Could she be a vital part in making sure no more families suffered or grieved? "...Guess what? Not all of us humans are evil, okay? What if I had something to help you? I think I know a little bit more about you than you do yourself," she said, holding a small bag which contained the journal she had found. The devil raised a furrowed brow.

"WHAT IS THAT?"

"A journal I found somewhere out here the other night. And I think...it was written by one of your sisters."

"ONE OF MY...SISTERS? I HAVE NO MEMORY OF ANY FAMILY BESIDES MY MOTHER, WHO WAS HANGED ON A TREE IN A CLEARING NEAR HERE. *SHE* CURSED THAT AREA."

"That makes sense. Your mother was hanged for giving birth to you. She didn't want you. Your father...he came back home from some journey and was very different from his former self. Her love warped into a confused hatred."

"W-WHY WOULD THEY KILL HER FOR GIVING BIRTH TO ME?"

"You were the thirteenth child in the family. You were destined to be evil by their superstitions. Some birth defects might have reinforced those beliefs, I'm not sure."

"MY FATHER...WAS SCUM?"

"I don't think he always was. Your sister was quite fond of him at one point." The silence between them was filled with the faint noise of the kids at the encampment.

"MY MOTHER'S SOUL IS FILLED WITH A RAGE I HAVE BEEN UNABLE TO TAME. I...WAS ROBBED OF MY CHILDHOOD. OF ANY NORMAL LIFE."

"Yeah...your story is pretty tragic. I'm sorry," she sighed. "You were never meant to be a 'devil'. I have no clue what happened to you afterwards, but know this: you were loved the moment you were born.

Your mother may not have wanted you, but your sister loved you. And I'm sure your other siblings did too."

The creature stood there and lowered his head. Lola could've sworn she saw a tear drop to the ground from its singular eye.

"DO NOT PRETEND LIKE YOU KNOW ME, TEACHER," it said, grasping its head in sudden pain. Lola watched on in cautious curiosity. It regained its composure and continued. "TONIGHT...WILL BE DIFFERENT NOW. THE STAGE WILL SOON BE SET."

"Stage will be set for what? I'm not a fan of this cryptic shit, y'know."

"LISTEN. YOU HAVE A ROLE IN ALL OF THIS. ARE YOU PREPARED TO BEAR THE BURDEN OF TRUTH?"

"What's going to happen?"

"THERE ARE FOURTEEN CHILDREN HERE. MORE THAN ENOUGH. A WRETCHED SOUL. A VESSEL..." The beast headed back to the camp and Lola followed, keeping her distance. *Burden of truth? What could that mean?*

CHAPTER 31

They all stood around the man in the hole. Lola had no idea who he was, but they all acted like he wasn't even human.

"Help me! Help me, god dammit!" She cringed at the sad state he was in, knowing there was no way she could help him even if she wanted to. His fate was already sealed.

"BEFORE WE BURY THIS PUSTULE, WE WILL SHOW SOME MERCY–LET'S GIVE HIM SOMETHING TO BREATHE OUT OF." The devil had a reed that could act as a breathing tube. He placed it in Pearson's mouth, gluing it on with a sappy substance. "NOW PILE ON THE DIRT."

It only took a few minutes for him to be buried. All they could hear was muffled screaming coming through the tube. The Jersey Devil walked away and came back, holding something in its hand. Lola could make out what she thought was a bunch of brown specks. They wriggled, desperately clinging onto the creature's hand. She knew what they were; she had just taken one off of Crash the other day. They were ticks. At least fifty of them writhing, hungry to lodge their heads into skin where the blood flowed the most. The devil carefully funneled every single one of them down the breathing tube.

Lola gagged at the sight. And again after hearing Pearson's choked screaming through the tube. At first, he had no idea what came down the tube, not until he felt their chitinous legs crawling around. He fought hard, blowing as much air from his throat as he could, but the ticks were tenacious little creatures. They made their way up into his gums, under his tongue, and down his throat. His breathing became sporadic and he moaned in agony. Lola looked around in horror, as she could tell that everyone was giddy and cheerful beneath their masks.

"BE GRATEFUL. IF I WANTED, HORNETS WOULD ACCOMPANY THE TICKS, BUT ALAS, I WISH NOT TO DISTURB THEM DURING THE HARSH WINTER." It spat on the ground. "SUFFER." The Jersey Devil walked away. He was headed towards the clearing with the giant oak tree. Once he arrived, he bent down, dragging a claw or two through the ground around the tree. Back at the camp, Lola went up to Caleb.

"Pardon my French, but what the *fuck* is going on here, Caleb!?"

Caleb chuckled. "Don't worry Ms. Santos. He deserved it."

Lola went and found a place to sit down, unable to bear the sound of the buried man suffering anymore. She thought about where she was and if she should escape, but figured it was useless. She didn't feel safe, especially after seeing the New Jersey Devil wander off into the darkness. He was hard at work, concentrating on drawing symbols within the circle he made around the large oak. The clearing still made him feel unwelcome and upset, but his resolve made it bearable. He kept muttering to himself.

"CURSE...THIRTEEN...VESSEL...WITNESS...SOUL...RELEASE...DIVISION." Over and over it spoke, intense, obsessed. Everything was coming together. Tonight was another part of its twisted fate. After setting down two vials of liquid at the base of the tree, the preparations were almost complete.

Twenty minutes later, amidst all the noise, all fourteen kids stopped what they were doing and faced northwest. The Jersey Devil was back, and he went over to where Pearson was buried and pulled him out by the glued-on breathing tube. He was still alive, but barely. The devil ripped off the tube and Joel Pearson coughed and gagged and clawed at his mouth, trying to get the parasites out. He moaned in pain as the beast grabbed him by the neck. The devil told everyone to follow him as he dragged Pearson back to the clearing. When they arrived it was a whole new scene: torches of dark crimson and deep jade lined the perimeter of the clearing. The large oak had a ritual circle drawn in the ground around it, toting arcane and unrecognizable inscriptions of symbols and words of forgotten languages. The circle had many lines drawn into the center of the oak tree like arteries. With two almost innocuous-looking swipes of its claw, the Jersey Devil slit both of Pearson's wrists as he wailed, afraid and desperate. It walked up to a deep marking in front of the tree within the circle and tossed Pearson's near-lifeless body into it. The night was cold and silent. The crowd watched from behind. He turned to address them.

"MY BELOVED FOLLOWERS, TONIGHT IS A NIGHT OF TRANSFORMATION AND RELEASE. WE HAVE ALL BEEN BROUGHT HERE, TOGETHER, BY FATE. WE ARE ALL OF ONE WILL BESIDES THE WITNESS. NEVERTHELESS, THE ROLES WE ALL PLAY TONIGHT ARE EQUALLY SIGNIFICANT. MY MASKED CHILDREN, PLEASE STAND AROUND THE CIRCLE." They did as he commanded without question. Lola stood there, a spectator with no say in the matter. Although she was perplexed by what she saw, she was starting to piece together what would soon transpire.

She was fully focused, burning it all into her memory. For some reason she felt obligated. She couldn't look away even if she tried. Caleb stood back as well, closer to her. She tried to get his attention, but he also seemed distant, under the influence of some spell, perhaps?

The Jersey Devil walked over to Caleb, bent down and whispered something in his ear. They both walked back up in front of the tree and stood there. The creature started chanting. For the first time, its voice didn't enter any of their heads. None of them knew what it was saying. But as it chanted and grew louder, a figure materialized on a thick branch of the tree jutting out to the right. It was the spirit of a woman, hanging by an ethereal rope. She glowed and gave out sullen screams. Lola stood there with her mouth open. She looked down at the man in the hole whose life had expired. The ghost's screams came to a stop and an opening at the base of the tree appeared. It was hollow and a dark echo came from it. Caleb looked up at the devil, who gave him an affirming nod. Caleb breathed heavy and entered into the tree's opening. The Jersey Devil turned around and motioned with its arm, pointing its clawed hand toward its neck. The masked followers standing around the circle mimicked the gesture. The beast then thrust its hand in a strong jabbing motion against the side of its neck, then pulled away. With the power granted from the creature coursing through their veins, they each pierced their necks with ease, falling down with their heads leaning into the circle, blood spraying into it. The blood came and kept coming, and soon an unnatural amount of it filled the circle, streaming towards the center–the giant oak.

Lola fell to her knees, as fourteen corpses now lay in front of her. Another thirteen children dead. Ripped away from their families. And even if they didn't have much of a family, they were still young lives with potential. It crushed her. Would they finally be the last from the hands of the Jersey Devil? Would it finally end? She was choked up and felt a tear run down her face. She didn't feel like she was in the woods anymore, either, but instead some dark space ripped from the world. It was alien. Unnerving. No matter what she did, she couldn't calm herself down or shake off the feeling of being isolated. *No one would ever find you, no matter the efforts*. She shook her head to get the thoughts out, as they were almost as overwhelming as the haunting seclusion. She heard the creature speak again, although much softer now, she could at least understand it.

"I KNOW YOU DIDN'T LOVE ME, MOTHER, AND I UNDERSTAND WHY. THE VOID OF LOVE HAS EXPANDED INSIDE OF MY CHEST EVERY DAY. BUT YOU CAN LET GO NOW." The hanging ghost of the mother gave out more soft cries as the noose burned away, and this time, with a faint smile on her thin, tortured face, ascended far away into the night sky, giving out a bright glow. She manifested herself into the painting of stars upon the winter night. With a sigh of relief, the devil entered the opening of the tree as well. The opening closed up behind them like it had never been there in the first place, and after some time the tree started to twist and contort its branches in an unnatural, jarring manner. The tree glowed up with more strange markings, then seemed to be set ablaze by that supernatural fire Lola had seen just the other night–just like those ghosts' torches. This time the fire, although ethereal, roared and sputtered. The twisting and contorting, along with the fire, slowly died down and the tree wallowed in what she felt was relief. All was still, and she noticed that the tree had lost its normal graying-brown coloring, and had turned an odd pale-green color instead. Then the opening reappeared. Lola squinted, confused– someone was coming out of it. It wasn't Caleb, nor was it the Jersey Devil. It was a different child. The child picked up the vials that were at the base of the tree and drank them both. It looked at Lola. A boy. He was missing his left eye. It dawned on her. Then she heard a loud, bleating growl come from the tree.

It ran out straight at her in a blur, but stopped in front of her. She flinched, shielding herself, but upon hearing it stopping, opened her eyes. The creature. The Jersey Devil? It was different, however. It seemed wild. Natural. Free. It stared into her with its fierce, sagacious eyes, steam coming from its nostrils. She stared back and watched as it lifted a hand up. It ripped off one of its claws and tore off some of its fur, only giving out slight grunts of pain, and held it out to her. She took it, unaware of more tears running down her face. It gave her an amicable huff from its nose before letting out a cheerful cry, flying off into the moonlit winter sky, the trees bending down at the force of its wings. Lola watched it off, then turned her attention towards the child. He walked up to her.

"C-Caleb…?"

"Not exactly, Teacher!" His voice was chipper and friendly.

"Your eye…" Lola was baffled. "It can't be."

"I can't wait to learn more about this world. For the longest time I've been on the outside looking in," he said.

"This world…is certainly a strange one."

CHAPTER 32

Reports of an unknown child emerging from the New Jersey pine barrens made national news. He was missing an eye and seemed to have amnesia. Many were touched, as this child was a sliver of hope for the parents in despair. Maybe *their* child would come back to them. Since the authorities couldn't gather any information on the child, his identity remained a mystery. But that didn't stop many families from wanting to adopt him and provide him with a childhood and a chance at experiencing life.

It was around this time that multiple rumors of an urban legend known as the "New Jersey Devil" spread throughout the country via news and internet posts. Most of the rumors were spearheaded by a Park Ridge Middle School teacher who wore an odd necklace of a long, black nail. Many believed her claims, as she was a local and sounded very convincing, even showing off some sort of old journal she had found in an ancient house in the pines. Some people took the rumors seriously, others found humor in it, and many more were insulted by the fact that people really believed something like the Jersey Devil existed and snatched away children.

It wasn't before long that more sightings of the Jersey Devil were soon reported. What was once a local legend had gained widespread attention. After the mystery child appeared from the woods, authorities saw a major downward trend in missing children cases. To the relief of many families, the children were playing outside again, but not without precautions. Still, even on Halloween, young ones put on masks and had their own little Jersey Devil costumes. One man went so far as to say he had found and killed the Jersey Devil, gaining the attention of major news networks. He had eerie pictures and everything to prove it, too. But it was later debunked to be false–this man had gone so far as to stitch a goat's head onto a partially skinned deer and glued wings onto its back. Strangely enough, a few weeks later that very man was found dead–his head had been severed and stitched onto a deer with his body nearby, his back flayed to resemble wings. The case stumped investigators–there were no leads besides some odd, black fur at the scene.

CHECK OUT OTHER GREAT CRYPTID NOVELS

RETURN TO DYATLOV PASS
by J.H. Moncrieff

In 1959, nine Russian students set off on a skiing expedition in the Ural Mountains. Their mutilated bodies were discovered weeks later. Their bizarre and unexplained deaths are one of the most enduring true mysteries of our time. Nearly sixty years later, podcast host Nat McPherson ventures into the same mountains with her team, determined to finally solve the mystery of the Dyatlov Pass incident. Her plans are thwarted on the first night, when two trackers from her group are brutally slaughtered. The team's guide, a superstitious man from a neighboring village, blames the killings on yetis, but no one believes him. As members of Nat's team die one by one, she must figure out if there's a murderer in their midst—or something even worse—before history repeats itself and her group becomes another casualty of the infamous Dead Mountain.

DOVER DEMON
by Hunter Shea

The Dover Demon is real...and it has returned. In 1977, Sam Brogna and his friends came upon a terrifying, alien creature on a deserted country road. What they witnessed was so bizarre, so chilling, they swore their silence. But their lives were changed forever. Decades later, the town of Dover has been hit by a massive blizzard. Sam's son, Nicky, is drawn to search for the infamous cryptid, only to disappear into the bowels of a secret underground lair. The Dover Demon is far deadlier than anyone could have believed. And there are many of them. Can Sam and his reunited friends rescue Nicky and battle a race of creatures so powerful, so sinister, that history itself has been shaped by their secretive presence?

CHECK OUT OTHER GREAT CRYPTID NOVELS

SWAMP MONSTER MASSACRE
by Hunter Shea

The swamp belongs to them. Humans are only prey. Deep in the overgrown swamps of Florida, where humans rarely dare to enter, lives a race of creatures long thought to be only the stuff of legend. They walk upright but are stronger, taller and more brutal than any man. And when a small boat of tourists, held captive by a fleeing criminal, accidentally kills one of the swamp dwellers' young, the creatures are filled with a terrifyingly human emotion—a merciless lust for vengeance that will paint the trees red with blood.

TERROR MOUNTAIN
by Gerry Griffiths

When Marcus Pike inherits his grandfather's farm and moves his family out to the country, he has no idea there's an unholy terror running rampant about the mountainous farming community. Sheriff Avery Anderson has seen the heinous carnage and the mutilated bodies. He's also seen the giant footprints left in the snow—Bigfoot tracks. Meanwhile, Cole Wagner, and his wife, Kate, are prospecting their gold claim farther up the valley, unaware of the impending dangers lurking in the woods as an early winter storm sets in. Soon the snowy countryside will run red with blood on TERROR MOUNTAIN.

www.ingramcontent.com/pod-product-compliance
Lightning Source LLC
Chambersburg PA
CBHW071506170626
46811CB00007B/2749